Every Inch Her Bodyguard

"Did you like what you saw this morning?" Smith's voice, deep and laconic, came from behind her.

Grace wheeled around and fought the urge to bring her hands to her cheeks.

He was standing in the living room with a steaming mug in his hands. As he took a drink, his eyes hovered over the edge, piercing her with blue flame.

She was picturing his bare chest. . . .

"Well, did you?" he prompted, one brow arching.

How had he known she was watching? He'd seemed totally focused on what he was doing.

Smith put the mug down on a side table and slowly raised his hand to her. She felt a soft caress move down her hair until his fingers rested on her collarbone.

"So answer my question, Countess." His voice was a low growl, delicious and provocative. "Did you like what you saw?"

AN UNFORGETTABLE LADY

J. R. WARD
Writing as Jessica Bird

A SIGNET BOOK

SIGNET
Published by New American Library, a division of
Penguin Group (USA) Inc., 375 Hudson Street,
New York, New York 10014, USA
Penguin Group (Canada), 90 Eglinton Avenue East, Suite 700, Toronto,
Ontario M4P 2Y3, Canada (a division of Pearson Penguin Canada Inc.)
Penguin Books Ltd., 80 Strand, London WC2R 0RL, England
Penguin Ireland, 25 St. Stephen's Green, Dublin 2,
Ireland (a division of Penguin Books Ltd.)
Penguin Group (Australia), 250 Camberwell Road, Camberwell, Victoria 3124,
Australia (a division of Pearson Australia Group Pty. Ltd.)
Penguin Books India Pvt. Ltd., 11 Community Centre, Panchsheel Park,
New Delhi - 110 017, India
Penguin Group (NZ), 67 Apollo Drive, Rosedale, North Shore 0632,
New Zealand (a division of Pearson New Zealand Ltd.)
Penguin Books (South Africa) (Pty.) Ltd., 24 Sturdee Avenue,
Rosebank, Johannesburg 2196, South Africa
Penguin Books Ltd., Registered Offices:
80 Strand, London WC2R 0RL, England

Published by Signet, an imprint of New American Library, a division of Penguin
Group (USA) Inc. Previously published in an Ivy Books edition. Published by
arrangement with the author.

First Signet Printing, July 2010
10 9 8 7 6 5 4 3 2 1

To Dianne Anderson,
and her love,
Scott Anderson.
And also the wee MacGregor.

Dear Readers:

An Unforgettable Lady came out in March of 2004 and was the third of four contemporary romances that I wrote at the start of my career. I just finished reading it for the first time in five years, and the nostalgia is overwhelming. I wrote this book at my mother's house on Cape Cod, in this big armchair in an alcove on the second floor. Plenty of light and sea air. Bliss for an author. I can remember going on a tour of the mansions in Newport, Rhode Island, in preparation for doing the scenes of Grace and John at Willings, her family's mansion. And I gave Grace, the heroine, anxiety attacks because at that time in my life, I was having a lot of them.

I can also recall being utterly lost while drafting the manuscript. More on that later, however.

Back to the book. Of all the one-liners and descriptions and dialogue on the pages, one particular line stands out to me. It's spoken by John Smith, the hero: "You better shut the fuck up before I cut your tongue out."

Sound familiar? First thing I thought of were the members of the Black Dagger Brotherhood. Definitely something they would say!

Back in 2003, when I wrote about John, he was actually a departure for me. My first two heroes were gentleman types (a horse rider/trainer and a corporate titan of industry). But with *Lady*'s main man, I wanted to go darker and more raw—do a romance with a true alpha hero. John Smith—former Army Ranger and covert ops man, now head of the Black Watch firm of security specialists—was right up that alley. He was tough and hard and not at all concerned with social proprieties, which made him the perfect foil for his heroine, the wealthy and polite Grace Woodward Hall.

In some ways, the romance between them reminds me of Butch and Marissa from *Lover Revealed*, that whole opposites-attract thing. And I also think, for a contemporary romance, their conflict is strong: as a man with a dangerous past, John Smith needs a low profile, but Grace is in the papers all the time. Further, extricating himself from the shadowy way he's lived (he has, as he says, no valid social security number and three passports, none of which is in his real name) is not only hard for him to contemplate; it puts Grace in jeopardy because if she's with him, his enemies become hers. The fact that both are willing to overcome these issues is a testament to how they feel about each other—and the lengths they will go to be a couple.

As I've said before, one of the great challenges in contemporary romance is finding valid and dramatic reasons for two people not to be together. In our current society, all those strictures about not having sex before you're married or not being able to choose freely whoever you want as your partner have largely gone by the wayside. The fear of social ruin or family disappointment is not as strong as it's been in other historical periods, which makes authors have to work harder at keeping people apart. (Otherwise, it's just a case of boy meets girl and she likes him and they ... er ... get married. Snooze.)

I like the fact that John and Grace had to choose to be together in spite of her present and his past, and that love triumphs in the end in so many ways. I'm actually surprised I liked the book as much as I did—when I started reading, I was critiquing it as an editor would and finding things I didn't like. But then it got rolling ... and I really got lost in the story. I also loved the fact that John does get to save her in the end—and in a very physical, grrrrrr kind of way.

Yum.

Now, for the author-as-lost-in-the-weeds part. When I wrote these first four contemporaries, I wasn't a big outliner. I was a true pantser—which meant I had only a vague idea where things were going when I started typing. I can remember struggling through certain scenes, trying desperately to ground myself in the story and the moving parts of the plot while feeling like the book was sand in my hands, falling through the cracks of my fingers. I've since learned that although I listen to my Rice Krispies and do whatever they tell me, I need to be one hundred percent disciplined when it comes to laying out a book before I type those two magic words: Chapter One.

For me, with the Black Dagger Brotherhood series and my new Fallen Angels books, I have to make sure that my inspiration for a given story is guided by a solid road map. With *Lady*, there were twists and turns in the suspense subplot that I had to work out on the fly in the manuscript itself—and a lot of those sequences had to be reordered or shifted or buttressed with earlier scenes. It was an incredibly inefficient process—after all, it's a hell of a lot easier to fix things in outline form than when you have to fish through what you've previously written to see where folks were left and what did or did not happen. Plus, while you're thinking so much about plot and you're in the weeds with your characters, you can't concentrate on the words you're putting down, so there's much more line-by-line editing and brushing up after you're finished.

This is not to say that the book doesn't work. I think it does. It's just that I remember relying too much on my editor and scraping a good hundred pages here and there. But here's the thing. There isn't one author I know who doesn't start out having to flail around and find their process. It took me four books to discover that I needed to learn about craft—previously, I had thought all that "craft" crap was bullshit. I also realized I had to figure out some way of harnessing my inspiration so that I could really get it down on the page well.

One last thing about *Lady*. I remember truly falling in love with John Smith as I wrote him. Don't get me wrong. I adored my other heroes, too—but that raw alpha-male thing really got my attention. I was also totally into the Brotherhood of the Black Watch and those other guys. And I was liking the suspense stuff. In this book, it turns out I was starting to head into vampire land—I just didn't know it.

Good thing I remembered how much I liked John Smith about a year later, however. When it came time to reinvent myself after my fourth contemporary (*An Irresistible Bachelor*, which is the companion to *Lady* and coming out next summer!), I went back to John Smith and his boys and drafted a romantic suspense series based on them. It was okay, but it lacked that certain sizzle—and then Wrath showed up.

And I leapt into the night with him and the Brotherhood.

Rereading the Jessica Bird books has proven to be really cool—it's kind of like walking back through the halls of your high school and checking out where your locker was and peeking into all the classrooms. When I wrote these manuscripts, I was at a different place in my life—but the commonality between now and back then is that I still have to write to be truly happy. That hasn't changed in the slightest.

I really hope you love John and Grace as much as I do— they're a great couple, but also really good people individually. And next summer look for *An Irresistible Bachelor*, which is all about Callie's love story!

Thanks for all your support and for coming along on this ride with me,

J. R. Ward
December 2009

1

JOHN SMITH checked his watch and looked around the Plaza Hotel's ballroom.

Things were going well. According to the report that had just come over his earpiece, the ambassador's plane had landed safely at La Guardia and the man would be arriving at the party on time.

Smith's eyes passed over the glittering crowd. It was the same kind of flashy scene that always revolved around $5,000-a-plate dinners. Women in jewels and long gowns, men in tuxedos, the collective net worth of the room up into the stratosphere. In the midst of the shifting throng, deals were being made, affairs were getting started, and social slights were exchanged with smiles. The place was choked with air kisses and hand pumping.

Underneath the chandeliers in the elegant ballroom, the whole lot of them looked as if they had the world by the throat. Smith knew better. He'd been hired by quite a few, had learned their dirty secrets and their hidden vices. He'd even watched as some got their wake-up call to real life.

Being the target of an armed stalker, that was something to worry about. Your kid gets pinched by some madman looking to hose you down for a couple million? That was a problem. Whether or not your mistress's boob job was symmetrical paled in comparison.

Danger, like illness, was the great equalizer, and the rich learned fast what really mattered when tragedy came knocking at their door. Courtesy of the visit, they also picked up a few lessons about their inner depths. Smith

had seen hardened businessmen break down, sobbing
from fear. He'd also witnessed great reserves of strength
appear in a woman who'd only worried about her clothes
before.

Being a personal security specialist was a dangerous line
of work but it was the only thing he could imagine doing.
With his military and intelligence background, and the fact
that he didn't take orders well, it was a good fit. An ob-
server, a protector, a killer if he had to be, Smith was at
the top of his field and his small firm, Black Watch, Ltd.,
handled everyone from statesmen to financiers to international figures.

For some, it would have been a hard life. His chosen profession had him flying around the world, sleeping in hotel
rooms, staying in other people's homes, moving on to the
next job without a break. To him, the lack of continuity was
appealing. Necessary.

An army duffel full of clothes and two metal briefcases
of equipment were his only possessions. The money he'd
earned, a tidy sum, was spread around in various offshore
accounts under several different names. Without a valid
social security number, and with neither the Internal Rev-
enue Service nor any other government agency having an
unclassified record of him, he was, for all intents and pur-
poses, a ghost.

But this didn't mean he went unnoticed.

A woman in a tight black gown sauntered by him, eyeing him with an invitation he imagined a lot of men would
find irresistible. He looked past her, through her. He wasn't
interested in a quick fling with a social diva. Experience
had taught him to stick with his own kind.

The women he'd been with tended to be members of the
intelligence community or in the military. They understood
his life and expected nothing more than a shared night or
two, a body to warm their bed. Civilian women tended to
look into the future after they had sex and dealing with
their misplaced expectations took time and patience he
didn't have to spare.

His earpiece went off. The "package" was in his limo,
heading to the Plaza.

"Thanks, Tiny," he said into a small transmitter on his wrist.

The ambassador had been receiving death threats, which was how Smith had ended up in a tuxedo at the party.

As he scanned the crowd, he didn't expect trouble. The place was crawling with his men. He knew and trusted them all, having handpicked them out of elite military corps. Black Watch was the only place he knew of where former Rangers, Marines, and Navy SEALs could work together without throwing punches. If something went down tonight, they'd work together and do their damnedest to protect the ambassador.

Except Smith wasn't worried because he knew something no one else did. The man after the ambassador had been killed about five hours ago, in a deserted outpost in his native country. Smith had been tipped off by an old friend of his, and considering the source, he was confident the intel was solid. It didn't mean the ambassador was out of the woods, as assassins could be easily replaced, but it decreased the odds of trouble on this particular evening.

Despite the reduced level of threat, Smith wasn't any less alert. He knew where all the bodies in the ballroom were, in what patterns they were moving, how they were entering and exiting the space. Even the best intelligence in the world wasn't going to change the accuracy of his peripheral vision or his rapid assimilation of information.

The watchfulness was second nature to him. As immutable as his eye color.

Smith sensed someone approach from behind. He turned and looked down into the worried face of Alfred Alston, the gala's host. The man was a typical Social Register type, with a full head of prematurely white hair and the requisite horn-rimmed glasses. Smith liked him. The guy had been easy to deal with.

"I'm terribly sorry to intrude, but have you seen my wife?"

There was a slight English cadence to his vowels, no doubt left over from when his family had crossed the Atlantic. Back in 1630.

Smith shook his head.

"She should have been here quite some time ago. She would hate to miss the ambassador's entrance." Alston's thin fingers came up and fiddled with his bow tie. "Although I'm sure she will turn up."

The strain around the man's eyes was more truthful than his words.

"You want me to send one of my men over to your place?" Because Alston had been such a good sport, Smith wouldn't have minded the extra effort. Besides, it wouldn't take long. His boys had a way of getting through traffic that made NYC taxi drivers look like they were from the Amish country.

Alston offered a worried smile. "Thank you, that's very kind, but I wouldn't want to trouble you."

"Let me know if you change your mind. The ambassador's on time, by the way."

"I'm glad you're here. Curt Thorndyke was right. You put a man's mind at ease."

Smith resumed looking around the room. In another twenty minutes, the ambassador would show up. There'd be the requisite photographs and genuflecting and then dinner would be—

Smith's eyes caught on something.

Or someone, rather.

He stared through the crowd at a blond woman who had just arrived. Dressed in a shimmering silver gown, she was standing in the elaborate entrance to the ballroom looking too damn radiant to be real.

He recognized her immediately. But who wouldn't?

The Countess von Sharone.

Conversation in the ballroom dropped to a hush as people registered her presence. The social status of the gala, already high, shot through the roof with her arrival, and the crowd's approval was palpable.

If these fancy types hadn't all been carrying drinks, they'd have burst out in applause, he thought dryly. As if she were the honoree, not the ambassador.

Still, he had to admit she was a looker. With her blond hair twisted up high on her head, she was a classic beauty with delicate features and dazzling green eyes. And that dress. Molded to her body, it moved like water as she stepped into the room.

Christ, she was *beautiful*, he thought. Assuming you liked that patrician, butter-wouldn't-melt-in-my-mouth type.

Which he didn't.

Alston went up to her. She extended a hand and accepted air kisses on both cheeks from him, her expression warming. Someone else approached her and then another, until she was carried into the room on a wave of ingratiation. Smith tracked her every movement.

She'd been in the papers recently, he recalled, although it wasn't like she was ever really out of them. Her clothes, her parties, that extravagant wedding she'd had, they were fodder for the tabloids and the real papers alike. What had he read about her lately, though? Her father had just died. That was it. And there'd been some spread about her and five other women in the Style section of the *New York Times*. He'd seen it lying faceup on the front desk of the Plaza.

Talk about being born with a silver spoon in your mouth, he thought, eyeing the heavy pearls and diamonds that were around her throat and dangling from her ears. Her family's fortune was in the billions and that count she'd just married wasn't exactly pulling down minimum wage either.

As she came deeper into the room, she turned in his direction and met his gaze. Her brows lifted regally when he didn't look away.

Maybe she resented being stared at. Maybe she sensed he didn't belong even though he dressed the part.

Maybe some of the lust he was feeling had crept into his face.

He hid his reaction as she scanned him. He was surprised by the shrewd light in her eyes and the fact that she lingered on his left ear, the one with the piece in it. He wouldn't have expected her to be so observant. A first-rate clotheshorse for haute couture, sure. The favorite arm candy of some wealthy man, yeah. But hiding half a brain under all that fancy window dressing? No way.

The countess continued into the room as Tiny's deep

voice came through the earpiece. The ambassador was fifteen minutes away. Smith glanced down at his watch. When he looked up, she was standing in front of him, having broken away from her admirers.

"Do I know you?" Her voice was soft, a little low for a woman. Incredibly sexy.

The smile she offered him was gentle and welcoming, nothing like the aristocratic, chilly grimace he would have predicted.

His eyes flickered over her. Her breasts were concealed by the silver gown but they were perfectly formed and the waist below them was small. He imagined that her legs, which were also covered by the dress, looked every bit as good. He also noticed her perfume, something light and tangy that got into his nose and then his nervous system.

"Haven't we met?" she repeated, putting out her hand and waiting for an answer.

Smith looked down. She'd given him her left hand and he caught a look at the jewels on her ring finger. She was wearing a monstrous sapphire and a thick band of diamonds.

The rings reminded him he'd just mentally undressed a married woman.

He glanced up into her eyes, wishing she'd go the hell away. They were beginning to attract attention as she stood there with her hand out.

"No, you don't know me," he said roughly, gripping her palm.

The instant he touched her, a flare of heat shot up his arm, and he saw an echo of it flash in her eyes. She pulled back sharply.

"Are you sure we haven't met?" Her head tilted to one side while she rubbed the hand, as if trying to get rid of an unpleasant sensation.

His earpiece fired up with another update on the ambassador. "Yeah, I'm sure."

Smith turned and walked away from her.

"Wait," he heard her call out.

He didn't stop, just kept heading for the back of the ballroom. Pushing open an unmarked door, he stepped into a corridor that was filled with extra chairs and tables. Bald lightbulbs were suspended from the squat ceiling and they cast harsh shadows on the concrete floor. The hall would take him to the service entrance the ambassador was going to use.

When he heard a clicking noise behind him, he turned around. The countess had followed him.

Even under the glare, she was breathtaking.

"What are you doing?" he demanded.

"Who are you?"

"What's it to you?"

She hesitated. "It's just that you were looking at me as if we'd met."

"Trust me. We haven't."

Smith started walking away again. The last thing the countess needed was another man panting after her. No doubt adoring simps were a dime a dozen in her life. And speaking of simps, why wasn't her husband drooling all over her tonight? She seemed to have come to the party alone.

Smith glanced over his shoulder.

The countess had turned back to the door. Her head was down, as if she were bracing herself before going back into the gala.

His feet slowed. Then stopped.

"What's wrong with you?" he called out, his voice bouncing off the bare walls. The instant he asked the question, he wanted to take it back, and muttered, "Someone show up wearing the same dress tonight?"

The countess's head snapped toward him. She straightened and regarded him coolly.

"There is absolutely nothing wrong with me." Her voice was steady, the words coming out clean and sharp. Maybe he'd imagined the vulnerability. "You, however, are sadly lacking in manners."

Smith frowned, thinking that she was damn efficient with the put-downs. With one sentence spoken in level, calm tones, she'd made him feel like a total heel. Then again, she'd no doubt had plenty of practice cutting people down, had probably perfected the skill on a whole retinue of servants and waiters over the years.

Well, he wasn't one of her lackeys. And she had no business getting in his way. Even if the ambassador's assassin was dead, the last thing Smith needed was to have someone like her hurt in the middle of one of his details. She needed to go back to the party now, so he could do his job.

Time to be a hard-ass, he thought.

Smith sauntered over to the countess and had to ignore the tantalizing scent of her while glaring into her eyes.

"Is there something you have to say?" she asked primly. "Or do you just want to loom over me?"

As she regarded him with that even stare, Smith was surprised. People backed off quickly when he glowered. The blonde was holding her own.

He pushed his face closer to hers, feeling irritated.

"I'm sorry if I merely offended you," he said. "I meant to piss you off."

"Now why would you want to do that?"

"Because you're in my way."

"How so?"

Time was passing, the ambassador was getting closer, and the countess's tenacity was beginning to get under his skin.

Just like her proximity was. Staring down at her, he felt an urgency that had nothing to do with timing.

And everything to do with hunger.

Wrong woman, wrong place, he thought. Get rid of her.

"Tell me, Countess, do you always beg for attention like this?" His voice was cold, disdainful.

"I'm not begging you for anything," she said smoothly.

"You pick the only man who has no interest in you and follow him out of the party. You think that's standoffish?"

He was itching to be free of her but there was more. His reaction to her, the strength and inappropriateness of it, made him wary. She was like standing in front of a fire.

And he was a man who had no intention of being burned.

He was surprised when her lips lifted in a slight smile. Instead of getting the reaction he'd banked on, some kind of huffy disapproval, he was being eyed with tolerant censure.

And then she shocked him by nailing the truth.

"You," she said decisively, "are threatened by me."

Smith was stunned and recovered with a jolt of anger.

Who did this blue-blooded Barbie doll think she was? He was in the business of saving lives and she paraded around in fancy dresses at parties. He dealt with murderers and thieves and psychos for a living. He was threatened by her? Screw that.

"You've got a hell of an ego there, Barbie," he said laconically, "if you think you're scary."

"And you seem increasingly antagonistic. I wonder why?"

Smith jabbed his thumb in the direction of the door.

"You better go on back to your friends out there in la-la land. You'll be much safer with those Ken dolls than alone with me in the service corridor."

In response, she had the gall to smile widely at him.

Didn't she understand he was a dangerous man? An armed man, for Chrissakes.

And did she have to smell so good?

The countess shook her head ruefully. "You know, I really thought you were someone different."

Different? She got that right. "You bet your sweet ass I have nothing in common with you."

"Out there, I thought you were really in control, in charge of something."

"Honey, I'm in charge of the whole world."

"Really? So why are you so upset? We're just talking."

"*We're* not doing anything. You're wasting my time."

She shrugged, an elegant lift of her shoulders. "You came back to me. No one is keeping you here."

As he towered over her, she raised her hands, the picture of innocence.

She turned back to the door and looked at him over her shoulder. "You also aren't very savvy."

"What the hell's that supposed to mean?"

"Sun Tzu, *The Art of War.* Some simple rules on human conflict. If your opponent is angry, irritate him." She shot him a glance from under her lashes while putting her hand on the doorknob. That big, relaxed smile of hers goaded him. "The instigation technique works particularly well, even with tough guys like you. Maybe especially with tough guys like you."

That did it.

In a surge of movement that had nothing to do with his conscious mind, Smith reached out and snatched her against him. She'd driven him to the brink of his self-control.

And one inch past it.

The amusement left her face as she braced her hands against his chest. "What are you doing?"

"Too late to go back now, Countess," he growled. "You pushed the wrong man, too far."

He took her lips in a punishing kiss, his arms contracting and holding her so tightly, he could feel every inch of her. The sensation of her body against his was a total shock. Her soft contours fit into his hard angles seamlessly and a wave of lust burned through him. She was like harnessing pure lightning, like nothing he'd ever felt before.

As he slid his tongue between her lips, a moan drifted up through her throat and into his mouth. He felt her grip his shoulders as she stopped trying to shove him away and began to kiss him back.

And then his earpiece went off. The ambassador's car had pulled up.

Smith broke the contact abruptly, stepping back and breathing hard. She opened her vivid green eyes and stared at him, wordlessly.

He paused, soaking in the way she looked. Her lips were swollen and red from his kiss, her breath was coming out in soft beats, and her cheeks were flushed. She was an unforgettable woman who would have to be forgotten. Otherwise he'd go insane, he was sure of it.

Smith turned away sharply and broke into a jog, knowing he better damn well be at that service entrance when the ambassador got out of his limo. He hadn't lost a client yet and he wasn't starting tonight.

Just forget you ever met her, he told himself as he pounded over the concrete.

Fat chance of that.

Dammit, why the hell did she have to follow him? And why hadn't he just kept going when she did?

Because it's just getting started between us, he thought grimly.

His sixth sense told him that their paths were going to cross again.

2

CUPPIE ALSTON was dead.

The words had been bouncing around Grace's head all day long, from the moment Alfred had called her with the terrible news. She still couldn't believe what had happened, couldn't comprehend that her friend had been killed the night before while they had been at the ambassador's ball.

The surrealism of it all had been a terrible companion on her long drive from New York City to the Adirondacks. Over miles of highways, county roads, and then winding mountain passes, her mind had struggled with the tragedy, churning relentlessly over happy memories that were now tinted gray with grief.

How could this be real, she thought once again as she pulled up to a sprawling mansion on the shores of Lake Sagamore. She turned off the Mercedes's engine and stared into the darkness.

She didn't like the silence or the lack of movement. With no distractions, her mind spiraled into something close to hysteria. Not only because Cuppie was dead but because she herself was now in danger.

Grace curled her fingers around the steering wheel and squeezed. Her conscious mind told her she hadn't been followed. A sliver of fear told her she might have been. She looked out into the night, searching for shadows. In the moonlight, she found them twisting and turning, thrown off by tree limbs waving in the wind.

Just a day before she wouldn't have gone looking for dark corners or wondered what they concealed.

But twenty-four hours ago, someone she knew hadn't been brutally murdered.

She lowered her forehead to the steering wheel.

The whole thing was inconceivable, like some bad movie. Cuppie found dead. In the foyer of the Alstons' lavish Central Park West penthouse. Next to the body, a recent article on the six most prominent women in the city. Cuppie had been the first one featured and her picture had been ripped out.

The piece had culminated by praising Grace.

Which was why she'd spent the afternoon at a police station. No one but the murderer knew for sure whether the other five women were next, but Grace could tell what the police believed. The lieutenant had treated her with kid gloves when she'd come in for questioning, even though he had a harsh, smoker's voice and the tired eyes of a man who wasn't impressed by much. He was, she realized, treating her like a victim.

When she'd walked into his cramped office, he'd done his best to cover up the crime scene photos but he hadn't been fast enough. She'd caught a glimpse of them and nearly retched. Cuppie's neck had been ripped apart, a gaping hole where her voice box should have been.

Grace didn't need a medical degree to see the violence in it all. Someone had stabbed Cuppie over and over and over again. Not just to kill her, but to defile her.

Nausea swelled and Grace pushed open the door, leaning out in spite of the seat belt. Because she'd left the keys in the ignition, the car chimed cheerfully, and she counted the passing moments by the electronic sounds. Looking at the gravel on the drive, she wondered what she'd clean up the mess with if her stomach followed through on its threat.

It'd be nice to have something pleasant to say when her oldest friend opened the door. *I just threw up in your side yard* was not the kind of greeting Grace wanted to offer. Much better to lead with *Congratulations on your marriage, Carter.* Or, *How does it feel to be Mrs. Nick Farrell?*

Grace looked up at the house. Someone walked past a window and she thought about how much she'd hated missing Carter and Nick's wedding. Her father had been buried the day they'd wed and the two life events, a beginning and an ending, had meant neither could be there to support the other in person. There had been plenty of phone calls, however.

And now there was another reason to reach out to her friend. Just when Grace thought she couldn't handle another awful surprise, when the loss of her father seemed an impossible weight in her chest and the failure of her marriage an embarrassing anchor to drag behind her, life had thrown another punch.

All things considered, it had been a horrible year. The high point had been her wedding in January and things had been on a downhill spiral ever since.

At least it was September and there wasn't much left, she thought.

The noise of the car got on her nerves so she pulled the key free. It was hard to marshal the energy to go inside even though the cold night air was working its way through her clothes. She didn't want to be less than perfectly happy for her friend but the effort of pretending seemed more than she could manage.

In a flash of memory, her father's voice, stern and commanding, came to her. *Buck up, Starfish. Let's see that smile.*

The refrain from childhood made her see him as he had been then, bending down, looking at her with love and determination. On command, she straightened and released the seat belt.

There'd be time enough to wallow in things she couldn't change on the trip back home. No amount of feeling sorry for herself was going to bring her father back and it wasn't going to change the implications of that article or the fact that Cuppie was being buried on Monday.

Grace flipped down the vanity mirror to check her makeup. The dark circles under her eyes were still hidden, but her lipstick had worn off. She fished through her purse, found a tube, and began to put some on.

The contact made her pause and she let her fingertips drift across her lips.

She could still feel his kiss. That soul-shattering meeting of mouths and tongues and bodies was as vivid to her as it had been just after they'd parted. She couldn't forget what it had felt like to be drawn in hard against that stranger's body, the way he'd touched her, the thundering in her blood.

She'd had, in that stark hallway, her first taste of passion.

Grace snapped the mirror up, disturbed.

It was too bad she was never going to see him again. She had no idea who he was or where he was from and she knew asking questions about a man like him would get talk started. She was still legally married, after all, and he was dangerously attractive. The last thing she needed was to spark rumors.

God knew, they bubbled up enough of their own accord.

What she needed to do was buck up, drag herself into that beautiful house, and share in her friend's joy.

As Grace stepped out of the car, she looked over her shoulder. Moving swiftly, she grabbed her Vuitton bags and rushed over to the house. Just as her feet hit the porch, Carter Wessex threw open the door with arms outstretched.

"Woody! You made it!"

Grace dropped the luggage and hugged her friend hard.

"Whoa, you okay?"

"Fine, just fine. I'm glad to see you." Grace smiled as they pulled away.

"Well, you look fantastic. Then again, you always do."

Grace glanced down at the Chanel suit she was wearing. She couldn't wait to take it off, get it away from her skin. It reminded her of the police station.

"Why don't you leave your bags here and let's go into the kitchen." Carter pushed her thick, black hair over her shoulder. "Have you eaten?"

Grace's stomach let out a wheeze of protest. "I'm not hungry, but I could use a glass of wine."

Or two.

"Well, I've got plenty of that," Carter said as she led the

way to the rear of the house. "I'm so glad you've come for the weekend. Nick's flying into Albany from London and driving up, too. He should be home within the hour. He's looking forward to getting to know you a little better."

"Me, too. Those big parties I always see him at are hardly the place to make friends."

Carter laughed. "Which was precisely why I gave them up."

When they'd settled down at a sturdy oak table in the kitchen, a plate of cheese and fruit between them, Grace raised her glass of Chardonnay. "To my best friend and comrade in arms. May your marriage be long and full of joy."

With a warm light in her intense blue eyes, Carter smiled. "I'm so glad you came."

"Me, too." Grace looked away. "So tell me about the wedding. Were you gorgeous?"

"How are you doing?" Her friend's voice had an edge to it.

"I told you. I'm fine, Mrs. Farrell. Now, I want details, although the CliffsNotes version of the wedding night will be sufficient."

"You look exhausted."

"You just told me I looked fabulous."

"You look fabulous and tired." Carter's expression softened. "I've been worried about you. I know how close you and your father were."

Grace glanced down into her wine. "Let's only talk about good things. Wouldn't you rather wow me with details of the honeymoon?"

The silence that followed told her that Carter, in typical fashion, wasn't going to be sidetracked.

Grace put her glass to her lips and emptied it in two swallows. Liquid courage, she thought, tilting the thing toward her friend.

Carter obligingly refilled it.

"Did you read in today's paper about Cuppie Alston's death?"

Carter frowned. "A gruesome tragedy. You knew her well, didn't you?"

Grace nodded. "I was at the reception last night. Waiting for her to arrive like everyone else."

"That must have been awful."

"It was. They kept extending the cocktail hour until finally they had to start the program without her. That empty chair on the dais . . ." Grace shuddered. "They found an article next to the body, about socialites in the city. Cuppie was one of the women covered by it."

"Don't tell me they think it's some kind of serial killer?"

Grace took a deep breath. "I was also featured in the piece. I was questioned by the police today."

Her friend's response was a shocked hiss.

"My God, Grace." Carter reached across the table, knocking over a saltshaker.

Grace gave her friend a reassuring squeeze while righting the shaker with her other hand.

Just then, the back door swung open and Nick Farrell strode into the kitchen. They both looked up.

Farrell was a big man, a powerful man, dressed in an elegant pinstriped suit with a pale blue shirt and dark tie. As he placed a lingering kiss on his new wife's mouth, Grace looked away discreetly.

"So this is not just Grace Woodward Hall," Carter said, nodding her head across the table. "This is my old friend Woody."

Pale gray eyes narrowed. "I've heard a lot of things about what you and Carter have done together."

As she shook his hand, Grace forced a smile. "It is true we were almost kicked out of Groton for smuggling in wine coolers, but that thing about the St. Mark's lacrosse team is a total fabrication."

He laughed and glanced back at Carter. Instantly, his expression changed. Dark brows crashed together. "What's wrong?"

Carter's eyes flashed across the table. When Grace shrugged, her friend explained. When she was done, Farrell wore a grim expression.

"Here's what we're going to do," he said.

"Please," Grace interrupted. "None of this is your problem. I don't want to—"

"We're going to call John Smith."

"That's a great idea," Carter declared.

"Who's John Smith?" Grace asked. "Other than a man with a ridiculously ubiquitous name?"

"He's helped me in the past," Farrell said. "He's a private security guy. First rate. And he's very discreet."

"I don't really think that's necessary."

Nick shot her a blunt look. "Whoever left that article is probably just getting started. You want to meet him some night when you happen to be alone?"

The picture of Cuppie's throat flashed through her mind and Grace felt a stab of fear in her chest.

Carter frowned and stroked her arm protectively. "You don't have to be so harsh, Nick."

"I apologize, but you both know I'm right. She needs a bodyguard."

Grace looked away from the man's intense, diamond-colored eyes. The last thing she felt up to was fighting with someone like Farrell about her own safety. She didn't have the energy to spare and, even if she did, she had a feeling he rarely backed down once he'd made up his mind.

"I'm calling Smith right now," he announced and left the room.

Grace took a deep breath and closed her eyes. She shouldn't have come, she thought.

Carter rushed to apologize. "I'm sorry. He can be a little . . . aggressive when he worries. We're working on that. It's really just because he's concerned."

Grace shrugged, feeling the tension in her shoulders. "I don't want to be an alarmist. I'm not a movie star who needs a posse and I don't want some doughnut-munching rent-a-cop following me around."

"From what I've heard about this guy, Smith seems more like a trained killer."

Grace flattened her lips. "I don't want that either."

When Farrell came back ten minutes later, he said, "Smith'll be here tomorrow morning."

Grace opened her mouth to protest but the two of them just stared at her with almost identical expressions of determination.

No wonder they were such a great pair, she thought. Although their arguments could probably level a city block.

"I guess it can't hurt to talk to him," she said, giving up.

As they smiled at her, Grace took another sip from her glass. Inside, she felt numb. As she had so often in previous weeks, she found herself wondering whose life she was living.

The next morning, Grace paced around the mansion's living room until she thought she'd wear a track in the Aubusson rug. She made herself stop in front of an Early American mirror and stared at her reflection. Her face was disfigured by the leaded glass and the contortion seemed right.

She didn't feel much like herself, either.

She ran a hand down her skirt and adjusted her silk shirt, though neither needed the fine-tuning. She'd thrown the suit she'd arrived in back on. It was business, after all, and Chanel made her feel in control.

Grace wore Chanel a lot.

Feeling restless, she checked the backings of the heavy diamond studs she was wearing. Both were secure. She glanced down at her shoes. Not a speck of dirt on them. She wouldn't have minded a tear or a smudge requiring an emergency blast of seltzer. Without anything to focus on, she just dwelled on the lack of oxygen in the sun-drenched, airy room.

She went over to a window and pushed it open, welcoming the cool autumn breeze on her face. Outside, the lake was calm, the sun was shining, the day seemed full of promise. Perversely, she wished it was raining.

"He's just pulled up," Carter said from the doorway.

Grace turned around just as Nick came up behind his wife, putting his hands on her shoulders.

"You ready?" he asked.

"Bring on Mr. Smith," Grace replied as the brass door knocker let out a thundering noise.

This was all wrong, she thought, as Nick went to open the door. She didn't want a security detail. What she wanted was for Cuppie to be alive. She wanted to go back to Thursday night at the Plaza and to see Cuppie sitting between her husband and the ambassador all the way through the dessert course.

Grace fiddled with her watch, looking down at the platinum dial. She wasn't going to hire whoever came into the room and regretted letting herself get talked into the meeting. Nick might have had her best interests at heart but she felt like she'd been pushed.

What was it about her that made her a sucker for controlling men? Her father had been utterly devoted to her but he'd also been domineering and heavy-handed. She'd learned to accept the good and the bad in him, reminding herself, when he made unreasonable demands or tried to take over her life, how much he loved her. But being able to see both sides of him was not the same as sticking up for herself and that had led to her marrying the wrong man.

Her husband, Ranulf, had been equally difficult. With his continental opinions about what ladies should and shouldn't do, he'd proven to be a close second to her father when it came to issuing orders.

Her mother was no damn walk in the park, either.

Grace took a shallow breath as she heard the deep rumble of men's voices and then the sound of heavy footfalls.

It was high time she stopped being polite and started taking control of her life. As a result of her caving in last night, some poor guy had come from God only knew where just to waste his time. She didn't want this kind of help. And she wasn't going to let Nick Farrell's aggressive concern, or her old friend's more muted variety, make her take on a bodyguard.

She grimaced. As for the man who'd come in hopes of getting hired, she'd be up front and apologize, tell him that it was a mistake. She'd pay his expenses, of course. Yes, that was the right thing to do.

Grace lifted her head and stopped breathing. She had to blink her eyes, to make sure she wasn't dreaming.

"It's you," she whispered as she stared into the hard face of the man who had kissed her.

Her heart kicked into overdrive.

What was he doing here? Was he a—

But of course, he'd been protecting the ambassador.

That was why he'd been at the ball. That was why he stood out from all the other men as someone harder, tougher, different.

Too bad it hadn't been Cuppie he'd been watching over.

She swallowed through a tight throat. He was exactly as she remembered him, larger than life, colder than ice. His face was drawn in bold lines, anchored by a square jaw and a nose that looked as if it had been broken at least once. His haircut was short as a military man's, his penetrating eyes an intense blue. This time, he was wearing a black leather jacket and a pair of well-worn blue jeans, but he looked every bit as commanding as he had in the tuxedo.

As he stood in front of her, she remembered exactly how it had felt to be kissed by him, but she couldn't tell what he was thinking. He didn't show a lick of emotion. There was no shock or disbelief as he starred at her, not even curiosity. His opaque gaze betrayed nothing except for his intelligence and a quiet, brooding menace.

"You know each other?" Nick asked.

When the other man didn't offer an explanation, Grace murmured, "We met . . . sort of, at a party. Recently."

Nick's eyebrow cocked as Grace stepped forward, offering her hand. She was nervous about getting close to John Smith, afraid that something of what had happened between them might show in her face.

"It's good to see you again."

As soon as he gripped her palm, she felt like she'd been hit by an electrical charge. The sensation ran through her fingers, up her arm, and pegged her in the chest. She pulled back abruptly.

Just as she had the first time she'd shaken his hand.

"Would you like us to stay with you?" Carter asked her. "While you talk?"

Grace shook her head and they left her alone. With him.

"Won't you sit down?" she asked.

A mocking light came into his eyes as he picked a chair opposite the sofa and lowered his body down in it. Even seated, he looked tall, she thought.

"You don't seem surprised to see me." Grace settled on the sofa, crossing her legs. His eyes followed the movement, lingering on her calves, before returning to her face.

"I don't put myself in positions where I'm going to be surprised." His voice was deep and gravelly, totally confident.

He was all male, she thought, with the requisite pride, arrogance, and ego that came with an overload of testosterone. Of course, he did look tough as nails, so maybe the faith in himself was justified. She sure wouldn't want to get him angry. She'd done that once already and all it'd gotten her was a fantasy life she could do without.

"So let's talk about why I'm here." He crossed his arms over his chest. Impatience came off him in waves, threading through his low voice.

Grace's fingers went to her heavy engagement ring and she began twisting it around in circles. When those sharp eyes of his flicked over the movement, she forced herself to sit still.

She should just tell him to go, as she'd planned to, as she would have if there was a stranger sitting in that chair.

He was a stranger, she reminded herself.

"I'm afraid you've wasted your time." When she paused, his eyebrow rose. "I mean, I don't think you can help me. Er—that I need help."

As she tripped over her words, she wondered where in the hell her head was. Probably down the same black hole her life had fallen into.

"I can reimburse you for your travel up here," she added quickly.

"I'm sure of that," he drawled, looking back down at her rings. There was a subtle disdain in his eyes, a tightness to his mouth, that suggested there were other places he'd rather be.

She bristled at his tone and the expression. She could tell he didn't think much of her. So why had he come? As a favor to Nick?

"And I apologize for any inconvenience."

"How polite of you."

Silence stretched between them.

"I just don't think I'm in sufficient danger to justify a bodyguard."

"That so."

"Yes. Nick insisted on calling you. It wasn't my idea."

"Oh really."

Grace glared at him. He sent her a bored look in return.

He could at least pretend to be interested, she thought.

She crossed her arms over her chest, realized she was mimicking his pose and put her hands back in her lap. She had an absurd urge to yell at him because he was getting under her skin with all his terse silence, making her feel foolish and frivolous.

She narrowed her eyes and gave in to a childish urge to talk at him. Just to prove she could.

"I live in New York City and I work there, too. Have you ever heard of the Hall Foundation?" Before he could respond, she kept going, feeling like words were a way to burn off a little anxiety. A little frustration. Maybe of the sexual variety. She almost cringed. "My family started it in the late 1800s. We give grants to scholars, art historians, archaeologists, anyone who is seriously studying American history—"

He held his hand up to cut her off. There was a scar in the middle of his palm and she wondered how it got there. Hand-to-hand combat?

"I'll pass on the infomercial. Tell me something I don't know. You can leave out anything in the public domain."

Grace frowned at the curt words. "I live on Park Avenue—"

"I know."

"My office is at—"

A dark eyebrow arched.

Grace shot him a level stare. "I hate musicals and Mexican food makes me gassy. I eat it anyway, though."

To her surprise, the corner of his mouth twitched.

So Mr. Tough Guy could lighten up after all, she thought with a flare of triumph.

"You didn't know either of those?" she challenged.

John Smith's eyes didn't waver from hers. "No."

"Good. Let's see, I'm a fan of romance novels. Gaelen Foley writes these fabulous historicals—"

"I don't want to know what you read," he interrupted sardonically, "and I could care less about your intestinal tract. Why don't you get to the point."

Grace tightened her lips. Any chance of dismissing him in a polite, thoughtful way was fading fast. Her temper was starting to rear its thorny head and he seemed perfectly content to watch her boil while being the model of calm restraint.

Well, two could play at the cool, haughty routine. Thanks to her mother's arctic example, Grace was a master of the deep freeze.

She cleared her throat. "Tell you what—why don't you share what you've dug up about me? So I don't keep boring you."

Their eyes clashed as she waited for him to speak.

3

SITTING ACROSS from the countess, Smith could feel his temperature rising. As improbable as it seemed, the pristine woman perched on the sofa was managing to get under his skin again.

She was so damn beautiful sitting on that fancy piece of furniture. She'd arranged herself with precision, her legs crossed at the knees, her hands clasped elegantly in front of her. With her hair coiled up on her head, and wearing that expensive, modestly cut suit, she was every bit the lady. Poised, graceful, elegant.

The countess shifted, recrossing her long legs.

His eyes traced her delicate ankles and her shapely calves and he felt a stab of pure, unfettered lust. He wondered what she'd look like without all those expensive clothes on and decided she'd probably fall over in a heap if someone asked her to put on sweatpants.

When he'd gotten the call from Farrell, he'd been tempted to turn the invitation down. His instincts told him that taking the Countess von Sharone on as a client would be a complicated affair and not just because of their kiss. She was world-renowned. An icon, for Chrissakes. And someone who, most likely, was a diva of the highest order, capable of making actors or opera singers look meek and self-deprecating.

But he'd come anyway. He was curious to see her in person one last time, if for no other reason than to prove that she was just a woman. A woman prettier than most maybe, but she was first and foremost a living, breathing person who would one day get liver spots and gray hair, just like everyone else. Nothing special.

Trying to find something unattractive, he scanned her closely, but only ended up focusing on the color of her eyes. They were a very icy green now that she was upset with him.

Damn fine color, he thought. Like a Granny Smith apple.

"Cat got your tongue," she prompted.

He frowned, thinking she was trying to bait him. It wasn't going to work this time. "You can't honestly be offended that I investigated your background?"

"It's more your attitude."

"I'm not here to charm you."

"What a relief. I hate pointing out the failures of others."

Smith felt an unexpected urge to smile. Her sense of humor was a surprise. So was the fact that she was fidgety. Her hands were busy braiding the fringe on a silk pillow.

"So are you going to talk to me or what?" she demanded sharply.

Yup, there was definitely some diva in her.

"I know where you live and work," he drawled. "I know you're very wealthy. And I know you're featured in that article on powerful women found with Cuppie Alston's body."

Grace's eyes widened as she paled. "How do you know that?"

"Quite a number of New York's finest are friends of mine."

"Oh." She hesitated and then brought a shaking hand up to her hair.

He was intrigued by the show of fear, considering she'd gone out of her way to tell him she didn't think she was in danger.

"So you want to tell me the truth?" he asked.

"About what?"

"How you're really feeling." He looked pointedly at her trembling hand.

She quickly tucked it into her lap.

"I—ah, I am a bit disoriented," she murmured. "I've never had any kind of a threat before."

"That's surprising."

"Why?"

He sensed she asked the question just to get him to talk, as if she wanted to buy some time to get herself under control. He decided to indulge her.

"You lead a high-profile life and have a schedule Amtrak would envy. You leave your penthouse every morning at the same time, go on a run, get into your office by eight o'clock. You work until seven, you go out, you're home by eleven. Weekends are the same as weekdays."

"You managed to find all that out in less than twenty-four hours?" Her expression was incredulous.

"Three questions. That's all it took. And my car was running at the curb while your doorman was talking." He glanced down at the rings on her finger. "I also know that your husband hasn't been around for much of the past month. In spite of the death of your father."

Abruptly, she rose from the sofa and went over to the windows. Although her walk was smooth and calm, he wasn't fooled. She was winding the rings around her finger again.

There was something going on with the husband, he thought.

When she stayed silent, he said, "So now that I've shown you mine, you want to show me yours?"

There was a protracted pause. She reached up to the window and rested one hand on the glass. Her fingernails were trimmed neatly but not polished. It was another surprise but it made sense. She didn't overdo it with the makeup, either.

When she finally turned to face him, her face was arranged carefully into an expression of tranquillity. It was a lovely lie, he thought as his gaze drifted down to the graceful line of her neck. Her slender hand came up and fussed with her collar, as if she felt his eyes on her skin.

There was an elegance in the way she moved, he thought, a smoothness. He was surprised by how attractive he found it.

When she spoke next, her voice was marked by a brusque urgency and he knew then she was going to tell him everything. Or most of everything.

"I noticed about three weeks ago that I was being followed. It was right after my father's death. I was walking into the Hall Building after dark and I thought I saw someone behind me. When I came out an hour later, there was a figure across the street. Waiting for me."

Her words came out fast and edgy, as if spilled, and he thought she probably kept a lot to herself most of the time. Preserving that beautiful image, no doubt.

"Was it a man or a woman?"

"I couldn't see clearly. But I assumed it was a man."

"And how do you know the person was waiting for you?"

"Because when I got in my car, he left. To be honest, it could have just been a paparazzo. They're hungry for candids of me looking mournful."

"But you don't really believe it was a photographer, do you?"

"He didn't take any pictures. And then a couple of days later, I know for sure I was trailed. I was going out to Newport by car with my father's ashes. My driver noticed it first. A white sedan behind us, all the way into Connecticut."

The countess's hands were busy with her watch, playing with the catch, releasing and closing, releasing and closing, a small noise marking each movement. He suspected she was screaming inside that fine skin of hers.

"Again, I told myself it had to be the press, that someone must have leaked that we were going to lay him to rest. There were photographers at the cemetery and I did see a white sedan just outside the gates."

"You still felt threatened, though."

She nodded, reluctantly. "And it hasn't stopped. I'll be coming out of a restaurant and I'll see someone step back, out of the light. I leave work and, I swear, I'll see a figure across the street. Yesterday morning, I came out of my building and I thought I·saw him on the corner."

The countess paused and looked out at the lake. Her brows drew tightly together, knotting the skin of her forehead. She was searching for answers, he could tell. He'd seen the same questing look before in people who felt their lives were slipping out of their control.

From out of nowhere, Smith felt like he should say something. He wasn't much for offering sympathy, even to women who were in danger. Emotions were just not his bag. He was into saving lives, not nurturing, but there was something about her that struck him as unique and worthy. She wasn't a hysterical woman manufacturing fear to get attention. She was scared, truly afraid, yet her chin was up and she was trying so damn hard to be strong.

He was fascinated by the show of will, especially considering how nervous she was.

She took a deep breath and turned toward him. "The police called the morning after Cuppie's body was found. They questioned me pretty extensively."

Smith thought back to that night, to the party. He remembered the tortured expression on Alfred Alston's face as the ambassador had arrived and been seated next to an empty chair. Alston's wife had never showed up because her plans for the evening had been intercepted by tragedy. Instead of enjoying the dinner and engaging in light and witty banter with an international dignitary, the woman had been struggling against her killer and then bleeding to death by herself, surrounded by lovely works of art and expensive antiques, none of which could save her.

According to the police, the murderer's identity was a mystery, the motive, unclear. The only real piece of evidence had been the newspaper article found with the body. It didn't take a genius to know the killer might get busy again soon.

"What does your husband have to say about all this?" Smith asked.

Her face tightened and she remained quiet, as if trying to form an answer.

"Countess, where *is* your husband?"

She stiffened. "In Europe."

"When is he coming back?"

There was a pause. "Why is that relevant?"

"The man's married to you. In fact, I'm surprised he's

not here today. Most husbands don't take it well when their wives might be on the short list of a murderer."

"He's a busy man. I don't want to bother him." Her gaze skipped away.

Smith's eyes narrowed. "And why don't the police know that you're being followed? You didn't want to bother them, either?"

She began twisting the rings again. "How did you know—"

"My buddies down at the precinct were pretty forthcoming as to what they knew about you. They didn't mention you were being trailed," he explained coolly. "Why keep it to yourself?"

She shrugged. "As far as I'm concerned, the less I tell the police, the better. Leaks happen and I'm tired of being on the front page after weeks of nonstop coverage. The last thing I need right now is some exposé about either my paranoia or my connection with the murder."

"So you'd rather be dead than in the newspapers?"

She wrapped her arms around herself. "That's a harsh thing to say."

Smith brushed a hand over his hair impatiently. He was surprised at how frustrated he was with her. "Sorry."

"Thank you." The countess cleared her throat. "As I said before, I'm not sure I need you ... your services. We have our own security force at the Hall Building and with a phone call I can get someone round-the-clock. Anyway, I'm sure this will just blow over."

"No, you aren't."

Her eyes leapt away from his again. "Don't tell me what I think."

"Then be honest with me and I won't have to."

The countess's chin rose a little higher.

As the urge to browbeat her into hiring him struck, Smith had to ask himself what he was doing. It was none of his business if she went and got herself killed. The fact that he was even entertaining the notion of pushing her to take care of herself rankled. What the hell did he care?

He got to his feet and started walking out of the room.

"Where are you going?"

He spoke over his shoulder.

"Despite the fact that you know about the article found with the body and you admit you're being stalked, you aren't ready to take this seriously. You haven't been up front with the police, I know you're not being totally honest with me, and you say you're not even sure you want help. We don't have anything else to discuss."

"So you're leaving? Just like that?" She began to follow him as he walked into the front hall.

"I'm not going to talk you into protecting yourself. But I'll give you a prediction for free. One of two things is going to happen. You're either going to smarten up and call me later or you're going to get hurt. It's your life and you get to pick."

Her voice was strained as she reached out and touched his arm. "You think it's that serious?"

He looked down at her hand and then into her eyes. She stepped back abruptly. "You're the one who can't sleep at night."

"How did you know I can't sleep?"

"Experience."

He reached into his back pocket. When he did, his jacket opened. He saw her catch a glimpse of his gun and thought she looked queasy.

"Here's my card." He scribbled a number on the back. "That's my cell phone."

She took it from him. "Will you come if I call?"

He shrugged. "Maybe."

"But what if I need you?"

"It's my life. And I get to choose who needs me."

She looked back down at the card. Her mouth opened, as if she were going to say something, but then she gave a resigned shrug.

"Sounds fair." When her eyes met his, that delicate chin was thrust out again, a study in determination. "I guess this is good-bye."

As he stared into her eyes, he had a feeling she'd move heaven and earth not to have to call him.

Good thing he didn't take it personally.

"So long, Countess." He opened the front door and stepped out into the fall sunshine.

"You kissed me just because you were angry, didn't you."

The words, soft and low, stopped him dead in his tracks. He hadn't expected her to bring up what had happened between them at all, much less in such a straightforward way.

Smith turned toward her. Pale sunlight was cascading over her face, highlighting her cheekbones and the tender curve of her lips. Her blond hair positively shone.

"Yes. I was angry."

"That's what I thought." A curious insecurity colored her expression, one that he didn't understand. "Thank you for being honest."

Well, he'd been mostly honest. The part about him continuing to kiss her because he couldn't stop, he'd kept to himself.

Then it dawned on him.

"It won't happen again if I work with you," he said, annoyed. That was one disclaimer he'd never had to make before.

She nodded. "Not again."

"*Never* again." He smiled grimly at her hesitation.

If she only knew how little she had to worry about. He had a reputation for having a cool head and a cold heart and he'd earned it. No Barbie doll sweetheart, no matter how beautiful, was going to change that. Or him.

The countess hovered in the doorway, neither in nor out of the house.

"Was there something else you were worried about?" he asked sharply. "You want references or something?"

She shook her head while staring at his business card. "No, I don't need references. I know you're the best because Nick Farrell says you are. And because you carry yourself as if you wouldn't stand for being anything less."

At least she got that right.

He paused for a moment.

"Take care of yourself," he said, turning away.

"Where do you live?"

"Excuse me?" He looked back at her. Glared at her, actually.

He was ready to leave, impatient to put her behind him, and he wasn't used to personal questions. His clients were usually so wrapped up in their own problems that the subject of his life never came up. It was one of the things he liked most about his job.

She shrugged. "I just wondered where you're headed."

"I'm going. That's all you need to know."

He walked briskly over to his car.

Grace watched as Smith got into a black SUV and drove off. In his wake, dust from the gravel drive was kicked up and it rose as a milky cloud. She looked down at the card again. It was made of stiff white paper and engraved with dark ink.

Black Watch, Ltd. There was a number in the lower left-hand corner but no address.

She turned it over and looked at the numbers he'd written in bold strokes. She brushed her fingertip over them.

She hadn't meant to tell him everything, had wanted to make the meeting short and sweet, but it hadn't turned out that way. She smiled bleakly. There was nothing short or sweet about John Smith.

And she certainly hadn't intended to bring up the kiss. That little ditty had leapt out of her mouth, a traitorous slip of the tongue. It was a stupid thing to ask. Had she really expected him to say he'd done it because he found her irresistible?

After all, he was one of the most aggressive, fierce men she'd ever seen, as tough as they come. Hell, he looked like he could chew steel and spit out nails. No doubt he'd want an earthy, luscious woman to complement that hardness, someone who was wildly feminine. Someone who could lie on her back naked, open and waiting for him, tempting him with her sexuality. Someone who became wild, unhinged while making love.

Not some tightly wrapped, goody two-shoes, paragon of polite society.

Disappointment burned in her stomach.

Forget about it, she told herself. Forget about him.

Grabbing the brass door handle, Grace threw her weight into closing the heavy door. As she pushed it home, she caught one last glimpse of the fine dust that floated in the air over the drive, like a promise of things to come.

4

THE FOLLOWING week, Grace was in her father's former office reviewing the invitation list for the Foundation's annual gala, when the intercom buzzed softly. She jerked and the pen skidded across the paper.

Her assistant's voice was tinny as it came through the speakerphone. "Mr. Lamont is coming to see you and I have something for you to sign."

Great, she thought. All she needed was another meeting with that man. Each time they talked, their relationship deteriorated further.

"Come on in before he gets here."

Grace tugged at the Hermès scarf around her neck. When she loosened the knot and it still felt like a noose, she took the thing off altogether. The tangerine-and-yellow silk fell into a vibrant pool on the desk.

She was getting sick and tired of jumping all the time. The spasms were triggered by a host of things such as phones ringing, footsteps in the hall, sudden noises. She felt like a marionette, yanked around by strings she had no control over.

It was a hell of an exercise program, she thought, putting her arms out against the desk and stretching.

The chair and the desk had been her father's command post. They were massive pieces of furniture, made of hand-carved mahogany and fitting for a man of Cornelius Woodward Hall's imposing size and demeanor. She'd always loved them. As a child, when he'd brought her into the office on weekends, she'd sit in his lap feeling utterly safe, surrounded by the strength of his arms and the heft of all the wood.

Now, with only herself to fill the chair, she felt loose in it, dwarfed by its high back and thick armrests. Still, she was loath to get replacements. They were such a part of her father, as were the dramatic landscapes that hung on the walls, the formal conference table he'd taken his meetings at, the leather-bound books on the shelves.

She thought of him every time she walked into the room.

Glancing past his pipe rack and a candy dish still stocked with the peppermints he'd loved, she looked into a bronze bust of her father's face. Cast when he was in his fifties, it showed a handsome man with a distant smile and sharp eyes.

Lately, her memories of him seemed like the only allies she had at the Foundation.

When he'd died following a heart attack, he'd left her almost a billion dollars in his will, as well as his title of president and CEO of the Hall Foundation. The money was hers to keep as soon as the estate went through probate. Her ownership of the titles was proving less absolute. The job was hers by birthright but also one she'd been training for since she'd started interning at the Foundation while in college. Unfortunately, Cornelius's intent had been clear only on paper and others had a different idea of who should be sitting on the throne.

Grace was up to the task of leading the Foundation. She knew the employees, the mission, the strategy for its future. She knew what needed to get done both on the business side and with the social set that poured millions into its coffers every year. She also knew there were those who thought she couldn't handle the job. That she was too young and inexperienced. That a change of guard might be a good thing.

Some of the older dissidents even objected because she was a woman. That particular criticism really got her steamed. As if wearing pants was somehow a prerequisite for success.

The nexus of her naysayers was a tight-knit group of

directors, led by Charles Bainbridge, the board's chair. They were all older men who had respected her father, but weren't content to have him rule from the grave if they thought Cornelius was wrong about something. They were men she had grown up around, who had come to the Hall family's Christmas parties and Fourth of July fetes. Some of them had probably seen her in diapers and still remembered her with braces.

She could understand why it would be difficult for them to view her as anything other than young and decorative and she was determined to bring them around. She just hoped she had enough time before they pushed her aside into some figurehead position and let Lou Lamont run the place.

The door to the office swung open and Katherine Focerelli came into the room. Kat was in her midtwenties and working her way through law school at night. Grace had hired her the day after her father's death, when she'd moved into the office. In a matter of weeks, Kat already seemed to know the ins and outs of the Foundation and didn't seem that impressed with Lou Lamont.

The latter was a huge seller in Grace's mind.

The young woman was also a welcome replacement for the gray-haired ballbuster who had served for years as Cornelius's secretary. Getting rid of that old battle-ax had been one of the first things Grace had done when she'd taken over.

"Here are the documents for the Randolph dig," Kat said, a dimple showing in one cheek as she smiled.

Grace leafed through the pages, checking that the changes she'd made had been incorporated correctly. They had.

As she scrawled her name, she said, "So what's Lamont up to now?"

"He said he needed ten minutes, but wouldn't tell me why. I put him on the calendar only because you told me never to turn him away. By the way, your five o'clock got bumped and the mayor wants you to call him at six thirty. Oh, and is it okay if I leave early tonight? I'm going on a blind date."

"Only if you fill me in on what happens tomorrow," Grace said, passing the papers back across the desk.

"Can't be worse than the last one."

"The one who wanted you to get in touch with your inner artist?"

"No, the last one was the guy with the Peter Pan fixation. The one who wanted me to body paint him with my lipstick was two dates ago."

"Hard to keep track."

"Hard to keep a straight face, too. God, when am I going to meet a real man?"

An image of Smith came to mind as Kat bustled out.

Grace dug her heels into the carpeting and pushed back the chair. The office was on the top floor of the Hall Building and took up the whole northeast corner. The windows and the view they offered were one of the space's greatest assets.

She looked out at the majestic New York skyline, a chorus of buildings rising from the earth, silver and iron gray and black. With the sun just dropping over the horizon, a peach glow was growing in the sky.

She was having a terrible time forgetting about Smith. The man had been lingering in her mind, like an impulse she couldn't shrug, since he'd turned away from her for the second time. She wondered again if she should call him and knew only one thing for sure. If she did, she better have made up her mind to hire him. He wasn't the type to tolerate having his time wasted again.

The intercom buzzed. "Mr. Lamont to see you."

Grace went back to the desk. "Tell him I'll be right there."

She crossed over the deep red Oriental rug and pushed back a pocket door to reveal her father's private bathroom. In the gilded mirrors, she checked her chignon and her makeup. Everything was holding up well. She looked elegant and composed, just like a Hall should be.

Good thing no one knew the truth.

She had indigestion, thanks to having eaten tic tacs and three old Fig Newtons for lunch. The beginning of a headache was digging in at her temples, her left foot had a blister on it from the new pair of Jimmy Choos she was wearing, and her bra had a little rough spot under the clasp in back that was irritating her no end.

She was coming out of the bathroom when her cell phone rang. Rushing behind the desk, she answered it curtly. When she heard Lieutenant Marks's hoarse voice on the phone, her blood ran cold.

"We've found another body," he said.

Grace gripped the phone, the plastic cutting into her skin. "Who?"

"Suzanna van der Lyden. Early this morning."

A wave of dizziness crashed over her and she fell backward into her father's chair. She'd seen Suzanna two nights before at a prominent museum's annual fund-raiser. The woman had chaired the event for the past few years.

"Where did it . . . happen?"

"At her home."

"Do you have any idea who . . ." She couldn't finish.

"We're still going through the crime scene. We found her late last night when her husband, who was traveling, called us when he couldn't reach her. Listen, I'd like to assign a detail to you."

"A detail?"

"A couple of my men. So you're protected."

Her first impulse was to say yes, but then she pictured a photo of herself surrounded by cops showing up on the front page of some tabloid.

"Don't worry," Marks said, obviously guessing what she was thinking, "they'll be in plainclothes."

"I'd like some time to think about it."

Marks hesitated. "Okay. You know where to find me."

When Marks hung up, she sat frozen in the chair, her phone in her hand.

She should do something, she thought. Call someone. Go somewhere safe.

Except there was no one to go to and nowhere to hide. Her mother was hardly the place for solace and good advice. She'd already leaned on Carter enough. And she'd rather be by herself than with Ranulf.

She was totally alone.

And how ironic, considering she'd spent the morning culling a list of the city's top five hundred luminaries.

When the intercom buzzed, her head snapped around.

"Mr. Lamont says he needs to go to another meeting."

"Right. I'm coming," Grace answered.

But in reality she was going nowhere. Her mind was clogged, her body unresponsive. Abruptly, she felt her chest tighten, as if she'd inhaled something toxic, and she bolted to her feet. She knew what was coming next.

The anxiety attack came on fast and hard, bringing with it a crushing sensation of suffocation. She couldn't breathe. She couldn't—there was no . . . no breath in her lungs.

Opening her mouth, she tried to reassure herself that she was in fact drawing in air. She felt it passing over her lips and her tongue but it seemed to travel no farther. As her body ran away from her mind, she braced herself on the desk and broke out in a cold sweat. Quick breaths went in and out of her. Frantically, she brought a hand up and wiped off her forehead. Hell of a lot of good that did. Her fingers were numb now and all they did was tangle in her hair.

Grace wheeled around, caught sight of the big windows and the overpowering view and let out a moan as her head spun. She doubled over, leaning on the back of the mighty chair and putting her head down on her arms.

She tried to picture happier times. Her father at her college graduation, beaming from the crowd. The way she'd felt when she'd finished her first marathon. That Thomas Cole she'd just bought.

Good things, happy things. Things that didn't have anything to with death. Invasion. Terror. Things that would block out that picture of Cuppie lying dead on a marble floor.

Gradually, almost imperceptibly, she began to notice that her legs were shaking. So were her hands. And her bra was still jabbing her in the back.

Her breathing began to return to normal. Her heartbeat slowed.

When she felt up to it, she raised her head and ran an

unsteady hand over the chignon. A piece of hair in the front had been dislodged and she tucked it behind her ear.

Exhaustion came over her in a rush but it was a relief. Anything was better than the crushing explosion of fear.

Oh, God.

She didn't know how she was going to keep going.

Minutes later, Grace walked across the office to the double doors that led out into the reception area. When she opened them and met the irritated eyes of Lou Lamont, she had herself back under control.

"Sorry to keep you waiting." She was proud of her smooth smile and casual words.

Lamont brushed by her, issuing a command over his shoulder. "Katy, whip me up some Earl Grey, would you? And make it hot this time."

Kat grimaced and rose from her desk as Grace shut the door with annoyance.

As soon as he took a seat, Lamont carefully unbuttoned his suit jacket and brushed something off his pant leg with a flick of the hand. A staccato beat sounded out, the rhythm of his shoe hitting the corner of the desk. His impatience was one of the first things she always noticed about him. Well, that and his cologne.

Grace covered a sneeze with her hand.

"God bless," he said solicitously. "Are you getting sick?"

As if he secretly hoped she had something lethal and efficient.

"Not at all." Grace sat down, watching his eyes flicker over her. She knew the attention wasn't sexual. He didn't want her body; he was after her job and the piece of furniture she'd put her butt onto.

His cell phone went off.

"Excuse me," he said, taking it out of the jacket of his slick suit.

As the man started in on a chorus of yeses and absolutelys, she reflected on how long she'd known him. He'd started years ago on the lowest rung of the ladder, working part-time as a grant application sifter while he got through a master's degree in art history at NYU. By the time she came on board full-time, he'd risen in the ranks and his pièce de résistance had been when her father had promoted him into senior management.

He was a good-looking guy, tall and thin, and as his salary had increased, so had the quality of his clothes. He'd also gradually left behind his Bronx accent until it was only noticeable when he was angry. Over the years, he'd grown adept at accumulating power and he got what he wanted by any means necessary—hard work, blatant bullying, or charming persuasion. He was also good at his job. He'd turned into a first-rate chief development officer, able to raise phenomenal amounts of cash for the Foundation from wealthy donors and major corporations. The flip side was that he was brash, ambitious, and frustrated that he'd been passed over in favor of Cornelius's daughter.

He was looking for other jobs and, with a wave of grief, Grace remembered that she owed Suzanna for the heads-up. Late last week, the woman had called to say that Lamont was sniffing around the museum, looking to take over their Development Office. Suzanna, as chair of the board, had turned him down flat, telling him that she didn't want to endanger the museum's relationship with the Hall Foundation. Evidently, Lamont had left angry.

He flipped the phone off and slid it into his pocket. "We need to talk about the Gala. It's six weeks away and I need to take charge. I mean, you're so busy getting a handle on things, it's going to be impossible for you to do it all."

Shooting him a smile, Grace reached over and picked up one of her father's gold pens. As she twirled it through her fingers, Lamont's eyes lit on the thing as if he wanted to wrench it out of her hand.

"That's a kind offer, Lou. But the Gala is under control."

"Is it? Then why hasn't Fredrique shown up yet?"

"I'm not using Fredrique this year and I already told him that three weeks ago."

Lamont's brows dropped down tightly over his eyes. "But we always use him. He does the parties for everyone who's anyone."

"Not anymore. After that fiasco last spring, when he tried to wedge live elephants into the Waldorf, people are seriously rethinking his creative urges. He also double-bills. Mimi Lauer says she's not using him again after the ballet's big event this season and I know that the museum wasn't happy with his performance, either."

She thought of Suzanna again.

"But I told him yesterday we were going to hire him," Lamont said through thin lips.

"Then you better call him back."

"So who are we using?"

"Me."

He laughed out loud. "We're talking about five hundred of New York's most important people and this is the first Gala now that your father's dead. You can't afford for it not to go well."

"We're a nonprofit charity. I'm not going to waste thousands and thousands of dollars just for advice on what color the tablecloths should be."

"He does more than that. He coordinates the food, the flow of guests—"

"All things I can do."

"But your father always—"

She cut him off with a level tone. "My father, as you pointed out, is dead. And Fredrique is an expense we don't need."

"Look, you know as well as I do, this town is a tightrope. The Foundation shouldn't fall off into obscurity just because you want to save a buck."

"Fredrique is not the answer. And I think you're going to be amazed by my sense of balance."

Lamont rose from the chair, frustration getting the best of him. "I hope when I get back from Virginia you'll be thinking more clearly."

"Oh, that's right. You're going to see about the Finn Collection. When are you leaving?"

"Tomorrow afternoon."

"Good, there still may be a chance for you to switch your ticket."

"Switch?"

"None of us should be flying first-class when we're on company business anymore. Not unless we're paying for the upgrade ourselves."

Lamont's eyes narrowed into slits and Kat picked that moment to come in with a tray.

"Make sure you save the teabag," he muttered as he pushed past the girl. "She's going to want to reuse it for her next meeting."

Kat steadied her load. "You want his tea?"

"No, thanks." But his head on a stick might be nice, Grace thought. "And you can throw out the bag."

Kat was laughing as she shut the door.

As soon as she was alone, Grace sagged in the chair, feeling utterly depleted. She couldn't imagine staying in the office a moment longer. She needed to think.

Picking up her purse and the discarded scarf, she went out to Kat's desk.

"Do me a favor and close up. I need a break." She wrapped the scarf around her shoulders and walked over to the closet to get her cashmere coat.

Kat was frowning. "Are you okay?"

"I'm just tired. And I want to see how the contractors are making out with my guest bath. If I leave now, I might still catch one of them who was going to stay late."

"Are you still going to go to the Met tonight?"

Grace took a deep breath. "Yes."

"Okay. And don't worry. I'll handle everything here."

Grace smiled. "I know you will."

The tiny digital clock on Smith's computer read 1:07 A.M. He'd been online doing research on a potential client but he hadn't made much progress. He kept finding himself mired in the archives section of the *New York Times*, looking at pictures of the Countess von Sharone.

Which was a total waste of time, he thought as he called up another one.

She'd been on his mind for the past week but even more so after Lieutenant Marks had tracked him down in the afternoon. Another socialite had been killed, the second woman mentioned in that article. He was waiting for

Marks to call again with an update on the crime scene, even though technically it was none of Smith's business.

Marks owed him. The lieutenant's boy had been under Smith's command in the Persian Gulf. Smith had dragged the kid out of a battle zone after he got in the way of a bullet and Marks was a man who returned favors.

The article that popped up on the screen was a little less than a month old and covered her father's funeral. On the right-hand side, there was a picture of the countess walking with her mother and her husband across a grassy expanse checkered by headstones. He leaned in closer to the computer. She was wearing a black suit and a small hat, carrying a black bag on one arm. With her head tilted down and eyes looking forward, her face was a study of beauty in grief. Her mother, by contrast, was all stiff reserve, showing nothing. Still, it was obvious where the countess's stunning looks had come from.

He studied the husband. The count was separated from his wife by about two feet and a million emotional miles, looking as if he'd been dropped into the picture from some entirely different event. His handsome face showed only bland indifference and, with his hands pushed into the pockets of his suit jacket, he looked as if he were sauntering.

Smith's cell phone rang. "Yeah?"

Marks's battle-fatigued voice sounded worse than usual. "I've got the lowdown if you want it."

"Shoot."

"Victim was discovered in her front foyer, just like the last one. Throat was hacked wide open again, a real butcher job. There were signs of a struggle but no forced entry."

"And both of the women lived in luxury buildings, right? Doormen, secured doors, sign-in sheets."

"That's right."

"So how's he getting in?"

"Don't have a good answer for that one. The boys checked all the common areas, the bottom floor windows and doors. No broken locks or panes."

"You audit the sign-in sheets?"

"We're in the process."

"So tell me the freaky part."

Marks laughed. "How'd you know there is one?"

"There always is."

"Okay, there was something odd. We didn't think much of it at the first scene but it really spoke to me at this one. It's about the victims' clothes. They were ripped, torn, bloodied but they were all arranged neatly on the bodies. Like he straightened 'em up before he left."

"You mean the slasher's got a neat streak?"

"Yeah. He kills them and then puts them back together, in a sense. The victim we found last night was lying on her fancy rug, blood everywhere, picture hanging off-kilter where he'd probably thrown her against the wall. But the suit she was wearing was all buttoned up. The collar was arranged. The skirt was pulled down. One of her shoes had popped off—we know 'cause we found blood in it—but he'd put it back on her foot."

"Freddie Krueger with OCD?"

"Yeah. That's it."

"You get prints?"

"Naw. Guy wore gloves. We've got some blood but it's mostly hers. We have a partial footprint but it's a goddamn Nike. Who doesn't own a pair of those?"

"What size?"

"Ten men's. So he's probably of average height. We're checking for hair and skin under her nails." Marks coughed. "Hey, what's all this to you, anyway?"

Smith shot a noncommittal noise back.

"Well," Marks said, "you can expect to hear from me again. This guy's just warming up."

"Who's next in the article?"

"Isadora Cunis. Daddy is an industrialist, married one of the top Wall Street stock guys. I talked to her earlier in the day, along with all the others. I've urged her to get out of town and I think she's going to take the advice."

"Call me with news."

"You betcha."

Smith put the cell phone down and logged off the site.

Restlessly, he scanned his room. The hotel he was staying in was a small one in the theater district of New York.

The place was clean and quiet, all it took for him to give accommodations a five-star rating.

He got to his feet and walked over to the window he'd wedged open. Through it, he heard the city below, the sounds of honking horns and rushing taxis steady on the streets even though it was late. He'd come into town from LA to assess threats being received by the CEO of one of the top multinational companies in the world. Smith and the sixty-year-old scion of industry had met over dinner in the man's luxurious suite at the Plaza. After an hour of conversation, Smith had turned the job down despite being offered seven figures for two months' worth of work.

It had been easy to walk away.

Mr. Corporate America maintained that he was being threatened by ecoterrorists. He'd recently leveled two thousand acres of rain forest to build a manufacturing and assembly plant complex in Brazil. The tree huggers, as the man had explained, were up in arms.

But Smith knew it was a lie because he'd done his home-work. The CEO had two lives. One was aboveboard as an icon of the American dream, a self-made billionaire who had a beautiful, pregnant, second wife less than half his age. The other involved arms, and not the kind you picked up a newborn with. Turned out, the guy had carried a lot more than widgets on his boats as they went back and forth through the Panama Canal.

In Smith's view, the man was probably trying to get out of the illicit trade and was just now learning that handling people who deal in guns is a lot different from negotiating over a boardroom table with guys in suits and ties. Both lines of work might get you rich but with one you got a golden parachute and a nice watch when you left. The other got you shot in the head and maybe cut up into little pieces. Your family was lucky if they had a body to bury.

From Smith's perspective, he couldn't justify taking the job. It wasn't that he wanted Mr. Corporate America to get killed. Watching a guy who was a king in his world cry over fennel soup wasn't pleasant, but Smith had rules. If he was going to risk his own life for someone else's, they had to be honest with him.

It also helped if they weren't in a pigpen of their own making.

But he didn't leave the guy flapping in the wind. Before Smith left, he'd passed along the number of another security firm.

Anyway, if he had taken the job, it would've involved some shuffling of clients. Tomorrow he was due in Paraguay and Tiny would have hated subbing on that job, even though he'd have done it at the drop of a hat. Tiny was big enough to make a linebacker look dainty and as tough as Smith was, but he hated the tropics. Something about spiders.

Going into the bathroom, Smith peeled off the undershirt he was wearing. In the light flooding down from the ceiling, his muscles stood out in stark relief, a powerful show of flesh and bone that he didn't stop to admire. He'd been in top physical condition all his life but his body was only one reason he was considered a heavy hitter in a profession full of tough guys.

What he did linger on were patterns across his skin, crisscrosses and streaks that distorted as the muscles underneath moved. They were scars, ragged testaments to the life he'd chosen. Some were twenty years old, from his violent youth, others were more recent. Some were the result of attempts on his life; others badges of his courage. He was so used to them, he didn't regard them as unusual or ugly. They were like his arms and legs, a part of him so intrinsic it was as if he'd come out of the womb with them.

Which of course, he hadn't. He just couldn't recall being unmarked.

Absently, he ran his hand over a pale pink scar that cut across his abdominal muscles. He thought about the countess and imagined her touching him with her delicate hands. The mere thought hardened him.

He cursed out loud.

It was a great fantasy but that's all it would ever be.

Besides, a woman like her would be used to the unmarred skin of investment bankers and aristocrats. Men whose professions didn't require they be stitched back together with a needle and thread. One look at Smith's map of horrors and she'd probably run shrieking in the opposite direction.

Then again, maybe she wouldn't. He thought of that chin of hers, kicked up high.

Oh, Christ, who was he fooling? He was never going to find out.

Smith shut off the light and left the bathroom. Shrugging out of his pants, he tossed them over the back of a chair, logged off his computer, and lay down on the bed. He didn't bother getting under the covers. The night was unseasonably warm for fall and he'd turned up the temperature gauge in the room so that the air-conditioning wouldn't come on.

He hated fake air.

Smith crossed his arms over his chest and shut his eyes, ready for blackness. He was an efficient sleeper. Out like a light, awake just as fast. A typical night was three hours flat on his back and then he'd be recharged.

Except he hadn't had "typical" in the past week. Lately, he'd had trouble sleeping, and sure enough, minutes later, he jacked himself up into a sitting position. With visions of the countess swirling in his head, Smith leaned back against the padded headboard, pissed.

That dreamless trance he went into every night was the closest thing to a normal routine he had. The fact that it was getting thrown out of whack on account of some woman was simply unacceptable.

Maybe he just needed to get laid.

He leaned over to the nightstand and slid a long, thin cigar out of a pack that was mostly full. The flash of his lighter was bright yellow in the darkness; the tip of the cheroot glowed orange when he inhaled.

That was probably it. He needed to have sex.

As he exhaled, the feel of the countess's body against his own came to him in a rush.

But Christ, not with her.

His cell phone rang.

Smith's head whipped around, and before the sound came again, he had the phone against his ear.

"Yeah?"

There was a long pause. "Is this . . . John Smith?"

His body knew the voice even before his brain recognized it.

"Yeah."

"It's Grace Hall," the voice said. "I need you."

When Smith put the phone down, he wondered what had taken her so long to call.

Tiny, it seemed, might be going to Paraguay after all.

5

TWENTY MINUTES later, Smith was on Wall Street, walking up the granite steps of her family's skyscraper. As he approached the banks of revolving doors, a uniformed security guard opened a side door for him.

"Mr. Smith?"

When he answered, the man stepped aside to let him pass.

"She's waiting for you," the guard said. "Up in her office, on the top floor. You want to take the elevators over there."

Smith gave the man a nod and got into the elevator. Fifty-two floors up, it eased to a stop and he stepped out into a plush hallway. At the end of the corridor, he saw light spilling from a pair of doors and he went toward it, his feet silent over thick carpeting. He passed by conference rooms and offices and thought, if it weren't for the spectacular oil paintings hanging on the walls, he could have been in the executive suite of any successful corporation.

Smith slowed as he came up to the doors. Without knocking, he pushed open one side and saw her.

Silhouetted against a twinkling view of the city, the countess was wearing a red gown and facing out toward a wall of windows. The flowing silk covered her long, lean body and left her back exposed. With her hair coiled on her head, she had the graceful curves of a ballet dancer.

A howling need hit him in the gut just as she caught his reflection in the glass. He heard her breath suck in with a hiss and she seemed to take a moment to steady herself before she turned. When she did, he saw her fine features were tight with tension.

"You move so quietly," she said.

He shrugged. "No sense announcing myself with a marching band."

Her lips lifted in a smile and Smith felt his chest constrict. He wasn't someone who got preoccupied by beauty but he found himself absorbing hers through his skin. She warmed him.

He resented the effect.

"What's going on?" he said sharply.

"Have you heard the news?" The treble of fear was in her voice, making it higher than he remembered.

"About Suzanna van der Lyden?" He nodded.

She wrapped her arms around herself. As she moved, diamonds shimmered.

"I can't believe it." The countess turned back to the view, as if she didn't want him to see her struggle for self-control. "God, how her family must feel. She has a young son. Had."

Her eyes flashed over her shoulder. She measured him for a long time, as if trying to delve into the space behind his eyes, into who he was as a man.

"Can I trust you?" she asked with quiet urgency.

"With your life, Countess."

There was a pause. She turned back around to him. "My husband and I have separated. We're getting a divorce."

She watched him closely, obviously wondering whether his word was his bond or a fiction. She was no doubt worried he might go to the papers and he didn't blame her. The separation of the Count and Countess von Sharone was going to be big news.

After a moment, she continued. "I am not prepared to announce it, not until the divorce is worked out. That's why I didn't tell the police I was being followed."

"You think your husband's stalking you?"

"He might be paying someone to keep an eye on me."

"Is he still in love with you?"

She shrugged. "I doubt it. But that doesn't mean he wouldn't try and find something to use against me."

"And you?"

"Still in love? No. I married him because I was supposed to." She let out a harsh laugh. "My father liked him. My mother liked his family. I thought there were worse things in life than marrying a handsome man from a royal family."

She looked back out of the windows. "I was wrong, of course. You should never marry for anything less than love."

Smith frowned.

"No offense, Countess, but do you honestly think you can keep news like this a secret? After that wedding you had?" He remembered reading about it on a plane as he flew to God only knew where. Hundreds of the world's überwealthy had attended the festivities in Europe. Her dress alone had cost over $100,000 if the papers had gotten the figure right.

"There are issues here at the Foundation and I need to be perceived as strong and in charge. If news of my marriage breaking up gets out now, people are going to assume I'm on the verge of an emotional breakdown."

"Are you?"

"Do I look like a nervous wreck to you?" Her voice was steady as she met his eyes in the wall of glass.

He shook his head. In that red dress, she looked enticing as hell—that's what she looked like.

The harsh laugh came again. "Good. I've learned in the last month to relish that particular illusion."

"Why don't we sit down," he said, abruptly. "You look like you're about to fall over."

Those graceful shoulders moved back and he waited for her to fight him. She would no sooner admit she was tired than she'd let out the fear she was holding in so tightly.

But instead of arguing, she settled behind a large desk and he took a seat across from her. He waited for her to speak again, waited for her to formally ask the question he was prepared to answer.

Grace was determined not to break down in front of Smith but she felt as if she might shatter and fall to pieces at any moment.

She'd spent the preceding hours thinking about how to best take care of herself and the only answer she came up with involved him. When she'd left the Met, but couldn't bring herself to go home because she was scared to be alone, she'd dialed his cell phone number.

He was the one she wanted, the only one. He was a tough-ass, hardheaded son of a bitch capable of making a killer turn and flee. He would keep her safe. With him protecting her, maybe she could get through a day without having an anxiety attack. Maybe she'd be able to concentrate on her job again. Maybe she could have part of her life back.

Her eyes flickered over to him. He'd chosen a chair just beyond the pool of light cast by the desk lamp. He looked dangerous in the shadows, so still and watchful. She couldn't see his eyes but knew they were on her. Even in the midst of her fear, she felt a surge of warmth and had to remind herself they had business to discuss.

Grace cleared her throat. "I'd like to hire you."

She held her breath, waiting for his answer.

He shifted in the chair, his leather jacket creaking softly.

"How far are you willing to go?"

"What do you mean?"

"What accommodations are you willing to make?"

Her eyebrows rose. "As in?"

Impatience flared in his tone. "Changing your schedule. Restricting your activities. Leaving the city."

Her eyes widened. "I can't leave the Foundation. We're getting ready for the Gala and—"

Smith shook his head resolutely and began to get up from the chair.

"Wait a minute." Grace put some command in the words. "Where are you going?"

He froze, suspended by his arms over the seat of the chair. The look he gave her told her he wasn't used to being ordered around.

"I mean, please don't leave. You're the best. And I want the best." More softly, she added, "I need you."

He got to his feet and looked down at her from his

full height. When he put his hands on his hips, his jacket stretched tightly across his shoulders.

No doubt he was all solid muscle, she thought. Actually, she already knew that, having been against him. Held by him.

The swirling desire that broke through her anxiety wasn't an improvement and she wanted to curse. Why couldn't she be blindsided by calm? Tackled by a wave of peacefulness? Swept off her feet by tranquillity and relaxation?

But no. Her relief pitcher was lust.

"Please," she said. "Don't go."

"Lady, I'm the best because my clients tend to live longer lives. The reason is because they do what I tell them to." His tone was bored, even though his expression was intense. "I have zero interest in arguing with a client over what I have to do to keep them alive."

"You don't understand." Grace got up so she could at least come close to looking him in the eye. "I need to be here right now."

"You'd rather plan a party than take care of yourself?" His voice was dark with disapproval as he began to turn away. "Look, I can recommend someone who'll do what you want. There are plenty of big pieces of meat who can trail after you."

She rushed around the side of the desk, placing herself between him and the door.

"Hear me out." Before he could argue, she pointed to the bust on the desk. "That's my father. I'm in this office because he's dead but *only* because he said so. I'm at war with the board and his second in command. I leave now and I get put out to pasture as a figurehead.

"I've got a bunch of throwbacks in my boardroom. My father's right-hand man is turning them against me because he wants to be in charge. If I disappear now, I'm going to lose control of this foundation because they're going to push me out. It will be the first time a Hall hasn't been in charge and I can't let that happen." Her eyes implored him. "There's a lot more at stake than just a party. But I just can't live in fear any longer. It's killing me."

He studied her for a moment. "Are you prepared to be completely honest with me?"

"I told you about my husband, didn't I?"

She'd felt uncomfortable talking to him about her marriage. Smith was, outside of her lawyer, the only person she'd told and she hadn't liked revealing the truth. The tabloids would pay a mint to get their hands on that kind of copy, but what choice did she have? She had to trust someone and John Smith hardly seemed the type who'd sell out for money. He seemed to have too much dignity for that.

"Are you aware of anyone who would want to hurt you? Any enemies?"

Grace frowned. "As I said, Lou Lamont wants my job. He's aggressive but I can't believe he'd—"

"You'd be surprised what people are capable of. Anyone else?"

She shook her head. "Not that I can think of."

"Do you have any lovers?" The words were curt.

"Good Lord—why do you ask?"

"If I'm going to work for you, I need to know everything."

"Are you taking me on as a client?" she countered.

There was a long silence. "I'll need to be with you all the time."

"Of course."

His eyes, vivid blue and glowing, narrowed into beams. "If I do this, you're going to have to be completely honest with me and do what I say."

At the moment, she didn't care if he wanted her firstborn.

"Absolutely."

"Then yes, I'll protect you."

Grace took her first deep breath in weeks. "Thank God."

"Now answer my question," he demanded. "Do you have any lovers?"

She frowned. "No, I'm not involved with anyone."

"Was there anyone else during your marriage?"

"I can't imagine why that would be—"

"Don't tell me you need a crash course on crimes of passion." His voice was clipped, like a drill sergeant's.

He was used to being obeyed, she thought. Like her father had been. Like her husband had expected to be.

And she'd just agreed to do anything he told her to.

Out of the frying pan and into the fire, she thought grimly.

But she was through with meek compliance. He was going to protect her and she was relieved to be his client, but that didn't mean she'd allow him to bully her around.

Unfortunately, he did have a valid reason for wanting to know about her love life.

Grace took a deep breath. "I was faithful to him. Always."

A fleeting emotion traced his face. Had it been disapproval?

And most people thought fidelity was a virtue, she thought.

"So what happens next?" she asked.

"I get on your security guys here at the Foundation. You start coming and going in an unpredictable manner. I move into your apartment."

She stopped nodding in agreement. "Move in?"

"I can't watch you if I'm not around you," he said dryly. "And it's not like the madman who's after you only works a day shift."

Grace was dumbfounded. It had never occurred to her he'd need to be that close. "Are you sure that's necessary?"

He gave her a dark look. "Is there a problem?"

"You're talking about living in my home." She raised her hand to her neck, feeling exposed. "I don't know anything about you."

"I'll bet you don't know much about the guy who does your taxes, either."

She pictured her accountant, who wore half-glasses and came up to her collarbone. Eugene Fessnick, CPA, sleeping in her guest room was not the same thing. At all.

"But you're ... different."

"I'm more on the level of the types who service your car, right?"

She frowned, ready to correct the mistaken impression that she thought she was better than he was, but he didn't seem bothered by what she'd said. He didn't care what she thought of him, she realized. To him, it was utterly unimportant. He was focused on the task at hand. On her safety. Nothing more.

Except she didn't want to come across as the kind of person people often assumed she was. Shallow, snobby, privileged. She'd worked hard to combat that image. Her "common" touch, as her husband had put it, had been yet another reason Ranulf had been dissatisfied with her as a wife.

She shook her head. "That wasn't what I meant. You're just—"

Smith turned and started walking to the door. "You coming, Countess? Or do you want to spend the night in your office?"

Grace refused to follow his lead. "It's just that I don't know many people who are as . . . hard looking as you are. It's a little intimidating, to tell you the truth. And having you come into my home, it makes this all so . . . real."

Smith paused by the door, pushing his hands down deep into his pockets and looking pointedly out into the hall. His profile was rigid, handsome. Unconcerned.

"Will you please look at me while I'm talking to you?" she demanded.

When his head snapped around, she braced herself for an argument. Or worse. His expression was so grim, she thought he might drop her as a client before they even got started.

His voice was stern when he spoke. "Countess, we need to get something straight. I'm not here to get to know you. I'm here to keep you alive. That's it. If you want to talk about your inner feelings and the way we relate, call a girlfriend. You'll get more out of it."

Her temper flared. "Well, pardon me for trying to put your mind at ease. I was trying to reassure you—"

"Honey, my mind is always at ease."

She shot him a derisive look. "That wasn't what it looked

like the night I first met you. You seemed downright hot and bothered to me."

"You were being a pest, Barbie."

"Only because you were staring at me."

"Yeah, well, you should be used to that by now. Or do you doll yourself up just because you like to play with makeup?"

"I do not doll myself—" She lost her train of thought. "What are we arguing about again?"

They glared at each other in silence.

And then, suddenly, he smiled. The expression took her breath away. If he was compelling when he was serious, he was close to irresistible when he lightened up.

Maybe she should pray for more of his dark moods.

"What's so funny," she muttered.

"You've got some steel under all that window dressing, don't you?"

She flushed. "I like to think of it as strength of purpose."

His smiled disappeared. "Well, whatever you call it, put it to good use on someone else. I don't take orders. I give them. Is that clear?"

Grace tightened her jaw and told herself now was an excellent opportunity to stand up and be counted. "I don't mind doing what you think is best. But some give-and-take will make this whole thing easier."

"I don't do give-and-take. Sorry."

She cocked her head to the side. "So I'm just supposed to go along for the ride? You can move into my home, take over my life, force me to answer intimate questions about my—my—" She stuttered because she couldn't make herself say the word *sex* in front of him and felt ridiculous. "But I can't ever challenge you, even when you might be wrong?"

"You're a quick study, Countess."

"That's not fair."

"Let's do a reality check. You need me more than I need you. So who gets to set the rules of the game?"

"I don't think I like you very much," she said. It was true. She wasn't sure what she felt about him but *like* was definitely not it.

"Good. That will make it easier on both of us."

She frowned, thinking the comment was strange.

"So do you still agree to the terms of my engagement?" he asked.

She took a deep breath and slowly nodded.

"Then let's go."

He looked around the room, eyes training on her purse and wrap, which were on the glossy surface of the conference table. He picked them up and went back to the door.

Grace approached him, head held high. Damned if she was going to let him know how much he disturbed her. She stopped in front of him and waited.

"What?" he demanded.

"Oh, I thought you were going to help with my wrap," she said, feeling foolish. Of course a man like him wouldn't worry about social graces. "Give it to me."

She watched him frown and look down at the hand she'd extended. He gave her the purse.

And then, in a flash of movement, he leaned in close and slipped the red silk around her shoulders. He didn't pull away immediately. As his hands lingered on the fine cloth, her breath caught and her eyes flashed up to his.

Her lips parted as he focused on her mouth.

But he made no move to kiss her.

"Remember, Countess, I'm not your escort. And I'm never going to be."

He stepped away sharply and she had to scramble to keep the wrap from falling to the floor.

6

When they got to the lobby, the security guard was gone.

"Probably on a walking tour," Grace said, her voice getting lost in the huge space. "They're supposed to do that. I'll call my driver."

As she took out her cell phone, she looked over at Smith. His eyes were tracing every feature of the tremendous atrium and its neoclassical appointments.

"I can see why this place is considered a national landmark," he remarked. "It was the sister of the Chrysler Building, right?"

She nodded. "They were built within two years of each other. The elevator doors are my favorite. The Egyptian motif, all that matte silver and shiny brass. And the ceiling's not bad, either."

They both looked up at the adorned stretch three stories above.

He turned toward a pair of massive doors, above which "The Woodward Hall Museum" was inscribed on a pediment of white marble.

"Is the museum open to the public every day?"

"Except for Tuesdays."

"How big is it?"

"It takes up the first four stories of the building and has its own elevator system. There are three floors of exhibit space and one that houses the library, the administrative offices, and the lab where we handle conservation."

"I'll need a tour of the building tomorrow. And architectural renderings."

"All right." She dialed her driver's number.

When her limousine pulled up in front, she and Smith slipped out into the darkness. They walked across about twenty yards of granite paving stones to the street, passing by a mammoth statue of George Washington and then going down a handful of shallow steps.

Grace glanced over her shoulder when Smith didn't walk next to her. His eyes met hers and then shifted away, as he scanned the plaza and the street around them. There were no other pedestrians and only the occasional taxi shot by on the street, but she didn't feel scared. At all.

What a change, she thought, compared to how frightened she'd been when she'd run into the building an hour earlier. Being with Smith, she didn't worry about a thing. She could feel his strength and protection radiating around her.

He was a trained killer. Indeed, a force of nature.

Her new roommate.

"Are you armed?" she asked abruptly.

"Always."

She shivered.

Her driver seemed surprised when he got out of the car to open the door and looked up, way up, into Smith's face.

"Good evening, sir."

Smith nodded, and got into the back with her.

Although it was cool in the interior of the car, Grace had the sudden urge to open a window, anything to give her a little more space. Even though he was sitting across from her, looking calm and in control, there was something completely overpowering about him.

Oh, get over it, she told herself. He's not the Messiah.

Grace smiled and looked out the window.

Because then he'd be in a white sheet and wearing sandals. Probably have a halo around his head, maybe some cherubs floating around. He would most certainly not be wearing black leather, an intense expression, and a gun.

As a fit of giggles struck her, induced by stress and the absurd picture of him in a toga, she knew she needed to get a grip. After all, he was no doubt riddled with imperfections. He probably sang off-key in the shower, snored like a bulldog, and had frayed waistbands on his boxers.

As an image of him half naked came to mind, she winced and started to massage her temples. The Calvin Klein ad running through her head was not helping, not if she was shooting to demystify the man.

Through her fingers, Grace's eyes went to him. He was staring out of the car as they sped up Park Avenue. With every streetlamp they went past, light flared over the harsh lines of his face and then faded.

How had he broken that nose of his? And how many times?

"Is John Smith your real name?" she wondered, aloud.

His head snapped in her direction. She thought his stony expression meant he wasn't going to answer her but then he shrugged. "Real enough."

"What do I call you?"

"Whatever you want."

"Will you answer to Pookie?"

He looked back out of the window but she caught the corner of his mouth lifting up. "No."

Her eyes traveled over his short hair to the proud length of his jaw and then lingered on his lips. In a flash of heat, she remembered their kiss.

Smith turned to her and his eyes narrowed, as if he knew what she was thinking about.

"Were you about to say something?" he said with disarming softness.

She glanced away.

"No more questions, Countess?" His voice was mocking.

"None that you would care to answer," she muttered.

And none she had any business asking. She'd been wondering if he was married. She hadn't seen a ring on his finger, but some men didn't wear them.

As they pulled up in front of her building, he leaned over to her. His voice was a low growl.

"Be careful with those eyes of yours, Countess. They may be asking for things you don't really want."

And then he opened the door and stepped out.

Oh God, she thought. How was she going to live with him?

Grace took a deep breath. At least she'd have tonight to figure it out because surely he wouldn't be moving in until tomorrow. Or maybe the day after. There'd be time to adjust.

Grace gathered her wrap around her shoulders and stepped out of the car. As Smith walked her under the green-and-gold awning of her building, she wracked her brain for a way to end the evening on a casual, confident note. While the doorman opened the door, she was trying to frame the kind of breezy, sophisticated comment she was known for.

Too bad her wit was shooting blanks, she thought. Under the circumstances, probably the best thing to do was say good night and leave it at that.

When he started to go inside, she froze.

"Er—you're coming up? Tonight?" The pitch of her voice was an octave higher than usual and the doorman discreetly dematerialized.

Smith waved to the driver and the limo pulled away.

"That was our agreement." His eyes were laconic. "Do we have a problem? Again?"

"What are you going to sleep in?" she blurted.

"My own skin usually does the job."

"Oh, of course. Yes." And she'd thought the underwear fantasy had been hard to handle. "Ummm."

"What are you waiting for?"

She couldn't very well answer that one truthfully. He didn't need to know she was trying to clear her mind of what he'd look like buck naked.

As she led him through the grand lobby of the building, her mind was lamenting that she had no time to prepare for him coming into her home. Sleeping in the bedroom next to hers.

Sharing a bathroom with her.

A giggle came out of her mouth as she remembered her guest bath was ripped apart. There wasn't even running water in it. He was going to have to use her towels, her soap, her shower.

"What's so funny?" Smith reached over and hit the button to summon the elevator. His blue eyes moved over to her lazily, as if he might not really care what was amusing her.

So she made sure to tell him.

"I'm wondering what you're going to think when you take a shower tomorrow morning and have to use my lavender-scented soap." She smothered another fit of laughter born out of tension. "Are you sure you don't need anything? A razor? A comb? Or do you roll out of bed looking like your badass self?"

"Well, what do you know. The countess knows a curse word," Smith remarked as the elevator arrived.

"I'm quite well-versed in the use of slang," she said. "Just the other day, I dropped a jar on my foot and swore a blue streak."

"Was it caviar?"

"No, shoe polish."

"Now that's another surprise." He bowed slightly at the waist as he held the door. "Your Highness."

She frowned. He was mocking her again and, stupidly, it hurt her feelings.

Because he was, after all, going to be living with her. Even if they were never going to be friends, surely they could both make an effort to be respectful of each other? She was certainly willing to work on getting along with him. Even if she vacillated between wanting to yell at him and ...

She wasn't going to let herself think about kissing him again.

"Just call me Grace, would you," she muttered while stepping inside. "That royal title nonsense is grating."

In the tight confines of the elevator, Smith was itching for the doors to reopen.

Grace was standing in front of him so he had a good look at the back of her neck, which was the last thing he needed. All the way up the building, he kept picturing his hands sliding around her waist and pulling her back against his body, tilting her head around so he could kiss her long and hard.

If the damn elevator was going up any slower, it'd be heading for the basement, he thought with a curse.

Working with the countess was going to be difficult. While riding in the limo with her, he'd had to stare out the window so he didn't linger on the generous expanse of leg revealed by her dress. And when he'd sensed her looking at him, he had been damn tempted to give her exactly what those eyes of hers had been asking for.

Hell, he'd even been annoyed to learn she'd been faithful to her husband. As if that aristocrat deserved it after the way he'd looked at her father's funeral.

When the doors finally slid open, he felt a surge of release as they stepped out into a hallway.

There were two unmarked doors at either end of the short corridor as well as a third that had a glowing red EXIT sign over it.

He heard the ringing sound of keys as she opened the door to the left. As soon as she stepped inside, she kicked off her high heels and sighed before padding around, flipping on lights.

Smith was impressed by her home but not surprised. He figured she'd live in one hell of a place. The penthouse had twelve-foot ceilings, a spectacular view, and period details from the turn of the century. The woodwork alone, from the moldings to the hardwood floor, was worth a mint, and it didn't hurt that her antique furniture and paintings were museum-quality.

"I suppose I should give you a tour," she said without much enthusiasm.

It was late and she must be exhausted but he needed to know the layout and he doubted she'd feel comfortable with him snooping around by himself.

"Lead on," he said, nodding.

As he followed her into the living room, he noted several sets of double doors that opened out onto a terrace, which was lit up. There was a lot of silk-covered furniture, antique side tables, and Oriental lamps. A grand piano took up one corner.

He walked over to an impressive, marbled fireplace. Over the ornate mantel was an oil painting of a mountain scene. In it, a British redcoat was bathed in a shaft of light breaking through a dark and troubled sky.

"Nice picture," he said idly.

"Thank you, I just bought it. It's a Thomas Cole. I collect Hudson River School works."

Smith got the distinct impression she was eager to get the tour over with but he wasn't going to be rushed. While he was looking at her decor, he was noting the motion sensors in the room, which were no doubt wired into a security system. She obviously hadn't bothered to turn the thing on, however, because she hadn't deactivated it when they'd walked into her home.

He paused next to a table with a series of photographs on it. She was in many of them, looking happy next to all sorts of people, some of whom he recognized as powerful or famous. One picture interested him most. It was a candid black-and-white of her and her father in a thick silver frame. Their smiles were radiant, her eyes full of love and affection as she looked at the man. There wasn't anything staged about it, nothing glamorous. Just a father and a daughter, enjoying each other's company.

"That was taken last year," she murmured. As she came up beside him, her perfume, that subtle blend of lemon and flowers, reached out to him. "We were at Willings, our Newport house. It was the Fourth of July. Neither one of us would have guessed there was so little time left."

She turned away sharply. "The dining room is through here."

But he wandered over to the piano, sizing it up. It was a Steinway and its black lacquered surface glowed in the soft light. He exposed the keys, his thumb and his pinkie easily spanning a C octave. The sound was rich and luxurious. His hand assumed a different position and he struck a major and then a minor chord. Good movement, perfectly tuned.

Nice piece of hardware.

"Do you play?" Her voice held surprise as the notes drifted away.

Smith shut the key guard. "No."

He was not about to tell her that music had been his

salvation when he was younger and one of the few ways he found peace as an adult.

For the most part, his life was not about tranquillity; it was about being sharp, hyperaware, on guard. On those rare occasions he needed a break, however, the piano could calm him, lead him to still waters. Tai chi was maybe the only other way he could truly relax.

Smith followed her into the next room, which was marked by a long mahogany table and twelve chairs. The crystal chandelier hanging from an ornate plaster medallion twinkled when she turned its lights on. As in the living room, heavy silk draperies in a deep cream were hanging at the windows, held back by tasseled satin ropes.

Smith looked across the gleaming table at her. In that red dress, in those diamonds, she belonged in the regal room.

He had to wonder what she looked like with her hair down. While making love. He imagined her head back in the throes of passion, those buffed nails gripping a sheet as her body shuddered in release, her mouth letting out hoarse words of need.

Now that would be something to see.

And it was a damn shame he never would, he told himself with resolve. Because unless she choked on a chicken bone and required the Heimlich, or fainted dead away and needed resuscitation, he wasn't going near those lips or that body of hers again.

When he'd grabbed her in that corridor, she hadn't been a client. She'd been a desirable woman who'd toyed with him and needed to be taught a lesson. Now, he'd accepted the responsibility of keeping her alive. That meant his fantasies could create all kinds of fiction if they wanted to but he wasn't going to do a damn thing to make any of it reality.

Smith followed her through a swinging door into a good-sized kitchen. There was a restaurant range in one corner, a tremendous stainless-steel refrigerator in another, and plenty of granite countertops in between. The place was surprisingly high-tech considering how old-world the rest of her home was.

"So now you've seen about everything." Her voice trailed off.

"Do you have live-in help?"

She shook her head. "I have a maid who comes during the day. Now if you don't mind, I'll take you to your room."

"And I'll need to see where you sleep."

Her eyes shifted away from him. "Of course."

On the way to the other end of the penthouse, she picked up her shoes and he was struck by how human she seemed. In spite of the diamonds and the fancy dress, she was just a tired woman with feet that had probably ached all night long.

"How long have you lived here?" he asked.

"About five years."

She led him to a large room with a set of double beds in it. The walls were done in dark blue silk and the Oriental rug on the hardwood floor was covered with plastic.

She hesitated before opening a pair of double doors. Inside, he saw a claw-footed bathtub on its side and various toilet parts lying on the floor. "As I mentioned, you'll have to use my bathroom to shower. I'm renovating this one."

Her eyes flashed to his and then looked away.

"My bedroom is down here."

She took him farther down the hall.

The master bedroom was done in various shades of creamy white. There was a set of French doors that opened out to the terrace and many more windows. He noted with approval the motion sensors.

As he looked around, he saw a photograph standing up on an Early American bureau. He went over to it and took a hard look at the face of Count Ranulf von Sharone.

"Handsome guy," Smith commented.

"What? Oh, that. I keep meaning to put that picture away."

"Hanging on to past illusions, Countess?"

When he glanced over at her, he was surprised. Her mouth was screwed down tight and her eyes were flashing vibrant, angry green, even though the comment had been a mere throwaway to him.

She wasn't over the marriage yet, he thought. No matter what she said about not loving the man.

"Let me be very clear, Mr. Smith. I don't appreciate being mocked."

As he looked at her, he enjoyed seeing the force of her will. "Please call me John. That mister stuff can be grating."

With a quick movement, she picked up the luxurious skirting of her gown and marched over to him, head held high.

As she met his gaze with righteous indignation, Smith felt a thrill go through him. There weren't a lot of people who faced off with him. Tiny was one. Maybe Eddie. The rich people who hired him always treated him with deference and respect, as did the high-level government agents and political leaders he dealt with. Civilians usually just stayed the hell away from him.

And yet this woman, who was easily five inches shorter than he, this *lady* who was in her stocking feet and a ball gown, was looking at him with an authority and command that reminded him of his Ranger battalion commander at Fort Benning.

He'd thought she was a looker when she was being all prim and proper. Pissed off, she was downright spectacular.

"*Mr.* Smith, if we are going to live in the same house together, you are going to have to dial down your ego and the condescending attitude that goes with it. I've already put up with a father who lorded over me and a husband who tried to. I don't tolerate heavy-handed men anymore."

God, he wanted to kiss her again. He really, really wanted to kiss her.

He grinned. Something close to sunshine was flowing through his blood and it was waking up parts of him that had lain dormant for years. He kind of wanted to laugh. Throw his head back and really let a belly-roll loose.

Who'd have thought all that fire lived underneath such an icy, elegant skin? But then why should he be surprised? He'd already felt the passion in her once.

"So do we understand each other?" she demanded. "I'm willing to put my life in your hands and take your orders, but I'm not going to be ridiculed."

He inclined his head once, in a way that could have meant anything.

He was thinking that after it was all over maybe they could spend the night together. That way, his fantasies wouldn't have to be a source of frustration. They'd merely be a prelude.

Not a bad idea, he decided, feeling pleased with himself.

She let out a frustrated noise and nodded at an open door. "That's my bathroom."

"What's through there?" He pointed to a set of double doors.

She walked over and opened them up. A light came on to reveal row upon row of hanging clothes. Suits, shirts, slacks, ball gowns. Shoes of every conceivable shape and color lined the floor.

She took a deep breath and he watched her shoulders sag as she turned toward him. Now that her anger was spent, she looked dead on her feet.

"When was the last time you slept through the night?" he asked.

Surprise flared in her face.

"Before my father died." She paused. "Actually it's more like sometime before my wedding."

She looked around, seemed to realize she had nowhere to go, and stalled.

"What time are you getting up?" he asked.

"Early. Six-ish. I'm going out for a run."

"I'm coming with you."

"Fine." She hesitated. "Will you be with me all day long?"

"Yes."

"Won't that be boring?"

"I'll be busy."

"Doing what?"

"Watching you."

Her eyes flashed up to his. They were full of vulnerability and an unconscious inquiry that turned him on.

She frowned, as if a thought just occurred to her. "Tell me something. Do you like what you do?"

When it came to watching someone like her, yeah, he

liked it just fine, Smith thought. But he didn't answer her question.

"You'll sleep well tonight," he said instead as he headed out of her room. "And keep the door open. I need to be able to hear you."

"Smith?"

He stopped and looked over his shoulder.

"Thank you. I really appreciate—"

He cut her off, telling her the same thing he did all his clients. "Don't waste time with gratitude. We have a professional arrangement. All you have to do is pay me at the end and I'll be happy."

Her eyes dimmed. "All right."

An odd sensation shot through his chest as he turned away from her.

It dawned on him that he'd hurt her feelings. Again.

And somehow, hurting her bothered him.

As he walked into his new bedroom, he was wondering what the hell was wrong with him. When had he started caring about the feelings of others?

About the countess's in particular?

7

GRACE CAME awake with a wild jerk, her arms pinwheeling through the sheets. Straining in the faint light of dawn, her body tense, she waited for some clue as to what had disturbed her exhausted collapse.

There was only silence.

She looked around her room. She was alone for all she knew.

She thought immediately of Smith. Had he been moving around? Or was it someone else? She slipped out of bed, debating whether to go find him. When the silence continued, she didn't think she had a reason to wake him up. He was her bodyguard, not a security blanket.

Feeling ill at ease, she went over to the French doors. The sun was just about to rise and high, thin clouds brushed across the horizon. Below, the streets were still marked with glowing lamps and Central Park was a dark, dense expanse.

So they'd gotten through their first night together, she thought. And it hadn't been that bad. Only one argument caused by the intersection of his sharp tongue and her nervous fatigue. All things considered, maybe it was a triumph.

Now, if she could just figure out how to share a bathroom with the guy, she was practically home free.

Grace was about to turn away when Smith walked out onto the terrace from the living room.

Her breath caught in her throat and she leaned forward until her forehead hit the glass. Cursing, she pulled back and rubbed the spot.

He was naked to the waist, wearing the black pants he'd had on the night before. His body was everything she'd suspected it to be. He was built hard and strong and there wasn't an ounce of fat on him as far as she could see. As he moved, she watched the shifting and contracting muscles of his back. They fanned out from his spine and filled his shoulders, giving heft to his upper torso.

It was then she noticed marks on his skin. Scars. Several on his back, one that went across his side, a jagged streak on his right shoulder.

She put her hand up, as if she could soothe him from afar, and tried to imagine the kind of life he must have led. Where he had been. What had been done to him.

The need to know about his past was intense.

No wonder he was so tough. He knew a hell of a lot about physical pain.

She watched, entranced, as he moved stealthily across the terrace, sidestepping plants and porch furniture, stopping only when he stood a couple of feet from the wrought iron railing. Facing the sun, he put his two hands together and bowed his head.

Grace wondered whether any tenderness could have survived in a man like him. She thought of his hard face, his impassive eyes, that bored tone she suspected he cultivated as another guise to hide his true thoughts. She wanted to know what was under the camouflage.

When he looked up again, he began to shift through the ancient gestures and positions of tai chi. She was amazed. He harnessed his masculine power, all those muscles and bones capable of such brute force, and disciplined them into movements that were fluid, calm. As the sun rose behind him, his silhouette pushed and pulled against the air in a graceful dance.

She stayed at the glass until he returned to his starting position. When he bowed his head again, and began to turn around, she scurried into bed, praying he hadn't seen her.

When she closed her eyes, she only saw visions of him. The sensual kaleidoscope was disturbing so she reached over and picked up her diary. Spilling her thoughts onto a page had always relieved her mind and she'd been writing in the small leather book a lot lately. Her pen flew across the page until there was nothing else to say about her attraction to him.

When she closed the book and lay back into the pillows, she thought she would just rest a moment but her body had different ideas. Much later, she surfaced from sleep in a plodding, heavy-lidded fashion. Enticing dreams seemed reluctant to let her go. Or maybe it was the other way around.

When she glanced at her clock, she groaned. She'd forgotten to set the alarm and had slept through her run. It was now 8:20 and she was late. Sitting up, she pushed her hair out of her face and stretched her arms over her head.

Again, her first thought was of Smith. After drawing on a silk robe, she went down the hall to the guest room. The door was open and she knocked on the jamb. When there was no response, she peeked in.

The bed had been made and there was nothing out of place, as if no one had been in the room at all. He was either one heck of a housekeeper or he'd slept on the floor. Or maybe not at all?

She headed for the living room. He wasn't there either.

In a flash of anxiety, she wondered whether he'd left her but the thought passed quickly. He'd have told her if he was going to quit the job and, as long as he stayed, he wouldn't leave her alone.

The doors onto the terrace were ajar and she walked over to them, feeling the cool breeze on her skin. He wasn't outside, but she lingered for a moment.

Everything was as she'd seen it last. The chrysanthemums were still cheery in their porch pots, their small white faces crowding through their thick green leaves. The wrought iron table, with its chairs pushed in and its umbrella wrapped in a tight bundle, was exactly where it had been last. The view was the same with the park and the buildings where they had been the day before and the day before that.

Except now there was a ghost in the familiar landscape. She saw him again in the light of dawn, moving.

"Did you like what you saw this morning?" Smith's voice, deep and laconic, came from behind her.

Grace wheeled around and fought the urge to bring her hands to her cheeks.

He was standing in the living room with a steaming mug in his hand. As he took a drink, his eyes hovered over the edge, piercing her with blue flame.

Fortunately, he'd put his shirt back on. But she was picturing his bare chest. When he looked down at what she was wearing, his mouth tightened.

She pulled the edges of her robe a little closer together, wishing she was wearing something more substantial.

Like a parka. Or a HazMat suit, for God's sake.

"Well, did you?" he prompted, one brow arching.

He seemed determined to get a response. Unfortunately, the only thing coming to her mind was along the lines of *Yeah, you're one smooth mover, but could you be naked next time?*

And how had he known she was watching? He'd seemed totally focused on what he'd been doing.

Smith took another sip from the mug.

"So you've found the coffee." She lifted her chin, thinking he couldn't make her admit anything she didn't want to. "Did you make enough for two?"

She gathered herself up to her full height and bustled by him, prepared to let his question drop.

His hand shot out, taking her arm, and she felt his fingers through the thin silk as if she wasn't wearing anything at all. She looked down at them, amazed that the contact was enough to make her body kick into overdrive.

When he didn't say anything, her eyes rose reluctantly to his.

"I'm a man who likes his privacy, Countess." He brought the mug up to his lips casually, as if he wasn't holding her in place. She caught a whiff of herbal tea, not coffee. "I don't appreciate intrusions into my time."

There wasn't a lick of anger in his voice or his expression but the warning was obvious nonetheless.

She forced herself to keep meeting him square in the eye. "I was only curious about what you were doing."

"Really?" he said in a lazy tone that didn't fool her.

"Yes, really."

She tried to get her arm back but, instead of releasing her, he jerked her closer. His eyes narrowed on her lips and she was amazed as hunger flared in his hard face, turning him into someone she didn't recognize. There was nothing self-controlled about what was coming out of his eyes.

She licked her lips, feeling parched, and had to look away. She glanced down at his forearm. The thick cords of muscle told her he could hold her for as long as he wanted and there wasn't much she could do about it.

"Let me go." Grace tried for something close to a command. She felt as though she should put up a protest so he didn't know the truth about what was going on under her skin. Unfortunately, the breathlessness in her voice held more invitation than rebuff.

His eyes narrowed and there was a subtle shifting in him that she sensed, rather than saw. As if he were considering a problem.

She gave her arm a tug but it was a halfhearted one. She wasn't all that interested in freedom.

Smith put the mug down on a side table and slowly raised his hand to her. She felt a soft caress move down her hair until his fingers rested on her collarbone.

"So answer my question, Countess." His voice was a low growl, delicious and provocative. "Did you like what you saw?"

Grace swallowed through a tight throat as she felt his fingertips under her chin. He tilted her face up with the slightest of pressure.

The obvious answer, the only safe answer, was no.

But she knew he would catch her lie. He was looking at her with such absorption, she didn't feel like she had any other recourse but the truth.

"Yes." The word was so quiet, no louder than her breath.

And that was when she realized she would make love with him. As crazy as it was, as dangerous as it was, if he asked, she would take him into her body and never look back. It was the perfectly wrong thing to do. Her life was already spinning out of control and falling into bed with a man like him would be like hitting the gas, not the brakes.

But she didn't care.

His grip on her arm loosened and he took a step closer, his hand going under the weight of her hair. He stroked the sensitive skin at the back of her neck.

Hesitant, she reached for him, placing her hands on the thick muscles of his shoulders. She felt the heat of his body through his thin shirt.

But the moment she touched him, he frowned, as if he'd just realized what he was doing.

He pulled away sharply.

"What's wrong?" The words left her lips on a hoarse breath.

"Are you trying to seduce me, Countess?" His voice had an edge to it.

Grace's mind, choked with sensations, churned over his words. "What?"

"How long's it been since you were with that husband of yours?" he said impatiently. "Or are you just interested in trying something from the other side of the tracks?"

Anger cut through her daze. "You were the one who— just now ... I never came on to you."

His eyes raked over her. "You stood at that door this morning, watching me in your see-through nightgown, looking like a hungry virgin. What the hell am I supposed to think?"

Grace put her hands on her hips. "I never looked at you like that."

He leaned toward her. "You want to try that again and shoot for the truth this time?"

"I don't know what you are talking about."

"So when you hired me last night, you weren't thinking of tacking on a little horizontal action with the security you're buying?"

Grace's mouth dropped open. She might be obstructing the truth a little but he was a goddamn revisionist.

She jabbed her finger at him in a decidedly unladylike fashion.

"You were the one with a death grip on my arm just now." The gesture made her feel stronger so she did it again and again, pushing her words through the air at him. "And I didn't ask you to touch me. Before you start playing holier than thou, you'd better look in the mirror. If anyone's starving around here, it's you."

She kicked up her chin and turned away from him. She'd gone about three feet when he caught her and spun her around.

His lips came down hard on hers and she met them with equal force. She grabbed onto his shoulders, pulling herself against him, while his arms came around her. The sensation of their bodies meeting was a rush.

Groaning, he broke off from her mouth, burying his face in her hair as if he were battling himself for control. But she didn't want him to turn away. When he started blazing a trail of kisses down her neck, she let out a sound of relief and desire and her head fell back as he took her skin in between his teeth and tasted her. His mouth explored further, down over her collarbone where his finger had once been, down into the valley between her breasts.

Roughly, he pushed the robe off her shoulders so it hung in waves from the sash around her waist. His eyes seemed to feast on the sight of her taut nipples pulling at the silk that draped over them. As he brought his hands slowly around until they rested under the weight of her breasts, her breath caught. Moving only his thumbs, he began to caress her, lingering over the hard peaks until she closed her eyes and moaned with pleasure.

"God, there is such heat in you," he said with wonder.

Her eyes opened and through the haze she saw a strange expression on his face, one that was a mix of passion and astonishment. She had the fleeting thought that if he knew she was watching, he would have hidden it.

He hooked his finger under one of the thin straps that held the nightgown's bodice in place and slipped it gently off her shoulder. The lace and silk melted away from her breast, leaving it bare to his eyes. Slowly, he dipped his head and took one of her nipples into his mouth. Shuddering with need, she drove her nails into his biceps. She watched as his tongue came out and licked at her tender tip. Biting her lip, she moaned again.

Through the haze, she recognized a foreign sound. Something vaguely troubling.

Keys.

Smith pulled away from her quickly, his eyes snapping toward the door.

"The contractors," she said roughly.

Grace struggled to get the top of the gown and the robe back in place but nothing was working right. Her mind was fuzzy, her hands were fumbling and the fabric seemed dead set against behaving.

"I'll deal with them." Smith's voice was ragged and he shielded her with his body as the door was thrown open.

Grace escaped into the kitchen just as three men came barreling through her front door. As she heard male voices talking, she leaned back against the refrigerator, struggling to get herself covered.

She put her head in her hands. How had that just happened?

Well, she knew the answer to that. Take one healthy male and a woman who'd been fantasizing about him since the night they met and put them in an enclosed space. It was lust, pure and simple.

It was just a kiss, she told herself. People do it all the time.

Well, yeah. But not like that.

Christ, what was wrong with her? She was two weeks away from being thirty, for heaven's sake, and about to be a divorcée. She wasn't some twenty-year-old, capable of believing that a couple of kisses were a transforming event. That a few sparks and some heat could turn a lonely, stressed-out woman into a femme fatale and a hard man into a romantic hero.

She knew she should do herself a favor and stay away from him but how was that going to happen? He was supposed to be with her every waking minute of every day.

The door opened.

She looked up into Smith's face. He was back to being self-controlled, arrogant, sure of himself.

But she knew she hadn't imagined his passion. The first time he'd kissed her might have been explained away by frustration and anger. What had just happened couldn't.

"I've taken their keys and told them you'll give a call when they can come back."

"Thank you. Er—I'm going to get dressed."

"We need to talk."

She shook her head. "No, we don't. Because—because it's not going to happen again. It should never have happened in the first place."

There was a pause. "I couldn't agree more on that."

"So there's nothing else to talk about."

Smith's eyes flickered over her face. "Weaknesses that aren't acknowledged have a nasty habit of turning into liabilities."

She began twisting her engagement ring around her finger, partially out of embarrassment, mostly out of gnawing frustration with herself and the situation. When Smith looked down at the heavy stone, she dropped her hands.

"I can assure you," she said with an edge, "I have no intention of throwing myself at you. If that's what you consider a liability, I think we're okay."

When he didn't reply, she prompted, "Are you going to leave?"

His eyes darkened with resolve. "No. I don't quit. Ever. But let's be very clear. All we have between us is the job, nothing more."

"I agree completely."

"I'm glad you see it my way."

His choice of words chafed. She lifted her chin.

"It's not your way. It's the truth." Grace looked away quickly and caught sight of the clock on the microwave. "I'll make it short and sweet in the bathroom. We're late."

After she'd left, Smith went into the living room and paced around.

In spite of his Sermon-on-the-Mount pronouncement that there was only a job between them, part of him was cursing that damn doorbell. It was tough luck she had the only contractors in the city who showed up on time. Nine o'clock sharp. The bastards.

But, hell, he should be thanking those guys with the tool belts and the pencils behind their ears. They were the only reason he hadn't made love to her then and there. On the carpet. Without the coverall brigade, he wouldn't have taken the time to spell out where the future had to lie. He'd have taken her, instead.

Which would have been a bad idea. Nursing a lonely, frightened woman through an inappropriate love affair was nothing he wanted to be a part of.

Even if she was like cozying up to a blowtorch.

It was a damn shame they weren't sleeping under the same roof in a different set of circumstances. The countess had genuine heat under that prim exterior. Fire and ice. He couldn't remember when he'd been so hot for a woman.

Smith shook his head. Never would have predicted this one, he thought.

He reached over and picked up a picture of her with the mayor of New York.

He wasn't worried by the fact that he wanted her. She was a stunningly beautiful woman with a good dose of kick ass underneath that glossy WASP exterior and he was a man, after all. But, though she was proving to be a tempting package all around, that didn't mean she was going to rock his world. When the threat was over, when they found her stalker, he was going to leave her life exactly as he had come into it. A clean break, a handshake, and then off to the next assignment. Exactly as he'd done with his other clients.

He returned the picture and went over to the mug he'd used. He hated herbal tea but it had been the only thing he'd found in her kitchen, apart from a sponge, that he could throw in with some hot water. When she'd mentioned him finding the coffee, he'd had no idea what she'd been thinking. After an extensive search, he'd only found a few jars of caviar, some crackers and a lot of empty space in her cupboards. The refrigerator was just as bad. Ancient, half-used salad dressing bottles and a tub of fancy mustard. That was it.

Smith's stomach growled and he went back into the kitchen. It was either hors d'oeuvres or nothing, so he got out the caviar and crackers and rooted through a few drawers until he found a knife. Breaking the seal on a jar marked Tsar Imperiale, he began ladling the stuff on some of Carr's best and tossing the piles into his mouth.

Not bad, he thought, but he'd have to stock the shelves if he was going to live with her.

When the knocker sounded, he went out into the front hall.

"Yeah?" he said without opening the door. He noticed with disapproval that she didn't have a peephole.

There was a hesitation. "It's—ah, it's Joey, the doorman. Who's this?"

"A friend of the countess's."

"Oh." The confusion in the guy's voice was obvious.

"Can I help you, Joey?"

"A package came for her yesterday. She forgot to pick it up."

"Leave it there in the hall."

"Ummm . . . okay."

Smith waited a minute or two and then began to unlock the door.

From behind him, he felt her approach. "Who was that?"

He glanced over his shoulder. Fresh out of the shower, she was wearing a terry cloth bathrobe and had a towel wrapped around her head. Her face was freshly scrubbed and a little pink and he tried not to think about what the rest of her looked like.

As he picked up a box wrapped in brown paper, he wondered if there was a way to make her keep wearing the fuzzy thing instead of that other, silky kind of robe she'd shown up in. No reason to torture himself.

"A package came for you." Smith carried the box inside. It was small, about a six-inch cube.

"Oh, thanks." She reached to take it from him.

"Not so fast," he said. "Let me open it."

She warily pulled together the lapels of the robe and followed him into the kitchen.

He put the box on the counter and reached into his back pocket, taking out the thin leather case he took with him wherever he went. It was about the size of a wallet and when he opened it up, thin, stainless-steel tools gleamed. "You got any rubber gloves around here?"

She plucked two yellow ones out of a cabinet under the sink, handing them to him with a worried look. He snapped them on and examined the package carefully, looking, listening, smelling. The countess's name and address had been written by hand across the top; otherwise there were no identifying marks.

"You recognize this handwriting?" he asked.

She shook her head as he continued.

"Where'd you learn all this?" She was lingering in the doorway, watching him work. The smell of the soap she'd used pleased him. He tried to ignore it.

"Here and there."

Unexpectedly, she let out a giggle. As he shot her a wry look, he watched her clap a hand over her mouth.

"Sorry. I have a tendency to laugh at inappropriate times."

"Somehow I doubt that." He slid a thin knife out of the kit.

"No, it's true. I used to drive my father mad. Once, during a holiday party, a guest got drunk and fell into the fountain. Everyone was stunned into silence as he splashed around except for me. As my father liked to tell it, from out of the crowd, a giggle rose like a bad smell."

Smith inserted the blade through the wrapping and began cutting around the top of the box. "Children can have rotten timing."

"Actually, it was two years ago."

He flashed her another look and then found himself pausing. It seemed inconceivable that someone as poised as she was could make such a gaffe and he wondered what other foibles and mischief she'd gotten herself into.

Her lips lifted sweetly into a smile and he felt his chest tighten.

Smith frowned and went back to work. "Let me guess, the guy in the drink was someone important."

"Bishop Bradford. Not the sort one laughs at."

"Where've I heard the name?"

"Bradford Bourbon. Kentucky's best."

"Hard to imagine a bourbon king with low tolerance," he muttered.

"Funny, that's what my father said."

When Smith was done, he lifted off the top and saw Tiffany's signature blue glowing from underneath a thin veil of tissue.

"What is it?" she asked nervously.

"If it is a mail bomb, they have excellent taste." He pulled the smaller box out gingerly and put it on the counter. "Mind if I do the honors?"

When she shook her head, he cut off the white bow and lifted off the lid. There was a card on top of the tissue.

He could feel the tension emanating from her as he picked up the envelope. After opening it, he read aloud, "To Woody with love, Bo. PS, can't wait to see you next week."

Grace began to laugh, a lovely sound of relief.

"What's so funny?"

"Bo happens to be Bishop Bradford's niece. You might know her as Senator Barbara Ann Bradford from Kentucky. What a coincidence."

Smith began pulling out tissue, creating a fluffy pile on the counter. "Assuming she's not paying you back for that giggle over her uncle, I don't think this is going to blow on us."

Nestled deep in the protective layers, he found a small porcelain box with flowers on it. He debated on whether to open it and decided it would be safe for her to. He had a feeling she'd appreciate the privacy if it was a personal gift and passed it over to her.

When she lifted the lid, she gasped.

"What?"

"Nothing," she said softly. She tucked the small box into her hands, curling it up and holding it close.

He restuffed the package, cramming the wrapping paper as well as the white fluff into its belly. He was surprised that he actually wondered what was inside the little box.

She nodded toward the caviar and crackers on the counter. "I see you've scavenged around for something to eat. Sorry about that. I wasn't expecting company . . . last night."

"Better than some other things I've had over the years." He snapped off the gloves and put them back under the sink. "About your maid."

"Therese?"

He nodded. "When she came this morning, I told her she was going to have a break for a while."

The countess frowned. "But she's completely trustworthy. She's been with our family for years and—"

"Do you have a regular driver?"

She nodded while regarding him warily.

"Call him and tell him he's going to have a little vacation. I want my own man at the wheel."

"But Rich has been my—"

"I want my man."

Grace dropped her head. He could feel her inner struggle.

"This won't be forever," he said gruffly. "Look, I know this is hard but you're not alone."

Her eyes flashed up to his. "You're right. I'm living with a trained killer and being stalked by a murderer. I should be praying for solitude." She took a deep breath. "I'm sorry. You don't deserve to get hit with my frustration."

"I can take it."

She looked at him for a long time, her green eyes the color of spring leaves. "I'm sure you can. You look like you could withstand anything."

And thank God for that, Smith thought, remembering how she felt pressed against his body.

"The shower's free," she told him.

"Okay."

Grace led the way down the hall to her bedroom.

"I put out some fresh towels and a razor." She went over to her dressing room, pausing in the doorway. "If you need anything . . ."

"I'll be fine."

She nodded and closed the double doors behind her.

8

A HALF hour later, they left the penthouse and went down to the lobby. As Grace introduced Smith to Joey, the regular doorman, she saw a black SUV pull up to the curb. It was big as a tank and, with its darkened windows, she was convinced only Smith's twin could be behind the wheel.

"Where's Rich?" the doorman asked as he took in the new car.

"On a little vacation," Grace said casually. "Oh, and the contractors won't be coming back for a while. Therese won't be here, either."

The man shot her a quizzical look while Smith gave him a card. "If anyone asks to get into her apartment, call my cell phone immediately. No one gets in unless I clear it, okay?"

"Yeah, sure thing."

"Have a good day," Grace said as they went out under the awning. Approaching the car, Smith went ahead and opened the door. She climbed up into the backseat, trying not to rip her skirt in the process.

"Good morning!" The cheery, booming voice was a shock. "Didn't mean to startle you. I'm Eddie."

A hand the size of a bear paw was passed into the backseat and as she took it, she looked into a face that belonged on a Christmas card. Round, rosy-cheeked, white bearded, the guy was a dead ringer for Santa Claus.

"Er . . ." Grace smiled and shook her head. "I'm sorry to stare. It's just that you look—"

"Like Brad Pitt? Yeah, I get that a lot." The New York

accent was thick, warping the words. She liked the sound of it. "So do I have to call you Countess?"

"Absolutely not. I'm Grace."

"Okay, Grace." He gave her a wink.

As soon as Smith climbed in the other side, the doors were locked with a stereo click.

"Mornin', Boss man," Eddie said, hitting the gas and throwing them out into traffic. Grace grabbed onto the armrest to keep from pitching into Smith's lap. As the Explorer's engine roared, and then Eddie slammed on the brakes to avoid sideswiping a taxi, she reached around behind her and put on her seat belt.

Heaven help her; she hoped they'd make it downtown in one peak.

Eddie looked up into the mirror. "Hey, Grace, what did you feed this one for breakfast? He looks a little drawn. A little peaked. A little—"

"Not in the mood for your antics," Smith muttered.

Grace's eyes flickered across the seat. Smith's tough face was relaxed.

"So come on, Grace," Eddie prompted, "whatcha feed him?"

The man was staring into the rearview mirror while pumping the gas and the brake like they were bike pedals. If only to get him to look at the street again, she said, "He didn't get a lot, I'm afraid."

"Ah." He addressed Smith. "What'd you make do with? A bowl of cereal that tastes like cardboard but's good for your colon?"

"Caviar," Smith said dryly.

"Jeez! Is that what you fancy people eat for breakfast?" Another wink was sent Grace's way. "Well, you can't keep a man like him going on fish eggs. Boss man, you want to pick up something on the way?"

The tone was light but the question serious. She had the impression that Eddie was used to taking care of Smith.

"I think I can make it."

"Well," Eddie huffed, "you aren't gonna lap me in a weight contest with that kind of attitude."

"That's a trophy you can take home."

Eddie looked back over to Grace in the mirror. "You know, not only can I eat him under the table, but I can bench press two of him. 'Course, he could probably bench-press two of me, come to think of it. Which is even more impressive."

Smith was staring out of the window, his face a study in calm concentration in spite of all the jerking and surging. She got the sense he was comfortable around Eddie and she wondered what had brought the two men together. Maybe they were related in some way.

She glanced at one and then the other. Or maybe not.

"We have to think of a reason . . . for you," Grace said abruptly. "I don't want people to think I need a body-guard."

Smith looked over at her, one eyebrow rising. "Understandable."

"A consultant. You're a consultant of some kind." She started smiling. "On organizational development."

He frowned. "What's that?"

"OD experts help companies overcome organizational stress by bringing staff together and helping them get along. Think Wall Street meets the Age of Aquarius."

He shrugged. "Sounds good to me."

"And it'll even explain the wardrobe."

"What's wrong with my clothes?" he drawled, obviously not prepared to change even if they were downright offensive.

She eyed his leather jacket with a smile. "You're not exactly pulling off the corporate pinstripe and wing tip routine."

Eddie laughed. "Well, the man's got basic black down cold. He's got more dark clothes than an undertaker."

"There's nothing wrong with black," Smith countered.

"Maybe if you're in the embalming arts, sure."

"You know that's just a side job."

The two shared a look and Grace's smile dropped from her face. She couldn't help wondering if Smith had had to kill anyone.

"Tell me more about your number two," he said.

"Lou Lamont is head of our Development Department.

As I mentioned, he's been fighting with me, in subtle and not-so-subtle ways, from the moment I took over."

"Well, maybe I can help him get used to you." There was a tightening of Smith's jaw and a furrow appeared between his brows.

"I thought you didn't know anything about OD."

Eddie laughed. "You're looking at a man who marshaled a team of Army Rangers through the desert. He can handle one guy in a suit. Trust me."

Grace flushed and looked at Smith. He must have been an officer, she thought. And fought in Desert Storm.

She stared at him, as if she could find answers in his face or his hands or the way he was sitting. He had one arm against the window and the other across the back of the seat. Spread out as he was, his jacket was gaping open and his black shirt stretched across his chest. The glimmer of his gun was barely visible. His confidence in himself was obvious.

But there were no hints, no clues for her.

She looked back out of the window, trying to distract herself by watching the people on the sidewalk. Anything to keep her from getting absorbed in him.

Although on that logic she'd need something big. The Macy's Thanksgiving Day Parade. A presidential motorcade.

Elvis, back from the dead.

When Eddie pulled up in front of the Hall Building, Smith leaned forward. "I've got stuff I need back at the hotel."

"No problem. Anything else?"

"Food. And lots of it."

"I know what you like."

"That's it."

Grace reached for the door handle but Smith stopped her. "Allow me."

He got out, looked around, and then opened her door.

Grace paused by Eddie's open window. "It was nice to meet you."

"You, too. Now will you feed him something real for lunch? A good sandwich. Some salad. Maybe a piece of fruit. It's good to keep the potassium up and protein is really important."

Smith rolled his eyes. "Don't tell me you're back at the extension school."

"Sure am. Just finished a class on nutrition. Now, I'm taking creative writing."

"Oh, boy." Smith lifted a hand as Eddie lurched back into traffic. "Here we go again."

Grace shot him a quizzical look as they walked past George Washington. She was surprised when he indulged her.

"Eddie never graduated from high school. When he turned fifty, he decided it was time to get educated. We've been through medieval history, French, and how to bake bread in the last year."

"That's wonderful."

"Yeah, except he made me eat his homework. He failed light and fluffy. Makes an excellent brick, though."

Grace glanced up at him and her quick laugh caught in her throat. His voice had been so casual, she'd assumed he was merely strolling through the plaza as she was. He wasn't. His eyes, calculating and impassive, were scanning the pedestrians around them, noting the revolving doors they were walking to, measuring the street behind them. His stride was even but she knew he could spring into action in the space of a breath.

As they stepped into the lobby, she thought about her attraction to him.

Was he right? Was her fascination with him because he was from a different world? She didn't think so. No matter what planet he was from, it was the electricity between them that tempted her. He could be another fancy-dressed, dandy blue blood like her husband or a garage mechanic. When she was in his arms, she wasn't thinking about his tax returns.

As soon as they were inside the Hall Building, people started coming up to her, greeting her, talking. It took them ten minutes to get into the elevators and she kept the conversation going with more staff while heading up the building. She asked about wives, husbands, children, family members, all by name.

When they emerged on the top floor and started down the hallway to her office, he said, "You know everyone here."

"My father inspired loyalty. A lot of the employees have been here for decades." Grace stuck her head into a conference room and waved at people in a meeting. They waved back.

"They're responding to you."

She glanced at him in surprise as they came up to Kat's desk. The young woman slowly put down her pen, eyes widening.

"Good morning, Kat," Grace said.

"Good morning."

The girl had yet to look Grace's way.

Grace smothered a smile and introduced them. "He's going to be with me for the next couple of weeks, doing some consulting work. Any calls yet?"

Kat cleared her throat and shuffled some papers. She looked up at Smith again and finally glanced over to her boss. "Ah—yes. Yes, I left them on your desk. Oh, and his lordship, the count, called. He said that he tried to reach you at home but had been unable to get through. He'd like you to call him and said you knew where he was."

"We'll be in my office for the morning."

"The count said it was urgent."

"Then I hope he's holding his breath," she muttered softly.

"What?"

"Nothing, Kat. Thanks."

When the doors were shut and they were alone, Grace put her purse down on the desk and planted herself in her father's chair.

She cleared her throat awkwardly. "So, ah . . . what will you do all day? I don't want you to be bored."

"I'm not a guest, remember?" Smith settled himself at the conference table. "I'm working. Just like you are. I'll need a set of plans for this building and your schedule for the next month."

Grace opened her mouth to speak but the intercom buzzed.

"Lou Lamont is here to see you."

"Does he look like he's going to want more Earl Grey?" Grace asked.

Kat laughed softly and whispered, "No. He doesn't seem to be in the mood to stay long."

"Make a note, will you? He's getting a tea cozy for Christmas from us. Also, can you print out my schedule for the next four weeks and get security to bring up a set of floor plans?"

"Floor plans? For the executive suite?"

"The whole building."

"Ah, okay."

Grace was just getting to her feet when Lamont burst into the room.

One look at Smith and he pulled up short.

"Who are you?" The man's tone was imperious.

Smith rose from his chair slowly and Lamont tilted his head up with surprise.

In a calm voice, Grace introduced them and fed Lamont the OD line.

"No offense," he said to Smith, in a voice meant to be subtly offensive, "but you look like a bouncer."

Smith's smile didn't reach his eyes as he sat back down without responding. He looked utterly unconcerned with the man and Lamont bristled.

He looked over at Grace. "What do we need an OD consultant for?"

"The Foundation has been through a big change and we need help."

Disgust clipped the man's words short. "This is ridiculous. You tell me we can't use Fredrique, who could really make a difference, only to bring on some New Age, touchy-feely—"

"Do you think Mr. Smith looks like a touchy-feely kind of guy?"

Lamont's eyes flickered across the room at the other man and then shot back to Grace. "And just what do you hope to accomplish?"

"We need to have a unified team."

"Unified—" He shook his head. "Your father and I ran this place for years. The Foundation doesn't need a team; it needs a strong leader at the top."

"You and I see things differently." Before he could argue further, she cut him off. "What I'd really like is to stop fighting with you."

"I haven't been fighting. You're just defensive."

"So those conversations you've been having with board members behind my back are somehow supportive? You must show me what I'm missing." Grace smiled calmly while Lamont tried to construct a response. "But enough about this. Shouldn't you be in Virginia?"

Lamont shoved his hands into his pockets and began to rattle his change. "That's the problem. I spoke with Herbert Finn the third this morning. They've changed their mind. We aren't going to be auctioning off the collection at the Gala."

Grace covered her disappointment quickly.

Every year, the Hall Foundation Gala offered an important piece of Americana for auction. The seller agreed to take half the money and got a hefty tax write-off. In return, the Foundation got a generous donation and the evening was injected with the kind of sizzle that made people scramble to buy tickets to the event. At the auction, inevitably the bidding was fast, furious, and, in a genteel fashion, vicious. In the past, they'd sold a handwritten draft of Martin Luther King's "dream" speech, a pristine set of Union battle plans for Gettysburg, and Betsy Ross's first flag.

Losing the Finn Collection of letters was a real blow.

Grace sank slowly into her father's chair. "That's a shame."

"I think they pulled it because they're waiting to see whether the Gala will still be a draw this year. This is exactly what I'd feared and another reason we need Fredrique."

Lamont's voice was unusually restrained and Grace realized he was legitimately disappointed. But she refused to broach the subject of the party planner again.

"It's not going to be a problem."

"Where are you going to find something on a par with

twelve perfectly preserved letters penned by Benjamin Franklin to Thomas Jefferson? That kind of thing doesn't just land in your lap. And let me remind you, it was your father who got us the Finn Collection in the first place, not you."

She smiled around gritted teeth. "I'll find something else."

"But while you diddle around with your OD consultant," he countered doggedly, "the Gala is getting closer by the day."

"Yes, so it is."

Lamont seemed ready to argue but then abruptly marched to the door. "Have it your way."

After the man had left, Grace shuffled a few papers on her desk impatiently. Unable to sit still, she burst up from the chair and went over to the bank of windows. She put her hands on her hips and stared down at the skyscraper across the street.

She was marching over to the bathroom, when Smith spoke up. "Go on. Say it."

She cleared her throat. "Say what?"

"What you're thinking."

"I'm not thinking anything." In fact, she was filled with riotous emotions that she didn't want to let out in front of him. It seemed somehow weak, given his self-control. She forced herself to go to her desk and sit down.

"Liar."

"What the hell do you want from me?" she demanded, glaring at him. The calm curiosity in his face really ticked her off.

"Why is it so important for you to be in control?" he asked.

"This coming from you?" He cocked an eyebrow. "A man who makes the Terminator seem loose and easygoing?"

"Now there's an original comparison," he said sarcastically. "Never heard that one before."

She looked away. "I think you're right. We don't need to get to know each other."

She felt Smith keep staring at her.

As soon as her anger dissipated, she was sorry she'd

snapped at him. Under normal circumstances, she wasn't prone to losing her temper. Clearly, the stress was wearing her down.

That and being around him. Even though he was quiet, she found him agitating.

Grace took a deep breath. "I know Lamont is going to blow this problem way out of proportion. He's probably calling Bainbridge right now. It's like I can't get a break around here."

She leaned back in the chair and stared at her father's bust. Had things been this tough for him? If they had, he'd never shown it.

"And the worst of it is, Lou's right. This is really bad timing. I don't have any idea where I'm going to find something that important to auction off."

The intercom buzzed.

"Yes?"

"Your mother's calling."

Wincing, Grace felt like she'd been put back into a headlock.

"Terrific," she muttered. When she picked up the receiver, her voice was light and cheerful. "Hello, Mummy. Tonight. Of course, I'd love to. Yes. Eight? Right. Bye-bye."

She hung up the phone. When she looked up, she gave him a tired smile. "You ever feel like just screaming out loud?"

Before he could respond, Kat buzzed again with another call.

The day passed in a blur of meetings and paperwork and people who wanted things from her. There was nothing unusual about it except that everything was complicated by Smith.

Even though he was silent, his presence affected her and everyone else. The men tended to be subdued around him, as if they were intimidated by his presence. The women had the same reaction Kat had. One look at him and they became all wide-eyed and fussy. It got to the point that Grace could time when the surreptitious check of the hair would happen.

And she knew she'd better get used to the floor show when the Hall Foundation's general counsel, a woman who took the term *sturdy* to a whole new level, came in for a meeting. Sitting across from Smith, the dour paragon of serious behavior let out a girlish giggle like nothing anyone had heard come out of her mouth before.

Frankly, it had been hard not to stare. Who knew she even had the estrogen in her?

But the truth was, Grace got a little irritated watching women fall all over themselves while trying to get Smith's attention. At least he never seemed to notice and that was probably why they worked so hard at it. His eyes never dwelled too long or inappropriately on any of them, even when one of the staff accountants removed her jacket and pushed her big breasts out in his direction.

At that moment, the idea of being totally autocratic and firing the Betty Page wannabe was very attractive, but Grace let it go.

And she refused to dwell on the implications of her passing impulse. Delving into why she was having a territorial reaction wasn't going to do her any good. She had a feeling she wasn't going to like the answer.

Fortunately, it had been the last meeting of the day.

9

When they returned to the penthouse in the early evening, Grace quickly changed into a short black dress. She'd grabbed a thick wrap and was heading out of the door when Smith put on his leather jacket.

"Where are you going?" she asked.

"With you."

She started shaking her head, resolutely. "Oh, no. You simply can't."

His brow rose as he gave her a bored look.

"How am I going to explain to my mother what you are?"

"I think I do a damn good impression of a human," he replied lazily.

Grace put a hand up to her forehead. "Forgive me. I didn't mean it like that. I just don't know what I'll say to her."

"How about the truth?"

She shook her head fiercely. "I couldn't possibly."

"You couldn't possibly tell your own mother that you have a bodyguard to keep you safe?"

"She doesn't know about . . ." She waved her hand around. "Any of this. My mother and I aren't exactly close."

Smith's eyes narrowed on her engagement ring. "And you haven't told her about the divorce, either, have you?"

Grace frowned, wishing he wasn't so observant or incisive. It made her wonder what other clues he'd picked up about her. Did he know how often she thought about him?

"Why does that matter?"

"It doesn't."

"So why did you bring it up?" Her voice was turning toward the hot side of disagreeable but she couldn't help herself. Smith had the ability to goad her into anger faster than anybody she'd ever met. It was almost as if he liked getting her in a bad humor.

He shrugged. "It's just an observation."

"Keep them to yourself," she muttered under her breath.

"Now, where's the fun in that?"

She glared at him and he held his hands up. "Okay, okay. You and your mother can eat alone."

"Thank you," she said grudgingly.

He started for the door.

"Where are you—"

"I'll sit a few tables away. That's the most I'm willing to compromise." He went out in the hall and pushed the elevator button.

She looked at his back, which was ramrod straight, and knew there'd be no further negotiation.

Smith walked into the dining room of the members-only Congress Club and felt like he'd been ricocheted back to the turn of the century. With its white marble floor, blood-red walls, and sweeping gold-colored drapes, the place looked like a bank lobby.

Or a high-class whorehouse, depending on your background and associations.

Hanging from the walls were dower portraits and Smith recognized some of the faces staring out of the gilt frames—they were on bills he had in his wallet and coins that jangled in his pockets. He wasn't surprised. The Congress, as the place was known, was all about old, establishment money and entrenched power. Its members had long shaped the history of the country, for better and worse, and were still doing so.

As he was led to his table, he looked over the diners. The people who were eating glanced at him, their patrician faces showing nothing but openness and welcome. Even though they didn't recognize him, they knew he was there only because he knew one of them.

The maître d' who'd led him through the room bowed as Smith sat down in a leather club chair. His table for two had a glowing candle in a brass holder, heavy silverware, and a lot of thick crystal. He figured the thing must have been braced up by an I-beam.

"Would you care for a libation, sir?" The man leaned forward and with a flourish put a leather-bound book down in front of Smith.

He shook his head.

As the maître d' disappeared, Smith tugged at the tie the club had lent him, hating it. The navy blue jacket they'd given him was also too tight but he didn't dwell on that either. Grace was being escorted into the room.

As she greeted the men and women whose tables she passed, her smile was radiant, her gestures elegant and refined. She seemed perfectly at ease but he could read her well. He knew she was nervous because her hand kept fluttering up to her throat and, in the dim light, her eyes were dull. She was clearly on social autopilot.

As soon as she'd taken a seat, a man came up to her. Smith frowned. The guy was probably in his late thirties and looked as polished as a new Rolls-Royce. He had dark hair that was on the long side, a handsome, rather ruthless face, and was wearing an expensive suit. A blue blood all the way.

When he bent down and kissed Grace's cheek, her face lit up for real.

And Smith felt an inappropriate urge to cross the room and help the guy roughly to whatever his final destination was going to be.

For the next ten minutes, the urbane man talked and Grace laughed. By the time they parted, she was actually looking relaxed. While Mr. Charm sauntered across the room, Smith stared at him, imagining all kinds of fun ways to break his leg bones.

It was a surprise when the man paused at Smith's table.

"Do I know you?" The tones were cultured, the voice deep, the smile on the aggressive side of social propriety.

Up close, he was a really handsome guy. Definitely one of her kind.

"I don't think so," Smith answered darkly.

"No?" The guy lifted a shoulder. "So why are you looking as if my imminent demise would be a great source of pleasure for you?"

"Maybe I'm not in the mood to be disturbed."

"You've got a low threshold if you think a little polite conversation is disturbing."

"No, wait—you're reminding me why I'm a misanthrope."

Mr. Charm smiled and leaned down a little. "Well, I hate to disappoint you but my overall health is fine. Enjoy your meal, stranger."

The guy had balls, Smith granted, as Grace's flirt walked away.

He glanced back across the room. She seemed anxious as she stared back at him, but the contact was broken as a stunning older woman was led to her table. He watched as Grace's face immediately assumed a false calm and the two women kissed the air next to each other's cheek.

So this was Mom.

Grace's mother was so thin he had to wonder whether she'd ever had a full meal. The two of them shared the same high cheekbones, the same ruler-straight nose, a similar graceful arch to their necks. Like Grace, the mother's pale hair was coiled up high on her head and she was wearing a black dress. As the woman unfolded her napkin and placed it gingerly on her lap, Smith caught sight of a sizable diamond.

A waiter came by Grace's table and Smith watched her mother look up imperiously. She said a few words, the waiter nodded with deference and then he faced Grace. She smiled, something her mother had yet to do, and started to speak. Her mother cut her off.

"Sir," came a voice next to Smith's table. "What may I get for you this evening?"

He didn't take his eyes away from what was happening across the room. "Anything."

"I beg your pardon?"

He frowned. "Just bring me some food. On a plate."

The tuxedoed waiter cleared his throat. "We have an excellent—"

With the look Smith shot him, the man clammed right up and hurried away.

Smith went back to the scene at Grace's table. Their waiter had left and the mother was speaking. As the woman's lips moved, a subtle disapproval floated in the air around her like a bad smell.

"I'm terribly sorry, sir," came another voice in Smith's ear. "But was there nothing on the menu to your liking?"

Great. The waiter had brought reinforcements.

Smith didn't bother hiding his irritation. "I haven't looked at the menu."

The eyes of other diners began to focus on the group at his table.

Christ, could these boys make more of a scene, he thought.

"Well, perhaps you might examine it," the new one suggested. He leaned in and opened up the leather-bound book. "We offer a wide selection of—"

"Is there a problem?" came a third voice.

Smith was getting ready to roar when he saw that the other two had come to attention liked they'd had their butts snapped with a newspaper. It was the maître d'.

"This gentleman—," the taller one started in.

"Is a guest of the Countess von Sharone," the maître d' said calmly. The other men looked at Smith in surprise and then offered smiles so warm and sincere they could have been missionaries.

Smith leaned back in the chair and crossed his arms over his chest. "I don't care what you bring me as long as it isn't roadkill."

"Of course, Mr. Smith. Right away." The maître d' bowed and the waiters bustled out of his way.

Smith went back to looking at Grace.

"Who is that man over there?" Grace's mother demanded.

"Which man?" she said, even though she knew precisely who it was.

"That man with Edward and the two waiters. I don't recall ever seeing him in here before. He seems to be causing a problem of some sort."

Grace took a small sip from her water glass. "How was your trip down from Newport?"

Her mother continued to stare at the tuxedoed knot around Smith, as if she could will away the disruption. "The trip was fine. Just fine."

"And how are you settling in?"

To her relief, her mother finally looked away from Smith's table.

"Mercedes Walker is coming down from Boston tomorrow. We're having a bit of a reunion."

"Jack is here tonight, by the way."

"Really?" This time when her mother scanned the room, her eyes were warmer. She waved in Jack's direction as he nodded.

Grace glanced over at Smith, wondering what had been said between him and Jack and what the problem with the waiters had been. His eyes, as they met hers, were so intense that a rush of awareness went through her. She frowned. If she wasn't careful, she was going to mistake his focus on her for being something more than professional.

Which would only take her further into dangerous territory.

She was paying him to watch her, she reminded herself. It was his job. He wasn't bowled over by her feminine mystique.

Mostly because she had none.

Ranulf had gotten that right, unfortunately. Whatever Grace's attributes, she wasn't one of those women who had a lot of sex appeal. Never had been. And her husband's obvious and well-shared disappointment with their love life had only underscored what she'd always believed about herself.

She thought about the kisses she and Smith had shared. He'd been passionate because he was a passionate man. His reaction had more to do with his own sex drive than with any special quality of hers.

"Grace?"

Her mother's strident voice brought her back to the present. "I'm sorry?"

"I was telling you about my forthcoming trip to Paris. I shall be staying with the vicomte—"

This time, Grace was careful to pay attention as her mother laid out her plans in minute detail. The only pause came when the waiter brought their entrées. As a salmon fillet was placed in front of Grace, she hid a grimace.

She hated fish.

"You'll like that much better than the beef, darling," her mother said as an identical plate was put down at her place setting. "Now, tell me about the Gala."

"I think it's progressing quite nicely." Grace picked up her fork. She didn't like to lie, but had no intention of speaking the truth.

"Your father always had such a talent for those events. He was responsible for securing Betsy Ross's first flag for auction. Do you remember that?"

Grace let the story she'd heard countless times wash over her. Reminding herself to nod as soon as she heard a pause, she brought her fork to her lips and took the salmon into her mouth. She had to fight to keep from gagging.

Her eyes left her mother's well-preserved face and traveled through the room she knew so well. The place made her think of her father. She'd loved coming to dinner with him all alone. It had started out as a birthday tradition when she'd been younger and, as she'd grown up, they had done it more regularly.

Her father would watch her intently as she spoke, all the while tracing the tip of a silver teaspoon on the heavy linen tablecloth. She could still hear the soft rasping sound of it rising up between them. He would move the spoon in circles while he was listening. When he would speak, he would draw invisible squares, turning the corners as he made his points.

Those moments had been the very best of him, of their relationship. A sense of loss made her put the memories aside for another, more private, time.

She looked over to Smith and stiffened. She sensed that those hooded eyes were seeing through her social smile and her carefully observed manners. He knew, she suspected, that she was exhausted, tense, and lonely. Did he know that she despised the dinner she'd allowed her mother to order for her, too?

"Grace," her mother said sharply.

She turned her head. "I'm sorry. What were you saying?"

"I asked after Ranulf."

Grace's hand tightened on her fork. "Oh, he's well."

"Your husband is such a marvelous man. Did you know he wrote to me?"

"When?" She tried to keep her face smooth. Unlined. Pleasant.

Inside, she was wondering why in the hell Ranulf was reaching out to her mother. Now that they were separated, he should keep to his own family. She made a mental note to talk with her lawyer about it.

"The letter arrived last week. He said that he was going to be in town and that the three of us should get together." The disapproving tone, the one that made Grace's shoulders tighten like a vise around her spine, came back, "I assumed you would have brought him tonight."

"He was busy."

"Well, I did call on short notice. Will you send him my regards?"

"Of course."

"Now tell me, when will you be having children?"

Grace choked on the fish. Coughing, she fumbled to get a napkin to her mouth.

Her mother didn't miss a beat. "Your one-year anniversary is coming. It's time, don't you think? Your father missed the opportunity of knowing his grandchildren. I don't want the same thing happening to me."

Grace took a sip of water. And another one. "I'm busy with the Foundation right now. I can't—"

An impatient hand waved away her words. "Let Lamont run the place. That's what your father really wanted."

Grace's eyes flared. Slowly, she put her glass down. "What did you say?"

"You can't honestly think he'd want you cooped up in that dreary office all the time. That's why he cultivated Lamont. Besides, what could you possibly know about running the Foundation? I was talking to Charles Bainbridge the other day, pointing out to him that you were really under too much stress. You need to be taking care of Ranulf right now, not worrying about business. Charles agreed."

Grace felt the blood drain from her face. Bainbridge was the chair of the board and the leader of the men who were rallied against her.

Her mother looked concerned. "Darling, you're not eating. Is the fish not to your liking? I'll summon Edward."

As her mother began to lift her hand, Grace rushed in, "No, no, the salmon is fine."

In the silence that followed, she tried to get her temper under control.

"Mummy, how could you do that?" she said quietly.

Her mother looked up in surprise. "I beg your pardon?"

"How could you undermine me like that?"

"Good Lord, are you talking about Bainbridge? I did you a favor. You really can't handle the responsibility—"

"I will be the one to decide that."

Carolina Hall froze. As her mother's expression turned icy, Grace fought against being submerged in her mother's censure.

"I find that comment and your attitude most ungracious."

Grace took a deep breath.

"I'm sorry, Mummy. But I know I can be what the Foundation needs and I want a chance to prove it. You going behind my back to Bainbridge is not helping me accomplish my goals." As her mother stared hard at her, she played her only strong card. "Besides, do you really want someone other than a Hall running the Foundation?"

That got through to Carolina. Slowly, the thaw came.

"You and your father were always alike. Once he got it into his head he was going to do something, nothing could sway him. I still believe, however, your focus should be on Ranulf and the family you will have with him. That's how I was with your father and look at how successful our marriage was. Don't you want that kind of accomplishment?"

As if marriage was a game to be won, a playing field on which to triumph over others.

All things being equal, Grace thought, she'd rather

have a good partnership than something worthy of a social trophy.

She made an effort to change the subject. "Mummy, did you know we're going to do a tribute to Father at the Gala this year?"

"Ah, lovely. You know, your father started the tradition of the Gala."

"I know." Grace kept most of the exhaustion out of her voice.

"It was in 1962 that he first came up with the idea. We had the first one in our own home . . ."

When their plates were cleared, the waiter asked if they would like dessert.

"None for us," her mother answered. "Just coffee. Black."

Grace was wishing they could have skipped the coffee when her mother said, "You don't look well."

"I don't?" She picked up her water glass again and rationed what she drank. She wanted to save the last inch or so in case her mother dropped another bomb and got her choking again.

"No. And you've seemed very distracted tonight. You haven't been sleeping, have you?"

"I've been busy."

"Do you grieve for your father?"

The words were so quiet, Grace almost didn't hear them. She looked up in surprise.

"Yes, I do. I miss him tremendously."

The coffee came with the check. Carolina carefully drew her signature on the bottom followed by WH1. She lingered with the pen in her hand, staring down at the slip of paper. Her eyes drifted upward, coming to rest on the candle that burned on the table between them.

"You and he were always so close. You worshiped him. I can remember, when you were a little girl, I found you in his closet once. He'd been gone for a week or two on business. You'd gotten into his clothes, had put yourself into one of his suits. You had a necktie around your neck that almost reached the ground. You must have been five or six."

Grace smiled sadly. "I remember that. You were furious because I wasn't allowed in your bedrooms."

"Was I? I don't recall. What I remember was your explanation. You told me that because he was gone, you needed to do his job for him, but you didn't have anything suitable to wear. It was really quite charming."

Her mother's eyes misted over, the smallest of changes, easily missed. Grace reached across the table for her mother's hand. She was surprised when they remained linked for a few moments.

"You always looked up to him," her mother murmured. "Your faith was enviable."

Grace frowned. Enviable? What an odd way to put it, she thought. Especially coming from her mother, who had made it her life's work to support the man.

Carolina pulled back, put the pen down, and lifted her coffee cup to her mouth. She blinked in quick succession a number of times.

"Do you miss him?" Grace asked quietly.

"Of course. I lived with the man for forty-six years. One gets used to having them around. How is your coffee? Mine is a little cool."

Grace sighed. She never drank caffeine late at night and had no intention of trying whatever had been placed before her.

"Mine is fine," she murmured.

"Which reminds me," her mother said. "We're closing up Willings late this year because of your father's death. I want you to come to Newport for Columbus Day weekend."

"All right."

"You and Ranulf will come together." Her mother's eyes sharpened over the rim of her cup.

Grace stiffened.

She should just get the announcement over with, she thought. She wasn't going to change her mind about the divorce and time wasn't going to alter her mother's reaction.

"Mummy, I need to talk to you about something."

A familiar male voice interrupted her. "Mrs. Hall, how are you?"

"Jackson Walker!" her mother exclaimed, accepting a

kiss on her cheek. "I was hoping you would come over. How are you?"

"I'm well." Jack smiled and his regal face looked less austere.

"How is Blair?"

"Perfect in every way."

Grace heard her mother laugh and let the conversation fade away. She looked over at Smith. He was drinking coffee while his eyes were fixed in her direction.

"Did you hear that, Grace?"

"I'm sorry—what?"

"Jack and Blair will come over Columbus Day weekend, as well."

"That's wonderful."

Grace offered an enthusiastic smile to her old friend but, as she looked into his eyes, she knew she hadn't fooled him. When he turned to go, he rested a hand on her shoulder. Leaning in to kiss her cheek, he whispered, "Call me if you want to talk, okay?"

She nodded, placing her hand over his. "Thank you."

Jack strode out of the room, waving to a few of the other diners as he left.

"Such a lovely gentleman, that Jackson," her mother said. "You know, if you hadn't found Ranulf, he was the one I'd hoped you'd marry. The Walkers are an excellent family and he is such a success."

"Yes, he is."

Her mother glanced over at a grandfather clock. "It's late. I must go."

As they were walking to the cloakroom, her mother said, "You were about to say something?"

"It was nothing, Mummy. Nothing at all."

10

EDDIE LET OUT a whoop of joy as Smith tossed his leftovers into the front seat. "Bonus! So what am I eating? Lobster Newburg? Filet mignon?"

They were waiting while Grace and her mother said good-bye in front of the club.

"I think it's spaghetti."

Eddie craned around. "Let me get this straight. You go into a place like that and you order freakin' spaghetti?"

"I didn't order it." Grace's face was showing strain as she smiled and nodded. He was amazed that her mother didn't pick up on it.

"What do you mean you didn't order it? Did a fairy just wave a wand and it appeared?"

"Don't know about the fairy but it was delivered by an evil little henchman."

Eddie laughed. "I'm not going to go there."

"Wise of you."

After her mother had been swallowed into a black Town Car, Grace came over to the SUV and Smith opened the door for her. While Eddie pulled away from the curb, Smith glanced across the seat. She looked like she'd been pulled through a wringer but she wasn't asking for pity. There were no heaving sighs of exhaustion, no emotional tirades about whatever was wrong with her mother.

Just quiet forbearance. Delicate strength.

Funny, he'd never thought the two words could be used together.

"Rough meal?" he said.

She leaned her head back against the seat and glanced at him sideways. Her eyelids were half closed. "It could have been worse."

She turned away.

They'd gone about three blocks when Smith said sharply to Eddie, "I think we're being tailed. Pull over."

Grace's head snapped up as the Explorer halted. A white car passed them.

"That looks like the sedan that tailed me to my father's funeral," she said.

"Follow it," Smith told Eddie.

The Explorer shot back into traffic. Smith did his best to get the license plate but taxis and other cars kept getting in the way. As they approached an intersection, he thought they were going to get lucky. The light was turning orange and only one car separated them from their prey.

But with an abrupt burst of speed, the sedan raced through the light and dodged down an alley. Eddie gunned the engine to shoot around the vehicle in front of them but a taxi blocked their way at the last moment. Smith watched the taillights of the sedan get smaller and then disappear.

"You get anything, Eddie?"

"Nah, I was too busying trying to get close to the damn thing."

Smith glanced over at Grace. "Take us home."

"Sure, Boss."

After they drew up in front of her building, Smith got out and helped Grace from the car. When she was standing close beside him, he reached into the back and pulled out the duffel bag and metal briefcases that Eddie had picked up from his hotel.

"Thanks for getting my stuff," he said to his friend.

"No problem. And the doorman accepted the grocery delivery twenty minutes ago. Told me he'd leave it in the hall. What time do you need me tomorrow?"

"Seven thirty."

"Right-oh."

And then, despite the fact that she looked like she was ready to fall over, Grace leaned into the car and smiled at Eddie. "When you heat up the pasta, do it over a stove if you can. High heat and move it around a lot. That way, the vegetables will stay crisper. I think you'll like the flavor. The head chef comes from Tuscany. Good night, Eddie."

Smith glanced at his friend. The man was wearing a bemused expression, having been thoroughly charmed.

" 'Night, Eddie," he said wryly.

"Yeah, Boss," the man said distractedly as he pulled away.

On the way up the building, Smith asked, "How'd you know what I had for dinner?"

"You aren't the only observant one."

When they reached her apartment, Grace's hands were shaking as she tried to unlock the door. It took her several attempts before she let them in. As she reached down for one of the grocery bags he told her to not worry about it.

"Then I'm going to go to bed," she said as he deactivated the alarm and shuttled the food inside.

He followed her down the hall, dropped his bag and the briefcases next to the bed he'd slept in the night before, and kept going into her bedroom. When she looked at him curiously, he told her he was just checking the rooms.

After doing a quick pass through the master suite, he checked the rest of the penthouse, unpacked the groceries, and went to his own room. He was taking off his leather jacket when he heard the sound of water rushing from down the hall.

As he tossed his coat over a chair, Smith imagined her stripped free of that black dress with her hair down around her shoulders. The locks would end just over the tips of her breasts and he'd have to gently push them aside to kiss her skin. He pictured the blond waves covering his chest and falling onto his face as they made love.

He heard the water fall silent.

All he had to do was go down that hall, he thought. Walk into her room and take her into his arms. Because he had a feeling, even though she'd agreed with his strict hands-off policy, she'd get carried away by the passion again.

One kiss and he would have her.

As blood pounded through his body, Smith stopped moving.

What the hell was he doing?

He shook his head.

What the *hell* was he doing?

Moving with deliberate motions, he took off his holster and slid his gun out. He stared at the black metal as the grip welcomed his palm and his fingers. The weapon had been handmade for him, to his precise specifications, and there were two more identical to it in the Kevlar briefcases.

The familiar weight of his gun was comforting.

His preoccupation with Grace was not.

He remembered that man at the Congress Club, the one in the suit who had kissed her on the cheek and made her smile. Smith hadn't thought much of it at the time but now his aggressive reaction to the guy struck him as way out of line. He was behaving like a jealous lover of hers.

As opposed to the woman's professional bodyguard.

Maybe he just needed a vacation. A little time off somewhere warm, where the drinks flowed like water and the women were easy.

Yeah, that's what he needed.

A goddamn vacation.

Smith frowned. And realized that in all his life, he'd never taken one.

Days later, Smith found his fixation on Grace was only getting worse. The result wasn't pretty. Sexual frustration was cutting into his sleep and shortening his temper.

And it wasn't as if he was known for his good humor to begin with.

From his seat at the conference table, he looked across the office. Grace had her head buried in some documents and he tried not to notice that her silk blouse had opened up and was showing more of her skin than usual.

Becoming aroused, he shifted in the chair.

Great. On the job with a hard-on.

Real professional.

Smith felt his mood sink deeper into dark and aggravated territory so he took out his cell phone and dialed Lieutenant Marks's number. He knew an update on the investigation would get his mind off that woman's damn blouse.

"How are things going, Lieutenant?"

"Oh, Christ, not good." The man sounded tired. "The chief of police is up my ass because those women's names are plastered all over New York's cultural institutions. The press is barking up a storm, wanting confirmation that the *Times* article was found on the first body—I'm trying to find out who the asshole was who leaked that little tidbit. And we don't have any suspects so far."

Smith kept his voice low. "Did you check with the doormen of those buildings?"

"Yeah. The day and evening shifts in both places have been covered by the same guys for the past five years. Their background checks have all come back clear and each one of them said they saw nothing suspicious on either of the nights in question. The delivery and visitor logs didn't tell us squat, either. Everyone signed in and out—no dropped balls there."

"Any names show up on both logs?"

"Quite a few. These wealthy types tend to use the same people. There were cleaning folks, caterers, tailors, plant people. Those places are a goddamn revolving door of help. We're chewing our way through the background checks on every single name."

"You find any connection between the husbands of these women? Business? Pleasure?"

"Haven't checked that, yet. Good idea." Marks paused. "So tell me, how's the countess?"

Smith's eyes flickered across the room. "Holding up, considering the stress she's under."

"Nice woman. Someone with her kind of money could be a real pain in the ass if they wanted to but she seemed surprisingly normal."

They talked for a little longer about the forensic tests that had been performed on samples from the crime scenes. When Smith hung up, he glanced back across the room. Kat had come in and Grace was laughing at something the girl had said. Kat was smiling broadly.

People tended to do that a lot around Grace, he realized. They came into her office or met up with her in the halls and they'd leave the encounter looking lighter, happier.

Surprisingly normal didn't go far enough.

"Thanks, Kat," Grace said, shuffling the papers around. "You were a big help on this."

The assistant beamed. "I'll make the changes now."

"Don't worry. It's past six. Let's all go home." Grace's eyes shifted to him and then she looked away quickly.

"Well, I'm in no hurry," Kat said.

"Don't tell me. Another date?" Grace's eyes were sympathetic.

"Just drinks. He's an IT guy. I'm hoping we'll talk about something other than Java programming or the Sims." Kat picked up the document and walked over to the door. "Good night, Mr. Smith."

Smith nodded without looking in the girl's direction. Grace glanced over at him and then looked back at the girl.

"Good night, Kat," she said softly, her expression growing concerned.

When the door was closed, her eyes narrowed at him. "You could be a little warmer with her."

"With who?"

"Kat."

He frowned. "What are you talking about?"

"I think she has a little crush on you."

Smith shrugged and began gathering the papers he'd been reviewing. He was consulting on a fraud case for a friend of his. "That's not my fault."

Grace rose to her feet. "True. But it isn't hers, either. When you ignore her like you do, I think you hurt her feelings."

Neither her eyes or her tone was combative but he felt defensive. The idea that his behavior hadn't lived up to her standards galled him for a reason he didn't want to examine closely.

Because he shouldn't care what she thought of him.

Smith smiled grimly. "You want me to take her out on a date or something?"

"Why don't you just shoot for being polite?"

His first instinct was to make a cutting comment to get her to drop the subject but the bravado faded as he realized she wasn't trying to control him. She was honestly concerned about the girl's feelings.

Smith wanted to curse. It was easier to fight against something than to give in to a thoughtful request and he'd have preferred the former, especially in his current frame of mind. His attraction to her, in addition to frustrating the hell out of him, was making him more aggressive than usual.

Which was saying something.

"Fine," he said darkly.

She smiled. "There now, that wasn't so bad, was it?"

As if he were a child in need of soothing.

The gently chiding comment was all it took to spark his temper. Smith got up and marched across the room. Her smile faded.

What he wanted to do, as he towered over her, was kiss her.

Instead, he said, "I'm willing to make allowances. I'm not too interested in being patronized, though."

Her startled eyes traced over his face and then bounced down to the span of his chest, as if she was remembering the feel of him against her. Her lips parted.

Sweet Jesus.

All he wanted to do was kiss her.

So before he did something stupid, Smith took his bad mood and his desire for her and went back to where he'd been sitting at the conference table. He packed up his things and used the time to berate himself.

Christ, of all women. Why did he have to be so damn hung up on her? He hated complications and there was nothing more complicated than a beautiful, rich woman who was a client. And why couldn't he just let it go? He'd forgotten plenty of women over the years. Nearly every one he'd ever been with, as a matter of fact.

But this one? She just wouldn't get out of his mind.

Every night, when he was at the height of his insanity, he convinced himself that they could jump into bed as soon as the job was over and everything would be fine. They'd spend a couple of athletic hours together, maybe a day or two. And then he'd move along.

Staring up at the ceiling in the dark, it sounded like a good plan, but in the daylight, he knew it was a terrible idea. If she was going to sleep with a man, she'd no doubt want all the things Smith couldn't give her. She'd want more than hours, more than days. She'd want a relationship. Some sense of security. A little stability.

And then there were the bells and whistles she'd expect. According to the papers, she'd been wooed by some of the most eligible bachelors in the world. Men who had nothing better to do than worry about pleasing her. Men who, no doubt, showed up on her doorstep in suits and wing tips with diamonds and pearls. They were men capable of whispering sweet nothings into a gentle ear and making the bullshit seem halfway believable.

Smith couldn't pull off that kind of act to save his soul, even if it was to get her into bed so he could get her out of his blood.

They were from different worlds. He lived on the fringes of society, in the dim stretch between criminals and civilians. She was an idol, a romantic dream to a whole country of people. She spent her days in the skyscraper her family owned, her nights in ballrooms, her weekends in Newport. He negotiated with low-life kidnappers and traded bullets with fascists and whack-jobs for a living.

She was satin and platinum. He was leather and gunmetal.

Oh, hell. Now he was starting to sound like a country singer.

He looked across the room. Grace had stood up and was staring out at the view as the sun went down. His eyes traveled from the crown of her head, where her blond hair was tightly pinned, all the way down to the pointed tips of her high heels.

Lust, hot and carnal, pumped through him.

Smith put on his leather jacket and smiled tightly, thinking they were both goddamn lucky he could control himself.

Because if it weren't for his years of military training, and the fact that his mind was stronger than his body, he'd be inside her this very moment.

*   *   *

Grace had the dream again a few nights later. The one of her father coming back to her.

She stirred from sleep, becoming aware that he was standing in the doorway to her room. In the dim light, she could see that his lips were moving but she couldn't hear his voice. It kept fading in and out, as if through a bad connection.

What? she asked him in her mind. *What are you telling me?*

His face had an urgency to it and she watched as he talked faster.

I can't hear you.

And then, for the first time since he died, she heard his voice.

Calla lily.

Grace shot upright, her heart pounding, her breath stuck somewhere in her chest. Pushing the covers away, she put her feet to the floor and braced herself before turning around. She looked toward the door to her room. He was gone.

He'd never been there, she corrected herself.

Stumbling over to the bathroom, she felt around in the dark for her water glass. Turning the tap on, she held her hand under the faucet waiting for the rush to get cool. She told herself that the sink was real, the marble under her feet was real, the pale glow coming through the windows was real.

But her father had not been.

She filled up the glass, took a couple of big gulps and tasted the familiar metal tang in the water. After putting it under the tap again, she took a deep breath and froze.

The smell of tobacco smoke tickled her nose, making her want to sneeze. As it always had when her father had lit up one of his pipes.

And the glass, like her sanity, slipped from her grasp.

Smith had just lit a cheroot and was staring out into the night when he heard the crash. Pitching the thing into an ashtray, he grabbed his gun and ran down the hall.

As he burst through Grace's door, he heard her voice from the bathroom.

"I'm in here."

When he flipped on the light, he saw her on her tiptoes surrounded by broken glass.

"I'm okay, I'm okay," she said, blinking against the glare. "I just dropped a glass and it shattered."

When she was able to focus on him, she stared at his bare chest and that was when he realized he was only wearing a pair of boxers. Her eyes widened and he knew she was looking at his scars.

"You sure you aren't hurt?" he said harshly, running his eyes down her body, trying to keep it clinical.

He failed. Like an answer to his fantasies, she wasn't wearing much, just a thin wisp of silk that was trimmed in lace. The sight of her breasts pushing against fragile cups made him want to fall on his knees and to hell with the glass shards.

"I really am fine. And I'm sorry I woke you." She started to look around the floor as if for a way out.

"Don't even think about moving. You're going to get cut." Smith put his gun on the counter.

She eyed the weapon warily. "I think I'll be fine if I just—"

"Stand still," he said sharply. "There's glass all around you. Give me a minute."

He went to his room and threw on a shirt and his boots. When he got back to the bathroom, he walked over the glass and grabbed her.

"What are you doing!" she yelped as he swung her up into his arms. He didn't reply. The glass crackling beneath his thick soles said enough.

As soon as he hit the carpet, he released her abruptly and she stumbled a little. He knew he'd better let her go fast or something was going to happen. Something like him pushing her down on the bed and covering her with his body.

In a rotten mood, Smith stalked into the kitchen, came back with a broom and cleaned up the mess. He was on his way out when he paused and looked at her.

She was wearing the thick bathrobe and sitting on the edge of her bed in the shallow pool of light cast by her reading lamp. Her back was to him and she seemed to be staring out at the darkness of Central Park.

Just leave her, he told himself. It's none of your business what's banging around that head of hers. You're paid to keep her body safe, not be her shrink.

"You okay?" he asked, anyway.

"Yes," she answered in a small voice. When he didn't leave, she looked over her shoulder at him. "Really."

"You want me to leave the light on?"

She nodded.

"Good night," he said, and got a mumble in return.

Smith went to the kitchen, put the broom away, and was on his way to his room when he heard a soft sound. It was barely audible and he waited to see if it came again. When it did, he realized it was a sob.

He walked silently down the dark hall until he stood on the brink of her doorway. She'd wrapped her arms around herself and was rocking back and forth on the edge of the bed.

"Grace?" he said quietly. It was the first time he'd called her by her name.

She jumped and hastily wiped her eyes. "What?"

"Why are you crying?"

"I'm not crying." He watched as her shoulders set like concrete.

"Tell me what woke you up earlier."

She waved him away. "I'm fine."

Smith took a deep breath. Sniveling women had never had much power over him. Any power, actually. He was attracted to strength, not weakness.

But he couldn't turn away from the sight of her so alone on that big bed, trying so hard to look composed.

"You're not fine."

When she turned to him, her green eyes were hostile.

He almost smiled, thinking he knew all about that kind of reaction. All about pushing people away.

"I thought we weren't supposed to get to know each other," she said hotly.

He shrugged. "Maybe I was wrong."

No, he was right. But, even though his instincts were screaming for him to go back to his bedroom, he was going to stay with her until she calmed down.

She regarded him steadily. "Okay, then you can go first."

With a determined sniffle, she crossed her arms over her chest. When he remained silent, she gave him a sharp look.

"What? There's nothing you want to share? No deep dark secrets you want to talk about?"

"This isn't about me," he said gruffly.

"Do you ever let it be about you?"

Not in a million years, he thought.

"Look," he said reasonably, "you're under incredible stress right now. Letting some of it out might help."

"Screw. You." She flashed him a glittering stare. "How's that?"

He smiled at her, relishing her backbone. "Pretty strong words for a countess."

"Well, I'm not feeling real royal right now. I'm tired of falling apart inside and having to pretend I'm—I'm *fine*." She took a deep breath. "The stiff upper lip routine can be an exhausting bore when your life is a mess."

He watched as she climbed in between the sheets and pulled the lace coverlet up to her chin. "Now do you mind? I'd like to get some sleep."

Smith approached the bed and watched her eyes widen as he sat down next to her.

"Tell you what," he drawled. "I'll do you an eye for an eye."

"What?"

"I tell you something about me but then you've got to talk. I'll even let you pick. You want to hear about the hell of Ranger school? How about the dry heat of the Gulf War? You want to know what gives me indigestion? It's not Mexican food."

She looked at his face for the longest time. "You serious?"

Dammit to hell, it appeared he was.

"Yes, I am."

She pushed herself up so she was sitting against the padded headboard. She was, he thought, temptation personified. Her hair, which was flowing around her shoulders in loose waves, glowed with blond highlights. Her beauty was classic as always, but with her parted lips and her nose a little red from crying, there was an enticing vulnerability to her.

He forced himself not to assess what the bodice of her nightgown might or might not be revealing.

"I want to know about the scars," she said abruptly.

Smith had to physically restrain himself from recoiling.

Shit. That wasn't what he'd had in mind.

He'd been prepared to give her a short take on how to handle a hard-ass battalion commander. Maybe a little wartime story with a happy ending, like when he'd saved that old man and his family. And being lactose intolerant was no big deal.

But the scars? He didn't talk to anyone about them, not even his boys like Tiny and Eddie.

Not all of the wounds had been inflicted on him as an adult.

"You said I could pick," she whispered. "And I have."

Smith cleared his throat, searched his mind for words and came up with a whole lot of nothing.

Her hand landed softly on his shoulder and he flinched. Through the undershirt, he could feel her fingers move slowly down his back as she explored his skin, lingering here and there.

Smith would have run, if he could have. But his body felt like lead.

When she got to a round scar on his side, one of the oldest, she went no farther. "Tell me about this one."

An image cut through his mind with the gruesome precision of a knife and he saw clearly events that were decades old. Feeling nauseous, he told himself to keep quiet.

"Please."

The soft word was a promise of comfort that he'd never had. That he'd never wanted before.

He responded to it before he could stop himself.

"Cigarette burn." Smith didn't recognize his own voice. Stiff and a little hoarse, he heard it from a far distance. "My father liked to smoke. He could always find a match. Ashtrays were a different story. Eventually, I got so I could outrun him but it took a long time."

He heard a hiss and realized it had been from her.

Smith didn't go further. She didn't need to know any more details.

"I'm so very sorry."

This was totally wrong, a voice inside of him yelled.

With all the women he had had, whose hands he'd allowed to touch him, he had never, *never*, let the subject come up. Even the ones who had had a few lacerations of their own had known not to speak of his map of horrors. And now, this achingly beautiful woman, this *lady*, who could know nothing about what had been done to him, about the kind of places he'd been and the people he'd dealt with, this delicate woman, wanted in on the nightmare.

"Are they all from . . ." She didn't finish her question.

A muscle began jerking in his jaw.

He forced his shoulders into a shrug. "Let's just say, I've been around the block a few times."

"I want to see them. All of them."

With a lurch, he pulled away from her. "This has gone far enough."

"I don't think it has," she said, moving toward him.

Smith was completely incapable of anything rational as her fingers went to the bottom of his shirt. He grabbed her hands in a brutal grip.

"You don't want to do that."

"Yes, I do. I'm not afraid of your past."

"You should be."

"I'm not. And I'm not afraid of you, either."

Gently, she removed his hands and slowly inched up the thin fabric. His breath began coming out in bursts and his body, caught between her will and his, began to quake in the conflict.

When the air hit his skin, he couldn't take it anymore. He exploded up from the bed and wrenched the goddamn thing off. He stretched his arms out wide, feeling his muscles expand.

"Here, I'll give you the whole show," he said ruthlessly. "Front and back."

Her eyes stayed on his face.

"Come on, Countess. You don't want to look now? Too much?" He was sneering at her, lashing out. She'd made him feel weak with her empathy and he resented how exposed he felt.

She shook her head and her eyes were grim, as if she'd taken his past deep down into herself and felt the echoes of pain in her own body.

"Not in such a big hurry to touch me anymore, are you. Now that you can see everything."

He was hoping if he pushed her hard enough, she'd back away. The others who had tried to get close had fled when he'd showed them the same rage.

But Grace didn't run.

Slowly, she rose from the bed and reached out a slender, gentle hand. When she touched his stomach delicately, he inhaled with a rasp.

His first instinct was to yell. He was infuriated that she had challenged him and exposed him. That she was near enough so he could smell her. That she was offering him compassion and understanding and warmth when he was battle-scarred and hard and ugly.

"I think you are beautiful," she said softly, looking up at him.

"Then you're fucking blind."

She shook her head slowly. "I see you, all of you. Clearly."

Grace traced a path across his stomach and stopped when she got to the waistband of his boxers. He felt himself swell for her touch and became instantly aware that he was half-naked and she was wearing close to nothing and they were alone in dim light.

He grabbed her upper arms and jerked her against him. Hard. Her only response was to tilt her head back so she could continue to meet his eyes.

"You might want to keep your hands to yourself." He made his words as cold as possible. "You touch me like that and I'm not thinking about what a courageous Florence Nightingale you are."

"So what are you thinking?"

He gave her a shake and watched as her hair swung around her shoulders and caught the light.

"Damn you," he growled. "Don't do this."

Her eyes were soft, luminous. Heated. He knew what she was thinking about and it didn't have anything to do with talking. In that hooded glance, she was asking for what she wanted. And she wanted him.

In spite of his anger. In spite of the marks on his skin.

The only honorable part in him spoke up.

"Listen to me, Countess. This body of mine is built for fucking. Do you even know what that is? We're talking one-night stands, up against a wall, don't know her name and don't care kind of shit. You don't want that."

She looked downcast, as if he'd robbed her of something.

"Hell." He let out some of his frustration with a deep breath. Everything that he'd been dreaming about was in his arms but the only thing he could do was let it go. "Don't you understand? You deserve better than what I can give you. You need someone who's going to make love to you. Not screw you and then leave you and your bed in a mess."

"You wouldn't do that."

"Oh yes, I would." Smith couldn't turn away but didn't want to kiss her because he knew he'd be lost.

So he pushed his hands into the waves of her hair and pulled them forward. The ends landed below her breasts, which were rising and falling as she breathed through her mouth. He lifted a strand and carried it forward to his nose. Breathing in, he caught the fragrance of jasmine. As he let the hair fall, he watched it settle between her breasts and curl obligingly around one silk-covered nipple.

Sweet Jesus, he wanted her.

He looked at her lips. They were parted, bow-shaped, tender.

"I don't want to hurt you," he said darkly. The truth was a surprise.

"I know." She reached up and touched his face, moving her palm down over the rasp of his beard growth. "But I don't want to be saved. That's not what I want. Not tonight."

Fighting himself was hard. Turning her down was ... impossible.

Smith bent forward and softly he stroked her mouth with his own. When he heard her moan, he put more pressure into the kiss and gathered her into his arms. As his tongue stole out to lick her lower lip, he felt her hands grip on to him. Moving even closer, he explored her mouth, delving deeper and deeper.

His fingers went to the straps of her nightgown. Slowly, he released the satin ribbons from her shoulders until she was bare to his eyes and the silk bodice was a pool around her hips. Blood roared in his ears and he pulled her down to the bed so that she was lying back against the lace-covered duvet. He began to kiss the skin at her collarbone and then went lower, ravishing her breasts and then her stomach.

With growing urgency, his hands moved over the swell of her hips and down her thighs. Going under the thin wisp of her nightgown, he stroked her legs, pushing the fragile silk up as he went.

When Smith slid his hand to her inner thigh, he felt the soft skin and the heat coming off of her. As he moved higher, he relished the sensation of her undulating underneath him and he looked up. The image of her with her arched back and her head cocked at an angle so she could watch him was the most erotic thing he'd ever seen.

He put his mouth on her stomach, just below her belly button, and prayed for self control. As his hands moved ever closer to her core, his mouth followed, kissing her skin through the silk. He had every intention of learning her intimately. With his fingers. His tongue. His body.

Smith's excitement grew to such heights that at first he didn't notice when her hands began to push against his shoulders. She started to thrash around but he assumed it was from the same passion he was feeling.

He was wrong.

"No! Stop!" Grace said, with alarm, jackknifing up straight.

She began to struggle with the nightgown and then gave up, pulling over a pillow to cover her breasts. She was shaking and pale.

Smith shifted to the edge of the bed and put his head in his hands. He was fighting to slow down the raging hunger in his body, cursing himself with every ragged breath.

"I'm—I'm sorry," she said softly. She reached out to him, touched his arm.

He yanked back. The last thing he needed was her hand on him. Not while he was trying to convince his inner caveman to get civilized.

"It's not that I don't want to . . ."

"But the wrong side of the tracks was tougher to visit than you'd thought?" His voice was hoarse.

"Good God, no. It's not that at all. It's just that . . . my husband—"

"I don't really want to hear about him right now, if you don't mind." Smith got to his feet. He needed to get the hell away from her. "Good night, Countess."

He left in a rush, walking back to his room in long, angry strides. He wanted to close all of the doors between them. Lock them tight, for Chrissakes. He felt like he needed something a hell of a lot more sturdy than his will to keep them apart.

11

The next morning, Grace fumbled to shut off the alarm. Her hand flapped around the bedside table, running into her diary, the lamp, everything except the clock. She opened her eyes, slapped the thing into silence, and collapsed back onto her pillows.

Outside it was storming and rain lashed against the windows.

She looked down and saw the shirt Smith had wrenched from his body. A flush went through her as she remembered what had happened next. She could still feel his mouth, hungry on hers, and his hands traveling across her skin. It had been a blur, going from his anger to their kisses, from the edge of reason to beyond control. She'd felt as if she was being possessed by him.

Pulling back, stopping him, had been an act of self-preservation.

Sometime after he'd laid her down, as he was kissing her belly and stroking her legs, taking her higher and higher into some kind of frenzy she'd never experienced before, she'd become overwhelmed and a little frightened. He wasn't hurting her but things had been moving so fast that she hadn't been able to process what bubbled up into her consciousness. Insecurities, insipid and disturbing, had cut through the passion and brought up memories she couldn't escape.

By the end of her marriage, her sex life with Ranulf had disintegrated into a painful exercise in humiliation for her. As he became more and more disenchanted with his wife, he grew rougher as a lover until she learned to dread the feel of the bed dipping down when he slid in next to her at night. What had previously been a pleasant enough experience became something she endured and her cool response to him only made the situation worse. He became impotent and laid the blame for his sexual dysfunction on her. With every failure, he railed against her, telling her she was frigid and hardly a woman. She had stood up to him once, explaining that a woman needed more than just rough hands spreading her legs to enjoy sex, and that had been the only time in her life she feared a man would strike her.

Although she knew Ranulf taunted her to be cruel, because he was humiliated as well as disillusioned with her and the marriage, a part of her wondered if he wasn't a little right. She'd had one lover before her husband and wouldn't have described her attraction to either of them as overwhelming. Between her past experience and Ranulf's vivid and disparaging vocabulary, she had doubts whether she could satisfy a man. And whether she herself could be satisfied.

Until John Smith had come along.

Her reaction to him blew the doors off the notion she was frigid. But it did nothing to dispel the other side of her self-doubts. If there was one man on the planet she wanted to satisfy, it was Smith. She just wasn't sure she could.

Knowing the basics of sex was no guarantee you could make all that thrusting anything more than a mild cardiovascular workout. Hell, she learned that from Ranulf—before he got mean.

When the doubts in her mind had cut through the desire in her body, she'd only wanted to slow down what was happening between them. She'd needed a moment to catch her breath, prepare to make the leap into unknown territory.

But when he didn't stop, she panicked because the struggle reminded her of Ranulf.

She didn't blame Smith for leaving in a foul mood.

Throwing the covers back, Grace got out of bed and picked up his white shirt. She didn't want him to think she'd pulled back because she hadn't wanted him. She might have lost her nerve temporarily but not her desire for him.

Pulling on a bathrobe, she left her bedroom and found him in his room, sitting on the chaise lounge by the window. He looked up from the book he was reading the instant she appeared at the door. His expression was totally closed.

"Are you skipping the run this morning?" he asked briskly.

She nodded as a gust of wind pushed the rain against the windows and the water landed in a pattern of sound.

"I—ah, I brought your shirt back." She put it on one of the beds and cleared her throat. "Listen, about last night—"

He snapped the book shut and stared out at the gray morning. "I owe you an apology."

Grace frowned. "What are you talking about?"

He shot her a dry look. "Aside from the fact that I never should have put us in that position, I didn't let you go when I should have. I didn't know you wanted to stop. The only excuse I can offer is that I don't usually get that ... preoccupied."

Her mouth slacked in surprise. She'd expected him to be mad because he hadn't gotten what he'd wanted. That had certainly been the first response of her father and Ranulf.

Smith's eyes were hooded as he cut her off before she could speak.

"I didn't mean to scare you. And don't deny it," he said when she shook her head and opened her mouth. "I know what I saw in your eyes last night. It was fear."

"But I want you to know why I couldn't—"

"It's none of my business and, to be honest, I don't want to hear the whys. They're not relevant. The last thing you need is to be afraid in your own house. Of me."

"I'm not threatened by you." Grace's voice was earnest.

He considered her thoughtfully but then shook his head.

"Even if that's true, it doesn't matter." Smith reopened the book. "Let me know when the shower's free."

"John . . ." He looked up with a dark expression. "I didn't pull away because I don't want you."

"Frankly, I wish that was the reason."

She frowned. "But why?"

He didn't reply. Instead, his eyes returned to the book.

Grace had no choice but to leave him. There was so much more to be said but she knew he wouldn't talk anymore.

When they reached the Hall Building, after a long, quiet ride through traffic, Grace paused to talk to some people in the atrium while Smith went over and checked in with the security officer on duty.

"Is that the consultant?" one of the staff whispered while nodding over at Smith.

So word had gotten around, Grace thought as she nodded.

"He looks a little . . . hard for an OD guy."

"He's a specialist," she said, hoping the subject would drop.

"I'll bet he is," another woman chimed in while looking Smith up and down.

Grace was in a bad mood when she got into the elevator with him.

As soon as it was just the two of them, he said, "Why are you looking like that?"

"Like what?"

"Like in your mind you've got your hands around some-one's throat."

"I don't know what you are talking about."

"Sure you do."

The elevator doors opened on her floor and she shot him a challenging look. "Do you really want to keep going with this? Because as I recall, this morning you were the one with the closed mouth."

Smith gave her a lazy smile as they walked down the hall.

"Touché," he said softly as they came up to Kat's desk and the girl looked up.

"Senator Bradford called," she said to Grace. She glanced at Smith warily, as if she expected him to walk right by her again. "She wanted to remind you to come to the Plaza on Friday. Seven P.M. Black-tie."

"Thanks. I'll be there with bells on."

"Morning, Kat," Smith said casually.

"Good morning." The girl's eyes flared.

"How was the IT guy?"

"Er—he was actually kind of okay." A tentative smile appeared. "He likes baseball, too, and, ah, I might go out again with him."

"Make sure he pays for dinner."

Her eyes bounced around a little, as if she was flustered by the attention. "Hey—do you need something? Coffee?"

"Coffee'd be great, thanks. Black."

After Grace and Smith walked into her office, he went over to the conference table and sat down, opening the files he'd spent days poring over. As he began to make notes, she knew he was deliberately avoiding the look of approval she was sending him.

When Kat came in with the coffee, she closed the door behind her.

"What's wrong?" Grace asked.

"There's a man outside," the girl said as she gave a steaming mug to Smith. "He doesn't have an appointment and he's demanding to see you. Someone named Fredrique."

Grace winced. "It's about the Gala. He did the party planning and the catering last year for us but I didn't re-hire him because he cost a small fortune. He probably just wants to pitch me for business I've already turned down."

"He seems like he's prepared to wait."

"Really?"

"He brought a cooler and a newspaper."

"Send him in then," Grace said, annoyed. "There's no sense turning the waiting area into a cafeteria."

When Fredrique came into the room, he smiled widely. Dressed in chef's whites, the man had a small picnic basket–like container in one of his hands. He looked as if he'd gained some weight, she thought, although maybe it was just the way the stiff cotton fell over his short, stocky build.

When he came around for an air kiss, she accepted the greeting with reserve.

"Please, have a seat," she said, indicating a chair across from the desk.

As he sat down, he looked over his shoulder at Smith. "And who is this?"

"What may I do for you?" Her tone was direct.

Fredrique faced her reluctantly, as if he would have enjoyed the introduction.

"I've brought you something to sample. From the new line of hors d'oeuvres I'm developing with Lolly Ramparr of NightWorx. You know Lolly, don't you? She and I go way back."

Grace narrowed her eyes, doubting that he was actually working with Lolly. After interviewing several firms, Grace had decided to use NightWorx as a caterer for the Gala this year because they had a good reputation and were reasonably priced considering their popularity. Lolly had asked specifically whether Fredrique was going to be working on the event and Grace had explained her reasons for not using him. Lolly, an up-front person who was not unkind, had indicated that she was moving away from collaborating with him for similar reasons.

Fredrique put the cooler on her desk, splitting the handles and popping off the lid. "I understand that you are using Lolly this year for the Gala," he said casually. "She's such a talent, as you will recall when you try these."

He took out a white plate. On it, there were three small mounds of peach-colored mousse atop some kind of cracker.

"I call them shrimp towers." He extended the plate, as if he were offering jewels. "Try them and fall in love."

"I'm sorry, Fredrique. They look lovely but I'm allergic to shellfish."

He frowned and retracted the plate. Glancing over to Smith, he said, "Perhaps you will do the honors?"

Smith, who had turned his chair toward Fredrique and been staring at him, just shook his head.

The other man took a moment to collect himself. "No matter. I'll bring you something else. Perhaps tenderloin on sesame-encrusted pita chips. Ooh! I have a wonderful lamb-stuffed mushroom—"

"I appreciate the thought but I have to remind you. We're not in the market for your kind of services."

Fredrique stiffened and returned the plate to the cooler. With precise movements, he put the lid back on and re-united the two handles over the top. "It's a shame for the Gala to miss out on my contributions. Mimi Lauer is thrilled with my work on the ballet's event."

Grace wasn't so sure about that, as Mimi had called recently to express her frustration with the man.

"I don't know what to say, Fredrique. We aren't using a party planner this year."

Abruptly, he smiled.

"Perhaps not at the Foundation, but privately?" He began gathering momentum again. "As you know, I do fabulous holiday parties in private homes. Although my book is filling fast, I could make sure I save you a date. I plan to meet with Isadora Cunis this week about the holidays but I could make sure you get first choice of the calendar. As long as you put down a deposit today."

"I don't think so." Grace didn't want to lead the guy on and knew she had to be clear. He was persistent and any polite prevarication would only be seen as a opening. "But I appreciate the offer."

She stood up, hoping he'd take the hint.

Fredrique stared at her and then slowly got to his feet, straightening his chef's uniform with a sharp movement. She forced a smile at him as he picked up his little cooler, and then led him across the room.

"Thank you for coming by," she said, wishing she could just push him out the door. Her day was jam-packed and the last thing she needed was to stroke the ego of someone whose food was second-rate and who'd overcharged them the year before to the tune of $20,000.

Fredrique, however, wasn't going to be hurried along. He took his time, looking around the office while she stood at the open door.

"Such a beautiful painting," he murmured as he stared at the landscape over the conference table.

"Thank you. Now if you don't mind, I have another appointment to go to."

She was taken aback when he came up close to her. "Are you sure you want to do this?"

Grace frowned but before she could respond, Smith's hand clamped on the man's shoulder.

"You want to step back a little, Fredrique." Smith's smile was on the north pole side of warm.

The other man looked up in surprise and immediately moved away from Grace. With a little bow, he murmured, "I'm sure I'll see you again soon, Countess."

As he walked away, Grace breathed a sigh of relief and shut the door.

"Thanks for putting some space between him and me," she said to Smith as he sat back down at the conference table.

"I can't be too careful."

She hid a shudder. "I should probably warn Isadora that he's on the hunt for business and she's next on his list."

Besides, she thought numbly, she and Isadora had other things to talk about. Their lost friends. That god-awful article.

Grace went through the rest of the week in a daze. There seemed to be an endless supply of problems to confront. The invitations for the Gala, which needed to be mailed out immediately, came back with a typo. The reprinting cost a small fortune and, when she'd looked at the final product, the absence of a major auction piece was obvious. She hoped no one else picked up on it but she knew they would.

Lamont had been right about one thing. Trying to do her father's job and pull a prestigious event together was a heavy load to shoulder. Dealing with the caterers, rental companies, sound men, publicists, and videographers was an incredible drain on her time. As the demands rose, and the event drew closer, she began to rely on Kat more and more. Fortunately, the girl welcomed the extra responsibility.

Grace was so distracted by work and the undercurrents between her and Smith that she almost forgot about the danger she was in.

Until Lieutenant Marks called again.

She and Smith had just walked into the penthouse after attending a late-night gallery opening when the phone started ringing. As soon as she heard the lieutenant's voice, the fear came back, vivid and awful.

"Don't worry," he said. "I'm just checking in. Have you seen anything unusual? Is Smith still with you?"

She felt a measure of relief as she sat down on the couch. "Yes, he is. And no, not really."

"Can you put him on?"

Grace called out to Smith. "Marks wants to talk with you."

As Smith took the phone, she watched him anxiously. She had no idea what they were talking about; all she heard were Smith's short replies. He hung up the phone and she was disappointed when he didn't say anything.

"Is anything wrong?" she asked.

He shook his head.

"So what did you talk about?"

He shrugged and started to walk down the hall. She hurried after him.

"Tell me," she demanded as she grabbed his arm. His wrist was thick and warm under her fingers, reminding her of what it felt like to be against his body.

When he looked down at the contact, she took her hand back but stepped in front of him, blocking his way to his bedroom.

"Don't hide things from me," she said bluntly. "I'd rather know bad news than have to deal with what my mind can imagine."

Smith gave her a level stare before speaking. "The only thing they know is that the victims have been killed by the same person. They've DNA-tested blood samples and hair fibers found at the scenes and skin found under the victims' nails and it's a match. Other than that, they have no leads. No suspects. No motive."

She leaned her hip and shoulder against the wall, feeling sick as she pictured her friends scratching at the killer. And the fact that the police hadn't made much progress was daunting. In the back of her mind, she'd assumed that they were picking up clues and hints that would eventually make some kind of sense.

"I can't believe they've found nothing," she said, looking down at the fine nap of the hall carpet. She moved the pointed heel of her Manolo Blahnik in a circle, making a half-moon trail in the otherwise smooth, cream-colored surface. It was an attempt to avoid his eyes and some of the harsh reality they were discussing but the distraction only worked on the former. "Have they looked hard enough?"

"Marks has a good reputation and I know he runs a tight ship. The bastard who killed those women has just been lucky so far."

"Or he knows what he's doing."

Smith's voice was harsh. "He's an amateur."

She cringed, thinking of the photos of Cuppie's body. "What makes you say that?"

When he didn't reply, she looked up at him.

"Are you sure you want to be talking about this?" he said gruffly.

"I asked, didn't I," she shot back as pride's sting surged through her fear. She didn't want him to think she was incapable of rationally discussing something that so obviously affected her life. At the same time, her stomach had started to roll with nausea.

Smith still didn't answer and her body went cold.

"Talk to me, for Chrissakes," she said sharply. "This sphinx routine is getting on my nerves."

Smith smiled faintly. "I'd asked Marks to look for any connections between the husbands of the women in that article. He said that other than social ties, there appeared to be no commonality. I wasn't surprised."

"So what do you think? Why is this happening?"

Hanging in the air was, *Why me?*

"It's personal. The connection is among you, not your husbands. Look, all I can tell you is that Marks is doing everything he can with what he has. He's a damn good cop. Something will turn up, eventually."

"But what happens until then? How many of us will . . ." Grace couldn't say the word that was bouncing around her head. Death was never easy to speak of, she thought, but it was damn near impossible to say the word *die* when you were thinking of yourself.

She wrapped her arms around her rib cage, missing the fog of security she'd been living in over the last few days.

"Grace. Look at me."

She lifted her head.

"You hired me to protect you." She nodded when he paused. "And that's what I'm going to do."

"I hope so. God, I truly hope so."

"Don't hope," he said. *"Believe."*

She stared into his eyes and saw self-confidence, power, control. It all seemed to promise that her faith in him would be rewarded.

When he reached out a hand to her, the gesture was unexpected.

"Let's go to bed."

Her eyes widened, but then she realized that he wasn't talking about sex. His words were a casual direction intended to get her to rest.

She took his hand, feeling his fingers wrap around her own, warm and strong. They walked down the hall together until they got to his room and then he broke the contact silently and left her.

She'd changed into a nightgown and was lying in bed in the dark when she heard him go into the bathroom. The sounds of water were muted and brief. Minutes later, he emerged.

"John?"

"What?" His voice through the darkness was smooth.

"I'm glad you're here."

There was only silence and she assumed he'd gone back to his room.

"Me, too," he said softly.

Surprised by his answer, she rolled over only to find that she was alone.

Hours later she was still awake. Feeling claustrophobic amid all the pillows and the thick comforter, she picked up her diary and a pen and went to the living room. As she passed Smith's door, the light was off.

Sitting on the couch, she curled her legs under her but found herself thinking instead of writing. When Smith had reached out his hand to her, she'd been surprised and, as she remembered the feel of his palm against hers, she thought of other things he'd done that had been unexpected.

The other morning, after they had come home from a blistering run, she'd been late getting out of the shower. She'd rushed into the kitchen to tell him that it was his turn when he pressed a cup of steaming coffee into her hand and pointed at a plate of toast he'd made for her.

She'd been dumbfounded.

"It's food," he'd drawled. "You may not recognize it because you haven't eaten much in the last week."

"Of course, I have. I—"

"That salad last night for dinner doesn't count. You're dropping weight you can't afford to lose."

She'd looked down at herself. He was right. Her skirts had been a little bigger at the waist lately.

"Eat." He'd pushed the toast at her.

She'd picked up a slice and noticed it was covered with strawberry jam. "I haven't had jam on toast for years."

As soon as she swallowed one mouthful, her appetite came back. After four slices, and having finished the coffee, she'd sighed with contentment. She'd been running on nervous stress for so long, she'd forgotten about feeding her body.

She remembered glancing up at him. All the while she'd been eating, he'd been standing against the counter, arms crossed, watching her.

"I'd like to thank you for this," she'd said wryly, "if you'll let me."

He'd shrugged but when no acerbic comment was forthcoming, she'd smiled at him.

"So thank you."

His sharp eyes had flickered over the empty plate. "Just taking care of my client."

Grace smiled at her memory of how he'd looked. The image of him being something close to sheepish was incongruous, but that's what he'd seemed. Her simple gratitude for his thoughtfulness had been hard for him to accept but he hadn't turned it down, either.

It was progress, she thought. Just like him reaching for her this evening had been.

But progress toward what?

In her heart, she wanted more of him. All of him.

And the desire was getting stronger as she got to know him better.

At first, she'd wondered whether he had another side, something to offer other than aggressive charisma. Now, she knew there were different, less harsh parts to him. He kept most of them hidden behind his mask of control but they came out in his actions, as simple courtesies that proved he was aware of others. Aware of her.

That breakfast was just one example of how thoughtful he could be. He never left the bathroom a mess. He'd made a point of being nicer to Kat. He cooked his own meals, cleaned up the kitchen, and somehow didn't track mud all over her white carpets, even on rainy days.

They were small things, but they meant a lot to her. They were also unfamiliar. Having a man in the house who didn't require constant attention or have a long list of demands was a new experience. Ranulf had expected her to organize their social calendar, make sure the penthouse was properly staffed, attend to his needs small and large, and entertain dinner guests nearly every night, even though she was working full-time and he wasn't. And all of this was done without thanks from him because, in his mind, it was her duty.

She was never falling into that trap again.

Grace looked down at the diary and the date she'd written at the top of the blank page. In the morning, she was turning thirty. At 7:05 A.M. to be precise.

Feeling whimsical, she wrote: *All I want for my birthday today is John Smith. In my bed with a ribbon around his neck and nothing else on him.*

Laughing softly, Grace pushed the book and the pen aside. She was being ridiculous, of course, but it was fun to fantasize. Certainly better than a lot of what her mind had been cooking up lately. Staring out at the night, she imagined things that made her blush. Eventually, she drifted back down the hall, pausing at the open door to Smith's bedroom. She toyed for a moment with going inside and finding him in the dark but forced herself to go to her own room.

The next morning, she took a shower and then went to find Smith. They'd fallen into a morning ritual. She'd go first and while she was getting dressed, he'd take over the bathroom.

"Smith?" She peeked in his room. The bed was made, as always, and there was no clutter around. The heritage of a military man, she thought. When she turned away, she saw a black bar in the doorway to his bathroom. A chin-up bar. So that was how he kept in shape.

Heading into the living room, she found him facing toward the morning sky. After days of gray clouds, the horizon was a pale blue and the sun was coming up over the city.

"Shower's free."

He showed no surprise at the sound of her voice even though she'd been quiet in her approach. She was getting used to his uncanny senses and the fact that he always seemed to know where she was. He was looking at her reflection now in the glass door.

When he didn't say anything, she cleared her throat. "Er—the shower?"

She pointed behind her with a thumb.

He didn't reply, just continued staring at her in the glass.

Her skin prickled in awareness as he remained silent. There was something different about him this morning, she thought.

When he finally turned around, his expression shocked her. There was heat in it, the kind of burning intensity she hadn't seen since the night she'd stopped him. She thought about his body against hers and what it had felt like to be touched by him. His eyes focused on her lips, as if he was thinking about the same thing.

When he crossed the room in long strides, she felt herself bracing for contact with him, ready for it.

"I'll make it quick," he said as he came up to her.

The letdown was tremendous. She'd been sure he was

going to take her into his arms and she tried to cover her disappointment by smiling nonchalantly.

But then he paused on his way by and bent his head down to her ear. "Happy birthday, Grace."

His breath brushed against her neck and she felt him run a forefinger down her cheek.

Electricity jolted through her and she gasped.

To her frustration, though, he just continued down the hall.

Feeling like she'd been tackled from behind, Grace sat down in a chair, wondering what in the hell all that was about. And why he hadn't followed through on what his eyes were promising her.

She frowned. How had he known it was her birthday?

Her eyes restlessly moved around the room as she tried to deal with her confusion. And then she saw, face open on the couch, her diary.

Oh, God.

She went over and looked at what he must have read.

Yup. Her little birthday wish.

Grace grimaced, feeling like a fool.

A wrinkle in time, she thought, closing the cover. That's what she needed. So she could go back to three o'clock in the morning and remember to take the thing down the hall with her.

A wrinkle in time or half an ounce of common sense.

12

STANDING IN the shower, Smith let the water run down over his head and his shoulders. It was hot enough to sting his skin but he needed some distraction and physical pain was always a good one.

He'd been lying in bed and staring up at the ceiling in the dark as she'd left her room the night before. When she came back down the hall, the pause she had taken in front of his door had been a temptation he'd barely resisted. He could still feel the sheet balled up in his fist as he'd let her go to her bedroom alone.

As soon as she'd settled down, it was his turn to pace around the penthouse. While walking from room to room, he'd thought about the fact that they were both sleepless and edgy although not necessarily for the same reason. That hesitation in his doorway could have been because of fear, but he wanted to believe there was another reason for it. He wanted to believe she couldn't sleep because she was as sexually frustrated as he was.

It was right about then that he'd passed by the couch and saw a small book lying faceup on the cushion. He'd bent over, looked at the elegant, neat script, and smiled when he finished reading it.

He'd love to be her goddamn birthday present.

Smith turned up the water a little hotter.

Christ, he thought. He wanted her. And, in spite of the fact that she'd pulled away before, she obviously still wanted him. What would be so wrong if they gave in to the urge? Just once?

Okay, it violated every professional standard he'd ever set for himself. But he was pretty goddamn tired of the frustration he was battling day and night.

Smith braced his arms against the marble wall and leaned in, feeling the muscles in his back stretch and the water hit behind his neck.

He liked clear divisions. Safe and dangerous. Smart and stupid. He'd always believed that life was pretty simple if you took care of business and made the right choices. It wasn't as if right and wrong were hard to discern.

For example, sleeping with a client was both dangerous and stupid.

Smith turned and let the jets pound into his back. He rolled his shoulders around, trying to loosen the tension, even though he knew it wasn't going to do any good. Nothing had eased him recently and he could feel the pressure building in his body. He suspected that the only release would be spending a night in bed with Grace.

Or maybe a week.

At least he'd know she was safe from the killer, he thought grimly.

As he stepped from the shower, the tactician in him came out. What he needed to do was assess the situation dispassionately. Review the assets and liabilities. Plan for conflict.

He'd been a Ranger, for God's sake. He was trained to reason himself out of no-win situations.

Smith turned off the water and stepped out of the shower. Picking up a towel, he started to dry off.

She wanted him. He felt the same way. Those were assets.

All right, maybe assets wasn't the right word. But it was reality.

He moved on to liabilities. That list was much longer.

First, there was the professional relationship. Waking up next to a client had sure as hell never been a career goal. He knew damn well that sex always carried with it the risk of emotional involvement on the woman's side but this was especially true when it came to someone he protected. It wasn't that he was such a great catch but people in vulnerable situations could easily get attached to their protector and sex would only encourage the inappropriate connection.

And then there was the way he ran his personal life. After he slept with someone, he left. There was no cuddling or snuggling or affectionate whispering in the dark. Usually he took off because he had to catch a plane, but on those rare occasions when he wasn't leaving imminently, he'd get the hell away from them because he felt trapped. The emotional aftermath of sex always felt forced to him. He just had nothing to say to the women.

Other than good-bye.

Grace might be one hell of a sophisticated woman but she clearly wasn't a player. He suspected she'd only give herself to a man she had some kind of emotional connection with and that was why she'd pulled back the night he'd almost had her. When she'd tried to explain, he hadn't wanted her to share her feelings. He knew damn well that confidences bred intimacy and he did not want to encourage that.

With any woman.

Smith let out a curse.

Talk about new and uncharted territory. He'd never thought about the ramifications of sleeping with a woman before. Previously, it had been a binary exercise. If he wanted one, he had her.

And then kept on going.

Smith tied the towel around his waist and wiped the steam off the mirror with his forearm.

He looked at himself with a hard, unflinching stare.

So what was the answer?

He had every confidence that he could sleep with her and not become emotionally compromised. Mostly because he was incapable of forging intimate relationships. His lifestyle had him jetting around to different parts of the world at the drop of a hat, to destinations he couldn't divulge. And if the constant dislocation wasn't a problem, his line of work sure as hell was. He didn't want to come back to someone who had had to live for a month without hearing from him, wondering all the time if he wasn't coming home at all.

Too much pressure.

When he was working, he needed to think about his clients' safety and his own. There was no room for worrying about some woman who might mourn him. This was why, at the age of thirty-eight, he'd never been married and had never spent more than a string of nights with any one woman.

Smith was alone in the world, except for his people at Black Watch, and he liked it that way. He didn't get lonely because he never stopped moving. And because he had no family, there were no guilt trips on those damn holidays that seemed to come around every fifteen minutes. He was free.

But what about Grace's emotions?

If they were going to make love, she had a right to know what to expect. Which was nothing but some really great sex.

Smith got dressed with an efficiency that had been drilled into him by the army. Shaving took a total of three minutes from the time he picked up the can of shaving cream to when he put down the razor. His hair was so short, he didn't even need to brush it.

He was about to leave when he caught sight of a splash of lavender silk hanging on the back of the door. He pictured Grace in it and imagined slowly peeling the delicate material from her skin.

What if he got emotionally involved, he wondered idly.

He didn't think it was even remotely possible but he shouldn't overlook the risk. What if he made love to Grace and began to care about her? He'd already come to respect her. And he found her attractive on so many levels.

Christ, for the first time in his life, he was actually thinking about how sex would affect things between him and a woman. That was how different things were.

So what did it all mean for him? Although it was best if she didn't get emotionally attached, it was goddamn critical that he didn't. Neither of them could afford his objectivity to be compromised and, with the heart engaged, the mind could weaken. Doctors didn't treat family members for precisely this reason.

Compartmentalization had to be the answer, he thought, touching the nightgown.

Fortunately, it was a technique he excelled at. His ability to segment his thoughts and his emotions meant that he could go into situations with a clear head and a calm body and stay that way after the bullets started flying. All he had to do was shut off portions of himself and suppress his feelings.

It was a matter of will.

He told himself there was no reason he couldn't distance himself from Grace emotionally. In the unlikely event he felt anything for her.

Smith gripped the silk tightly in his hand.

He wanted her, but he wasn't prepared to lie to get her into bed. He'd give her the choice. He'd be up front with what he could offer, which was nothing but physical contact, and she would choose for them.

After all, she was a grown woman. He'd spent enough time with her to know that she was smart and honest with herself. If anyone would be able to make an informed decision, it would be Grace.

When Smith opened the door, he was smiling.

"Smith?"

He turned toward her voice.

She was standing in the doorway to her dressing room, her silk shirt partially tucked into the waistband of a black skirt. She'd obviously been waiting for him.

"About what you read . . . out there." Her eyes struggled to hold his but she looked away as she flushed.

"I didn't know it was your diary until it was too late," he said, unable to keep the smile off his face.

"Yeah, well, ah . . ."

Smith went to her, stopping only when he could see the flecks of yellow in her green eyes.

"I liked your idea of a birthday present," he said. His voice was even lower than normal.

Her eyes widened.

He bent his head down so he could talk in her ear. "Even though I shouldn't, I want you to want me."

He brought up his hand and touched the pulse beating at the base of her throat with the pad of his thumb. Her heart rate was fast, so fast the beats blurred into one another.

"I think I've been wrong about us," he said, moving his fingers to her collarbone. Her skin was warm and smooth.

"About what?" she croaked.

Her eyes were luminous as they looked into his, full of fear and anticipation.

He put his lips closer to her ear.

"Tell me," he whispered, "what you want me to do to you."

Her breath left her mouth on a gasp.

He moved her hair aside and slowly, deliberately, took her lobe in between his teeth. "What do you want?"

Her hand rose to his shoulders and she pushed him away.

"John," she mumbled. She cleared her throat. He could see her willing herself to be strong and, as he watched her leash the fire in her blood, he respected her for it. Her voice was clear when she finally spoke. "Why don't you tell me what *you* mean."

He took a step back and shoved his hands in his pockets.

"I don't think there's any reason we shouldn't . . ." He was going to say *Have sex* but that seemed a little tough. "Be lovers."

And how about right now, he thought. Let's ditch the clothes. Dive into each other.

Grace's hand came up to her throat. "What's made you change your mind?"

Good goddamn question, he thought, knowing she deserved an honest answer.

"Because I want you like no other woman I've ever met," he said roughly.

Before she could reply, he went on, reminding himself of what else he had to tell her.

"Look, I can give you pleasure. But you need to know, the job ends and I'm out of your life. No permanence, no happy ending." He stared at her, willing her to take him seriously and still go to bed with him. "Until that happens, I can promise you, no one will make love to your body like I will."

He heard the desire vibrate in his own voice.

"Think about it," he said before moving away from her. "And let me know what you decide."

Grace watched him go.

He couldn't have surprised her more if he'd told her he was Superman.

She'd assumed he'd forgotten about what had happened in her bedroom that night, that he'd brushed it aside with the same casual disregard he treated most things. Obviously, he hadn't.

The idea that he wanted her was deeply satisfying. What he was proposing was less so.

Could she really have an affair? A short, intense relationship based on a physical connection and nothing more?

She remembered what his voice sounded like, deep in her ear, and thought yes, she sure as hell could.

Grace went back into her dressing room, sat down at her vanity and began brushing out her hair.

Except, if she was truthful with herself, she knew it wouldn't be only physical on her part. She was attracted to him but her emotions were already involved.

No happily ever after.

Putting down the brush, she twisted her hair up and began pinning the chignon.

Before her marriage to Ranulf, she'd been capable of believing in happily ever after. Or at least, moderately-happy-in-a-stable-kind-of-way ever after. Now, she didn't.

The question was, it seemed, whether she could be with Smith and still keep her head together. She'd have to be able to resist looking for, and then believing in, a future that he'd explicitly told her would never happen. Because she knew better than to assume he'd change his mind if she lost her heart to him. If he told her he was going to leave and never see her again, he would. She didn't doubt it for a moment.

Grace regarded the chignon from various angles and tucked one more hairpin in the back.

If she got hurt, it would only be her own fault.

She thought about his kisses and wanted to give him an answer right away. It was tempting to tell him yes and deal with the consequences later, to go to him this very moment and fall into his arms.

But that kind of spur-of-the-moment decision-making was at the root of her problems with Ranulf. He'd asked her to marry him and she'd agreed, pushing aside her doubts. If she'd taken some time to think about the situation, she might have followed the inner voice that was telling her they were ill-matched.

This time, she would make her decision carefully. In spite of how much she wanted to be with John.

From now on, she was going to choose her way more deliberately.

At the end of the workday, Grace looked at the stack of papers on the desk and felt as if she was staring up at a mountain. The pile had grown in spite of all the things she'd delegated, thrown out, or asked Kat to file. She was tired and distracted and the last thing she wanted to do was go to the Plaza for the birthday party Bo was throwing her.

"I can't do it," she muttered.

Smith looked up from the conference table.

"I can't go out tonight," she said more loudly. "I'm sorry."

He shrugged. "Why are you apologizing to me? We weren't going on a date."

His pragmatic words stung but he was right. They weren't going out together as a couple. They were just two people going to the same place.

And she thought she might be able to make love with him and not get more emotionally involved?

All day long, her answer to his proposal had been solidly in *yes* territory. Yes and *now*. But maybe she was deluding herself.

Grace picked up the phone, dialed the Plaza, and asked for Senator Barbara Ann Bradford. As soon as Bo picked up, she said, "I'm so sorry. Something has—"

Bo laughed and her smooth Southern drawl brooked no argument. "Don't even try that with me. I'm in town for forty-eight hours for your thirtieth birthday party. You will be coming for dinner, you will have a good time, and we will give you a royal razzing about getting older."

"I'm just exhausted."

"Everyone who's coming tonight is a friend. The real kind. If you end up falling asleep during dinner, we'll prop you up on a sofa. You'll be as elegant as ever, just a little more quiet."

"Maybe we should just meet tomorrow for—"

Bo's voice grew gentle. "Woody, you need us right now. That's why I sent you the gift."

Grace struggled to turn her father's chair around so it faced the view, wishing she were by herself. She didn't want to cry in front of Smith and tears were milling.

"Oh, Bo, I don't know what to say."

The gift was a relic of their girlhood together, a short length of braided hair, blond and auburn intertwined. They had woven it at the age of twelve when they'd been at summer camp and had cut each other's hair.

As soon as Grace had seen the lock in the porcelain box, she'd remembered exactly where they'd been sitting as they'd put a pair of scissors to work. It had been on a dock, on the shores of Lake Sagamore. The sun had been low in a very blue sky and the breeze mild. It had been toward the end of summer, she recalled, and the warmth in the air had been welcomed because their swimsuits had been damp. She could still hear the sound of the water clapping through the crib underneath their towels.

With great chops and slices, they had transformed themselves on the outside, eager to get closer to their grown-up selves. As locks of hair had fallen onto the bleached wood of the dock, they were convinced that with shorter hair they would look older. They would be further along on the path to their great destinies.

With shorter hair, things would somehow be easier.

When they were finished, they had taken some of the strands and made the two braids, one for each of them. They had brushed off the rest of the hair into the water where it lingered on the surface like a spider's web and then floated away. They'd laughed at how funny it felt to be free of the weight that had once lain on their shoulders.

Somewhere along the way to adulthood, Grace had misplaced her braid and the ache she felt from the loss would have astonished her younger self. Having grown up, having reached that maturity she'd yearned for, it was a surprise to find herself wanting to return to that simpler life, to that moment at the edge of the lake with her friend. To that summer day that she'd believed was going to last forever.

"Bo, how did you know how much it would mean to me?"

"Because I was with you then and I'm with you now. Someday, when I'm hurting, you can send it back to me." Grace felt tears prick the corners of her eyes as Bo laughed. "Think of it as emotional fruitcake. We'll just keep mailing it back and forth to each other."

"I don't know how to thank you."

"I do. Tell me you and Ranulf are coming tonight."

Grace hesitated, overcome with the need to see her friend. "Ranulf is . . . busy. I think I'll bring someone else."

"Great. Who is she?"

"He. Actually. Ah . . . He's a friend."

"Really? Is he single?"

"Er—yes. I guess so."

"Think he'd be interested in a thirty-four-year-old, over-worked, single mother?" Bo chuckled. "Now there's a personal ad guaranteed to get results."

Grace wasn't sure how to respond to her friend's innocent suggestion. The idea of John with another woman made her sick to her stomach.

When she hung up, she looked over at him and wondered whether there was a woman in his life. She couldn't imagine him being married but that didn't mean he was alone.

Might be something to explore before she made her final decision, she thought grimly.

"So I'm putting on the tux?" he asked. His keen eyes told her he had missed none of the emotions she was feeling.

She nodded slowly. "Bo is a hard lady to turn down."

"Obviously."

It was almost six thirty when Grace came out of her room. Smith was standing in the living room dressed in his tuxedo, the jacket hanging loosely over his arm. Grace slowed down as she approached him, thinking that the white of his shirt made his hair look darker.

Everything faded as she saw that he was looking at her lips.

"That's a beautiful dress," he said in a low, very male voice.

She glanced down at the lemon yellow chiffon. The gown was shoulderless, long, and simple.

"Thank you."

He walked over to her. "The necklace, too."

He reached out and touched one of the canary diamonds. There were six of them, linked by clusters of white diamonds.

"It was my grandmother's." Her voice was breathless as his fingertips hovered above her skin and she gripped her wrap and purse tightly.

His hand slowly went down to his side and she watched as the simmering emotions in his face were shut off.

"Are we ready?" he asked sharply.

She nodded and thought, as they went down in the elevator, there was a very real possibility she was going to get her heart broken by him.

Eddie took them down to the Plaza. As he pulled up in front of the hotel, he said, "I hope you have a splendiferous evening."

Smith shot him a look as a doorman stepped forward and let the cold air in. "That's a fancy word."

"Yeah, isn't it great? I'm liking adjectives. You need to work your vocabulary; it's like a muscle. Ummm—happy birthday, Grace, by the way." Eddie passed a small, carefully wrapped present back. "I know this isn't the best time or anything but I figure, what the hell, give it to her now."

"Why, thank you, Eddie."

"You don't have to open it."

"Of course, I do! This was very thoughtful of you." She ripped off the paper. "Why, it's . . . Mace."

She smiled at him.

"I know it's illegal in New York but you should really keep some with you all the time. Do you know how to use it? Just slide your finger in here and point it toward the face." He showed her the discharge mechanism and was satisfied only when she practiced twice. "Put it in your purse. You take it everywhere, okay?"

"Okay, Eddie. I'll do that." She slipped it inside her little silk bag and then leaned in and pressed a kiss to his cheek. "Thank you again."

Eddie was smiling as he pulled away from the curb.

"That was really kind of him," she said as she waved.

"Yeah, it was. He likes you. But then so do most people."

She looked up at Smith but he was scanning the park, the street, the pedestrians in front of the hotel.

"You sound surprised," she said softly.

His eyes came to rest on her face. "There's a lot about you I find surprising. Let's go."

She wanted to pump him for specifics, but she lifted the hem of her dress and walked up the red-carpeted stairs. As they passed the Palm Court, Grace stopped to talk to a couple and then they headed for the elevators.

When they got to the suite, Grace knocked on the door and her friend opened it wide, sweeping her into an embrace.

"Here she is!" Bo exclaimed.

Grace wrapped her arms around her old friend. "I'm so glad to see you north of the Mason-Dixon line."

"The air's a little thin up here but other than that it's okay."

Grace turned to introduce Smith. "And this is John . . . Smith. My friend."

The senator offered a welcoming smile and, as they shook hands, Grace had to wonder what he thought of Bo. She was a tall, handsome woman, with auburn hair, hazel eyes, and a high-voltage smile. The deep red suit she was wearing enhanced her dramatic looks and was tailored to fit her curves. Standing next to her, Grace felt washed out, a paler version of the feminine air Bo exuded like an exotic scent.

When they stepped forward into an elegantly appointed room, a crowd of twenty let out a chorus of greetings. A glass of wine was pressed into her hand and Grace tried to relax and enjoy herself as Carter and Nick came over. She was so happy to see them.

Throughout the cocktail hour, she always knew where Smith was. He lingered on the fringes of the crowd, looking comfortable in the group.

She was staring at him, thinking that he fit in well in the elegant atmosphere, when he shifted his eyes to hers. He lifted his eyebrow and sent her a nod.

And that's when she realized it was too late.

Staring at him across the room, seeing the light falling on his hard face, she knew that she was falling in love with him.

That, more than even the passion, was the reason she'd decided to go to bed with him.

Grace looked away quickly, in case he could read her thoughts. Flustered, she escaped the small group she was talking to on the pretext of putting on more lipstick.

As her mind churned over the whys and whens, she knew the jumbled searching was just mental gymnastics. It didn't matter when it started and knowing why wasn't an answer she needed. The truth was in her heart, not her mind.

She was in one of the bedrooms, bending toward the mirror with her lip liner when Mimi Lauer appeared in the doorway.

"I'm so sorry I'm late," the woman said with a smile.

Grace froze as their eyes met in the mirror. She thought of Cuppie and Suzanna before turning and opening her arms. Mimi was in that article, too.

"Mimi, I'm so glad you came! I figured we wouldn't see you because tomorrow is your big night."

Grace hadn't known the Lauers for very long but she'd liked both of them immediately. They'd moved from the West Coast four years ago because their son suffered from a bad case of juvenile arthritis and the treatment options for him were better in New York. Mimi's warm personality and flair for entertaining had served her well in her new environment and she'd risen quickly up the social ladder. For the past two years, she'd been chair of the ballet's annual event.

As they pulled back, Mimi said, "The performance tomorrow night is going to be splendid. They're doing a series of Balanchine favorites, just quick sketches of some of his best."

Grace frowned. "I'm sorry that I won't be going this year."

She and Smith had discussed her going to the big party. He didn't think it was a good idea for her to be in large crowds if she could avoid it and she'd taken his advice.

"Please, don't worry. You'll be missed, of course, but I can understand the kind of pressure you're under."

Mimi's eyes narrowed, as if she was tempted to bring up the very thing that was on Grace's mind. The killer. Their lost friends.

There was an awkward pause.

"So how are you holding up?" Grace said. "I imagine you have every detail taken care of."

Mimi shook her head. "On the contrary, things are a mess."

"Good God, why?"

"Fredrique has become a bit of a problem." Distaste flickered across the woman's face. "It's gotten so bad, I'm thinking of firing him even though the event is less than twenty-four hours away. He wanted to feature a shark in a tank at the party. A shark. What does *Jaws* have to do with ballet?"

Grace smiled and put her lipstick back in her clutch. "He wants to make a big splash, evidently."

"Well, he can do it somewhere else. Maybe Long John Silver's is looking for a party planner," Mimi replied dryly. "On another topic, what's going on between you and Lamont?"

"Why do you ask?"

"He called me today and said he was looking to make a change."

Grace pursed her lips. "Doesn't surprise me. He and I have never gotten along and I know he's approached a couple of other people."

"Well, I told him that I didn't think we had anything to offer him but I think he knew the real reason. You've been very supportive of me. Neither the ballet nor I would ever take one of your key people away."

"To be honest, I wouldn't mind if he went."

Mimi smiled. "In that case, we really wouldn't want him. If he can't get along with you, he must be impossible."

"That's a kind vote of confidence," Grace said with a laugh.

There was a pause as Mimi glanced downward.

"Grace . . . may I ask you something?" The woman's voice dropped to a whisper.

"Of course."

"What are you doing to . . . be safe?"

Grace felt her heart sink as Mimi looked up. There was naked fear in her eyes, the same thing Grace felt whenever she thought about what had happened to their friends.

"I've hired a bodyguard." Grace reached out for the other woman's hand. "Are you protecting yourself?"

"I've got a plainclothesman following me around and Marks has been really supportive, but I don't know. Ted and I were thinking about heading back to San Francisco for a while until this whole thing passes, except we really can't. Our son needs to stay with his physical therapists." Mimi paused. "Do you know if Suzanna had any help?"

"Marks has been pretty vague with details. I've been wondering whether whoever's doing this is following that article's sequence."

"You're lucky then. Because you were the last one mentioned."

"So Isadora is next."

Bo appeared in the doorway. "Am I interrupting something?"

Grace forced a smile. "Not at all."

Mimi gave an awkward laugh. "I don't mean to be hogging the guest of honor. I better go say my hellos to everyone."

"I'll call you," Grace said. "We'll have lunch and you can tell me all about tomorrow night's success."

"I'd like that. I'd really like that."

They shared a meaningful look as Mimi left. Grace had tacked on the party bit for Bo's benefit and they both knew it.

"So I have to ask," Bo said with a grin. "What does Ranulf think about you being squired around on the arm of that handsome man out there?"

"John's just a professional acquaintance."

"Business? Really? He looks more like a military man to me. He has the same quick eyes and broad shoulders my father did. And Daddy, as you know, was a general."

Grace tried to muster a casual smile and say something that wasn't a lie. Before she could reply, however, they were interrupted by one of the waiters who said dinner was ready to be served.

Bo grinned. "Well, I hope you don't mind, I've seated him next to me. Seemed only fair since I haven't been around a man like that for a long time. Those politicians I'm with daily, I don't know. They tend to be soft around the middle and in the head."

Grace smiled weakly and Bo frowned. "What's wrong?"

"I'll tell you all about it later."

Her friend's face took on an obstinate cast and Grace had the distinct impression that dinner or no dinner, Bo was prepared to lock them in the bathroom until the story came out.

"Don't go hitting me with Mother-vision," Grace retorted. "You save that maternal concern for your little boy. You've got twenty people out there ready for dinner and I'm rather hungry myself."

Bo shot her a look. "We'll finish this later, you hear?"

"Yes, ma'am."

They rejoined the party and Grace accepted another glass of wine, drinking it quickly as they went into the dining room. She was seated down the way from Bo and Smith and, as dinner arrived, she watched them. Bo was a consummate conversationalist and, even though Smith didn't say much, he seemed to be enjoying himself.

Or at least that's what Grace assumed and seeing his eyes flash toward her friend was hard to witness.

The man who had been a stranger only weeks ago was capturing her heart.

But he only wanted her body.

When Bo dropped her napkin and Smith bent over and picked it up for her, Grace asked for another refill of her wineglass.

13

SMITH FROWNED as he saw the waiter pour more wine into Grace's goblet. He'd never seen her drink much of anything and yet she'd already had three glasses of the stuff. As she turned to her right and smiled at Nick Farrell, he thought that the stress was getting to her. She was pushing food around her plate and her laughter, as it drifted over to him, sounded strained.

His little proposition that they go to bed together had sure as hell added to the confusion in her life, he thought. So much for all his professional standards.

In a remarkable exercise in delusion, he'd somehow managed to throw out every lick of training and common sense he had in order to come to the conclusion that having sex with her was acceptable. He had to wonder why it had made sense to him twelve hours ago. Now, seeing the exhaustion that pulled Grace's skin tightly across her face, watching her drink, he was feeling . . .

Regret.

Which for a knee-jerk risk taker was about as common as a signpost in the desert.

"So Grace never did tell me how you two met," Senator Bradford said to him. She casually lifted her napkin and blotted her lips. Her eyes were very direct.

He shrugged. "At a party."

Going by the dry look he was given, the evasive answer didn't satisfy the senator and she was prepared to follow up. He had the sense that the woman's good manners hid an iron will and it reminded him of Grace.

"Do you know her husband?"

The mention of the man made him want to curse because it reminded him once again that not only was she a client—she was also legally married. Usually, he didn't have any qualms about adultery, figuring that if a woman wanted to cheat, it was none of his business. But the fact that Grace was someone's wife rankled and not because he was worried about hurting the count's precious little feelings.

He wanted her all to himself.

When he was surprised by his reaction, he told himself he should have known better. Nothing about Grace was typical and neither were his reactions to her.

"I asked, do you know Ranulf?" the senator prompted gently.

"No, I don't," he said, putting down his fork and knife and leaning back in his chair. "And I don't have any interest in him."

A perfectly arched eyebrow rose. "Most people want to know him. He's considered quite an international figure."

"Based on what? Winning the heredity lottery? That's luck, not an accomplishment."

Bo studied him and then said softly, "There are some who do wonder what the allure is. Still, he cuts a dashing figure and for many good style and a royal title is enough to earn their affection. Frankly, I was surprised that Grace married him, although I understand that her parents were very pleased."

"No offense, Senator, but her marriage is none of my business. We're only professional associates."

"Really? She can't keep her eyes off you and you've spent most of this meal looking down the table, returning the favor. Unless the two of you are merely pursuing ocular endeavors, I might presume something deeper is going on."

He glanced over at Bo, who was smiling at him warmly. He couldn't help liking her even though she was irritating the hell out of him with her talk about Grace. "I think you're jumping to conclusions, Senator."

"I come from a family of bourbon makers, Mr. Smith. Trust me, I know a lot about love." She looked pointedly at

Grace who was taking another long drink from her wineglass. "Affairs of the heart have kept my family in business for generations. Love has a way of making people need solace and the liquid variety seems to work particularly well. I believe that is why our Grace has been imbibing this evening."

"You might want to rethink that pronoun."

"Fine. *Your* Grace," she said, with a wink.

Bo rang the silver bell that was next to her place setting and uniformed waiters came into the room. As the dinner plates were being cleared, the senator leaned over to him and whispered, "I'll tell you what, I think you're her lover."

Smith cocked an eyebrow. "Well, I'm not."

He just wanted to be. Goddamn desperately. And evidently at the expense of doing the job he'd been hired for.

Bo sent him a knowing glance as she refolded her napkin and laid it neatly in her lap. "Well, I'll let you keep your secrets, but only because my momma raised me right."

He shook his head wryly. "And somehow that proper upbringing included drills on interrogation technique?"

"Oh no. Those I got from Daddy." The smile she gave him was full of delight.

Bo nodded over her shoulder to a waiter who began putting tall, thin shot glasses in front of each guest. They were about three inches in height, an inch in diameter and were filled with amber liquid.

She reached over and put an elegant hand on his arm.

"Just don't hurt her, okay? She's had quite enough of that already. Even though she tries to keep up a good front, I happen to know the count isn't all he's cracked up to be. He tried to throw a pass at me the night of their rehearsal dinner. I disabused him of the notion he was irresistible with a swift knee to the crotch, but he's a shit and always will be. She deserves better."

"Why are you telling me all this?"

"Because I like the way she looks at you."

Smith smiled slowly. "You're a good friend, aren't you?"

"You bet your ass."

"I didn't know senators were allowed to swear."

"Doesn't count up north. Have to get 'em all out when I'm up here." The woman stood and the table fell silent.

Smith looked over at Grace as her friend spoke.

"And now, I'd like to propose a toast. If you all could pick up that glass of Bradford's finest, let's toss back a little bourbon for our dear friend, Grace. All love on your thirtieth, darlin'."

As a flaming birthday cake was brought in, Smith put his glass back on the table without having tasted it. He was thinking that Bo had a point about alcohol and love and finding a little transitory relief in the bottom of a bottle. He was so pent up, he could have used a few shots, but he never drank on the job.

That, at least, was one rule he was still hanging on to hard and fast.

An hour later, the party started to break up. People dispersed until only Bo, Grace, and Smith were standing in the foyer of the suite.

"Thank you," Grace said, raising a hand to her temple. She squinted and looked up at the chandelier as if she was bothered by the light. "This has been lovely."

"I think you better get on home." The senator smiled. "You never could hold your wine."

"I didn't think I had that much."

"Much is a relative term, darlin'."

After the women hugged good-bye, Smith offered his hand to the senator. "Good to meet you."

"Likewise," she replied. "Get her home safe, will you?"

Smith nodded, thinking he wasn't the only one watching over Grace.

When they emerged from the hotel, Grace paused and looked up at the sky, drawing her wrap around herself. Overhead, a hazy moon hung over the city, its radiance dimmed by the glow of the streetlamps and the skyscrapers.

"It's warm tonight," she said, taking a deep breath. "Let's walk a little."

Smith positioned himself between Grace and the street and shot a holding motion to Eddie, who was waiting in the Explorer.

As they walked toward Fifth Avenue, their footsteps over the sidewalk were in sync, the sound of their shoes rhythmic and slow. Taxis passed by, their red taillights glowing, and occasionally another pedestrian would come their way. A soft breeze was blowing at their backs, periodically sending a whiff of her perfume his way.

"I've always liked the way the city looks at night," Grace murmured, looking up at the buildings.

Abruptly, she caught the toe of her shoe in a crack and lurched forward.

Smith grabbed her around the waist and felt her relax against his body. She was warm and soft and his fingers tightened around the narrow span of her waist. He didn't want to let her go, even though walking with his arm around her wasn't smart. All they needed was a photograph of the two of them together and there'd be even more complications in her life.

"We shouldn't be so close," she muttered a moment later.

When she shrugged away from him, he let her go.

"After all," she said, in a louder voice, "I'm a married woman. A goddamn married woman."

Smith looked over at her. She was frowning.

"Bo isn't, you know. Married, that is."

He resumed scanning the street and the sidewalk. "She mentioned that her husband had died."

"Three years ago." She paused. "You two seemed to get along well at dinner. She's beautiful, don't you think?"

He cocked an eyebrow, wondering where she was taking the conversation. "She is."

"Tell me, Smith." She repositioned her wrap with a sharp movement. "What makes a woman beautiful to you? What was beautiful about Bo?"

As they strolled under a streetlamp, the light fell over Grace's delicate features and Smith knew exactly what his definition of beauty was. Before he could frame an appropriate response, she spoke up.

"Oh, don't answer that." Grace batted her hand about as if to erase the question. "I don't know why I asked. Probably to torture myself."

She seemed surprised by her own admission and said in a hurry, "Bo's husband was a wonderful man and she loved him deeply. Now that was a marriage that really worked. It was cruel, that it ended so soon."

Smith's instincts came to attention.

Glancing behind them, he felt, and then saw, a shape disappear into the darkness. Nonchalantly, he released the button on his tuxedo jacket in case he needed to get to his gun.

"I think it's time to head back," he remarked, taking Grace's arm firmly. She looked up at him. Not wanting to alarm her, he said smoothly, "It's getting late."

"Someone is following us, aren't they?" she whispered.

"Maybe."

He could tell she was frightened by the tension running through her body and the tight hold she took on his biceps but she showed no outward signs of fear. She just kept walking with her head up.

Good girl, he thought.

Smith looked around casually, searching for an opportunity to get her off the street. They came up to a lively restaurant.

"Let's go in here," he said, drawing her into the fashionable eatery. As soon as they were inside, he flipped open his cell phone and called Eddie.

Through the thicket of people waiting to be seated, the maître d' made a beeline for Grace with a wide smile. "Welcome, Countess. Will you be joining us this evening?"

As Grace struck up a conversation, Smith stayed by her side and looked for Eddie out of the wide windows that faced the street. When the black Explorer pulled up, he took her arm and ushered her outside. They had just stepped free of the door when a man jumped out at them. Smith covered Grace with his body as a flashbulb went off.

Moving before the blinding light had dimmed, Smith pushed her into the Explorer, slammed the door and went after the paparazzo. He caught the man in three strides and dragged him into the alley next to the restaurant. As the guy started yelling, Smith grabbed his camera, stripped out the film, and bulldozed him against the brick building.

"I'm sorry. What were you saying?" Smith pressed his forearm against the guy's throat as he smiled amiably.

"I'm going to sue! That's my film—"

"Here, take it." He shoved the exposed negatives into the guy's pocket.

"Let me go!"

"Not until you promise to leave her alone."

"It's a free country! You can't hurt me. If you do, I'll sue her!"

The man continued to struggle, his face growing red with anger. Smith held him easily, wondering how long it would take before the guy tired himself out.

"She's public property!" The photographer sneered. "Although why anyone would care who's fucking an ice princess like her—"

Smith stopping smiling. "What did you say?"

"I said—"

Smith shifted his weight, pushing his forearm harder against the man's throat and cutting off his words. "On second thought, I don't think it's in your best interest to repeat it. I might get upset and then things would get ugly."

"Oh, yeah?" the guy choked out. "What are you going to do?"

Smith put his face down close to the photographer's and the man fell completely still. "You don't want to know what I'm capable of."

The guy began to look worried, his eyes shifting up and down the alley as if he were looking for help. There was no one around.

Smith kept him trapped against the brick wall so he had plenty of time to imagine all sorts of grim injuries. He was kind of hoping the paparazzo would say something else, something that would give Smith an excuse to hit him. Hard.

Hearing a lowlife talk about Grace like that had really pissed him off.

"You had enough?" he asked the guy.

The nodding was fast and furious.

"I'll just assume you and I are in agreement about the

countess. If I see you around again, I'm going to do a hell of a lot worse than rip the film out of your camera. Got it?"

When Smith let go, the photographer slumped against the building and grabbed his throat. Smith turned and started walking away.

"I'm not afraid of you!" the man called out when there was a good distance between them.

A single glance over the shoulder shut the guy up.

When Smith got into the Explorer, Grace stared at him in silence. She seemed to be in shock and he couldn't blame her.

"You move so fast," she murmured, as they pulled away from the curb.

"When I have to. Eddie," he said, "take us around back when you drop us off. In case our little friend with the flash-bulb called any of his buddies."

The day before, at Smith's request, Eddie had scouted out the back entrance to the building. There was a walk-way that wound through the basement and came up into the lobby. It looked as if they were going to have to start using it.

As they were speeding through traffic, he felt Grace looking at him.

"That photographer . . . Did you hurt him?" she asked in a small voice.

"No."

There was a pause. "Are you sure?"

So that was the reason she was eyeing him like he was a stranger. She'd never seen someone haul another person into a back alley and come out alone.

"Yeah, he's going to be fine."

While she wrapped her arms around herself, Smith was glad she didn't know what he'd wanted to do to the guy.

Ten minutes later, Eddie pulled up behind the building and Smith squired Grace in the back door and through the musty-smelling corridor to the lobby. The doorman was asleep at his station and Smith rapped the guy sharply on the shoulder.

"Get up. They're not paying you to sleep," he said roughly.

The guy shook his head, although whether it was from shame or just as a way to wake up, Smith wasn't sure.

He pushed the elevator button and cut off the doorman's apologies. "If you can't stay up, find another shift or another job."

Grace's voice was much more gentle as she offered the man a soothing smile. "That's okay. I know your new baby's probably running you ragged."

The two talked about the man's family until the elevator came.

As Smith and Grace rode up to the penthouse, he watched her eyes dim again and he didn't blame her for being shaken. Getting jumped by a rabid photographer and watching her bodyguard manhandle a guy was no fun for anyone.

Smith thought back to what had happened in that alley. He'd been ready to let loose on the photographer, really hurt him. Making sure the picture never saw the light of day didn't seem to go far enough, considering the man had scared Grace and then insulted her.

In retrospect, his reaction was disturbing. Defending a client was one thing; avenging Grace's honor was altogether different. He reminded himself that she was paying him to protect her, not be a hired thug.

As they stepped into her home and he shut off the alarm, Smith knew they were heading for trouble. All kinds of lines were getting blurred with Grace and his clarity of mind was a casualty neither of them could afford.

She deserved to have him at his very best. He owed her that.

And wouldn't have settled for anything less himself.

Grace heard the door shut as she walked into the living room.

"You need anything?" Smith asked her.

She turned around. He was waiting for her to speak, a tall, dark shape lit from behind by the hall light.

She couldn't get the confrontation with the photographer out of her mind and kept seeing the scenario end in a different, violent way. When Smith had lunged forward to shield her with his body, only God knew whether it was a camera or a gun pointed at her. Still, he'd been prepared to take whatever was coming, whether it was a bullet or a knife or a fist or a flashbulb.

She thought of how easily the outcome could have been fatal. And how, in that moment as he surged ahead of her, John had been willing to give his life for her. She was grateful and angry at the same time because, if he was willing to do that for her, surely he put his life on the line for his other clients. Didn't he care that he could get himself killed?

Suddenly, looking into the future seemed a pointless exercise in optimism. He was with her now. Tonight they were together.

And she wanted him.

To hell with happy endings, she thought.

Taking courage from the lingering effects of the wine, Grace approached him slowly and let her wrap fall from her shoulders. In the dim light, she saw him follow the silk as it slid down her arms, past her waist and onto the floor. When his eyes came back to hers, they gleamed.

She reached out and touched the satin lapel of his tuxedo, letting her fingers float down the material. Easing herself against his body, so that her breasts pressed into his chest, she stretched up to his ear.

"Make love to me," she whispered against the skin of his throat.

She felt a shudder go through him.

The hesitation that followed was not encouraging.

"What's wrong?" she asked.

"This isn't right," he said, removing her hands. "I'm sorry, Grace."

She frowned in confusion, struggling to touch him again. "You told me I could choose. And I have."

"I never should have put you in that position." He stepped away from her.

Grace stared at him, unable to comprehend what he was saying.

As he met her eyes unrelentingly, she got angry.

"God*damn* you." When he remained silent, she demanded, "Why did you do this to me? Did you just want to see me beg?"

"Of course not."

"So why? If I'd known this was just some kind of game—"

"It has never been a game," he said fiercely.

Frustration made her lash out. "Well, then I never pegged you for a coward. If you really are king of the one-night stands, what's the big deal with a little sex? You've done it before and managed to survive the experience with your I-am-a-rock routine still intact."

With lightning speed, his hands gripped her arms so hard it hurt.

"Don't press me, Grace. I'm not in the mood."

"Then get in a better one. Kiss me," she murmured, looking up into his eyes.

"Stop it."

"No."

With a surge of power, he pinned her arms behind her and pushed her back against the wall.

"Christ, is this all you want?" He pressed his arousal into her body.

She looked at him boldly. "Tonight? Yes."

His eyes closed. And then they snapped open and his lips came down on hers.

His kiss was hard and she wanted it that way. Pulling her arms free, she grabbed on to his jacket and wrenched it from his shoulders as she felt his hands come up to the bodice of her gown. There was a tearing sound as he ripped the delicate chiffon from her body and covered her breasts with his palms.

His mouth was hot and hungry over hers, his tongue thrusting inside of her as he pressed against her body. Digging her nails into his back, she moaned.

At the hoarse sound, he froze. Looking into her eyes, he pushed her away abruptly.

Raking a hand over his short hair, he bent down and picked up her wrap.

"Go to bed," he told her, throwing it over.

Grace caught the silk but refused to cover herself, aware that her breasts were bare and he was having a hard time not looking at them. "You want me."

Smith came back at her in a rush, planting his hands against the wall on either side of her head with a loud noise. As he leaned in close, she felt no fear as his eyes passed over her body.

"Yeah, I want you. So bad it fucking hurts. Satisfied?"

"Not even close," she said softly, her words dripping with intent. She reached up and stroked his cheek.

His gaze narrowed on her lips but then he closed his eyes and stayed like that for a long time.

When he looked at her again, he was cold as ice. He calmly stepped back.

"What changed?" she whispered.

"You're not thinking clearly tonight. And I wasn't this morning."

He turned away and walked into his room. She heard his door shut quietly and realized it was the first time he'd closed her out.

In the silence, reality came back and hit Grace so hard she felt like crying out. She looked down in mute shock at the ruined gown. With fumbling hands, she pulled the bodice back up so that her breasts were covered and went to her room.

She couldn't bring herself to look at his door as she passed by.

Grace's first thought the next morning was that maybe it had all been a crazy nightmare. Then she looked over and saw the torn dress hanging off a chair.

Oh, God. She really had tried to seduce him and he really had turned her down.

Groaning, she went into the bathroom and took two aspirin. After having a shower, she threw on her thick robe and went out into the hall.

His door was ajar.

"Smith?" she said softly. When there was no answer, she walked into the room.

One bed had been slept in, or at least sat on. Two pillows

were propped against the wall and a book was splayed out on top of the covers. The other bed was neatly made and had his leather jacket and the tuxedo draped at the foot of it.

She was about to leave when she saw his wallet on the antique bureau. Next to it were his gun, holster, and a set of keys.

"Looking for something?"

Her eyes flew up to the mirror over the bureau. He was standing in the doorway with a cup of coffee in his hand. He looked rakishly handsome, wearing only a white T-shirt and that pair of low-hanging black pants. Her mouth went dry as she thought about kissing him and she wanted to curse. There seemed to be no end to her vivid imagination or her willingness to throw herself at him. After last night, she should have learned a thing or two.

"Shower's free," she said.

She left quickly, trying not to notice the wide berth he gave her when she walked by him. As she went to her room and began to dress, she decided that she'd gone from one extreme to another. From an ice queen to a harlot.

Not exactly an improvement, she thought ruefully.

When Grace and John came into the office on Monday morning, Kat looked up from her desk with a grin. "The place has been hopping today. Mr. Lamont has already stopped by twice. There are ten messages for you to return. Oh, and the caterers called. They said Fredrique had come by and discussed the Gala menu with them. They seemed a little confused, but they're sending you a first pass on the food anyway. I think they were under the impression he wasn't involved this year."

"He isn't." Grace swallowed her irritation.

"Oh, and one more thing. A Lieutenant Marks just called you from the NYPD. Said you'd know what it was about."

Smith's cell phone went off and he put it up to his ear.

Grace felt her stomach flip-flop.

As they stepped into her office and closed the doors, she heard him say, "Yes, I'm with her now."

Grace watched Smith anxiously as she sat down. He was on the phone for a few more minutes but she couldn't tell anything by his monosyllabic responses.

As soon as he hung up, she said in a frozen voice, "Who?"

He came around the desk, getting closer to her than he had for days. His eyes were gentle and that terrified her.

"Who?" she repeated.

"They won't release the name because they're still trying to notify the family. It happened last night. A maid found the body."

Grace shut her eyes.

She felt his hand cover hers and thought it was the first time he had touched her since that awful scene on the night of her birthday.

"It's a good thing we're going to Newport this weekend, isn't it," she said with false bravado. "They all seem to die in New York."

She tried to smile gamely and couldn't pull it off. Grimly, she glanced over to the windows so he wouldn't see her fear.

"Look at me. Grace?" Reluctantly, she shifted her eyes to him. "I'm not going to let anything happen to you."

"I want to believe that."

When Kat buzzed in that her first meeting had arrived, John went over to the conference table.

Grace pressed the intercom button and said she needed a moment.

She was thinking of Mimi Lauer and picked up the phone. The idea that Isadora could be dead was horrifying and she needed to talk with someone who knew firsthand exactly how out of control and saddened she felt.

When voice mail kicked in, she left a message.

As she hung up the phone, she felt a fine sheen of sweat break out across her forehead. A wave of dizziness followed closely on the flash of heat in her body, turning her vision into a checkerboard. Trying to draw breath through lungs that had turned to stone, she told herself she wasn't going to die. Nobody died because of anxiety. You'd just rather be dead.

She winced, thinking of the killer and the woman who had just been murdered.

That was one expression she wasn't going to use anymore.

14

THAT NIGHT, Grace could not get to sleep. After an hour of trying in vain, she wandered out to the kitchen.

Earlier that evening, she'd taken a couple of potential donors to the Congress for dinner, in hopes of securing an auction piece. Trying to concentrate on business had been impossible and maybe that was why she'd been turned down when she'd asked the Staffords for their collection of Early American needlework. The samplers would have been a good auction item. Even though they weren't as flashy as the Franklin/Jefferson letters, the pieces were still noteworthy for their rarity and excellent condition.

She opened the refrigerator and thought of Smith. The shelves were full of fresh vegetables, meats, and cartons of orange juice and soy milk. She figured the appliance was probably grateful for being used as more than a graveyard for condiments.

She was on the way back to her bedroom after having had a sandwich, when the phone rang. Smith materialized in the doorway as she reluctantly picked up the receiver in the living room.

"Grace?" It was a male voice. A shaky, grief-stricken male voice.

"Yes?"

"It's Ted Lauer."

She felt the blood drain out of her head. "Oh, God no . . ."

"Mimi is . . . She's gone, Grace . . ." Ted choked and cleared his throat.

Letting out a small, wounded sound, she collapsed into a chair, picturing Mimi as the woman had left Bo's suite. The idea that she'd been dead when Grace tried to reach her that morning was horrifying.

She tried to imagine Ted having to tell their son that his mother wasn't coming home ever again.

"Is there anything I can do for you?" she asked.

"There's nothing anyone can do."

When she finally put the phone down, after offering words of condolence and sorrow that felt pitifully insubstantial in the face of the man's suffering, she looked up at Smith.

"That family's life is ruined. Her son . . ." She stood up, shaking her head desolately. "We can't go to Newport. The funeral's this weekend."

"I don't want you to go."

"To the funeral?" She frowned. "How can I not?"

Smith shook his head. "I'm not taking chances."

"But I'll be perfectly safe. You'll be with me—"

"It's going to be a mob scene. I told you, no big crowds if we can avoid it.'"

"But she was my friend." Grace crossed her arms over her chest, battling tears of rage and frustration and fear.

"Grace, we've got to be reasonable."

"They'll be plenty of policeman there. You manage to protect political figures, right? People like the ambassador," she shot back. "So why is it any different for me?"

"That night, I had the Plaza crawling with my men."

"So bring them on, make me a damn coat out of them, I don't care."

His eyes grew dark. "We have an agreement. You'll do what I say is right."

Grace started shaking her head. "This isn't fair. I have to go."

"It's got nothing to do with fairness. This is about risk and going to that funeral is an avoidable one. Serial killers enjoy seeing the aftermath of their work. There's a good possibility he'll be somewhere in the crowd and I don't want you anywhere near him."

"So what's next? Are you going to tell me I can't go to

the Gala?" When he didn't answer her, she thrust her chin out. "I'm going to the Foundation's Gala, John. No matter what you say."

"Then we may have a problem."

"What the hell's that supposed to mean? Are you threatening to leave?"

"I told you from the beginning. I'm here only on my terms."

She was ready to argue with him when a surge of hope broke through her anger. "But maybe he'll be caught by then. Maybe this will be all over in a couple of weeks."

"Maybe."

His tone was more along the lines of *maybe not.*

"The Gala is still over three weeks away," she said. "Can we at least discuss this later?"

"You can't bargain with me."

She cursed out loud. "Fine! Can I yell at you, then? Because I'm getting pretty sick and goddamn tired of having no say in my life."

She felt wetness on her cheeks and realized she'd begun to cry. Impatiently, she wiped under her eyes.

"Christ," he muttered, holding out his arms. "Come here."

Grace hesitated and then went to his embrace, collapsing into his strength, laying her cheek on his wide chest. He held her for a long time, stroking her back with his big hands.

"I despise you right now," she said against his shirt.

"I know."

Smith cradled her in his arms for some time, trying to ease some of her frustration and fear. He'd decided even before Mimi Lauer's death that he might have to pull Grace out of the Gala and knew the conversation was going to be a tough one.

She was right. He had protected people like the ambassador, people who were being hunted by assassins who liked taking down targets in public. And the killer who was after Grace had a pattern of working in private. He probably preferred an intimate setting, which was why he killed in the victims' homes. Still, though Smith trusted his men and he had confidence in himself, when it came to Grace the slightest elevation in risk seemed unacceptable.

As he held her tightly against him, he couldn't bear the thought of her getting hurt and felt a real shot of sympathy for that Lauer woman's husband. To find out your wife had had her throat slashed open and bled to death in your living room. What the hell was that like for a civilian? Death was hard enough to deal with if you were trained to handle it and it took out your colleagues or your enemies. But a wife?

Christ.

He recalled what Marks had told him over the phone earlier. The murder had been along the lines of the other two. No forcible entry. Vicious knife work. No prints. And the woman's clothes had been neatly arranged after the struggle. The killing fit the pattern although it was out of order. Isadora Cunis should have been next if the killer was following the sequence of the article but Smith knew that didn't mean that woman was out of danger. Marks had said Cunis and her husband had left the city and were not coming back until her big event later in the month.

Lack of availability had undoubtedly trumped the order, to Mimi Lauer's tragic disadvantage.

Smith wondered how the killer had gotten to the woman. She'd been watched by good cops. Marks's men had been in the building and outside at the curb.

Just not in her damn house, evidently.

He felt Grace pull back. Her eyes were luminous from a haze of tears and her voice was a mere whisper when she spoke.

"I don't want to be alone tonight. Stay with me?"

Smith smothered a groan and stiffened. Sleeping next to her was not the kind of support he felt capable of offering. No matter how god-awful she was feeling, or how much sympathy she deserved, nothing was going to change the way he felt when her body was anywhere near his. He wanted to ease her suffering but lying next to her all night wasn't going to keep him in a compassionate mood.

"Are you sure?" he said gruffly.

When she nodded, and they started to walk down the hall, he told himself there were tougher tests of his strength.

Of course, they mostly involved moving heavy machinery or large household appliances. With an arm tied behind his back and his legs in goddamn shackles.

Still, he didn't think he could turn her down.

After she got into bed, he lay down on top of the sheets. He was thinking it wouldn't be so bad as long as they stayed on opposite sides but then she moved into his arms and curled up in a small ball. Gradually, her breathing slowed and the tension in her body dissipated until she became exactly what he'd dreaded.

Soft, yielding, warm.

He could feel her breath against his forearm, her tight little butt tucked into the cradle of his hips, the weight of her head on his shoulder.

Christ.

He was a tough guy. He'd gone through Ranger School with no problem—just a little mud, sweat, and sleep deprivation. Getting shot at? Healed up just fine, thank you very much. Same with getting stabbed, clonked on the head with a tire iron, and hit by that Chevy Nova.

Okay, so he'd needed some time in traction after the Nova and even now his knee ached a little when it rained. Still, all that was nothing compared to what spending a night lying next to Grace was going to do to him.

He had to wonder when he'd last lain down with a woman in his arms. Other than when he was having sex. He couldn't remember how long it had been. Maybe never.

Grace shifted in her sleep, rubbing against his hips.

As he gritted his teeth, he knew he wasn't going to get any sleep. And he had to imagine, if lying next to her and being separated by blankets, her bathrobe, and his clothes was this difficult, making love to the countess would only land him right where the Chevy Nova had: stunned and on his ass.

He closed his eyes, thinking it was a damn shame they hadn't met under different circumstances.

Although he didn't know what other state of affairs could possibly have brought them together.

                          *   *   *

On the Friday afternoon of Columbus Day weekend, Grace rubbed tired eyes and stretched in her father's chair. Smith was at the conference table, talking on his phone. He did that a lot while they were in the office and she'd grown used to hearing the deep rumble of his voice.

Grace studied him covertly, thinking back to the night they'd spent together. Sometime before dawn, she'd woken up to the feeling of heavy arms holding her tight and a big body pushed in close against hers. She'd rolled over carefully, trying not to disturb him, because she'd wanted to see what he looked like when he was sleeping.

But his eyes had been alert and glowing as she'd looked into them. The expression on his face had been intense in the morning light and he'd stared at her for what seemed like a long time. She'd wondered if he was going to kiss her but then he'd jackknifed off the bed in a smooth motion and walked out of the room without so much as a good morning.

The soft whir of the fax behind the desk brought her back to the present. Absently, she reached over and picked up the pages as they came through the machine.

Since that night, he'd avoided getting too close to her and it was hard not to feel like a leper as he sidestepped around her if they met in the hall or they passed while going in and out of her bathroom. She told herself not to take it personally but that didn't really help.

As the fax kept going, shooting out page after page, she looked down at the list of signatures and frowned.

"That's for me."

Grace jumped at the sound of his voice. He'd managed to cross the room without a sound and she wondered whether she'd ever get used to how quietly he moved.

"What are they?" She handed the documents to him.

"Delivery and visitor logs." He went back to the conference table.

"From what?"

When he didn't answer, she knew they had to do with the case.

"Tell me about the investigation," she said quietly.

He looked up. "I don't want to upset you."

"I told you before, I'd feel better knowing what's going on."

"I'm not so sure about that," he muttered. When she stared at him pointedly, he shrugged. "I'm going through the buildings' logs with a fresh set of eyes. Looking for patterns Marks and his team might have missed."

She went to him, leaning over his shoulder and staring down at the columns of signatures and dates and times. She saw a lot of the same names and recognized many of them.

"Isn't it time to go to the airport?" he asked abruptly.

"Yes. I suppose so."

Although she wouldn't have minded putting off the trip altogether. She still felt as if she should be going to Mimi's funeral and she wasn't looking forward to seeing her mother. The conversation she'd had with Carolina the day before, when she'd had to explain that Ranulf wasn't coming, hadn't gone well. The disapproval coming through the phone had intensified when she'd mentioned she was being accompanied by a male "friend."

When she and Smith left the office, Grace was hoping that the time would just fly by. She loved her mother, as much as the woman would let her, but a little of Carolina Hall went a long way.

Eddie drove them out of the city to Teterboro Airport where the Hall family plane was waiting, fueled up and gleaming on the tarmac. The Gulfstream jet had been used frequently by her father, but Grace was thinking of selling it, feeling that the overhead expense outweighed the convenience. The trip wasn't a long one. It was little more than an hour of air time to T. F. Greene Airport, which was located just outside of Providence, Rhode Island. As they stepped from the plane, she saw a familiar black Mercedes waiting at a special side entrance of the field.

"Hello, Wilhelm," Grace greeted the driver as they approached, a uniformed porter behind them pushing their things on a cart.

"Miss Grace," the man replied, doffing his chauffeur's hat. The German accent was heavy in his pronunciation.

"How is Marta?"

As the man opened the rear door, he replied, "Well. She's just as well as always. She's looking forward to having you in the house again, even if it is only for the weekend."

"Wilhelm, this is John Smith. A friend of mine."

The older man bent at the waist briefly. "Sir."

Smith nodded and slid into the back.

It took a full hour to reach Newport and, as they scaled the majestic bridge going onto the island, Grace felt a lick of anticipation in her stomach. The house at Newport was her true home, a place she loved as if it were a living member of the family. The vivid summer days and soft summer nights of her youth at the ocean's edge were more clear in her mind than what had happened the day before at the office.

And with the way things were going with the Gala, the chronological amnesia was a good thing. She still didn't have a suitable auction piece and there were some serious problems with the food for the event.

Thanks to Fredrique's interference, the caterer had come up with an obscure menu of Asian fusion that was so kinky and over the top, Grace had had to ask them to start all over again. Serving blowfish at the Gala just wasn't what she had in mind—it was expensive, and deadly if prepared incorrectly. She wanted to offer the guests fine fare, not a trip to the Lenox Hill emergency room.

She put the responsibility for the menu snafu firmly in her own court. She'd assumed that her call to Fredrique when she'd first learned of his meddling had been sufficient to get him to back off but clearly she'd been wrong. According to Lolly Ramparr and her staff at NightWorx, he'd showed up at their shop and refused to leave when they told him it was their understanding he wasn't involved with the Gala this year. When he kept giving orders, Lolly had tried to reach Grace, who'd been in a meeting and unavailable. Fredrique had then demanded Lamont be called and Lou had promptly vouched for the authority the man was assuming. Lolly had done what he'd said.

Obviously, Grace was going to have to try again with the man. Perhaps in writing.

It was damned inconvenient to have to fire someone you never hired, over and over again, she thought.

Grace lowered the window, leaned her head into the cool sea breeze and took a deep breath. The turmoil of everything seemed slightly removed as she looked over the ocean and she was grateful for the respite.

"You like it here a lot, don't you," Smith remarked.

"I love it here," she murmured, watching a sailboat charging through the waves.

"Your family's place is right on the ocean, isn't it?"

She nodded. "Willings isn't the largest of the estates, but it's got beautiful sea views and a wonderful garden."

"Interesting name."

She smiled, remembering the story.

"My great-great-grandmother, who was from Grosse Pointe, Michigan, hated the idea of summering in Newport after her marriage. Her family had always spent July and August in the Adirondacks and she regarded the lack of crisp, clear air at the ocean's edge as a respiratory insult."

"I can think of some worse ones," he said dryly.

"She was a woman with high standards." Grace looked over at him, pleased that they were talking about something other than the logistics of the job he was doing for her. Since the night he'd spent in her bed, she'd had the impression he'd deliberately kept the conversation professional. "After much cajoling, and some serious architectural planning, my great-great-grandfather presented her with a set of house plans. She indicated that if the place lived up to its potential, she might be willing to come seaside. Two years later, in 1879, the builders were finished, she was indeed willing, and the mansion had its name."

They turned onto Bellevue Avenue, passing Marble House and the Breakers, the former summer homes of the Vanderbilt family that were now open to the public through the Preservation Society of Newport County. A quarter of a mile later, Wilhelm pulled off onto a circular driveway and halted the car in front of a three-story mansion.

Grace hesitated before looking up at the towering white house with its terraces, columns, and porches. It was the first time she'd been back since the funeral. Then, she'd been distracted and overwhelmed by the guests offering their condolences. Now, in the quiet, she could feel the absence of her father much more keenly.

"Your mother is awaiting your arrival anxiously," Wilhelm said while opening the car door for her.

Grace stepped out and slowly approached Willings's formal entrance. Five white marble steps led up to a pair of massive, wrought iron and glass doors that were set inside a columned portico. Above the doors, dangling down from the ceiling on a thick black chain, there was an old-fashioned, heavy lantern still lit by beeswax candles at night. A pair of boxwood topiaries in stone urns framed the doors and Grace recalled having decorated them with red, white, and blue ribbons on the Fourth of July when she was young.

Wilhelm walked by, holding some of their luggage and glancing repeatedly over his shoulder. Smith was close on his heels, carrying the rest of their things easily and thus breaking one of the butler's hard-and-fast rules. The old man had never been comfortable with guests being self-sufficient and had long disapproved of Grace's own independence. He regarded her unpacking for herself or merely driving into town to get her own groceries as a failure in the natural order of things. His Old World ways were part of the reason she loved him.

Grace followed the men through the front doors and, as the sound of their footsteps echoed through the vast foyer, she tried to see her home through Smith's eyes. The typical response of people as they came inside for the first time was of awe and wonder and the architects had planned for just such a reaction. There were marble fireplaces on either side of the hall with enormous gilded mirrors hanging above them. Massive brass doors opened to the formal dining room and a parlor but neither they nor the glittering chandelier hanging from the ceiling was the main attraction. Ahead, rising up like the wings of a great bird, was a bifurcated marble staircase. Among all the home's details, the stairway, with its two arms joining together to form the second floor's landing, had been photographed the most.

She glanced over at Smith. He wasn't looking at the art

or the architectural details. He was marking the doors and windows, and she smiled to herself. For all the interest he was showing the decor, they could have walked into a dim cave, and she liked the fact that he wasn't impressed.

As she shrugged off her coat, she saw her father's stand of walking sticks in the corner. They were a variety of shapes and sizes, some ivory handled and thin, some thick and gnarled as tree roots. She could remember her father taking them on their walks around the grounds, a stylish ornament he would use to point out flowers that interested him or boats on the horizon.

Wilhelm was taking her coat just as her mother came in from the parlor. Carolina was dressed in a pale cream suit, looking elegant as a tea rose.

"Darling, how was your trip?" As they embraced, her mother's attention was on Smith. "Grace, won't you introduce us?"

"This is John Smith. Er—John, this is my mother, Carolina Woodward Hall."

Her mother offered him a thin hand and a thinner smile. "We don't know many Smiths. It is s-m-i-t-h, correct?"

He nodded.

"Yes, I had a feeling it wasn't with a 'y' and an 'e'," she murmured. "Didn't I see you at the Congress Club recently?"

"Maybe."

"Whose guest were you?"

Grace interrupted. "When are Jackson and Blair coming?"

Turning to her daughter, Carolina said, "They should be arriving any minute. We will be ten for dinner tonight, with Mr. Cobith, the Raleighs, and the Blankenbakers. Marta is working on a fabulous roast beef."

There was a pause and Carolina glanced back at Smith, fixing her eyes on his leather jacket. "We dress for dinner here."

When he neither looked away, nor showed any reaction, her mother's brow rose.

Grace jumped in again. "I think we better get settled. Why don't I show John to his room."

"He is in the green suite."

With Wilhelm and Smith behind her, Grace headed up the staircase. On the upper landing, she asked Wilhelm to take her bags to her room and took Smith down the hall in the opposite direction.

When she opened the door to a masculine room steeped in dark greens and wood, he didn't even bother looking inside.

"Where are you sleeping?" he asked.

"At the other end of the house. This is the guest wing."

"How far away?"

"Down the hall, take a left, go past the stairs. I'm the corner room, ocean side."

"Show me."

Grace noticed that he kept his bags with him as they went to her room.

"Who's across the hall from you?" he asked as she opened her door.

"I don't know. Probably no one."

"Then I'm taking that room."

"But you can't—"

His cocked eyebrow stopped her. "Unless you want me sleeping on your floor?"

When she shook her head vigorously, he walked into the other room.

As his bags landed with a thump, Grace tried to corral her anxiety into a manageable bundle of snakes. It was highly unlikely her mother would venture outside the new first-floor master suite to check exactly who was sleeping where.

Although it wasn't completely outside the realm of possibility.

Grace went into her own room, feeling frustrated at her mother. At Smith. Most of all at herself. In the grand scheme of things, she had to wonder why she was so scared of giving a guest of hers another room to sleep in. She was thirty now, for Chrissakes. When was she going to be enough of an adult to stand up to her mother?

If she kept on her current course, she was going to be

gumming soft foods and using a walker before she found her backbone with that woman.

As Grace looked around, she felt time contract. She'd spent some, if not all, of every summer at Newport and the room hadn't changed in thirty years. The drapes and wallpaper were the same pale yellow they'd always been and the furniture hadn't been moved since she'd graduated from the nursery into her "grown-up room" when she was three. The windows, which overlooked the ocean and the gardens, still let in the light in a familiar pattern across the floor. And the French doors, which opened out onto the terrace, made that comforting, chatty noise as the offshore breeze came up against the house.

Grace opened one of the doors and stepped onto the second-story porch, which ran around the house. Down below, past the gardens and the lawn, the ocean rushed and retreated at the shore. It was a sound she associated with the house, with her room. With happy times.

When she heard footsteps behind her, she stiffened.

"I just wish you weren't so conspicuous—" She turned. "Jack!"

Grace laughed out loud and threw her arms around her friend. She was pulling back, a wide smile on her face, when she caught Smith watching the two of them from the hall with narrowed eyes.

"Er, John," she said, stepping back into the room. "I'd like you to meet an old friend of mine, Jack Walker."

Jack smiled in the direction of the doorway but then cocked an eyebrow. "Well, this is a pleasure. How are you doing, stranger?"

Tensions rose as Smith came in from the hall and the men shook hands. As they squared off at each other, she remembered that night at the Congress and wondered what had sparked such friction between them.

"Where's Blair?" she asked, hoping to diffuse the testosterone surging in the air.

Although if that was the goal, she'd probably have better luck giving the two of them a manicure and a makeover.

Jack looked over at her. "Blair cracked a molar and

needed a root canal. She stayed behind to have a bonding experience with her endodontist and a hell of a lot of Novocain. She'll be here, on Motrin, sometime tomorrow."

Grace grimaced. "Sorry to hear that."

"And Ranulf?"

"Not here. Busy." The words rushed out of her mouth. "He's been very busy. He's in Europe. Being busy."

Oh, that sounded believable, she thought, remembering wryly that there must have been a time when she'd been articulate.

Jack gave her a wink and slipped a casual arm around her shoulders. "It's just as well. What they don't know can't hurt them."

Grace watched as Smith stalked out of the room.

It was going to be a hell of a long weekend, she thought.

15

By the time drinks were served in the library, night had settled in and the temperature had dropped. To cut the chill, Wilhelm had started a fire in the fireplace and Grace stood with her back to the flames, sipping a chardonnay.

The room was one of her favorites in the house because, unlike most of the others, it wasn't cavernous. The walls were covered with bookcases of leather-bound volumes and she'd always liked the way the gold lettering on the spines glowed in the firelight. Armchairs and couches, covered in dark red silk, were stationed strategically by the windows for reading and heavy velvet drapes fell to the floor in great sweeps. A dark ruby Oriental rug added to the jewellike color scheme.

When she was younger, she'd been convinced it was a wizard's room, relocated from some fantastic place.

Jack came over to her, looking handsome in a black suit. With his patrician features and hooded eyes, Grace wondered why she'd never been attracted to him. Plenty of women were. Most women, as a matter of fact.

He smiled at her. "So, your friend doesn't say much, does he."

Grace glanced over at Smith, who was leaning up against the doorjamb across the room. He was wearing all black, though not a suit, and in the dim light, his eyes seemed especially dark.

She offered Jack a smile. "You just don't know him."

"And I'm not in a big rush to. As dinner companions go, that guy makes a cold draft seem damn appealing."

"You know, I'm really looking forward to seeing Blair tomorrow," she said, eager to stop talking about Smith. "Tell me, when are you two tying the knot?"

Jack laughed and took a drink from his bourbon. "Changing the subject. Good defensive maneuver and a particularly well-chosen topic, too. Shall we talk about the weather?"

Grace laughed. "You are going to ask her, aren't you?"

Her friend's eyes narrowed as he looked down into his drink, swirling it casually. "I'll get around to it at some point. Who knows? Maybe even sooner rather than later."

"What are you waiting for?"

An elegant shrug was followed by a wicked smile. "The planets need to be properly aligned. My moon needs to be ascending, but for the past thirty years or so, it's been sinking fast. Or maybe it's the other way around."

"She's a lovely woman."

"I know. And she puts up with me, which makes her a saint." Jack looked up. "Just don't ply me with the whole marriage is fabulous routine. My mother's been using that line a lot lately and it's losing its punch."

Grace raised her glass to her lips and remained silent, thinking that would be the last thing she'd tell anybody.

When Marta announced dinner was served, Jack raised his elbow and she took his arm. As they walked through to the dining room, she felt Smith's eyes boring into her back. She had to fight the urge to wheel around and tell him his intensity was making her nervous. She was in her own home, among friends, for heaven's sake. It wasn't like Hugh Blankenbaker was going to rush at her with his salad fork or something.

Although, as soon as they sat down, she had other things to worry about.

In the middle of the soup course, her mother's voice cut through the conversation like a scythe. "Now tell me, Mr. Smith, what do you do?"

Everyone stopped talking and all eyes went to John, except for Grace's. She looked down at her plate, wondering if there was a way to deflect her mother's attention.

She could always bring up her impending divorce, she thought wryly.

"I'm in the service industry," John said, sounding bored.

"What kind of service do you offer?"

Grace answered before he could. "He helps with organizational development. I asked him to come to the Foundation and work on team building after Father's death."

Carolina's eyes shifted down the table and held her daughter's for a long moment. "Well, if you must. Although I still can't understand why you don't let Mr. Lamont run things. Your father had the highest confidence in him."

Maybe so, Grace felt like tossing back, but he didn't leave the guy in charge, did he?

Instead, she smiled graciously around tight lips. "Thank you again for the suggestion."

As the conversation surged again, Grace met Smith's eyes across the table.

Jack nudged her arm. "So?"

"I'm sorry?"

"What are you auctioning off for the Gala this year?"

Before she could answer him privately, the others at the table quieted down again and looked her way. She pinned a smile on her face and did a little PR dance.

"We've relocated the event this year. We're having it in the atrium of the Hall Building instead of at the Plaza. It's going to be spectacular in that space, assuming we can get the acoustics right."

Mr. Blankenbaker leaned forward while pushing his glasses higher onto his little nose. "What *is* the auction piece?"

"We're trying to decide," she answered.

And it's a bitch of a choice. Between nothing and nada.

"Would you be interested in Copley's portrait of Nathaniel Walker?"

Grace slowly lowered her spoon to her plate, sure she'd heard him wrong. "Excuse me?"

"John Singleton Copley's painting of Nathaniel Walker. It was done in 1775, I believe. Right before the battle of Concord in Massachusetts, wherein Walker was captured by the British and spirited away to Fort Sagamore. Surely you recall the history."

"Of course, I do. And the Foundation would absolutely be interested in the painting."

Mr. Blankenbaker nodded to Jack. "Your ancestor has been hanging over our fireplace for a rather long time. My wife purchased it from your father."

There was a subtle disapproval in the tone, as if the man couldn't fathom why such a family treasure would have fallen out of a Walker's hands.

"I remember when he sold it," Jack muttered, obviously sharing Blankenbaker's sentiment.

The man nodded, acknowledging their accord on the matter.

"Well, Walker looks outstanding in our parlor but my wife, she just keeps acquiring things whilst our wall space remains constant. I think donating the portrait to the Foundation would meet with her approval. Especially if you end up being the buyer."

"If it comes up for sale, he will come home with me. Whatever the price." Jack's smile did not temper the fierce light in his eyes.

Blankenbaker turned to Grace. "Tomorrow, you shall come to Edge Water and view the painting. I must say, it needs to be cleaned. He's rather dark, but it's an excellent example of Copley's early work, before he went across the pond and made a name for himself in London."

As she thanked the man, Jack leaned over and whispered in her ear, "Does this mean you don't want that old pair of long underwear I've got in my closet? Word has it they were worn by Benedict Arnold."

Rolling her eyes, Grace elbowed him, then looked up.

Smith was staring at her from across the table, his eyes stern. She felt as though he were offended in some way and thought maybe it was her mother who had put him out of joint. God knew, Carolina Woodward Hall had done that to plenty of people.

As she took a drink from her water glass, Grace wondered whether her father and Smith would have gotten along and decided they probably would have. Cornelius had liked strong people and Smith was certainly the dominant type. She doubted, however, that her father would have approved of Grace's attraction to the man.

When she'd confessed the poor state of her marriage to him a couple of months before his death, his response had been emphatic. He'd told her she should immediately go home and make things right with her husband. He took great pains to stress the international significance of the von Sharone family and point out all the good that came out of her having a royal title. Of having royal children. When she'd pressed him, explaining how unhappy she was, he'd glossed over the fact that she didn't love the man she was sleeping next to at night. In his eyes, he felt that she'd made a commitment to a worthy man and had better live up to it.

Her father had disappointed her that day. But she'd gone back to Ranulf.

Grace looked over at the portrait of Cornelius that hung on the wall behind the head of the table. He stared out of the frame sternly, his dark red hair brushed off his autocratic forehead, his eyes hooded, judging.

No, he wouldn't have approved of the way she felt about Smith. Not at all.

After dinner was over, and the party had dispersed, Smith saw Grace to her bedroom and went across the hall. Pacing around the room he'd commandeered, he was not a happy man.

Watching Grace and Mr. Charm flirt during dinner had really gotten on his nerves. And that Pepsodent grin the man was sporting when he'd said good night to her had been the kicker. Smith couldn't help wondering if Walker was looking so damn cheerful because he planned on spending the night with Grace.

Smith wrenched a hand over his hair and caught his reflection in a mirror. He looked like a caged dog and wondered what the hell was wrong with him.

You're jealous, stupid.

"I am not," he muttered, turning away.

He told himself to get real. He had no claim to Grace.

He had no reason to care what she did after dark. Who she did.

Smith had turned her down so she was moving on. And why shouldn't she have a fling with some two-bit, Hugh Grant look-alike? She was a beautiful, vibrant, young woman, free to do what she wished.

He cursed out loud, thinking that was a great rationale, real logical. Too bad it hit him like a pair of brass knuckles.

The idea of her with Jack Walker put him in a commando kind of mood. He wanted to go find Walker, drag him out behind the house, and rearrange those pearly whites of his. Which was utterly ridiculous.

Still, getting physical on something was damn appealing.

Smith looked across the room, sized up the highboy in the corner and rejected the temptation. The thing would have been a fine opponent, for an inanimate object, but he'd feel like an idiot trashing the place. He wasn't a rock star, for God's sake.

No, he was just a sexually frustrated man who was going to have to try and sleep across the hall from the woman he wanted . . . while she was making love to somebody else.

Oh, hell. *She* was not the problem. The trouble was this possessive streak he had going. After years of not giving a crap what anyone else on the planet was up to, let alone who they were sleeping with, he couldn't believe he was finally interested in someone else's love life.

But damn, he'd managed to pick a bad time for the transformation.

Smith groaned as a thought occurred to him. He needed to give Grace a panic button in case something happened in the middle of the night. They were out of the city, but being at Willings didn't guarantee her safety.

He walked over to his bag. When he'd found what he was looking for, he gave himself a lecture. He wasn't going to waste a second in that room of hers. He was going to give her what was in his hand and then get the hell out of there.

He had no interest in meeting up with Walker.

After all, he had faith in his self-control. But he wasn't going to push his luck.

Grace was sitting at the vanity in her bathroom when she thought she heard a knock at her door. She put her hair-brush down and listened.

When another knock came, she traded the towel she'd wrapped around herself for a silk robe and went to the door. She was surprised to see Smith standing in the hall.

Going by the expression on his face, his mood hadn't improved.

"Mind if I come in?"

"Please." She stepped back, acutely aware that she was naked under the robe.

When he shut the door, his eyes lingered on her damp hair but his voice was gruff and standoffish.

"Take this." Smith held out a small black box the size of a pager. "It's a panic button. Press it and I'll come."

"Thank you," she said, examining it.

He turned to go.

"Smith?" She hadn't meant to speak, but his name just jumped out of her mouth. As he looked over his shoulder at her, her heart began to pound.

There were so many things she wanted to say to him. None of them were easy. Few made sense. And he didn't look like he was in the mood for talking.

"Never mind," she muttered.

There was a long silence between them. And then he turned around, his mouth lifting in a humorless smile.

"You seemed surprised it was me knocking at your door. Expecting someone else?"

She frowned. "No."

"You sure about that?"

"Who would—you mean Jack?"

"Seems like just the kind of guy who could juggle two women well. Probably discreet, too. Good choice, if you're looking for an affair."

Grace pulled the lapels of her robe closer together. "I'm not looking for one."

"You sure about that, Countess?"

His eyes were glittering as he looked her over and she was confused but drawn by the change in him. Sexual energy started coming off him in waves of heat.

"John?" she whispered, aware that it was an invitation of sorts.

He shook his head, although she wasn't sure whether it was to turn her down or because he was disappointed in himself.

"You are so goddamn beautiful," he said, his eyes moving over her face, down her neck, over her body. "I almost hate you for it."

"I don't want you to hate me."

"Yeah, well, it'd be easier to handle than what I'm feeling now."

"What are you feeling?" Her voice had gone breathless.

"Like I want you naked and underneath me."

Involuntarily, Grace took a step toward him and, in a blur of motion, he took her into his arms. His lips came down on hers in a kiss that was hard and full of demand. Opening her mouth, taking him inside of her, she moaned. This was what she had wanted for so long, since that night that they had almost made love.

And tonight, she wasn't going to turn back.

She felt his hands loosen the robe and slip underneath, on to her skin. As he brushed over her breasts, she strained to get closer to him. Grabbing the front of his shirt, she fumbled with the buttons.

Suddenly, there was a sharp knock at the door.

"You decent? I hope not," Jack said, throwing it open. "I brought the wine—"

Grace and Smith pulled apart, panting. As she yanked her robe back into place, she could feel the blood rush into her face. In the awkward moment that followed, she thought of the contractors who'd interrupted them that morning so long ago.

She and John had god-awful timing, she thought. Or maybe it was the rest of the world with the problem. Either way, it was maddening.

Jack's brows shot up into his forehead. "I didn't mean to—"

"I was just leaving," Smith growled. As he strode past the other man, Jack stepped out of his way.

After the door was slammed shut, her friend looked at her ruefully. "I didn't know you and he were—ah . . . It sure as hell explains a lot."

Grace cleared her throat and wondered what she should do. She wanted to rush across the hall to John and disabuse him of the conclusion he'd obviously jumped to. However, if the look on his face as he'd left was anything to go by, the last thing he'd want would be a visit from her.

In the meantime, her friend was waiting for an explanation.

"Ah—we're not together. Or at least, it's not what it looks—looked like." She paused. "Oh, hell."

She went over to a window and stared out at the ocean. Moonlight was falling on the waves, dancing across the swells.

"What's going on, Grace?"

She threw up her hands, feeling like she couldn't keep up the guise of being happily married any longer. "You might as well know that Ranulf and I have separated."

Jack let out a low whistle. "I'm sorry. When did this happen?"

"A month ago. I'm filing for divorce."

"Because of the man who just left?"

She shook her head. "No, it doesn't have anything to do with John. Ranulf and I should never have gotten married in the first place."

"Jesus, I really am sorry." There was a pause and then Jack let out a soft laugh. "Is it all right for me to say I never really liked Ranulf? For all that fancy lineage of his, he wasn't good enough for you."

"That's sweet of you to say." She turned to her friend, a sad smile on her face.

"So who's this Smith guy?"

"It's complicated. But there's nothing . . . going on between us." She shot him a dry look. "In spite of what you walked in on."

"You sure about that? I think I understand now why he's been looking at me as if I had a bull's-eye on my chest and he was carrying a fistful of darts. He's being territorial. Over you."

Grace shook her head. "Look, I don't want to talk about him, if you don't mind. It's . . ."

"Complicated. I can tell."

She smiled softly. "Listen, my mother doesn't know about Ranulf, yet. So keep it quiet. I'm going to break the news to her before I leave."

He shook his head. "This is going to be a long weekend."

"I've been thinking that from the moment we came over the bridge."

Jack hesitated. "I need to say one more thing about John Smith, though."

"Yes?"

Her friend's expression was very serious as he nodded at the door. "Be careful with that man. Your heart is in your eyes when you look at him."

Grace felt a chill pass over her skin. Clearly, Jack saw through her brave front and her little white lies.

"It wasn't like this with Ranulf," she whispered. "It hasn't been like this with anyone."

Jack put the wine and the glasses down and came over to her. "We don't get to pick who we fall in love with."

Grace sighed unhappily. "I'm not in love with him."

Jack put an arm around her and she leaned her head on his shoulder for a long while. When she pulled back, he smiled and tucked a strand of hair behind her ear.

"Why don't we save the wine and reminiscing for another time."

"Thanks, Jack. You're a good friend."

He leaned down and kissed her on the cheek. As he was pulling away, his cell phone went off. Somehow, he managed to answer it, pick up the bottle and glasses, and leave without dropping anything.

Grace shut the lights off and got into bed. Her last thought was of the anger on John's face as he'd turned away.

She'd give him some time to cool off and then she'd talk to him.

*   *   *

As Smith shut the door to his room, he felt like an idiot. A stupid idiot.

A vision of her in that goddamn silk robe taunted him with what he had been denied.

That Walker and she were together at this very moment was—

He was having trouble finding the right words.

Jesus.

And he'd thought getting through dinner was bad? Being cooped up in a room across the hall from the bed she was putting to good use was intolerable.

He disarmed himself with jerky motions, thinking the last thing he needed was to be anywhere near a gun.

What he needed was air.

Using the door at the end of the hall, he went out and walked around on the terrace until he had a full view of the ocean. Hearing the waves and feeling the cool, damp air on his face, he took a couple of deep breaths while trying to remember when he'd felt so out of control.

It had been a while.

He'd had a damn fine stretch of being on top of his game until he'd met Grace. Courtesy of destiny's vicious little whim, he was feeling a lot of things, but in control wasn't one of them. He was frustrated. Horny as hell. Juiced up with aggression.

Smith braced his hands against the railing and leaned forward. Staring off into a dark, star-studded horizon, he realized he was searching for some kind of answer in the night sky and this surprised him. He typically wasn't one for moments of reflection and the yearning he felt was as unfamiliar as the ache in his chest.

Turning away from the silent heavens, he faced the house, only to realize he was standing outside Grace's bedroom. Through the glass, he saw her talking with Jack and then he watched her step into the other man's arms.

Pain ripped through him, sleek and cold.

His first instinct was to tear down the door and rip the two of them apart. To keep from acting on the impulse, he

200 *Jessica Bird*

reached behind and gripped the cool wood of the railing until his palms burned.

When she lifted her head from Jack Walker's shoulder and met the man's eyes, Smith absorbed the image like it was a stain. With terrible clarity, he saw her body arching toward Walker's, her blond hair tumbling in waves down her back, her arms reaching up and coming to rest around the man's shoulders.

Walker stroked her face and then slowly bent down toward her lips.

Smith wheeled away, heading back to his room.

He didn't want to see any more for fear of what his reaction might be.

16

EARLY THE next morning, Grace went to the gardens looking for a little peace of mind. As she wandered among the flower beds that had been prepared for the coming winter, she remembered what they looked like in full bloom. Planted in a studied manner, the tea roses and the foxgloves, the peonies and the lilies, the many hybrids that her father had enjoyed cultivating, all of them blossomed into a great profusion of color and life in the summer months.

As she continued down the lawn, the sound of the ocean grew more insistent. Overhead, a few gulls surfed high above the water as the dawn's rays fanned out across the pale blue sky. It was chilly and she was glad she'd put on a thick sweater.

At the edge of the property, overlooking the drop to the sea, there was a shingled bathhouse, white-trimmed, green-roofed. It had a shallow porch with two white wicker chairs on it and she sat down in one, hearing the weave creak as her weight was accepted in the seat. She kicked off her flats and stretched out her legs so that her heels rested on the railing.

Wiggling her toes at the arriving sun, she watched as a gull shifted direction and came in for a smooth landing a couple of yards away. She was about to tell him she wasn't a good bet if he was looking for breakfast when she realized she wasn't alone.

Grace shifted in the chair and saw Smith standing at the other edge of the property under the arms of an old maple tree. He was leaning up against the trunk and staring out at the ocean. She wondered how he knew she'd left the house. She'd been so quiet.

Figuring she had nothing to lose, she got out of the chair and walked over to him. When he didn't acknowledge her approach, she was tempted to leave him alone.

"Hi." She wasn't surprised when all he did was nod at her. Wearing a black T-shirt under his leather jacket and a pair of well-washed jeans, he was very handsome in the morning light, in a hard and remote kind of way.

"You know, Jack is just a friend," she blurted.

He frowned. "Who you sleep with is none of my business."

"I'm not—" When he shot her a look of disbelief, she let out an exasperated breath. "You know, I feel pretty asinine defending myself over something I haven't done."

When he didn't reply, frustration got the best of her. "Come on, John. Why don't you just admit you're upset? And while we're at it, why can't we talk about what's happening between us?"

He sounded disinterested when he answered her. "Unless you want to alter the terms of our employment agreement, there's nothing to say about *us.*"

"Jack is not my lover. Last night—"

He cut her off with a harsh laugh. "This may come as a royal surprise, Countess, but the world doesn't revolve around you. You may have an interest in rehashing your nocturnal exploits but I find the subject boring."

He looked back out to the ocean.

Maybe she was going about this the wrong way, she thought.

She put her hand on his arm. "I wanted to be with you."

Smith shrugged her off impatiently. "That's not really an exclusive club, is it? Now that you're getting free from your husband."

Grace sucked in a breath. "I can't believe you said that."

Smith pushed off the tree trunk and loomed over her. "You want to talk? Fine, but let's get real. Mr. Charm's got a whole lot to offer you, doesn't he. I bet he's goddamn front and center with the flowers and jewelry after he gets his rocks off. Hell, he'd even make a great second husband. All I can offer you is a one-night stand with a member of the lower classes. Weighing your options, I think you made the right choice."

"Excuse me," she said, hotly, "but if you recall, you were the one turning me down the night of my birthday. And I did not sleep with Jack!"

Smith glared at her. "That lie is a waste of breath, Countess."

"Don't call me that," she snapped.

"Fine. How does whore sound?"

Grace hissed as she was blinded by anger. With a sharp movement, she drew back her hand, ready to slap him.

"You want to hit me?" he growled. "Go ahead."

She stood there, shaking, unable to comprehend what she was doing.

Smith leaned in closer, jutting out his chin. "Hell, because you're supposedly a lady, I'll even make it easy for you. Aim high and follow through."

Grace blinked and slowly dropped her hand. In a voice rough with emotion, she whispered, "God help me. I wish I had never met you."

With her heart in her throat, she ran toward the house.

Grace closed her bedroom door and paced around, waiting for her body to stop trembling. She couldn't remember being that mad at anyone before and knew the strength of her emotions was about so much more than just the words he'd spoken or the tone he'd used. She had the sense they were circling around what they wanted and avoiding the truth. Clearly, it was driving them both mad.

She was convinced Smith was beginning to care for her. It was the only explanation for his behavior toward Jack. And she knew damn well how she was feeling about him. The fact that they couldn't just admit what was between them upset her the most.

Sitting down on her bed, she saw the panic button and picked it up, resenting the reminder of the real reason John was in her life. She was finding it difficult to separate her feelings for him from the reality that he worked for her. And would be leaving, perhaps someday soon. She couldn't imagine what it would be like not to see him. Even when he was frustrating the hell out of her, she wanted him around.

When a soft knock sounded, she threw the little black box down onto the pillow and straightened her clothes.

"Yes?"

When John came in, she stood up, surprised.

"This won't take long," he said, shutting the door and leaning back against it. His expression was remote.

She offered him a lopsided grin, pleased that he'd come and found her. "Don't worry if it does. It's not like I had any big plans before breakfast."

"Listen, I'm sorry I lost it down there," he said gruffly. "What I said was totally inappropriate and unprofessional. I should've just kept my mouth shut."

"I don't think that's the best strategy." She tucked a pillow into her arms and looked at her tumbled sheets and blankets. Evidence of her deepening relationship with insomnia, she thought. "I don't know if I can keep living under this pressure."

She heard him release a long breath, like he was switching topics in his head. "I don't blame you. I promise, the police are going to find whoever killed those women—"

"No. I'm talking about you. About us." She glanced up. "I don't like what just happened. I don't like turning into such an angry person. But being around you with so much left unsaid and unexplained is tearing me up. Frankly, I think it's tearing us both up."

He crossed his arms over his chest. The stance, she thought, was so typical of him.

"John, we can't ignore what's happening between us. And don't you dare tell me that it's nothing. Last night, you looked like you wanted to kill Jack when he came through that door."

"I'm sorry if I made you uncomfortable." He shifted his weight impatiently and she got the impression he was anxious to leave.

Exasperation tightened her voice. "John—"

"Look, in spite of what I said down there, it's none of

my business who you sleep—what you do in your personal life."

"You can say the words, but I don't know if I believe them."

For once, Smith was the one looking away. Pushing his hands deep into his pockets, he seemed to be debating within himself. When he finally spoke, the words came out rigidly.

"I watched him kiss you. I was out on the terrace."

Grace frowned. "I don't know what you think you saw. But Jack has never kissed me anywhere except on the cheek."

He started shaking his head, as if he was frustrated with himself. "Dammit, we shouldn't even be having this conversation."

He made a move for the door.

"John, we *need* to talk about this. Don't go."

"I have to."

"What are you so afraid of?" she whispered fiercely.

"You."

It was the last thing she expected him to say.

"But why? You must know how I feel about you." She squeezed the pillow. "I think I'm falling in love with you."

"Jesus *Christ*." He pushed his hand through his hair.

She winced. "Not exactly the response I was hoping for. When the next woman springs that declaration on you, you might try for something a little less like a reprimand."

"This is precisely what I wanted to avoid," he said under his breath.

"Why?" she demanded. "What's so wrong about me loving you?"

He waved away her words. "First of all, you don't love me."

Grace frowned. "Don't tell me what I feel."

"You're in danger. You're in the middle of a divorce. Right now, you're vulnerable. If we had met under different circumstances, you never would have gotten emotionally attached."

"How dare you!" She tossed the pillow aside and got on the bed.

"It's the truth," he said darkly. "And when I'm gone, you'll realize it, too."

"Who the hell made you an expert on my emotions?"

"The sooner you recognize the reality of the situation, the better off we're both going to be."

She shook her head vehemently.

"I refuse to let you reduce my feelings—my heart"— she pounded her chest—"to some kind of—of rebound theory."

"It's not a theory," he said, holding her eyes harshly. "This has happened to me before. You're not the first client to think they were in love with me, Grace."

That quieted her for a moment.

As she measured the span of his shoulders, she wondered how many other women had clung to them.

"And what happened?" she asked, bracing herself for the answer. "Did you . . ."

"Sleep with them? No, I didn't." His mouth lifted in a cold smile. "I was never tempted . . . until you."

"Well, at least that's a start," she muttered.

"No, it sure as hell isn't."

"Why? As you said, the threat hanging over me isn't going to last forever. You're not going to be working for me for the rest of our natural lives."

"Christ, Grace, this isn't just about the damn job. I've spent the last twenty years alone. By choice. I don't do relationships and you're not the kind of woman who can handle having sex without one. This isn't going anywhere."

"How would you know what I can and can't handle, exactly?"

"Think back to when I took you to bed that night you broke the glass. You put a stop to it, Countess, pulled away pretty damn fast when things got heavy. Not really the kind of thing a woman does when she's comfortable with casual sex, is it?"

Grace could feel the heat rush to her face.

He cursed softly. "Look, I'm not thinking straight anymore and you're not paying me to be distracted. We've got a problem and I'm trying to make it better, not worse."

"We don't have a problem," she countered doggedly.

"Then you're deluding yourself. And you're the one who's going to get hurt."

She wrapped her arms around herself. "I don't know that for sure and neither do you."

He shot her a level stare. "If my brain gets scrambled in the wrong situation, you could end up dead. I'm still leaving at the end of this job. You want to pick between those two finales?"

"Who says they're the only options."

"There's no happy ending to this. I told you that before."

"Well, dammit, maybe there could be!"

He brushed his hand over his hair again. "Grace, don't fall . . . for me."

"Why? Because you're worried my heart's going to inconvenience you in some way?" she snapped.

"It's for your own good."

She put her hands on her hips, pegging him with hard eyes.

"Let's get one thing straight, you arrogant son of a bitch. I'm capable of surviving a lot worse than a love affair with a goddamn *ghost*. The truth is, when you hit the road, there isn't going to be much to miss because not much of you has been here. And you've got a hell of a nerve telling me what's for my own good. You're a coward under all that muscle. You," she pointed at him, "are so busy protecting yourself it's a miracle you have time to take care of your clients. For my own good," she muttered. "Why don't you work on yourself first? Then you can play Dr. Phil on someone else."

John let out a curse with such force she stepped back.

"Just what do you think your life would be like if I hung around?" he demanded. "You think you're going to have a ball staying up nights, wondering where I am and whether I'm coming home—ever? You think you can handle not being able to reach me for weeks, maybe months at a time? Are you tough enough for all that? Or do you expect me to turn into some goddamn party favor, someone you can have on your arm like a purse at all those fancy parties you go to?"

She shook her head and tried to respond more evenly. "I wouldn't want that. I'd never expect you to be something you're not. All I want is to give us a chance."

"You want to play out this whole relationship fantasy? Fine." Smith's eyes were sharp, assessing. "You can't tell your own mother you're getting a divorce from a man you don't love. How are you going to break the news to her that the two of us are sleeping together? I'm her worst nightmare."

Grace lifted her chin. "You don't need to worry about my mother. She's my problem. And as for your job, is the line of work you're in now the only thing you can do? I doubt that."

He shot her a humorless smile. "People without a valid social security number, people who have three different passports, people like me, don't just walk into an office somewhere and apply for a job."

"Don't hide behind logistics," she said with dismissal.

"Logistics? What the hell do you think I do for a living?"

She sent him an annoyed look.

"Well?" he demanded.

"You're a bodyguard." When he shook his head in disbelief, she said, "Come on, Smith, I know you're a tough guy but even the most decorated military men manage to get back into civilian life when they leave the service. You can choose another path."

She was taken off guard when he just stared at her and she got the sense she might be off base.

"Don't they?" she whispered with doubt.

"Here are some buzzwords for you," he said. "Hand-to-hand combat specialist. Munitions expert. Sharpshooter. Assassin. Now, you want to tell me what kind of job those qualify me for in your world?"

"If you gave us a chance, we'd make it work, together."

"Don't fool yourself, Grace."

Frustration surged. "I'm not. You're the one who won't see—"

"I'm sorry."

"*Damn* you! Don't be sorry when you could so easily

make things different." Tears blurred her vision. He was like talking to a statue. "Oh, hell, maybe you should just leave."

As she walked over to open the door, he grabbed for her hand. She struggled against his hold with an angry glare but stopped as his eyes went nearly black with emotion.

"Think about all those scars you were so interested in, Countess. How do you think they got on my body? It sure as hell wasn't from sitting behind a desk."

She looked away.

"I have enemies, Grace," he said in a deadly quiet voice. "The kind who don't use lawyers to fight their battles for them. The kind who wouldn't hesitate to kill you just because you're sleeping next to me at night."

Her eyes widened as he let go of her hand and started to pace.

"Even if I leave Black Watch, I can't just wipe the slate clean and start over. These people have long memories and the fact that you're such a public figure is a problem. I don't want my face or where I live to be on the front page of the newspapers. I haven't had a home, ever, because I don't want to be easily found. With you, any degree of anonymity would be impossible and that would not only put me in danger. It would put you at risk, too."

She took a deep breath. "Good Lord, John, what did you used to do?"

There was a long silence.

"Covert ops."

"Can you tell me why you got out?"

He hesitated. She had a sense he was sifting through the truth and cleaning it up for her.

"I got wounded. After a couple weeks in the hospital, I decided if I was going to get wasted on a job, I wanted to be running the show, not taking orders. In the military, no matter how high up you go, there's always someone over you unless you're the president. As soon as I was back on my feet, I began taking some subcontracting work. When I had more than I could handle, I snagged Tiny and a couple others who were really good. We've been working together for five years now."

"It must be a hard life." Grace lowered her eyes. "Can you go on like this forever?"

"I know I can get through today and tomorrow. That's all I think about."

"But don't you get lonely? Don't you want someone in your life?"

"No."

"What about your family?" There had to be someone, somewhere who he relied on. A mother. Sister. Brother.

"I don't have any."

"None at all?"

When he didn't answer, she tried to imagine what it would be like to be so alone.

"I find it hard to believe you can live without . . . anyone."

"I have Black Watch."

But that was business, she thought.

"You've never thought of getting married? Starting your own family? Haven't you ever wanted some kind of relationship with a woman?"

"If I want sex, I have it. And then I leave. Permanent ties are time-consuming, draining, and not something I want to deal with."

Grace felt her heart sink as she wondered how she would feel, watching him walk out of her door and never look back. "Haven't you ever wanted to stay?"

He shook his head. "I can't remember the last time I woke up next to a woman."

"Well, actually, that would have been me. Wouldn't it?"

Reluctantly, he nodded. "Yes, I guess it was."

"When I rolled over and looked into your eyes that morning, I knew you wanted me." She spoke softly and looked up.

"Sure, I wanted you then. I want you right now. But I can't change my whole life for you and that's what it would take for us to be together."

She went over to him and touched his face. "You can't protect my heart, John, and neither of us can predict the future. I'm already falling in love with you. If you don't want to be with me, fine. But don't make decisions for me because you're afraid I'll get hurt."

His voice was low, husky. "I never thought I'd meet someone like you."

He took the palm of her hand, pressed his lips to it, and placed it on his thick chest.

Then he stepped back.

"But whether you know it or not, you're looking for love in return, Grace. And I can't give you something I don't have inside of me."

He was out the door before she could respond.

17

GOING DOWNSTAIRS for breakfast, Grace had to pin a smile onto her face. She would rather have eaten alone, but meals were a command performance at Willings and her absence would have led to another confrontation with her mother. Because she was holding herself together with only loose threads of dignity, she wanted to avoid any further upheaval.

Only two more days, she thought, walking into the dining room.

She was surprised to see both Jack and his girlfriend seated at the long table.

"Blair!" she exclaimed. "When did you get here?"

The other woman got to her feet and they embraced.

"Late last night."

Blair, tall and slender with closely cropped blond hair and dazzling gray eyes, was the perfect complement to Jack's sleekness. With their expensive clothes and their classic looks, they were a matched set.

As Grace stepped back, she saw Smith come into the room and became instantly aware of him.

"How's the tooth?"

"A little sore." Blair laughed, rubbing her jaw. "But I was feeling better than I thought I would and came late last night."

"She's a real trooper, all right," Jack said.

The woman looked over at him. "Although I'm going to have to miss today's sailing excursion. I am not strong enough to hit the ocean with you and Alex."

"Funny, you managed to get out of it the last time he

asked us." Jack chuckled. "Are you sure you didn't plan the root canal?"

"Alex is in town?" Grace asked, sitting down as Jack pushed her chair in.

Alex Moorehouse was one of the country's best America's Cup sailors and an old friend of Jack's. Grace had met him on a number of occasions and liked the man.

"He is and I wouldn't miss a chance to get out on the open sea with Moorehouse. That man's pure adrenaline."

Carolina entered the room and they all stood up. She was dressed in a fine tweed suit, her hair precisely arranged in the chignon she'd worn it in for years. As her mother's eyes passed over her, Grace touched her own hair, which was down and flowing over her shoulders.

Carolina eyed Smith's blue jeans with disapproval before smiling at her newest guest. "Blair, darling, how are you? Sit, sit, everyone."

Jack helped her with her chair and then she rang the bell. Marta came in with a breakfast of scrambled eggs and cut fruit on a large silver tray. The woman paused by each guest, holding the load with ease.

When it was her turn, Grace didn't take much of either.

"It looks lovely, Marta, thank you," she said. "Mother, today we're going to go to Mr. Blankenbaker's. Would you like to come?"

"No. I'm having lunch with Harrington Wright. First, however, I must go to see Stella Linnaean, who is not feeling well. And then . . ."

Grace let her mother's recital of the day's activities pass over her like a mist. She thought instead of John and what he'd said earlier that morning. She was surprised he'd revealed so much of himself, although it was a damn shame that so little of it worked in her favor. She replayed their conversation in her head over and over again, looking for a way to make him see the possibilities instead of the obstacles between them.

His past was one of the harder things to counter. She didn't doubt him when he said he had dangerous enemies, but she had to believe there was a way around even that impediment.

"Grace?" her mother said sharply.

She shook herself out of her reverie and looked down the table. Her mother had folded her napkin into a neat square, placed it next to her plate and was getting to her feet. Evidently, breakfast was over.

"Sorry. What?"

"I would like to see you for a moment."

Grace grabbed a piece of toast and reluctantly followed her mother across the foyer into the lady's parlor that her mother used as a study.

The room was painted in a cornflower blue and filled with delicate French antiques. Grace had never felt comfortable in it. Everything seemed small, dainty, and breakable. Booby-trapped. It was as if each of the chairs had been calibrated for her mother's birdlike weight and anything heavier would cause a collapse, embarrassment, and censure.

Carolina shut the double doors behind them and Grace's chest contracted. It was hard to imagine how such a bright, elegant room could feel like a dungeon, but it did.

"It's good to see Blair looking so well," Carolina said, pausing to inspect a bouquet of flowers on a delicate side table. She picked off two petals from a white rose and threw them into a little decoupage wastepaper basket that was otherwise empty. "Although it was a dreadful story about that tooth."

"Yes, it was."

"She's just lovely, don't you think?"

"Yes, she is."

Grace knew damn well she hadn't been called inside to discuss Jack's girlfriend and waited for the real conversation to get going.

Carolina walked smoothly over to her desk, a Louis XIV masterpiece with few things marring its pristine surface. In one corner, there was a silk box of her personal stationery that had her name at the top and Willings's address underneath. Laying on the stack, there was a single gold pen as thin as a flower stem and a tiny leather-bound address book.

"Sit down, Grace."

She carefully lowered herself into the chair next to her mother's desk. The sunlight coming through an east-facing window streamed into her eyes, making it hard to see. She blinked.

"I'm surprised you're wearing your hair like that. It's a bit unruly, don't you think?"

There was a long silence.

"Mother, what did you want to talk about?"

Carolina crossed her legs at the ankles and smoothed down her perfectly flat skirt with a scrupulous hand. "I'm afraid you have put me in a rather awkward position."

"How so?"

"I saw you this morning. With that man."

Grace felt herself tightening up all over. "Which man?"

"You know exactly to whom I am referring."

"And?"

"You were arguing with him. On the lawn. I saw you from my bedroom window."

Her tone suggested she would rather have woken up to a rotting Winnebago on the grass.

Grace fought the urge to look down at her fingers, which was what she'd done when she was young and facing the same refined condemnation. Reminding herself that she was a grown-up, she tried to stare back at her mother. With the sun making her eyes hurt and her back rigid in the uncomfortable chair, she had a clear vision of herself at the age of fifty still playing the apologetic daughter. Her stomach lurched.

"So?" she said in a low voice.

"Grace, ladies do not argue in that manner. And most certainly not out in public"—there was a meaningful pause—"with a man other than their husband."

Grace shifted in the chair, felt it wobble underneath her and realized she was fed up. For the first time in her life, it occurred to her that she didn't have to take her mother's prim displeasure.

It was a powerful epiphany.

She just wasn't sure how to act on it.

"Well?" Carolina demanded. "What do you have to say for yourself?"

How about just leaving, she thought.

Grace rose from the chair, stepped out of the sunlight and looked across the room at the closed doors.

"Where do you think you're going?" Her mother's voice was brittle.

Anywhere, she thought. Anywhere away from you.

"I want an answer," Carolina said sharply. "Why were you fighting with that man?"

"I don't have an answer for you, Mother," Grace murmured, walking away.

Her hand was reaching for the knob when her mother said, "Tell me he is not your lover."

Grace glanced over her shoulder and saw that, behind the iron voice, her mother was looking pale.

Grace breathed in, long and slow, and spoke clearly. "Even if he was, that would be none of your business."

Carolina rose from her chair. "You are a married woman. How can you disgrace yourself by—by carousing with that . . ."

"With what, Mother?"

"That ruffian!"

Grace fought the urge to giggle inappropriately at the antiquated word.

"Don't be ridiculous," she muttered.

"He wore *jeans* to the breakfast table."

"For Chrissakes, Mother," Grace snapped, "this is a private residence, not a consulate. He can wear anything he wants."

"He is unsuitable as a guest and I don't understand why you insisted on bringing him here. May I remind you that you are married to a man of royal descent—"

"Spare me the ad copy, okay? Ranulf doesn't live up to any of it. If he were half the man Smith is—"

Carolina gasped. "Don't say that!"

"It's true."

"You—you . . ." And then, as if a switch had been pulled, Carolina snapped her mouth shut. After a deep breath, she said, "I don't believe I have anything more to say to you at the moment."

"Which is good, because I was just leaving."

As Grace shut the doors behind her, she wasn't sure whether she had won or lost the argument and realized it didn't matter. At least she had held her own.

An hour later, while Grace was outside playing croquet with Blair, her mother came and announced that the evening's party had been canceled and she would be dining elsewhere. With no more explanation than that, she returned to the house, without once looking at her daughter.

She did make a point, however, of sparing a withering glance for John.

The afternoon was spent at Mr. Blankenbaker's looking over the portrait. Grace was thrilled by the masterpiece, although disappointed that Jack had missed the preview. Mr. Blankenbaker agreed to draw up papers making the gift official and to ship the painting to the Hall Museum in time for the Gala.

They returned to Willings when the sun was hanging low behind the house and the ocean was quieting down for the night. As she walked into the foyer, Grace decided a good long soak in some very hot water was just what she needed to relax.

Either that or a brain transplant.

"Where are you headed?" John asked.

She looked over her shoulder at him. He'd been silent for much of the day but never far from her side. After everything that had been said in her bedroom, being so close to him was a bittersweet torment.

Abruptly, she was struck by an idea. When she and John had talked, he'd been using his head. His reasoning. His logic.

Perhaps she just needed him to stop thinking so much.

Grace offered him a slow smile. "I'm going to have a bath."

He nodded and followed her up the stairs.

She'd never seduced a man before, she thought as she hit the second-floor landing. And it was time to give it a try.

He'd said he wanted her. Maybe his body could override that mind of his.

*   *   *

Smith paused outside of her room, telling himself that he was going to use the time she was in the tub to do some push-ups and sit-ups. He had a hell of lot of energy he needed to burn off.

"I'll be across the hall," he said. "Take the panic button in with you."

"I can't."

"Why the hell not?"

"I think it's broken."

He frowned. "I tested it before I gave it to you."

She shrugged and went through her door. "I don't know. Maybe I'm wrong."

And then she shut the door in his face.

He pounded on it. "Grace? I've got to check the damn thing."

There was only silence.

"Oh, for Chrissakes. Grace?"

He threw the door open and froze.

She was stepping out of her pants. Had taken off her sweater. All he saw was a lot of creamy skin and a few strips of silk.

Smith blinked like he'd been sucker punched.

Sweet heaven, he thought.

Moving deliberately, and without bothering to hide herself, she folded her pants and put them in the bureau.

As the sight of her flooded his brain, he tried like hell to hold on to reality.

Which was goddamn close to impossible with his fantasy three feet away in her bra and panties.

"Where's the panic button?" he growled.

She shrugged. "I don't know. It was somewhere in my bed."

"Jesus Chri—"

Grace reached behind her back and unclipped her bra. Slowly, she peeled off one satin strap and then the other. When the lacy cups fell to the floor, and he saw her breasts in the sunlight, he felt his knees get weak.

"What the hell are you doing?" he demanded.

"I'm getting ready for my bath."

She turned around, flashing her picture-perfect butt at

him, and walked into the bathroom. He watched as she bent over and worked the faucets.

It was the kind of sight that could blind a man, he thought numbly.

Smith fell back against the door. He tried to think about his options, which were limited as he couldn't seem to make his body leave the room. The only thing that came to him was a vision of picking her up and carrying her over to the bed.

Grace spent an inordinate amount of time making sure the water was the right temperature and then turned around to face him. Even though she was behaving provocatively, her eyes revealed a nervousness that was totally endearing.

She had no idea what she was doing, he thought, wanting to smile.

Bur then she locked her thumbs under the waistband of her panties.

And Smith got deadly serious.

She moved the silk down her hips and her thighs and then kicked it off with one foot. Standing in the bathroom with steam from the hot water billowing up around her, it was clear she was waiting for him.

Get the hell out of this room, right now, he thought. Before you can't go back.

It took every ounce of willpower he had to turn around and leave.

Going out onto the terrace, he walked around until he could see into her bathroom. By the time she was back in his sight, she was in the tub, covered by the water.

He cursed out loud as he felt the lust pound through his body.

Taking out a cheroot, he lit it and assiduously ignored the fact that his hands trembled slightly.

It was a while before he could string any coherent thoughts together.

As he leaned against the railing and smoked, he thought about her declaration of love. Could it be true? Could a woman like her actually love him?

And what would he be willing to sacrifice to have her

in his life? He thought about Black Watch, his work, his clients. Images flashed through his mind of a thousand hotel rooms, of airplanes and private jets, of people looking up at him with fear in their eyes and hopeful faith in their hearts.

Grace had challenged him on something he had begun to wonder about himself. How long could he go on? His rootless existence had sustained him for so many years, had been the only way he could conceive of getting through life. But what if there was another way?

And what if it involved Grace?

His eyes narrowed as she leaned back against the porcelain rim of the tub and closed her eyes. Her hair was coiled up on her head and a few tendrils were curling around her face from the heat and humidity. Her profile was a perfect composition of planes and angles that added up to great beauty, but that wasn't what held his attention. He realized he'd started looking past her physical perfection. He was a hell of a lot more interested in the jumble of strengths and weaknesses that was inside of her.

He watched as her hand came out of the water and brushed over her cheek. When she did it again, he realized she was crying.

"Oh, Grace," he said, softly.

She was right. They were tearing each other up.

Smith watched her until she started to get up from the tub. Before she stepped free of the water, he went back inside and was waiting next to her door when she emerged twenty minutes later, dressed for dinner. She was silent as they went down the hall.

Before they hit the stairs, he reached out and took her arm.

He put his lips close to her ear. "You are the most sensual woman I've ever seen. I'm going to take the image of you standing in front of that tub to my grave."

Her steps faltered and she let out a sad, self-deprecating laugh. "Somehow, I doubt that. I've been known for a lot of things but sexy isn't one of them."

He stopped her. "What the hell are you talking about, woman?"

She shrugged and her expression showed a kind of defeat he didn't associate with her.

"You didn't get in that tub with me, did you? Which was my sole motivation for behaving ... Anyway, I should have known better. Ranulf always told me I was beautiful but not enticing. It was probably the only thing he got right about me."

"What did he tell you?"

When her eyes refused to meet his, Smith thought back to the night she'd tried to pull away from him and had panicked when he hadn't let her go. Maybe there was more to it than her not wanting to have casual sex.

"Grace? What did he do to you?"

She hesitated. "Let's just say he was less than satisfied with me as a lover. And he let me know it."

Black rage hit Smith. As he tried to calm down, he wondered what the hell was wrong with the man and how he could get his hands on the aristocratic asshole.

"Let me tell you something," Smith said darkly. "Ranulf was full of shit. You're incredibly erotic."

She rolled her eyes. "You don't have to say that."

He moved close to her, took her hand, and placed it on his arousal. She gasped.

"I'm totally serious." He lowered his head so his mouth was an inch from hers. "All I have to do is think of you."

Grace swayed against him.

"I wanted you to stay," she whispered.

Christ, so had he.

"Know this," he said roughly. "The reason I left had nothing to do with how badly I want you. I'm trying to do the right thing by you. I really am."

He kissed her hard and quick and then held out his arm.

Together, they descended the grand staircase.

Smith leaned back as Marta cleared his plate. When a dessert tray was wheeled next to him, he shook his head at whatever sweet, sauce-covered thing was on it.

Crossing his arms over his chest, he stared through the candlelight at Grace, who was twirling her wineglass on the table. Her eyes were on the faceted crystal as she laughed at something Walker was saying.

"Of course I turned you down today," she said. "Blair needed company more than you and Alex need a mate on that sailboat."

"Come on, you just said no out of habit. You started turning me down in kindergarten and haven't let up. Fortunately, my ego can take it." Walker smiled urbanely as he poured himself some more wine. "If only because I've gotten used to it."

The man pushed his chair back from the table, kicked his legs out in front of him and crossed one loafer on top of the other. The wineglass dangled from one of his hands as he reclined.

"At least you love me," he said to Blair.

The woman leaned over and kissed his cheek. "Yes, I do."

"How long's it been now?"

"Five years or so."

"You know, I've been thinking about us lately."

Blair rolled her eyes as she smiled at him. "What have you dreamed up this time?" She glanced over at Grace. "Last winter, he scooped me up in a plane, told me to take a little nap, and I woke up over the Atlantic Ocean. We were heading for Portofino. It was lovely but a bit disorienting."

Walker laughed and put the glass back on the table.

"Well, this one doesn't involve plane travel and I hope you won't sleep through it." He reached into the inside pocket of his jacket and took out a small velvet box. "I'd like you to be my wife. You want to get married?"

Smith's eyes snapped to Grace's face. Her expression was joyous as she clasped her hands together.

Walker cracked open the box and pushed it over to Blair. He was sporting a half smile as she stared down at the sizable diamond, speechless.

"You know, I really enjoy surprising you, Blair."

The woman's eyes rose from the engagement ring. "Are you serious?"

There was an imperceptible pause.

"It's time for us to settle down." He smiled. "And I did

it in front of witnesses so you'd know I have no intention of backing out."

Blair took the ring from the box and slid it onto her finger. She took a deep breath, but then smiled. "Okay. Let's do it."

Walker leaned over and kissed the woman. While the two whispered to each other, Smith studied Grace. She was staring into the flame of a candle, a soft smile on her face.

A little while later, the small party broke up and everyone headed to their rooms. Smith was walking behind Grace when she got to her door.

"May I come in?" he said.

"Of course."

As he followed her inside, she went over to the bureau and started taking off her earrings.

"I really jumped to the wrong conclusion about you and Walker, didn't I?"

She turned around, fingers twisting the back of a diamond solitaire. Her voice was tired. "What made you finally believe me?"

"The way you looked at him tonight. You would have to have ice in your veins to be so genuinely happy at his engagement. Especially considering it happened in front of you."

Grace nodded and went to work on the other ear. In the dim light, her skin was translucent. He wanted to touch her.

After she put the other earring down, she sat on the edge of the bed and began to take off her shoes. "Well, thank you for saying something."

He nodded, watching her kick off a high heel and start to unbuckle the ankle strap of the other one. He lingered on the graceful curve of her calf and the arch of her foot.

"And you're right," she murmured. "I am thrilled for Jack. I hope everything works out for them. Marriage, even under the best of circumstances, is a challenge. Except for my parents, of course. Who were perfect together."

"You sure about that?" he said quietly. "Perfection's pretty damn hard to find in this world."

"True," she said, "but my parents came close. He was the

business and philanthropy star. She was his social publicist. Real 1950s stuff but they were so right for each other."

"Is that what you thought you were getting with the count?"

Her eyes registered surprise but then she shook her head. "No. I never wanted to be a cheerleader for someone. I wanted to be on the field. I thought Ranulf understood that, and to some degree he did. He was happy enough to spend both the money I had as well as the money I made."

He had a vision of her at her office, working those long hours, being a rock to so many people.

"You deserve better." Smith's words were low and intense.

She looked up at him and nodded. "I'm just starting to figure that out."

Even though he knew he shouldn't, he went over to her. Reaching out, he ran a finger down the silky skin of her cheek.

"Good for you," he said softly. "See you in the morning, Grace."

18

AFTER JOHN left, Grace changed out of her dress and went over to a window. As she stared out at the ocean, she was sorry she'd just let him walk out of her room. When he'd touched her face, she should have taken his hand and pulled him down to her.

As a matter of fact, she should just walk across the hall and kiss him.

After all, the striptease had worked better than she'd originally assumed, Grace thought. Maybe she had some vamp in her, after all.

Shoring up her courage, she stuck her head out of her door and listened for sounds that anyone was moving around in the house. Silence seemed to stretch in all directions so she figured Jack and Blair were likely celebrating their engagement privately. Her mother wasn't home yet, either.

Rapping on John's door softly, she waited with her breath held.

There was no answer.

Frowning, she knocked a little louder.

When there was still no response, she stuck her head inside.

"John?" she said into the darkness.

She went through the door. As her eyes adjusted, she could see shapes inside the room. The bed, the highboy, some of his things like his bag and his Windbreaker. The door to the bathroom was open and she saw, in the glow of the night-light, a towel bunched up on the marble counter and another hanging off the shower door. There was a razor and a can of shaving cream next to the sink.

Feeling like an intruder, she returned to her bedroom and left the door open so she'd hear him come back. When he hadn't returned twenty minutes later, she began to get worried. She went over and picked up the panic button.

Holding it in her hand, she wondered whether she should use it. With a curse, she put the thing down on the bureau next to her. She wasn't in any danger, after all. She just wanted to know where he was.

A half hour later, she was getting antsy and worried, wondering if something had happened to him. It was hard to imagine what could take down a man like John, but things happened.

She thought of Cuppie, Suzanna, and Mimi.

Awful things most certainly happened.

And he'd made it clear that the kind of people who might want to hurt him wouldn't do it with cruel words or threatening innuendos.

She told herself not to be ridiculous. What kind of bad guy was going to hunt John down in Newport, Rhode Island? And who'd even know he was at Willings?

Time passed. And her reasonable side got ambushed by the terrible pictures flying through her head.

Grace looked at the panic button. If she activated it, and he didn't come, she'd know he was in trouble.

Yeah, and then what was she going to do? Arm herself with a hairbrush and go hunting for him in her nightgown?

No, she'd go get Jack, she thought. They'd figure out what to do.

She went over, picked up the panic button and pressed the red pad.

In a nanosecond, Smith came crashing through the balcony doors, wood splintering and falling to the floor as he broke the lock. His gun was drawn and his eyes were black as hell while he scanned the room. As she looked at him, she knew without a doubt that he was capable of deadly force.

And that she'd made an awful mistake.

"Oh . . ." Words failed her. "Shit."

After he'd looked around the room and over her body, he demanded, "What's wrong?"

Grace felt badly. And foolish. "Er—nothing."

"Why the hell did you hit the panic button then?"

"I'm so sorry. I didn't know where you were and—"

"Jesus," Smith swore as he tucked his gun into its holster. "That thing is not a pager."

"I know. I really shouldn't have used it unless I had an emergency." She offered him a chagrined smile. "Believe me, I'm never touching that thing again."

"No, I want you to use it. Just make sure there's a good reason to." He went over and inspected the door. "This is going to need a serious repair job."

Shaking his head, he shut the doors and propped them closed with a chair.

"What were you doing out on the porch?" she blurted. "Did you need anything?"

There was a long pause. She met his eyes.

Do it, she thought. Just say the words.

"I need you."

Before he could get a word out, she approached him.

"You told me that we could have one night together. I know you've regretted the invitation but you have to admit the two of us are driving each other crazy. If you're worried about being distracted or whether I'm going to get hurt, do you honestly think things can get any more complicated? Whether you want to admit it or not, we are involved, John. I think we should stop talking. And start making love."

With sharp movements, he took off the jacket he'd worn to dinner, as if the room had suddenly grown hot.

"You know I'm right," she said softly.

His eyes fixed on the door to the hall and, when he finally moved, she was sure it would be to leave. Instead, he came over and wrapped his arms around her.

"God help us," he said.

Grace raised her mouth for his kiss but he pulled back his head.

"If we spend the night together, it won't change the ending," he said. "I'm still going to leave."

Staring into his eyes, she said, "I know. But you're here now, aren't you? So shut up and kiss me."

With a sardonic smile, he murmured, "Are you getting tough on me?"

"Yes." She pulled his mouth down to hers.

As their lips touched, she heard a groan of need rise from him. His tongue dove into her mouth and she met the thrust passionately. The kiss quickly took on a wild edge.

Roughly, he stripped her robe from her shoulders and then she felt her nightgown drift down to the floor. As the cool air hit her skin, she circled her arms around his shoulders but stopped when she felt the gun. He pulled back and took off the holster and then his shirt. As he undressed, his eyes never left her face and she relished the expanse of his chest and his ribbed stomach. She reached out, touching warm, male skin.

"I want to see you," he said, moving her over to the bed and into a pool of light. As he looked at her, she heard a hiss and was stunned by the dark need in his face. He sat, or perhaps it was even collapsed, onto the bed.

He reached up and took her breasts into his palms, his thumbs rubbing the nipples, which were already taut. They peaked even further with his touch and her head fell back as a moan of desire escaped her. Leaning forward, he took the tip of one breast into his mouth and she gripped his shoulders, then his neck, then his head. His mouth went lower, down the flat plane of her stomach and over to her hip, his teeth gently nipping at her skin.

And then, as if he couldn't stand it any longer, he pulled her forward on top of him. His arms gripped her body tightly and his arousal was thick and hard, pressing into her. She reached down in between them, searching for his belt buckle, as he continued to kiss her. With one fluid motion, he rolled her over, pulled back and took off his pants. The first moment she felt him totally naked against her, Grace felt a surge of heat that was almost pain.

Time halted as he explored her body, kissing her neck and her breasts, covering her skin with his hands. She thought dimly that no one had ever taken such care to arouse her before and she felt herself come alive.

"I need you to touch me," he growled against her mouth.

With confidence she never would have thought herself capable of, she began to stroke him, from his wide shoulders and his chest, down the rigid contours of his stomach, to the curve of his hip bones. When she went lower, taking him in her hands, he braced himself against the headboard as spasms wracked his big body. Marveling that she was the one he needed so badly, she began to pleasure him.

She didn't get far. With a flash of movement, he grabbed her and drew her to him, his tongue thrusting into her mouth, his hands going over her back restlessly. She sensed that he was trying to be gentle but that his need made him rough. She wasn't afraid. She only wanted more.

"I can't hold out longer," he groaned against her mouth. He rolled over on top of her and his eyes bored into hers as his weight pressed her down into the mattress. Arching under him, feeling a swelling, pulsating need at her core, she brought up her knees. He settled in between her legs with an expression that was close to anguish.

John pulled back, looking down into her eyes. "Are you sure?"

She nodded and pulled him to her mouth.

With an aching slowness, he entered her, filling her body with a lush thickness that was her undoing. She cried out and he swallowed her incomprehensible words as he began moving inside of her. Harder and faster he mastered her body until they came together, exploding with hoarse cries, holding on tightly to each other.

In the stillness that followed, a glow settled in her, but she wasn't sure what he was feeling. She glanced at him from under her lashes. His eyes were shut and the harsh planes of his face were startlingly relaxed.

"You okay?" he said.

She smiled. "Yes. I am."

He looked at her, stroking back a strand of hair from her face. "You're one hell of a woman."

"Really?"

"Yes. Really." He kissed her. Long and slow.

She reached up and grabbed on to his back.

As he grew hard inside of her again, she sighed and gave herself up to the pleasure.

Grace woke up alone and she could tell it was late in the morning. The sun, which was streaming in through the windows and wandering lazily across the floor, had reached as far as the end of her bed. She stretched, feeling all kinds of new sensations, and smiled to herself as she looked at the mess they'd made of the bed.

After making love to John all night long, she felt like a new woman. He'd been everything she'd hoped he would be, both passionate and tender, and he sure as hell knew how to use that hard body of his. It had been the single most satisfying night in her life.

Looking across the room at the chair that was braced against the French doors, she did wonder how she was going to explain the damage, however.

She was just getting up and drawing on her robe when she heard a knock on the door. She was surprised to find her mother standing outside in the hall.

"This is early for you," Grace said, trying to smooth down her hair. She was well aware it was a matted mess.

"No, it isn't. You slept through breakfast."

Her mother stepped forward, forcing Grace to move out of the way. Her eyes went to the broken door. "I thought I heard something in here last night. What happened?"

Grace shrugged. "I locked myself out on the terrace by mistake."

"Why didn't you use the door at the end of the hall?"

"That was locked as well."

Carolina went over and inspected the broken handle. "I will have to get Gus up here to repair this."

"Do you want something?"

Her mother turned. "Why is the bedroom that I gave Mr. Smith uninhabited?"

Grace hesitated. "Because he's not staying in it."

"And where is he staying?"

"Across the hall."

There was a terrible pause. Grace straightened her shoulders as her mother's eyes turned cold.

"Is there any particular reason his original room was not to his liking?"

"Mother—"

"You lied to me, didn't you?" The words were whispered fiercely.

"About what?"

"About—about . . . that man being your lover!"

Not exactly, Grace thought. Yesterday, he hadn't been.

"Mother, you're blowing this out of proportion."

"Am I?" Carolina pointed a finger at Smith's coat, which was hanging over the back of a chair. "Then perhaps there is another explanation for why your bed is in disarray and that man's jacket is in your room."

Grace prayed her flush wasn't as obvious as it felt. "We went for a walk. I was cold and he gave it to me."

"And you expect me to believe that?" Disgust cut lines through her mother's carefully tended forehead.

"You know, this conversation didn't go well yesterday. And it's not getting better with time."

"Is it too much to ask that you fulfill your obligations as a member of this family and behave like a lady?"

Grace sighed in exasperation. "For heaven's sake, this isn't the Victorian era."

"And more's the pity," Carolina said with bite. "Back then, people understood the importance of manners and appearances."

"Just who do you think I have to impress, Mother? Other than you, that is."

"Don't be argumentative. You know people are always watching. And I assure you, there is nothing quaint or nostalgic about breaking your wedding vows." Carolina pointed to the open door, through which Smith's room was visible. "I want that man out of this house."

Grace's eyes widened. "I can't do that."

"Yes, you will."

"Mother, John Smith works with me."

"I don't care if he's your doctor or your lawyer or your garbageman. I don't want him under your father's roof."

"Then I'm going, too."

Those four words brought the conversation to a halt.

"I beg your pardon?"

Grace raised a weary hand to her temple, trying to rub away some of the tension that had crawled up her spine and into her head. "Look, I don't want to upset you."

"It's a bit late for that."

"But I think it might be better if we just go."

Carolina sniffed with disapproval. "There's no reason to be theatrical, Grace. And I'm only looking out for your best interests."

"It feels as though all you're doing is making accusations."

"Better me than the press." Carolina's eyes narrowed shrewdly. "It would be so very public, if you were to indulge in any indiscretions. You know that, don't you?"

Grace nodded through her frustration. "Of course I do."

"We may have lost your father but we still have the power of his name. I don't want anything to happen to this family's reputation."

Grace stiffened as the implications of what her mother said sank in.

"Would that be the greater tragedy for you?" she whispered. "Harder to bear than losing him?"

Carolina ignored the question. "You are the only valid heir to his legacy. I don't want you to throw that all away for some . . . man. You married into royalty—"

"Stop it, Mother," Grace interrupted. "Please."

Turning away, she went over to the closet and pulled out her suitcase.

"You are truly going?"

She found her mother's shock grating. "Yes, I am."

"But what will I tell the guests? After I already rescheduled the party to this evening due to your outbursts."

With a resigned shake of the head, Grace murmured, "I'm sure you'll think of something."

As she began taking things out of the closet, her mother made a disparaging sound in the back of her throat.

"Well, if this is going to be your attitude, perhaps it is best that you go." Carolina paused at the door. "Although do me the courtesy of saying your good-byes, will you? It's the least you can do."

As soon as Grace was alone, she slumped on the bed and looked over at the clothes she'd thrown haphazardly into the suitcase. The idea that she might not ever be comfortable at Willings again, that the division between her and her mother would only get larger now that her father's buffering influence was gone, disappointed her.

But maybe staying away was the only option. There was something about her mother that sucked the will to live right out of her, she thought. All that cold elegance, that indefatigable censure, it was like being next to an emotional black hole.

When she heard the soft tones of the grandfather clock down the hall, she realized she'd better tell John they were leaving.

She went across the hall and knocked on his doorjamb. "John?"

He came out of the bathroom wearing a T-shirt and black pants. There was a towel hanging around his neck and his hands were gripping both ends, making his biceps stand out.

A flush sped through her but, when their eyes met and he showed little response, disappointment had her squaring her shoulders.

"Good morning," she said.

He nodded. "Morning."

She sure could have used a smile. Some hint of warmth. The touch of his hand. Instead, he seemed to have retreated into himself and she was reminded of when she'd first seen him and wondered whether there was anything behind the hardness.

"Ummm—There's been a change in plans. We're leaving," she said.

"Fine."

She frowned. The night before, he had held her tightly against him, whispered her name hoarsely as his body had come into hers. Staring at his impassive face, she thought it was as if everything that had happened the night before had been a dream.

One of hers. Not his.

She hesitated. "Right. I'm going to pack."

"I'll be ready in ten minutes."

As he turned away, her eyes clung to his back. "John, what's wrong?"

"Nothing." The word was said over his shoulder as he walked into the bathroom.

She heard water rushing into a sink and the soft hiss of a shaving cream can.

Grace followed him. "Why are you being this way?"

His eyes were fixed on the mirror as he picked up a razor and cut a swath through the white beard he'd given himself.

"What way, exactly?"

"Talk to me, please."

"I don't have anything to say."

"Nothing?"

His eyebrow cocked as he rinsed the razor off and went back to work on his beard. "You want me to make something up?"

"Just so you know," she said roughly, "if your goal is to prove there's no happy ending in store for us, your mission's accomplished."

Going back to her own room, she realized she'd made a rash miscalculation by assuming things couldn't get any harder if they made love.

19

As THE jet descended over the runway at Teterboro, Smith looked out the oval window next to his seat at the rushing ground. He'd spent the hour of air time with his eyes closed, but he hadn't been sleeping.

Ever since he'd woken up next to Grace that morning, he'd been trying to convince himself he wasn't falling in love with her. The lecture wasn't going well, even though it was based on totally rational principles. Hell, he of all people should know that one night didn't mean anything. It was just two bodies in the dark, fulfilling evolution's prime directive.

So why did he feel like his center of gravity was off?

And why the hell did he behave like such a jerk to her?

He remembered how she'd looked standing in the doorway to the bathroom as he'd shaved. Her words before she'd left had made him feel despicable.

Christ, what a hypocrite he was. Telling her that she deserved better than the way her husband had treated her only to lay on the silent treatment after they'd . . . made love.

Made love. Those were the right words, he realized.

The night before had been about so much more than a good lay, and he was struggling to come to terms with his response. Things like sticking around or even wanting to be with a woman again after he'd had her once were not what were usually on his mind the morning after.

He wanted to talk with Grace. He did. He just felt like he had to get his mind straight. He needed something to say that made sense to him.

Well, at least he knew where the hell to start. He needed to apologize for not handling his confusion better. A little introspection was one thing. Shutting her out completely was unacceptable.

As the plane landed on the tarmac and the reverse thrusters began to slow them down, he looked across the aisle. Grace was going through her monthly reports and had spread papers out everywhere: on the seat next to her, on the floor, across the built-in table to her right. She was dressed casually, wearing a well-fitting sweater and a pair of light wool slacks, but she still managed to look elegant.

He never would have imagined being attracted to someone who was so refined. Or so expensive-looking.

He tried to narrow down why she was so different from the other women he'd known. All kinds of images came to mind. Her reaching out to touch his scars, her chin kicked up in the midst of her fear, her shy eyes as she stripped for him. She was such a contradiction, assertive yet vulnerable, regal yet down-to-earth, passionate yet reserved.

And she was sexy as hell. All he could think about was taking off her clothes so he could taste her again.

The plane pivoted, sending a shaft of sunlight through the cabin. As the flash traveled around, it fell on the count's sapphire engagement ring. The gem sparkled brilliantly.

A rich man's fancy jewels, he thought. On a rich man's fancy woman.

He wanted her to take them off, but knew he had no right to be possessive. Especially after the way he'd treated her.

"Grace?"

She didn't look up and her voice was brisk. "Yes?"

"I'm sorry."

He watched as she circled a paragraph and wrote something in the margin. "About what."

"This morning."

She looked up toward the front of the plane, as if she'd just noticed they'd landed. "Don't worry about it."

She began picking up the papers, shuffling them together into neat piles and putting them into folders.

"Grace. Look at me." When she didn't, he unbuckled his seat belt and went over to her. "I'm honestly sorry that I hurt you this morning."

Her hands stilled. There was a long pause.

"You didn't hurt me. I hurt myself because I knew what the rules were." She looked up at him, her eyes somber. "You told me all along what you wanted and what you could give. My ego made me look further into what you did to my body than I should have."

"Grace—"

"Are you going to leave?"

"No." He frowned. "What makes you think I might?"

"That's pretty obvious, isn't it?"

"I'm still going to take care of you," he said, meeting her eyes directly. "Nothing's changed."

She took a deep breath and let it out. "Unfortunately, I suppose that's true."

The plane came to a standstill.

"I wasn't prepared for what happened last night," he said grimly.

"Look, you don't owe me anything. Apologies or explanations." She shot him an overly bright smile. "I'm a big girl. I can take care of myself. You should just forget about it."

Throwing off her seat belt, she reached down for her purse, gathered her folders in her arms, and rushed off the plane as if she couldn't wait to get rid of him.

Christ.

He knew that getting involved with her would be one hell of a complication. Now he was acting like a head case, she was hurt, and they were back in New York, where the killer had probably spent the weekend sharpening his knives.

If this job were going any worse, Smith thought, someone would be bleeding.

Eddie was waiting for them in front of the terminal and he helped get the luggage into the Explorer. The man was in a sunny mood.

"I was surprised you came back so early," he said as they got into the car. "What with the good weather and all."

Smith grunted while Grace offered the man a tight smile.

"Say, how are the creative writing classes going?" she asked him.

Eddie smiled into the rearview mirror as he pulled away from the curb. "They're going real well. We're doing dramatic tension right now."

How appropriate, Smith thought.

The ride into the city was quiet and strained. When they slowed to a stop in front of the penthouse, Smith got out first and was looking around as Grace stepped onto the sidewalk.

When the release on the back hatch popped, Smith went around to pick up their luggage. He'd grabbed Grace's bag and was pulling it free of the car when she went to take it from him and stumbled on the curb. He had just slipped his arm around her waist to keep her from falling when they heard her name being called out.

They both looked to the sound just as a photographer leaned out of a car window and started snapping pictures. With the flashbulb going off like a strobe light, the car careened into traffic.

Smith cursed and almost ran after the guy but he didn't want to leave Grace. Even as he trained his eyes on the license plate, he knew it was too late. The pictures had been taken and there wasn't much he could do about it.

As he looked at Grace, he saw exhaustion settle into her eyes.

"It's going to be everywhere tomorrow," she said, wearily.

It was past eleven o'clock when Grace decided to take a warm shower in hopes of making herself sleepy. She was on her way to the bathroom when the phone rang and she let it go into voice mail. There was no one she wanted to talk to at this hour.

If it was Lieutenant Marks with another gruesome announcement, he'd call John. And if it was her mother, she definitely didn't want to pick the thing up. She'd left a message at Willings with a warning about the pictures, but she didn't want to fight about the situation. Not tonight.

As she took off her robe, she had a deadweight in her stomach even though she hadn't eaten dinner. Smith had cooked up something that smelled appetizing, but she'd turned him down when he'd asked her to sit with him. If she was trying to shut him out, however, she didn't have much luck. He had a stranglehold on her mind.

He'd told her he was sorry and she believed he had regrets. They'd been pretty obvious both in his eyes and in his apology. She told herself she couldn't be surprised. And, at least he had the decency to care that she was hurt. She had a feeling he hadn't spared the effort with a lot of the other women he'd had.

She groaned, remembering again how it had felt to have him on top of her, kissing her, touching her.

God help her, she wanted to be with him again. And yes, even if it meant getting hurt in the morning.

It was hard not to be disappointed with her libido and she wondered why she couldn't be attracted to someone more reasonable. After all, Eugene Fessnick, CPA, was single. She could probably even get her taxes done for free if they were dating.

But no, she had to pick someone who was never going to settle down. Someone who was hot and passionate and managed to create chaos and havoc in her life. The El Niño of men.

Clearly, her sense of self-preservation needed a serious overhaul.

She was toweling off when a dark shape appeared in the doorway. Quickly covering herself, she looked at John's silhouette in surprise. In the quiet stillness, he was overpowering and she sensed the tension in his body.

Had it been Lieutenant Marks after all?

She licked her lips nervously. "Is there something wrong?"

His voice was deep and husky. "I wanted to make sure you were okay before I went to bed."

"I'm fine." When he didn't leave, she pulled the towel up a little higher and tucked the loose end in. She couldn't see his face clearly but sensed there was something upsetting him.

She frowned. "Are you okay?"

He pushed a hand through his hair. "No, I'm goddamn not."

"What's the problem?"

"I want to make love. With you. Now."

Grace sucked in her breath as words exploded out of him.

"I know I really screwed up this morning. I'm inexperienced at this whole—" He moved his hand back and forth as if he were searching for the right word. "Man-woman thing. It's a goddamn nightmare. I'm pissed off at myself and have spent all night dreaming up apologies that are like something out of a goddamn soap opera. I'm wondering where in the hell my logic's gone, I can't get rid of this ache in my chest, and if there was a way to go back to this morning and do it over again, I would. Every time I close my eyes, I see you naked in my arms, looking up at me with trust in your eyes and I want to put my hand through a wall."

He started pacing. "It's driving me crazy. I'm driving me crazy. Christ, there's got to be an easier way than this. How the hell do people put up with this confusion when they finally meet someone who matters? It's like being thrown into a cave without a goddamn light. I've never felt so fuck-frigging disorientated in my life and, let me tell you, I've been in some pretty hairy messes before."

Speechless, Grace watched him as he continued to talk. She'd never heard him say more than a couple of sentences at any one time and he'd certainly never been so candid about his feelings.

"This is awful. I feel bad. You feel bad. All I want to do is hold you in my arms. I don't know what's happening to me. I only know that I want you and I wish I hadn't hurt you. And . . ."

He took a deep breath as he rambled to a halt.

Grace shook her head and smiled ruefully. "That's quite a mouthful."

"Well, I thought about it over dinner."

"Obviously."

It was hard not to forgive him when he seemed so sincerely at odds with himself and she could feel her body warming. But she reminded herself that even though he'd apologized for what had happened, it wasn't as if he was promising to stay in her life after the job was over.

They had tonight, though, she thought. And tomorrow morning. After he left, she was only going to have her memories.

"Come here," she said, holding out her arms.

His eyes widened, as if she'd done the unexpected, and his body threw off waves of intensity as he stepped forward. She put her hand on his chest. The warmth of him came through his shirt and she could feel his heart beating under her palm.

"I'm glad you told me all that."

His eyes closed, as if he were reliving the disappointment he felt with himself.

"You've got to believe me, the last thing I want to do is hurt you."

Grace lifted her lips for his kiss and pulled his head down. His mouth was soft on hers, a surprisingly gentle brush, and she felt him take her left hand into his.

"Will you take off those rings tonight?" he asked.

She didn't hesitate. With careless movements, she removed her sapphire and diamonds and tossed them onto the marble counter.

John picked her up and carried her to her bed. When he put her down and laid on top of her, bracing his powerful arms on either side of her body, she felt anticipation flow through her veins like a drug. As his mouth took hers, she surrendered to the desire.

Grace was sound asleep in John's arms when the phone began to ring at six thirty the next morning. When it started in on a third course, she picked up the receiver.

"Where have you been?" her mother demanded before Grace had time to squeeze out a hello. "And why didn't you answer the phone last night?"

"Was that you?" Grace sat up, pushing her hair out of her face.

John stirred and moved with her, keeping his arm around her waist. She was relieved he didn't leave right away.

"Of course it was me," her mother snapped. "I thought you might appreciate knowing that I took care of your little problem. I spent most of last evening entertaining phone calls from Cameron Brast. In the middle of my party, I might add."

Grace grimaced. Brast was the publisher of one of New York's rags.

Her mother went on. "The picture of that Smith man with his arms around you will not be appearing in the papers this morning. It took all my powers of persuasion to block its publication and, courtesy of your indiscretion, I am now indebted to that odious little Brast man."

"I'm sorry you—"

"Equally outrageous, however, is the fact that your husband called me to say that some reporter had reached him in Paris for a comment. Ranulf was practically inconsolable last night. He'd tried to phone you, and when he was unable to get through, he called here. Have you no shame!"

Grace shut her eyes. "Mother, Ranulf and I are getting a divorce."

Carolina's swiftly indrawn breath came through the phone like a draft. "Oh, my God. It's that *man*, isn't it? You're leaving Ranulf for some—"

"Ranulf and I separated right after father's death. Before I even met John."

"My God . . . But why is he divorcing you?"

Grace was almost able to keep the frustration out of her voice. "I'm the one who's asking for a divorce."

She could practically hear the gears in her mother's brain grinding to a halt.

"But, whatever for?"

"We have irreconcilable differences."

Starting with the fact that we never loved each other, she thought.

"Come now, how different can you two be? His family is very well thought of. Perhaps you could just try again."

"That's just what Father said," Grace replied.

There was a pause. "You spoke to him about this?"

"Yes. Over the summer. He told me to go back to Ranulf and I did. Things only got worse."

"I don't understand. What happened? You always looked so happy together."

"Appearances can be deceiving, Mother."

There was a long silence on the phone.

"Oh Grace, I can't bear the thought of all this. First your father and now your marriage. When will it end?"

"I'm sorry this has upset you." It was hard to keep the disappointment in her mother to herself. She could have used some support from the woman, but knew full well that had never been how their relationship had worked.

"You know, your father and I had difficult times," Carolina said, a sliver of hope in her voice. "We worked through them. It can be done."

Grace found it hard to believe her parents had faced anything more arduous than what to wear for a dinner party.

"Mother, the truth is, I never should have married Ranulf. I had doubts from the very beginning. Even at our engagement party."

As Smith got out of her bed and walked naked into his bedroom, she momentarily forgot her mother.

"But what are you going to do? As a woman alone?"

"I'll manage somehow," Grace said with an edge of sarcasm. "It's amazing what girls are allowed to do these days. Were you aware we can vote now?"

"There's no reason to be hostile. And I must say, I am seriously distressed that with your marriage ending, your first instinct is to throw yourself into some turgid affair with that . . . Smith man."

"John is my bodyguard."

Her mother fell silent. "Your bodyguard?"

"That was why he needed to change rooms. He needed to be closer to me."

"Good Lord, what do you need one for? Are you okay?"

"I—I'm fine." She released a frustrated breath. Having just consoled her mother about her impending divorce, she didn't feel up to soothing the woman over the murders of her friends. "I'd better go, Mother. It's time for me to go to work."

"But today's a holiday. Columbus Day."

"I know it is, but I still have a job to do. I'll talk with you later."

Pushing the conversation out of her mind, Grace hung up the phone and went down the hall. She was about to ask Smith if he wanted to join her in the shower when she heard his voice drifting out of his room.

"I don't know when I'll be free. It could be another couple of weeks before I can leave New York, which means I wouldn't be able to go to the Middle East until early November."

Grace turned around and went back to her room, feeling sick to her stomach. The pain told her how much she was deluding herself. Somewhere deep inside, she'd been harboring hope that he would stay. Hearing the logistics of his leaving was a slap in the face.

She took a quick shower and, before shutting herself in her dressing room, she called out to him that the bathroom was free.

Sitting down in front of the vanity's mirror, she felt like crying. As she heard the sound of the water being turned on, she decided that what she needed to do, instead of mope around feeling sorry for herself, was to get out of the penthouse. She realized it had been days since she'd gone for a run and the idea of being free for a little bit was irresistible. All she needed was something short and quick, enough to clear her mind and help her get through the day without tearing up in front of him.

She just needed something to remind herself of her strength.

Throwing on a pair of sweats and her running shoes, she was on the street in a matter of minutes. As she stepped out from underneath the awning, she looked up. A soft rain was falling from a gray sky but the soggy day didn't bother her as she started off at a quick pace.

Out of habit, she took her normal route, heading up Central Park West and then going into the park. She picked one of the jogging trails that would keep her close to the street, yet still get her away from the noise and pollution of the traffic.

As she ran, her feet kicked up water from puddles which drenched her legs. She could feel the sweat of her skin meet the cold dampness seeping through the sweats and she pushed herself a little harder.

She'd gone about a quarter mile when she realized someone was following her.

Her first thought was that it must be John and she wanted to curse when she realized what she'd done. He was going to be irate that she'd taken off without him and had every right to be.

What the hell had she been thinking?

Not much at all, she thought as she slowed down and turned around.

It wasn't Smith.

Fear flooded her senses, temporarily wiping out the feel of her body, the sounds in her ears, everything. She quickly assessed the person behind her. She couldn't see the face because whoever it was had on a raincoat with the hood up. She didn't wait to get a good ID.

Grace started to sprint, looking left and right in hopes of seeing some other joggers. Because of the rain, she was all alone on the path.

Running as fast as she could, she hurled herself head-long through the trees and across the grass, trying to remember how to get to the street. Her heartbeat was ripping through her chest and her legs were numb from exertion, but she pressed on.

She looked over her shoulder. Whoever it was, they were keeping pace.

Images of Mimi, Suzanna, and Cuppie, all dead with their throats cut out, came to mind. She reached down into her legs for more speed. Angling toward home, she tried to reassure herself she could make it back.

But she wasn't sure she'd be able to.

Was this it, she thought with terror. Here in Central Park? In a flash of panic, she remembered what Smith had said about his clients living longer lives because they did what he told them to do.

She had broken one of his simplest rules.

Suddenly, through the rushing sound in her ears, she

heard a hoarse voice calling out. She realized the person following her was yelling something.

And then a word she never again thought she'd be referred to as broke through her fear.

"Starfish!"

Her father's voice came to her, *Buck up, Starfish, let's see that smile.*

Grace's stride broke as she wrenched around in surprise and tripped. Hitting the pavement in a slide, she felt her shin and knee getting scraped, but that was the least of her worries. As the stranger came upon her, she raised her arms up as if to ward off blows.

"I—I'm not going to hurt you . . ." Grace was surprised to hear a woman's voice, one that was harsh from heaving breaths. "Really . . ."

When her pursuer did nothing threatening but instead propped her hands on her knees and tried to catch her breath, Grace thought she might just have been spared.

As soon as she found her own voice, she said, "Who are you? And how did you know my name—"

The stranger pulled back her hood and Grace frowned.

There was something familiar about the woman's face, as if she'd met her before or seen—

Oh my God, Grace thought, going cold.

Her father.

The stranger had the same coloring he'd had, the same shaped face, similar deep-set, blue eyes.

Squinting against the rain and the impossibility of what she was seeing, she wondered if she was losing her mind.

"I'm . . . your . . . half sister. Callie," the woman said, still breathing heavily.

20

SMITH GOT out of the shower, thinking it was a damn shame he'd missed taking one with Grace. Even though they'd made love three times during the course of the night, he wanted more. He couldn't believe he'd thought a single night with her would be enough. He was going to need months, maybe even years.

It was a tragedy they didn't have that kind of time.

Waking up next to her had been another revelation. After years of leaving women as soon as he could get his pants back on, he'd rolled over next to Grace and had no interest in being anywhere else. He'd watched her as she'd slept, absorbing the look of her lashes against her cheek, the slight parting of her lips, her hair as it flowed over the pillow.

Smith toweled off, threw on some clothes and went out, expecting her to still be in her dressing room. When she wasn't, he looked at her bed and got caught up in remembering what she'd done to him in the night. As she'd grown more comfortable and confident with him, she'd become bold, demanding . . . innovative. His body began to overheat.

He was definitely taking a shower with her tomorrow morning.

Smith was about to go out and find her in the kitchen when he saw the count's rings on the top of her bureau. He picked up the engagement one. The thing was heavy, the stone a glorious dark blue, the diamonds on the sides sparkling with white fire.

What kind of ring would he give her? It'd be nothing like the carats and carats of sapphire he was holding. It would be simple. A band, maybe—

He shook his head. He wasn't buying rings for anyone.

And certainly not for her.

He was a reformed juvenile delinquent, an ex-military man, a former spy. He sure as hell wasn't the right guy to become the second husband of Grace Woodward Hall, previously known as the Countess von Sharone.

Period, end of story.

He let the sapphire slip out of his fingers and watched as it bounced and then wobbled to a standstill.

He was surprised he'd even thought about marriage at all, even if it was just hypothetical. Wives were even more of a no-no than girlfriends in his line of work, because families were the ultimate threat to clear thinking. The more ties you had to people, the more stability you courted, the more chances you had to be vulnerable.

He'd always thought it was a mistake for people to assume that if they had a home and a wife and a couple of kids that somehow the world was a safe place. A lot of them figured that just because they had a cup of coffee sitting across the table from the same person every morning they were somehow secure. Smith knew otherwise. Like everyone else, those folks were bargaining with fate; they just didn't know they were at the negotiating table.

He knew he was better off alone, because as long as he was a solo operator, all he had to worry about was death. And that was one force of nature that didn't scare him. Once you were dead, nothing mattered.

His clarity of thinking about the pitfalls of families had always been a source of pride but now he wasn't feeling quite so self-satisfied. Meeting Grace was changing what he thought about having a home. For the first time, he could understand the attraction of dependents. The truth was, he liked hearing her move around at night. He liked seeing her in her bathrobe in the morning with her hair a mess. He liked the way she snored softly when she slept on her back. He liked her warmth next to him—

Smith's instincts pricked to attention.

He listened carefully to the silence of the penthouse for only a moment and then he ran down the hall. He looked in the living room, the dining room, and then pushed his way into the kitchen. When he burst out into the front hall, a voice inside of his head had started screaming.

As Grace stared up at the woman, she blinked away the rain that was falling into her eyes. She felt the hard pavement under her butt, the cold, wet sweatshirt hanging off her shoulders, a hot stinging pain in her leg.

So this had to be real, she thought.

"I don't have a sister," she whispered even though her eyes were telling her otherwise. The resemblance to her father was subtle but undeniable and a feeling of betrayal came over her in a sickening rush.

"How do you know about Starfish?" she demanded roughly.

The reply was soft and full of pauses, as if the woman wasn't sure how Grace would react.

"When I was little, I saw a picture of you and him in the newspaper and I asked who you were. He said you were his other daughter and I wanted to know what your name was. He told me it was Starfish. I've always thought of you as that. Even when I learned your real name."

Grace felt a sting of jealousy go through her, that this other person, this stranger, knew the special name her father had given her.

How dare he be dead when this all comes out, she thought, irrationally.

As she struggled to her feet, the woman put out her hand but Grace refused the gesture.

The woman's arm slowly fell to her side. "I should have written to you first but I figured you'd think I was some kind of kook. You probably do, anyway. I just needed to meet you in person. I've seen you in pictures for so many years. It was like you weren't real. So beautiful and glamorous. I used to pretend . . ." A sad smile stretched her lips. "I just wanted to meet the other part of him. The bigger part . . . of my father."

Grace stared at the woman. Rain was darkening her

red hair, laying it flat and wet on her scalp. Her blue eyes seemed to have old shadows behind them.

"What's your name again?" Grace asked.

"Callie. Actually, it's Calla Lily."

A shiver went through Grace. The name. The name she'd heard her father say in the dream.

She shook her head, feeling reality shift and spin as her brain struggled to reorder her life.

Grace refocused on the woman. "You look like him."

"I know. It's the red hair, I think."

"Your eyes, too." Grace heard the anger in her own voice.

She wanted to tell the woman to go to hell, to accuse her of lying. At the very least, she wanted to have never gone out for the run, as if that would have somehow magically prevented their meeting.

"I know this must be a shock."

Now there was an understatement.

Grace began to wrack her childhood memories for signs of her father's double life. He had been gone a lot. He was a very successful man, so of course, he always seemed to be on the way to a meeting or coming home from one. Had those trips been excuses to go to his other life? She thought about how busy her days at the Foundation were. Before he'd died, he'd done everything she was doing as well as looked after the family's extensive investments. Where had he found the energy?

Well, obviously it had come from somewhere, she thought. Somehow, he had found the time to lead another life. To create another life.

Callie raised a hand and wiped some hair out of her face. "Now that I'm standing here with you, I don't know what I thought I'd accomplish."

Grace looked deeply into the woman's eyes.

Her father's daughter.

"It was you," she said abruptly, focusing on the slicker. "Watching me when I went in and out of work, waiting for me outside of restaurants. You followed me to the funeral, didn't you."

"Yes." Callie looked away. "It was hard to approach you. I kept thinking I could just go up to you but you were never alone and I—I didn't want to cause a scene. As for the funeral, I just had to see him buried because a part of me refused to believe he was gone. The papers didn't say where the services were going to be held, just the date. I followed you because I didn't know how else I could say good-bye to him."

Grace's stomach lurched and she started shaking her head again.

"I have to go," she mumbled.

As she began walking blindly, she felt the rain flowing down her face. Or it might have been tears.

Calla Lily.

Her father's voice echoed in her head.

She'd gone a couple of yards when she paused and looked back.

The woman was staring after her, looking small underneath the slicker.

That coat was not expensive, Grace thought. Just a cheap, plastic rain jacket. And her shoes were old, serviceable. She wasn't dressed like someone who had money.

Was she looking to contest the will? Was she really just after some cash?

Grace thought of John. He could find out exactly who the woman was and sniff out whether she was someone with ulterior motives.

"It's cold out here," Grace said. "Do you live nearby?"

"Not really. My apartment's in Chelsea."

Keep your friends close and your enemies closer, Grace thought. Words to be damned by.

"Then come back with me and get dry."

Blue eyes regarded her warily. "Are you sure?"

No, she wasn't.

Grace nodded anyway and Callie approached with caution.

"You're bleeding," she said, pointing with alarm.

Grace glanced down at herself. She could see the scrape on her leg through a tear in the sweatpants. Blood was staining her running shoes.

That should probably be hurting, she thought. Funny, she felt nothing at all.

"Are you sure you can walk?" Callie asked. "I can get us a cab."

"I'll be fine."

Whenever this horror movie of a life of mine stops adding new scenes. And new characters.

They went back to the street together, moving slowly in spite of the rain because Grace was limping.

"You really didn't know, did you?" Callie said softly. "I'd always wondered if you might have guessed. It must be really hard to find out . . . It's been twenty-seven years and I still find the whole thing difficult to deal with."

Hearing Callie's age set off another cascade of anger. Twenty-seven years. Her father had been living a lie for over a quarter century. He'd made them all live a lie.

Grace thought bitterly back to that lecture of his on the importance of staying with Ranulf. He'd even thrown in a line about the significance of the vows they'd taken, a comment that was now harder to stomach than his recitations of the von Sharone family's prominence. Courtesy of Callie chasing her down, his words stank with hypocrisy and Grace found herself wanting those three extra months she'd spent with Ranulf back.

As well as all those years she'd believed her father was an honorable man.

When they stepped under the awning of Grace's building, Callie paused and shook the rain out of her jacket and her hair. Looking uncomfortable, she followed Grace inside, her eyes moving over the uniformed man who opened the door for them, the luxurious lobby, the brass and glass elevator.

"This is a beautiful building," she murmured as they rode up to the top floor.

When they stepped out of the elevator, Grace frowned. Her front door was wide open and an unfamiliar blond man, who was big as a linebacker and dressed in black, was standing in her front hall. When he caught sight of her, his smile wasn't friendly.

"I believe your countess is back," he said dryly.

John exploded into the doorway and Grace took an involuntary step back. He was livid with rage.

"Where the *hell* did you go?" he bellowed.

She had to fight the urge not to get back on the elevator and disappear again.

Clearing her throat, she said very quietly, "I went out for a run. I'm sorry I didn't come and get you—"

"What the fuck were you thinking!" He jabbed his forefinger at her. "You don't go *anywhere* without me. That's our agreement. You want to tell me what the fuck was going through your head?"

She glanced back at Callie, who seemed to be trying to melt into the wall. Grace didn't blame her.

"You need to calm down," she whispered to John. "Everything is fine."

"Yeah, everything is just fine. I'll go call off the police now and tell all my men to go home because everything is a-okay. No fucking problem, *Countess*." As he marched back into the living room, he put his phone to his ear and started talking in short, angry bursts.

"Maybe this isn't the best time," Callie said softly.

"No, he'll calm down."

Hopefully, she added to herself.

As Grace stepped inside, she saw three other men in her living room, all tall, wide-shouldered guys in dark clothes. They looked like some kind of military squad even though they weren't wearing uniforms. When their eyes settled on her all at once, she felt like a kid who'd violated curfew.

Or an agitator who needed to be eliminated.

"Hello," she said to the group.

The man who'd been at the door when they'd arrived, the handsome blond one, barely inclined his head. The rest showed no response at all.

John clipped his phone shut and addressed them. "Marks and his boys are turning around and heading back to the station. Thanks for coming."

"Glad she showed," said the blond one. He shot John a sardonic grin. "Otherwise we were going to hog-tie you to a chair before you hurt yourself."

"Fuck you, Tiny."

Tiny threw a beefy arm around John and grabbed him

on the back of the neck, giving him a shake. In a much lower voice, he said, "You okay?"

John said something under his breath and Grace watched as the two men's eyes met and held.

"Okay, we're outta here, ladies," Tiny said to the men. As they walked past her, he paused and said, "Do us all a favor, Countess, and stick close to home, will ya?"

"Good-bye, Tiny," John said with warning.

The man rolled his eyes and smiled over his shoulder. "If I keep talking to her, you gonna start calling me Itty-Bitty?"

Tiny waved over his shoulder as he led the men out the door.

Grace looked at John. He had his hands on his hips and he was staring at the floor. His jaw was rigid.

Callie spoke up. "Look, I really think I should go."

John's head snapped upright. "Who the hell are you?"

"This is Callie," Grace offered. "My—er . . . half sister."

John's eyes narrowed on the woman. "I didn't know you had one."

"Neither did she," Callie answered.

"Well, welcome to the goddamn family. I'll talk to *you* later," John said to Grace before heading down the hall.

"Will you excuse me?" Grace said quickly as she went after him.

She was right on his heels when he stopped her in front of his room. "You need to get the hell away from me until I calm down."

With that, he shut the door in her face.

Grace released a breath.

As she returned to the living room, she regretted bringing Callie back with her, especially because she should have known how upset John was going to be.

She was just making bad call after bad call today.

"Would you like to take your jacket off?" she asked the woman.

Callie's eyes were somber as she shrugged the raincoat from her shoulders. She put it over her arm, holding it close to her body even though it was wet.

"Here, let me have that." Grace noted that Callie's damp

clothes were clean but not fashionable and that she wore no jewelry of any kind.

When she turned around from the closet, Callie was standing over the picture of Grace with their father. As she picked up the frame, Grace's heart contracted.

Damn him, she thought.

"Ah—I'm going to go take a shower," she said in a strained voice. "Would you like some clothes to change into?"

Callie put the picture back and looked down at herself. "That would be great."

A little while later, Grace sat at the edge of her bed in her bathrobe and waited for Callie to come out of the dressing room. When she did, Grace was surprised by the transformation. The woman's long red hair was drying into loose curls and, dressed in a pair of Grace's slacks and a fitted jacket, she looked sophisticated, not at all the drowned waif.

We wear the same size clothes, Grace thought.

"This is a gorgeous outfit." Callie stroked the fine cloth.

"The red is perfect for your coloring." Grace tilted her head to one side. "What do you do?"

"I'm an art conservationist, but right now I work as a receptionist at a gallery. I need to find another job, but for the past few years, things have been . . . difficult."

There was an awkward moment.

"How can I reach you?" Grace asked, going over to the bed stand and taking out a small pad of paper. As Callie's eyes lit up with what seemed like genuine happiness, she felt a spasm of guilt. The woman seemed to be looking for a friend, but Grace didn't think they could ever have that kind of relationship.

Callie jotted down a number and Grace was struck by the fact that she wrote with her left hand. Just like Grace did. Just as their father had.

"You know, you don't have to call," Callie said, handing the pad back. "I really only wanted to meet you. To see you up close once. To make sure you were real."

Grace looked down at the number.

"Can we give you a ride home?" she offered, wondering

where the woman lived in Chelsea. "We'll be going downtown very soon."

Callie glanced out of the window at the rain, which was still coming down. "That would be great. Thanks."

As Callie went out to wait in the living room, Grace approached John's door cautiously. Knocking quietly, she opened it when she heard his curt answer.

He was doing pull-ups at the bar he'd installed in the bathroom doorway. At a driving pace, he was pumping his body up and down, the muscles in his arms hard and heavily veined from exertion. She wondered how long he'd been at it.

"I'm really sorry I went off like that," she said tentatively as she shut the door. "I just needed to get outside for a minute. I wasn't thinking straight."

He stopped and dropped from the bar. "It was a goddamn dumb thing to do."

"I know. I won't do it again."

"You better the hell not. I'm not even going to bother telling you what could've happened." He reached for a towel and wiped the sweat off his face. "Are we going down to the Foundation?"

As he refused to look at her, she wished there was a way to take it all back, wished she could return to the moment when she'd put her running shoes on.

"I'm sorry I upset you."

"I'm not upset." He walked over to the bureau and began checking his gun. She heard the clicking sound of metal moving against metal.

"Yes, you are."

He turned to her, his eyes narrowed with anger. "Go get dressed, Grace."

Instead of cowering from him, she saw through the harsh words, to the fear she sensed was underneath them.

"I came back. I'm fine." When he didn't reply, she said, "John, I'm okay."

He put the gun back on the bureau and slipped on a black watch. "Did you think maybe the police had caught that nut job who's knocking off your friends? Because they haven't, you know. You could have damn well not come home after a stunt like that."

"But I did."

John cursed. "You should be smart enough not to believe in luck."

She tried to approach him but he stepped away. "You hired me to make sure you come out of this alive. Don't put me in the position of failing you again."

He went over to the door and threw it open.

"Countess?" he muttered, motioning with his arm.

She waited for him to look at her. He didn't.

As she brushed by him, she said softly, "Please don't use this as an excuse to push me away."

She didn't wait for his response.

As soon as Eddie pulled up behind the building, the three got into the Explorer. Callie gave out an address in Chelsea and Grace watched as the neighborhoods went from luxurious high-rises to brownstones to walk-ups. When they pulled up in front of one that was not quite as dilapidated as the others, Callie opened the door.

"Thanks for the ride," she said. "And I'll send back the suit."

"Don't worry about it," Grace replied.

The woman shook her head. "Thanks, but I can't keep it."

With a parting wave, she shut the door and disappeared into the dingy building.

Grace turned to John as the car surged forward. He was staring out the window, a brooding expression on his face.

"John?" His eyebrows rose but he didn't look across the seat. "Would you be willing to check into her background?"

"I've already started."

She stared at his profile, getting the terrible sense that something had changed between them. Perhaps irrevocably.

Ten minutes later, she and John walked into the lobby of the Hall Building. There were few employees around because of the holiday, but there were plenty of tourists visiting the museum. After stopping briefly to check in with the security guard at the front desk, they went into an elevator.

When they got upstairs, Grace was surprised to see Kat at her desk and a man standing in front of her. He had his hands on his hips and a cocky expression on his face.

"I didn't know you were coming in today," Grace said to Kat in an even voice. She gave the man a quick once-over. Slick suit, slick hair, god-awful tie.

It had to be a lawyer, she thought, wondering how he'd gotten past the security man downstairs.

Kat smiled tightly. "Mr. Lamont called and said he needed me to come in. I guess his assistant has quit again. This man—er, won't leave."

The guy flashed Grace a sparkling smile as he stuck out his hand. "I'm Fritz Canton. I believe you know who I am."

"Oh, of course, you're Ranulf's attorney. Did we have a meeting scheduled?" she asked, knowing they didn't.

"No, but I'd like to have a word with you." The man's gaze shifted over to John. "Alone, if I may. I won't take long."

When Smith approved as long as the door was left ajar, she said, "Very well."

Grace led him into the office and took a seat behind her father's desk.

Canton looked around and smiled. "This is some beautiful art you've got."

"Thank you." Grace leaned forward. "I don't mean to rush you, but could you tell me why you're here?"

He sat down across from her, put his hands together in a bridge and leaned his chin on them. "My client isn't satisfied with the cash settlement you're proposing."

Grace frowned. "Considering how much of my money he's already run through, I don't think one cent is appropriate. And frankly, I resent having to pay him for the privilege of a divorce."

"He only wants what's fair."

"Then let him leave with what he came with. I'll even give him back the ring."

Canton's eyes flashed and she knew he was estimating the sapphire's value. "You and I both know it's not that simple."

"Mr. Canton, if you're here to try and negotiate, you need to call my lawyer." She got to her feet. "Now if you will excuse me."

The attorney smiled. "I think you'll want to hear me out."

"Why?"

"I understand that you were photographed yesterday evening with a man. Outside of your building. My client received a copy of that picture." Canton rose. "It would be quite damaging to you if such a thing made it to the press— and your mother didn't have a chance to get it buried again. Adultery never looks good, especially on a woman, and I can imagine how important it is for you to be perceived as an upstanding citizen right now. With your father having passed and your just taking the helm of this venerable institution, it would be bad timing if a scandal were to come out now. Very bad."

As he ambled over to the bank of windows, Grace thought of that joke about lawyers, that a hundred of them at the bottom of the sea was a good start. She had an urge to get the trend started.

"Are you blackmailing me?" she asked.

"Not at all." He turned to her. "And neither, of course, is my client."

When she remained silent, his brows rose.

"So, what do you say, Countess? If we come to an agreement on a figure right now, this messy part can be over with. The two of you can issue a joint statement to the press indicating that it is all very amicable and no one will ever see the photo that suggests you've cheated on your husband. Ranulf and I, we were thinking something with eight digits will be sufficient."

Grace's first thought was that he and his client could go to hell.

Instead, she smiled calmly. "Thank you for coming by."

"There's nothing you want to say to me?"

Telling the guy to go screw himself probably wasn't such a hot idea, she thought.

"I believe you've stated your position clearly and I'm not negotiating anything without my own counsel present."

Grace walked over to the door and waited for the man to leave.

As he was walking out, he said, "Don't be foolish about this."

"Thanks for the advice," she said wryly.

21

THAT NIGHT, Smith called Eddie. It was getting late, pushing eleven o'clock.

" 'Lo?" came the groggy greeting.

"We're having an early start tomorrow."

A groan came through the line. "What time we talking, Boss man?"

"Six."

Another groan. "You'd figure a looker like her'd be into the whole beauty sleep thing. We headed anywhere special?"

"She has a breakfast meeting just over the border in Connecticut."

"Okay, I'll be there with bells on. But they may be hanging off my pj's."

"Eddie?"

"Yeah, Boss?"

"Tell Tiny to give me a call when he checks in tomorrow."

"What for?"

Smith pushed a hand into his hair. It had grown in since he'd been working for Grace. He needed to get it cut again.

"I'm thinking about giving up this job."

"Why do you want to pull out?" When he didn't answer, Eddie said, "What's going on?"

Smith was reliving what it had been like to discover Grace was gone. Part of his horror over what had happened was his own failure. When he'd left the bathroom, he'd been distracted, dawdling with those rings, thinking about marriage, for Chrissakes. Because he hadn't been focused on the job, it had taken longer than it should have for him to figure out she'd left and that delay was bald evidence his objectivity was shot to shit.

The first rule in the security business was pretty damn straightforward: Always know where your client is. She'd risked her life by taking off without him, but he'd compounded the danger by flaking out. It was precisely what he'd feared would happen, a perfect storm of bad thinking on both their parts.

"Boss? You still there?"

"Yeah, I'm here." Smith sat on the edge of the bed.

"Doesn't she need you anymore?"

He deflected the question. "Turned out she was being tailed by her half sister."

"She's got a half sister?"

"She does now. I'm running a check on the woman but so far, she is who she says she is."

"But why are you leaving? Did they find the killer?"

"No."

"Boss, do you want to tell me what's really going on?" When he didn't reply, Eddie said, "You worried about being involved with her?"

Smith opened his mouth but the lie sputtered and died on his tongue. "Is it that goddamn obvious?"

"No, I've just known you too long. Hey, not that you're asking, but that's a good woman, there. And she's got the eye for you. Like you're wearing her home address on your chest, you know what I mean?"

"You're getting real poetic as you age," Smith said, growing uncomfortable with the conversation.

"It's the writing course."

"Look, I'll see you tomorrow."

"Hey, Boss?"

"Yeah, Eddie."

"It's about time you settled down."

"Men like me don't settle down. You know that."

"Don't you ever think about it?"

Not until recently, Smith said to himself.

"You know," Eddie barreled along, "Black Watch can keep going without you. Tiny, he's as on top of the boys as a hammer on nail heads."

"Now you're into metaphors?"

"That was a simile, Boss."

After he hung up, Smith began pacing around the room, realizing that somehow, in the midst of all his discipline and self-control, he'd lost his way.

For years, he'd had one and only one goal. He wanted to make a lot of money doing what came naturally to him without getting himself killed. It was a simple and straightforward kind of life, assuming you knew how to handle yourself with a gun, which he did. But, after years of succeeding admirably, he was confused and conflicted. Black Watch and all it stood for felt arbitrary.

Holding Grace in his arms did not.

He tried to remember when he'd last taken stock of what he wanted or needed as a man and thought about something she'd thrown at him when they'd been arguing once. She'd told him he was a ghost. That she wouldn't miss him because he'd never really been in her life.

She was right, he thought, on a practical level and maybe in some deeper, more troubling way. What had he really given her except pleasure? And some heartache? She didn't even know his real name, for God's sake.

Come to think of it, he hadn't used his real name in years.

A ghost.

It dawned on him that maybe he'd disappeared a while ago and it was only now he was noticing. Perhaps he'd just been hiding behind the drive to succeed in his peculiar, violent, and dangerous line of work. After all, what could possibly be more distracting, if you didn't want to think about yourself, than protecting other human lives?

He wondered when the dissolving had started. Way back when he'd escaped his father's brutality? During his stint with the Rangers? Or was it during those shapeshifting years right after he'd left the military, when he'd relied on aliases and subterfuge so his enemies couldn't find him?

More likely, it was an accumulation of all the shadows he'd masked himself with.

How fucking ironic, he thought. The culmination of his life's work was to make himself disappear.

He thought back to what Eddie had said about settling down, starting over. The idea would have struck him as ludicrous coming from anyone else, except maybe Tiny. But if he unplugged from Black Watch, then what? What would he do with his hours, his days? Would he and Grace ever be able to have a life together? As he contemplated the expanse of time ahead of him, he felt the choices he had as a deadweight on his chest.

Nice frigging simile, he thought.

While he was cursing Eddie and his candor, Grace appeared in his doorway. She was wearing one of those nightgowns that hung from her delicate shoulders like a cloud of mist, the kind he could almost, but not quite, see through. His eyes traced the outline of her hips and waist and traveled up to her breasts.

"What is it?" he asked roughly.

"We're all set for tomorrow?"

"Yeah."

Silence stretched between them and Smith could feel the air change as their eyes met. Time began to melt. Slow down. Halt altogether.

He went over to her, thinking there was nothing he wouldn't do to protect her.

Even if that meant leaving.

He reached out to touch her, his fingers brushing across her collarbone and continuing downward over silk and lace. He came to a stop at the low point of the gown's bodice, right over her heart. He felt it pounding.

Wrapping his arms around her, he pulled her body against his and put his lips down to hers. She let out a long sigh, which he swallowed, better than air, into his lungs.

He lifted her from the ground and carried her to his bed. Pausing before lying down with her, he drank in the sight of her head thrown to one side, her back arched, her hair spilling over the fine fabric of the pillowcase. It was how he had wanted to see her, those many days and weeks ago when she'd first showed him her home. It would be how he would remember her always.

An unforgettable lady.

Wrenching off his shirt, he felt her hands come hungrily to his skin and he shuddered as she explored his chest and stomach. His need to be in her was so great, he felt his own hands shake as he slid the nightgown from her body and tore off the rest of his clothes. He pleasured her over and over again with his mouth before he entered her in a powerful thrust that carried them to another world.

After he came back to reality, he rolled over, taking her with him so that Grace was sprawled over his body.

"I will never be free of you," he whispered against the sweat-covered skin of her neck.

"Promise?" she asked huskily.

He nodded, feeling cursed.

Because he knew he had to leave.

Rolling over again, he tucked her into his side.

As she fell asleep, he thought it wasn't right to torture them both by delaying the inevitable. The sooner the transition was made, the better; he would ask Tiny to come right away.

And as for their long-term future, after the danger to her was gone, he didn't think it was fair of him to bring it back into her life. She deserved a normal existence, with normal trials and tribulations. She didn't need to be exposed to the kind of baggage he dragged around with him. The last thing she should have to deal with would be some madman showing up with a gun in her bedroom, ready to shoot her lover in the head.

When he was sure she was sleeping, he slipped out of bed, picked up his phone, and went into the living room. He wasn't going to wait for Tiny to call.

His oldest friend was the best man he had at Black Watch, almost as good as Smith himself. Actually better, in this case, because the guy would be coming at the situation with a clear head as well as a strong body.

If he could trust Grace with anyone, it would be Tiny.

As soon as the man's voice came through, Smith said, "What are you doing right now?"

Tiny laughed. "I'm up to my balls in spiders, to tell you the truth. God, I hate these tropical details. There's always something crawling into your clothes, only it's rarely of the feminine persuasion."

"I need you to take over a project."

"When?"

"Now," Smith said gruffly.

"Sorry, what?"

"Now."

Tiny let out a little hiss. "Jesus, you're bailing on the countess. What the hell'd that woman do to you?"

Smith let that one fall by the wayside. "When can you be here?"

"Ah—I'll see what I can do. Does this mean you'll be free to cover Senator Pryne on his trip to the Middle East? Flat Top was going to do it, but he'd be better down here."

"If you can get to New York, I'll go."

"Good deal. I'll call you tomorrow with my ETA."

Smith clipped the phone shut.

He stared ahead without really seeing anything. It was a while before he realized he was staring at the piano.

He walked over to it. Anytime he'd run across one, he'd made a point of playing if he could. They'd been few and far between while he was in the army, but once he was out, he'd played in hotel lounges, in private homes, the occasional bar.

He raised his hands and looked at them. They had been trained to do many things, few of which were uplifting.

The playing had come naturally, though.

Grace came awake the moment she heard the music. It was soft and low, powerful yet quiet.

She picked her nightgown off the floor, slipped it over her head, and went out to the hall. She paused before going into the living room, entranced by the sounds but afraid if John knew she was listening, he might stop playing. Leaning against the wall, turning her head to the sound, she closed her eyes. He was good. Better than good.

As he played, she allowed herself a few tantalizing fantasies. Of him staying in her life. Living with her. Giving her children.

When the music died away, she stepped out into the room. He was sitting on the bench, head down, long fingers still on the keys. He was wearing only boxers and the contrast between his bare skin and the glossy piano was appealing.

"How long have you been listening?" he asked without looking up.

"Some time."

He turned his head. In the dim light, his eyes glowed. "I didn't mean to wake you."

"I'm glad you did. You play beautifully." As he got to his feet and closed the guard, she asked, "Did you train somewhere?"

"I just make it up as I go along." He faced her, putting his hands on his hips. His expression was grave.

When she'd gone to him earlier, ostensibly to say good night, she'd been surprised and relieved when he'd kissed her, because he'd been so distant during the day. As he'd made love to her, it had been tempting to believe all was forgiven, but afterward she'd had her doubts.

The poignancy with which he'd held her while she fell asleep had been curiously troubling. It had been almost as if he were saying good-bye.

"We've got to talk," he said.

Grace's stomach rolled. "About what?"

"I called one of my boys tonight. I want to put him on this job."

Grace took a deep breath, relaxing some. "I don't care how many members of Black Watch back you up. Especially if it means I can go ahead with the Gala."

"That's not what I have in mind."

Instinctively, she put her arms around herself. "Then what are you saying?"

"I'm leaving."

Grace heard the words but instantly rejected them. "What do you mean? You can't leave. I—we—they haven't found whoever killed—"

"Tiny's a good man. I'd trust him with my life. And yours."

"I don't want Tiny. I want you."

"I've taken another assignment."

Her mouth fell open and then she laughed bitterly. "Quitting on me?"

"Changing jobs."

"It's the same line of work, though. Right?"

"Different"—he paused—"client."

He'd told her only after it was done, she thought. Only after he'd taken care of everything and there was no way to argue.

She turned from him as tears welled in her eyes. She refused to let them fall, blinking furiously.

"Grace," he said roughly. "I have to go."

She wheeled back toward him. "No, you don't."

"I can't trust myself with you any longer. I'm not the right man for this job."

"Don't you think I should decide that? I'm the one who's paying you."

"You aren't qualified to judge my skills."

She shot him a glare. "Thanks for the vote of confidence."

"You're no more objective than I am at this point."

Impatiently, she pushed her hair over her shoulder. "And when did you decide all this?"

"Tonight."

"You—you make love to me and then you tell me you're leaving?" she exclaimed. "What? Worried you wouldn't have a chance to get laid before your next assignment?"

He frowned, his brows drawing tight over his eyes. "You know it's never been like that between us."

"Oh, really? Then maybe you'd like to tell me what happens after you leave? Will I ever see you again?"

His silence was the answer.

"Oh, God," she said.

"I don't want it to be this way."

"So make it different," she snapped.

When he stared at her in stony silence, she shook her head. "I can't believe you're prepared to just walk away."

His response was quiet. "I'm sorry, Grace. I really am."

She thrust her chin up and brushed by him, going over to her desk and taking out a checkbook.

"I think you should just leave now." She began hastily scribbling with a gold pen. She ripped the check free and held it out to him. "Go on. Take it. Let's just end this now."

"Not until Tiny's here."

"You said you wanted to leave, so pack your things and get the hell out. I have no interest in being passed off to one of your *boys.*"

Tension crackled in the air as the check hung between them. He slowly came forward and took it out of her hand only to put it down on the desk.

"I'm not going anywhere until Tiny shows up."

"I don't think you understand," she said, pointing at the front door. "You and Black Watch are fired. Get out."

His voice was flat when he spoke, belying in its softness his awesome will. "I'm not leaving until I know you're safe."

Rage, borne out of hurt and frustration, had her blinking tears away. "This is incredibly cruel of you. To say that you're going and then force me to—"

"You have no idea what it was like when you disappeared."

She threw her arms up.

"I'm sorry. I said I was sorry." She bunched her hands into fists. "And I came back."

He cut her off. "I have seen death up close before, Grace. Imagining yours was the closest I've come to crying in thirty years."

She shut her mouth, stunned.

"I don't know what I would do," he said with stark emphasis, "if anything ever happened to you. The depth of my fear tells me I have to leave you in someone else's protection. And that I can't see you again."

Impulsively, she reached for his hands. "No, you're wrong. If you care that much for me, you shouldn't go."

"Grace, don't delude yourself. Those three women who were killed weren't careful enough. You need to be ruthless about your safety, as ruthless as that man who's cutting up your friends. You don't want me to be watching you and you don't want me hanging around in your life. Trust me on this."

"So let Tiny or whoever come. That doesn't mean you have to leave. We can figure out the future, together."

He shook his head. "A clean break is the only way."

She dropped his hands and turned away, sensing there'd be no negotiating with him. He was leaving and there was nothing she could do about it. In a rush, a numb feeling washed over her, taking away some of the pain.

"I don't want Tiny," she said. "I don't want him."

Because he will only remind me of you, she thought.

"Grace, don't let your anger at me impair your judgment about letting someone take care of you. You know it's not safe for you to be alone right now."

She thought about her three friends.

As much as she was mad at John, she wasn't going to be stupid about her own life. No man, even him, was worth getting killed over.

Although, Christ, with the pain in her chest at the moment, she felt half-dead already.

Grace squared her shoulders. "When will Tiny be here?"

"Twenty-four hours if all goes well."

"And what about the Gala? You realize it's this weekend. I still have every intention of going."

"If he can get a few men to cover him, and you allow Marks and his squad in the building that whole day and through the event, the risks could be mitigated. The killer does seem to like getting them at home. But it's Tiny's call. Myself, I wouldn't take the chance."

The hell it was Tiny's choice, she thought.

She was willing to concede that John was right. She still needed a bodyguard. But not one from Black Watch. She had twenty-four hours to find another firm.

And one day until she never saw John again.

She lifted her chin.

"I want to make something clear," she said. "I think you're making a terrible mistake by walking out on me and I have to question whether you really feel as deeply about me as you say you do. It strikes me that if you were truly concerned for my well-being, you would move heaven and earth to be by my side."

"Grace, I—"

"Stop lecturing me. And while you're at it, stop being so convinced you have all the answers and listen. I think you love me, John, and for a man who's lived his life alone, that's probably scaring the hell out of you. I can't help wishing you'd find the strength to stay but I'm done with begging. If you leave me now, know this. I'm not going to wait for you. I'm going on with my life. And I may never be able to open my heart to you again."

She shook her head sadly as she turned away from him.

22

WHEN GRACE rolled over at five A.M. the next morning, she caught a whiff of coffee brewing and knew John was up.

Facing him was something she needed to prepare for, so she took a bracingly cool shower and put on one of her power suits. It was black and formfitting, with lapels that were trimmed with a thin red piping, and she felt stronger wearing it. With a pair of high heels and a splash of vibrant red on her lips, she felt like she'd armored herself to get through the day.

When she came down the hall, John was on his cell phone, pacing back and forth between the living room and the dining room. The expression on his face was grim and he looked up at her.

"No, let me do it," he said under his breath and then hung up.

She shot him a cool stare.

"Isadora Cunis was attacked last night."

Grace's throat closed up.

Feeling her defensive pose crumble, she began to shake. "I thought she and her husband had gone out of state. What happened?"

"She came back to get ready for her event. She was found in the lobby of her building. She'd evidently been attacked in her home and somehow managed to drag herself into the elevator. Considering how extensive her wounds were, that maneuver was a miracle. She's in a coma at Lenox Hill."

Grace reached out a hand to steady herself and felt the

cool plane of the wall under her palm. "How did he get to her?"

John shrugged. "There's only one explanation. She knew him and she let him in."

Grace fumbled with the buttons of her jacket and took it off, throwing it over the arm of the sofa. Against the creamy fabric, she thought the splash of black looked violent.

"Good Lord," she whispered, sitting down. She crossed her legs at the ankles and folded her hands in her lap.

As if arranging her body would somehow order her mind.

"I—I don't think I'm going to go to Connecticut," she said.

"I'll call Eddie."

She heard the electronic beeping from his phone as he dialed and then the rumble of his voice.

She imagined Isadora lying in a hospital bed and grieved for the woman's suffering.

"Grace?"

At the sound of her name, she looked up and saw that he was kneeling in front of her.

"Grace? Do you want me to tell Kat that you're not going in today?"

She started to nod but then looked around the penthouse. The fact that the women were being attacked in their homes made the place feel somehow contaminated.

"No. I think I'd rather go to work."

Grace started to get to her feet and John offered a hand to help her up.

She forced herself not to take it.

"I need some time to myself," she said, heading for her room. "If you'll excuse me?"

She didn't wait for a response.

Later in the morning, when she walked up to Kat's desk, Grace flashed a steady smile that the girl apparently didn't fall for.

"Are you okay?" Kat asked.

"Fine, just fine."

"How was Connecticut?"

"I had to reschedule." Before Kat could ask any more questions, she said, "Will you do me a favor and cancel my regular meetings today? I have to work on the Gala preparations and I need some uninterrupted time."

"No problem."

With her schedule cleared, Grace spent the rest of the morning in a daze. She tried to do some work, but nothing she read sank in and nothing she wrote made any sense. In a last-ditch effort to accomplish something, she tried to finish the seating chart for the Gala.

After she'd been staring at it for twenty minutes, she pushed it away and looked up at the bust of her father. She hit the intercom.

"Kat? Will you please call maintenance? I'd like to move something down to the museum. Oh, and tell them I want to change some of the paintings in here. The ones on these walls have been here too long."

She released the button and looked at John, who was talking on his phone. He'd been doing that all morning, gathering information, she imagined, on what had happened to Isadora. She wanted to ask him for details, but wasn't sure whether that would make her feel any better. Bad news coming from him seemed liked a double hit.

Grace looked back at the bust and then at the candy dish and the pipe rack. She was thinking that she would get rid of them, too, when Callie's image came to mind.

When John put the phone down, she asked, "What do you know about Callie?"

He finished writing some kind of note and then looked up.

"She lives in the building we dropped her in front of. She's twenty-seven, never been married, lives alone, nothing in the bank. Works at a gallery, did very well in school. Graduated summa cum laude from NYU as an undergrad and then excelled in her master's program in art conservation. Her mother's dead."

Grace lifted her brows. "When?"

"Two years ago. Of MS."

She was about to ask if Callie had any siblings when Kat buzzed in. "Mr. Lamont is here to see you."

Grace pursed her lips in annoyance, tempted to send

him away. With the Gala only a day away, however, she didn't think she should chance it. He might actually have something constructive to say. "He can come in, but it's not going to be for long—"

Lamont threw open the double doors.

"Why, hello, Lou," she said dryly.

As he marched up to the desk, she looked over his sharp suit and perky tie. She noticed dimly that the folded handkerchief in his jacket pocket was the same kind her father had worn.

"Your auction piece has arrived," he said with a humorless smile. "They just unpacked it. That thing is so dark, God only knows what it really is."

She fought against responding to the cutting tone in his voice. "I believe that painting's documentation speaks for itself, Lou. Or perhaps you'd like to argue with the Copley scholars who've authenticated it?"

He let out a disparaging noise.

"You better be prepared to duck and cover tomorrow night because you're going to look like a fool. This whole thing has been a mess from start to finish. The invitations were wrong, it took you weeks to set the menu, and I haven't even seen that retrospective on your father yet. The portrait is a nightmare and God only knows how you're going to stage the party in the atrium downstairs. I tell you, Bainbridge is very uncomfortable."

"Stay away from my board," she said sharply.

"I'm just trying to save you from yourself."

Grace bit her lip to keep from snapping back. She was sick and tired of him stirring up trouble, of meeting his censure with nothing other than calm detachment. Frustration hardened her voice.

"Thanks, but I don't need to be rescued by you."

An angry flush deepened the color in his face. "Oh, I'm sorry. I forgot. You've got an amazing sense of balance in this tightrope town. I'll have to remember that when our donors want to know why the single most important event of the year turned out to be nothing more than a bad dinner and an embarrassing exhibition of a painting no one wanted to buy."

She massaged a knot of tension at the base of her skull. "Lou, I can't keep fighting like this."

"We wouldn't have to if you'd just do what I say. But no." He threw his hands up theatrically. "You're still so jealous of my relationship with your father that you can't show me respect."

"I beg your pardon?" Grace was honestly surprised. She didn't like Lou as a person, but it had nothing to do with how close he'd been to her father.

"You always hated the way he appreciated me, mentored me."

She shook her head. "My father did enjoy grooming you, but I wasn't threatened by that. You were a hobby of his, Lou, never his surrogate son. Don't let your ego rewrite reality."

Lamont planted his arms on her father's desk and leaned toward her, full of anger. "You little—"

A hand clamped on his shoulder.

"You want to relax, big guy?" Smith was smiling grimly as he loomed over the other man.

"Get your hands off me!"

"As soon as you calm down."

Lamont glared at Smith and then pulled away roughly.

"You're a really great OD consultant, you know that? I come in to give her a heads-up that *her* board is dissatisfied with her performance and you crawl all over me." Lamont snapped his suit back in place and smoothed his tie. "Don't tell me you went to school for this?"

Grace started shaking her head. "Lou, maybe you should leave."

"You're right about that. I've got a meeting with my staff in ten minutes to tell them they all need to come to the Gala this year, even the damn secretaries. Just so you know, it's to fill empty seats at the tables."

"No, I mean, really leave. The Foundation."

His eyebrows shot up to his hairline. "Are you *firing* me?"

Grace rose from the heavy chair. She'd been afraid to let Lamont go, even though he was trouble, because she was concerned that he might be right. There was a part of her that questioned whether she knew what she was doing and she'd hoped that Lou would eventually come around and be a help.

Looking into his face, she knew it was time to give up.

"Yes, Lou, I am firing you. I don't want to, but it's obvious that we can't work together."

"You're going to be sorry if you let me go," he said with soft menace. "I've been nothing but loyal to this place and your father."

"I know you've approached several people for jobs."

"I have not."

"Yes, you have. Because Suzanna van der Lyden and Mimi Lauer told me so after they turned you down."

Lamont's mouth tightened as he twisted in his own lie.

"Lou, we're at an impasse. You're not happy working under me and I will not step down. I suggest that you let us buy out your contract. As long as you leave civilly, we'll make sure you get to review the press release and I'll give you a satisfactory reference."

His eyes narrowed, but she couldn't tell whether he was adding up the zeros in his separation package or measuring the distance across the desk so he could hit her.

He jabbed a finger through the air. "I promise this will come back to haunt you."

As soon as he left, she buzzed Kat. "Get security to escort Lou out of the building. Make sure they get his badge and his keys, okay?"

The last thing she needed was to have Lamont stealing the donor lists, assuming he hadn't already.

As she sat down in her chair, she was trying to figure out who she could get to head the Development Department. She'd have to start searching now, because filling a job like that could take months.

Sitting at the conference table, Smith was impatiently tapping a pen against the pad of paper he'd been using.

Christ, why the hell hadn't Tiny gotten back to him, yet?

He picked up his phone and tried again. When he actually heard the man's voice, he said, "Where the hell have you been?"

The phone connection was fuzzing in and out and Tiny sounded like he was underwater. "I'm trying to get the hell out of South America. Flat Top has finally taken over for me down here and I tried to call you three times this morning. I couldn't get through."

"When are you going to be here?"

"I'm trying to get on a plane right now."

"Don't waste any time."

"Do I ever?"

Smith hung up and dialed Lieutenant Marks's private line. As soon as the guy got on the phone, he said, "What have you got?"

"She's still out cold. They think she's going to pull through, though, which means we might be able to get a positive ID. The crime scene's being combed over but I'm not holding out for anything too goddamn illuminating. Christ, I wish we knew more about this guy."

"Those women in the article were all attacked around the time of the social events they chaired and you know those big parties are exercises in exclusion. Who gets in and who doesn't is a big deal. We should be looking for someone who's getting shut out, someone who's either being denied entrance into the inner circle or someone who was in and is now getting turned away."

He glanced over at Grace. She'd picked up the phone and was speaking, a grave expression on her face. He wondered who she was talking to.

"That's sound reasoning," Marks said, "but at the level we're talking about, the social maneuvering is so aggressive, a boxer would think twice before going to one of those damn events. Who isn't ascending or descending at any given moment?"

"Those six women in that article, that's who. They're at the top. They're the arbiters of taste in this city, which means they make the decisions as to who gets cut from the A-list. I tell you, this is someone who's been stepped on, either in fact or through his perception of the way they're treating him. And every single one of those women know him personally. That's how he's getting in."

"But we've got no loose ends. You've seen the logs of

those buildings. No irregularities and everybody's checked out so far. They all had a reason to be in those places on those days and even more to the point, they all *left* before the time of death. In and out."

Smith thought about the rear entrance of Grace's building. "Maybe he's coming back in."

"What do you mean?"

"What if this guy signs in and while he's inside he props open the service door or a window. When he leaves, he signs out, makes sure the doorman notices him, but then comes in again the back way. These old buildings are labyrinths. He could wait around for hours if he knew where to hide. It would explain why there's been no forcible entry and why there are no discrepancies with the logs."

Marks was silent for a moment. "Christ, you may be right."

When Smith hung up, he saw Grace watching him. She looked like hell, he thought, her eyes a dull shade of green and her mouth slack. It was as if the light inside of her had been smothered.

"I'm going out to lunch," she said quietly.

"Fine. Where to?"

"Chelsea. I'm having lunch with my half sister."

After muscling through a traffic jam caused by a water-main break, Eddie dropped them off in front of a pretentious modern art gallery. As Grace was studying its steel and glass facade, Callie came out. With her hair pulled back, she looked less like their father and Grace had to admit she was relieved.

"Hi. Where do you want to go?" Callie asked.

Grace suggested a small, out-of-the-way place where they could have some privacy.

As they walked, the fall wind kicked up a fuss around them, making brightly colored leaves tremble on the small trees planted into the sidewalk. John stayed close, only two steps behind.

The silence was awkward.

"I was surprised you called," Callie murmured. "I'm glad you did."

"Me, too." Grace wasn't sure she meant the words but she didn't know what else to say. The only thing they had in common was their father and he wasn't exactly the stuff of small talk.

When they were seated in the café, John took a table next to them, to give them some space.

After they ordered, there was more awkward silence.

Grace was trying not to stare at the woman and failing, while questions with no outlet flooded her brain. The things she wanted to know could only have come from her father and his death made her irate. Still, no matter how frustrated she was, Grace knew it wouldn't be fair to take it out on Callie. The woman hadn't asked to be born into such a mess.

While the waiter filled their water glasses, Grace wondered what they were going to talk about, but then, surprisingly, the conversation began to flow. It started with something trite, the decor in the restaurant. Callie commented on the floor, which was a massive decoupage of images of dancers. Grace pointed down to a 1920s flapper she'd always liked and Callie picked out a cancan girl. This led to a discussion about the reproduction French lithographs on the walls, and Grace's most recent visit to Paris. Slowly at first, then with increasing ease, they traded stories. By a kind of unspoken agreement, they stayed away from their childhoods and focused instead on more recent years, but the past was always between them.

Most particularly in the pauses of their conversation.

"I went to NYU for undergrad and graduate school," Callie was saying as their plates were cleared. "I wanted to be with my mother as she got sicker."

"Did you nurse her for long?" Grace asked, trying to imagine the pressure Callie must have been under at the time.

"A few years, but the hardest was the last four months. She refused help from my . . . our father." Callie's eyes flashed upward with uncertainty. When Grace nodded, she went on. "He wanted to put her in a private hospital, but she was adamant, more to spite him than anything else. She was a very independent woman. The loss of control that came with the multiple sclerosis was very hard for her to deal with. Those last few months were the longest in my life. And in hers. It was a sad relief for both of us when she died."

Grace watched as Callie picked up a teaspoon and started drawing on the linen tablecloth idly. An image of their father came to mind and she had to force herself not to look away. Tracking the smooth movement, hearing that soft sound, she felt an awful sense of loss. And an odd kind of relief.

Although the beginning of the meal had been awkward, she was glad she'd called. The woman was smart, honest, and seemed very up-front and there was little about her that suggested she was a gold digger. What did come across, however, was the impression of someone who had lived a hard life. There were glimpses here and there of what Callie had had to face, not only with her mother's illness, but also with the isolation of being unacknowledged as a daughter.

As coffee was brought to the table, Grace sensed Callie didn't want to talk about her mother anymore. "So do you like art conservation?"

"I'm passionate about it and I wish I were working in the field instead of answering the phone at a gallery. I had some great project experience in school but the real world is hard. Conservation jobs are very competitive and, because my mother was ill, I didn't want to look outside of this city." She shrugged. "It's probably time for me to get my résumé out there. Now that I'm alone, I can go anywhere in the country. Or the world, really."

"Where would you like to go?"

Callie laughed and sipped her coffee. "I have no idea. I've always wanted options, but now that I have them, I'm overwhelmed and find that I only want to stay where I am."

Grace thought of the Foundation's own conservation department. Part of her didn't want Callie anywhere near the Hall Building. What if someone picked up on the family resemblance? She stared into the woman's face. The likeness to her father was subtle. Probably only noticeable if someone were looking for it and who would? No one had known about Cornelius's other life.

She hesitated but decided there was something very unattractive about refusing to help someone just because she was afraid of a remote consequence.

"Callie," she said, "perhaps you'd like to come in and talk to Miles Forsythe. He's our conservationist at the museum. He might be able to steer you to some positions. At the very least, he could give you the names of some people to talk to."

Callie slowly put her coffee cup down. Her eyes were startled, as if she never would have expected help from Grace. Or anybody else.

Looking as she did, it was impossible to believe she could be after money, Grace thought.

"I'd be very grateful," Callie answered.

After they were finished, they strolled back to the gallery and said good-bye on the sidewalk.

"I'll talk to Miles and get a date from him."

"Thank you." Callie shifted her small purse up farther on her shoulder. "And you didn't have to pay for lunch."

"I know."

As the woman turned her head and glanced at a taxi driver who was blaring his horn, sunlight fell on her face and picked out those lofty cheekbones Grace had always admired in her father.

Callie looked back. "I would have brought your suit in today but I didn't know you would call and it—"

"It's okay. There's no hurry."

Callie smiled. Standing in her modest clothes and a shapeless, floppy jacket, she seemed vulnerable and yet she clearly wasn't looking for handouts.

"Will I see you when I meet with Mr. Forsythe?" she asked.

"Yes," Grace said. "You will."

23

THE NEXT day, Grace came into work feeling overwhelmed. The Gala was twenty-four hours away and the big night was looming over her like an avalanche.

But it was Smith's imminent departure that was really on her mind.

"Good morning," Kat said as she handed over some papers. "Miles Forsythe stopped by. He's free to meet that woman later this afternoon. Oh, and Jack Walker called. He wondered if he could see the Copley tonight and I told him he could. I figured you wouldn't mind."

"Fine."

"And Fredrique is back."

Grace looked up in surprise. "He is?"

"He went after the caterers again. They said if you don't get him off their back, they're going to quit."

"I'd better take care of it."

Grace went into her office and phoned the caterers. After thirty minutes of soothing feathers, they were back on the job.

Still, she cursed when she hung up, feeling as if Fredrique's tenacity was one more problem she could have done without.

From across the room, John's eyes flipped up from something he was writing.

"Sorry," she muttered.

He shrugged and stood up. When he started to stretch, she looked down at her desk. Even though her mind had begun to accept the loss of him, her body had no such pragmatism. She wanted him, even now.

Even after he'd broken her heart. After he was leaving and never to be seen again.

She imagined that in some part of her, she would always want him. Always love him.

"I have something for you," he said briskly. He walked over and handed her an envelope.

Frowning, she opened it and took out a thick, folded wad of paper. She spread the documents out and began leafing through them. They were printouts of bills, from a casino in Las Vegas, a hotel in Monte Carlo, another on the French Riviera.

"What's all this?" She looked up.

"I took the liberty of doing a little research on your husband. Those are unpaid hotel charges and gambling debts. He's been on quite a bender since you kicked him out and he's been using his family's name and yours to secure credit. In addition to being lousy at the tables, he's evidently got a hearty appetite and an affinity for top-drawer liquor. Doesn't seem to care much for paying up, however."

She looked at the totals. "This is a lot, but not to a von Sharone."

"Well, that's the thing. Apparently, the family's not as wealthy as it once was. Were you aware they're selling their winery in France?"

"No." She frowned again. "But why? Those vineyards have been owned by them for generations."

"They've put several other properties on the market, as well as some paintings and sculpture. It's all been done very discreetly, of course, but when you add it up, they're off-loading a boatload of assets."

"Good Lord. What's happened to them?"

He shrugged. "Too many descendants with too much interest in the high life. The bottom line is, the family's out of money and that international existence your husband's been enjoying is going to get pretty provincial, pretty goddamn fast."

"Which is why he's trying to milk me in the divorce settlement," she murmured. It was all so much clearer. She'd assumed he was going after her because he was being vindictive. Instead, it was a matter of survival. God knew, he was wholly incapable of making the kind of money he needed.

John pointed to the bills. "Sent to the right journalist, these will set off an investigation into the von Sharone finances and they would do anything to avoid that."

"Because appearances are everything," she said softly. Grace glanced back at him, knowing he'd just handed her the ticket to her divorce. "Thank you."

"I had a feeling when his lawyer showed up in your office looking so damn pleased with himself that they were trying to hold you over a barrel. Probably leveraging that picture of us, am I right?"

She nodded.

"So let me tell you, finding all this has been my pleasure."

Grace looked down at the bills. Ranulf relished his international image of wealth and status and this kind of news would ruin him. She could just see the article in *Vanity Fair.*

She didn't want to hurt him. All she wanted was her freedom without having to pay exorbitantly for it.

"Kat, get my lawyer on the phone, will you?" she said into the intercom.

Toward the end of the workday, Grace and John went down to meet Callie in the atrium. As they cut through the throngs of people milling about, Grace saw the woman standing by the museum's marble entrance. She was dressed in black slacks and a thick black sweater, looking calm and composed.

Callie offered a tentative wave when she caught sight of them approaching.

"Welcome," Grace said. "Miles is looking forward to meeting you."

They left the noisy mosaic of movement and sound behind as they entered the quiet interior of the museum. Grace waved at the guards and the docents and began walking quickly toward the back when she realized Callie had fallen behind, having paused in front of an exhibit.

It was the one noting the Woodward Hall family's contributions to the study of American history. There were photographs and paintings of various generations, as well as of Willings. Grace's picture had been added, next to her father's.

Their father's, she corrected herself. She tried to imagine what it would be like to stare at a history that was hers by right, but not practice.

"Sorry," Callie murmured, coming forward.

"Do you want to—"

"We should go, shouldn't we?" Her voice was strained and Grace nodded.

Callie was silent as they went past exhibits on archaeological digs that the Foundation had sponsored and through a gallery featuring Early American portraiture.

When they got to a large freight elevator, Grace slid her pass card through a reader. As the doors opened and they stepped inside, Callie said, "Thank you for doing this."

"I'm glad to," she replied, meaning it.

Grace punched the fourth-floor button and the elevator lurched upward. She realized that, had they been alone, she would have asked Callie what she was thinking, because she wanted to help. She had a feeling the emotions she herself was struggling with were similar to the ones that had drawn Callie's lips tightly together and caused her brows to ride low over her eyes. Grace just wasn't sure what she could do.

Maybe they could help each other, she thought.

When the doors reopened, they stepped out into a long hallway. "Miles's office is down here to the right."

Grace took Callie to him and then decided to stay and chat with some of the museum's administrators while she waited for Jack to arrive. To her relief, everyone was excited about the Copley and, in spite of Lamont's dire predictions, the consensus was that the bidding at the auction was going to get lively.

A while later, Jack emerged from the elevators and a couple of the staff members who were waiting to get on stepped out of his way with deference. He was dressed in a black suit, walking in his forceful gait, and Grace thought he cut a powerful figure. Like John did, only in a different way.

"I'm all ready to see my ancestor again," he drawled as he kissed her on the cheek. He and John nodded curtly at each other.

At that moment, Callie's voice drifted into the hall.

"Again, thank you for the advice." She was backing out of Miles's office, a smile on her face as she waved.

Jack's head snapped in her direction just as she turned around. When she met his stare, her eyes widened as she looked up into his face.

Grace smiled, thinking Jack tended to have that affect on women. And then she hesitated, unsure of how to introduce Callie.

Her friend took care of it by putting his hand out. "I'm Jack Walker."

Callie paused before sliding her palm against his. As soon as contact was made, she retreated and looked at Grace. "Er—thank you for getting me in to meet Miles. It's always good to talk to a fellow conservationist."

"What's your name?" Jack asked, his eyes scanning her face.

Her eyes went to his. "Callie Burke."

"And you are?"

Grace flushed, aware of her own rudeness. "She's a friend of mine. She came here to meet with Miles."

"You're in the art world?"

Callie nodded, looking as if she wished the man would stop focusing on her. Grace had to wonder if Jack had offended her, but then saw the way Callie's eyes went back to him.

As if she were intrigued as well as wary.

"If you like art, then you must come meet Nathaniel," he said laconically.

"Nathaniel?"

Grace explained. "It's John Singleton Copley's portrait of Nathaniel Walker. Why don't you stay and have a look? It won't take long and I'd be curious to hear what you think of it."

Callie's eyes flipped to Jack. And then, with a nod, she followed the small group into the conservation workshop.

Grace loved visiting the lab and seeing the works in progress. The room smelled like varnish and paint and there was always some kind of classical music playing in the background. At stations all around the room, paintings in various stages of conservation were held upright in wood blocks. Next to each was a rolling cart of supplies that carried dark jars full of solutions as well as paintbrushes and cotton swabs.

The staff had left for the evening but she knew where the Copley was.

"He's over here, in lockdown," she said, going over to a bank of cabinets that were segmented into five-foot-wide, shallow drawers. With a key ring she'd brought with her, she unlocked one, slid it out, and rolled back a cloth. She heard Jack's sigh of satisfaction as he looked at his ancestor.

"Let's take him out," Grace said. She reached in and tried to lift the painting, but because of the massive, gilded frame she could barely budge the thing. Smith picked it up carefully and walked it over to one of the worktables, laying it down flat.

"He's beautiful," Callie murmured, standing to the side.

"But the brooding sort, or so I understand." Jack leaned over, looking closely at the face staring up out of the canvas. "This is a particularly good likeness of him, I think."

"His eyes are extraordinary," Callie murmured. "So expressive. Too bad they have the look of a tormented man."

Jack stared across the portrait at her for a long moment. "Yes. They do."

Grace stepped forward, pointing to the lower right-hand corner. "Here's the signature and date. This was right about the same time Copley did the portrait of Paul Revere that hangs in the MFA in Boston."

"Do you mind if I take a closer look?" Callie asked.

"Not at all."

Callie turned on one of the crane-necked lamps on the table and angled it toward the surface of the painting. Getting in close, she hovered about three inches above the canvas, moving slowly around the edges toward the center. When her body got close to Jack's, he didn't step away.

A soft smile was playing across her lips when she stood up.

"What do you see?" Jack asked.

"He needs some work. There's about seventy-five years of smoke and dirt stuck to a varnish coat that has yellowed with age. He's going to have to be handled very carefully, with a lot of love, but the canvas is sound."

"Maybe you'd like to do the work."

Callie glanced at him in surprise. "Excuse me?"

Grace tried to cover up the awkward silence that followed by laughing softly. "You have to buy him first, you know, before you hire someone to work on him."

"No matter what he costs, he will come back to the family." He turned to Callie. "Are you interested in the project?"

It was a long time before she answered. "This painting carries a huge historical significance because of both the subject matter and the artist."

Jack shrugged. "So are you saying you're not interested?"

"It's more than I've ever handled before."

"Then if you do it right, it'll make your career."

"I do it wrong and both the painting and my reputation are ruined."

Grace glanced back and forth between the two of them. Callie was staring at Nathaniel Walker. Jack was looking at her.

She wondered what he was thinking and decided that perhaps he just saw in Callie the opportunity to give someone a chance in the big leagues.

Smith had just lit a cheroot and was leaning back against the headboard in his room when his cell phone rang. "Yeah?"

"Hey," Tiny said. There was a lot of static cutting through the connection.

"Tell me you're somewhere over New Jersey."

"Not even close. We were delayed because of a bomb scare, then rerouted away from bad weather. I won't be in New York until midmorning tomorrow. Where do you want me?"

Smith cursed and then gave him the Hall Building's address. "We'll be in her office. Top floor."

"Righto. Now what's up with this Gala thing?"

"Standard-issue glamour party. About five hundred people coming. I've talked with Marks. If you decide it's safe, his boys are willing to crawl all around the place. You'll have plenty of backup if you need it."

"Good to know. What do you think?"

Smith blew out his frustration. "I don't know. The victims have been killed in their homes and I'm pretty sure the guy works alone. You need to get a sense of the space before you decide. If you think you can keep her safe, it would mean a lot to her to be able to go."

"Will you be reachable?"

This was something Smith had been debating. If he wasn't on the job, he shouldn't be floating around in the background. One person, and only one person, had to be in charge and there was no way he could play second fiddle, even to Tiny, in a situation involving Grace. The best course of action was for him to get the hell out of town, but he couldn't bring himself to leave. Not until the Gala was over and she woke up the next day safe and sound.

"I've booked a room nearby. You can reach me anytime and I'll be there in a heartbeat if things head south."

"Sounds good to me."

"Vic," Smith paused. He never used Tiny's given name. "Take good care of her."

Crackling came over the line and then his friend said, "Look, I've got to ask. What's this woman to you, anyway?"

Everything, Smith thought.

"Just another client." He stabbed out the cheroot.

"Yeah, sure, Boss. In five years of working with you, I've never seen you like this."

"All you have to do is make sure she stays alive, okay? Do that and I might even promote you."

"To what?"

"Maybe I'll start calling you Medium."

Tiny laughed.

As soon as the call ended, Smith dialed another number. Senator Pryne's private line was answered briskly by the man's chief of staff.

"It's Smith," he said. "When does he want to leave?"

"Will you be able to be in Washington the day after to-morrow?" The smoothness of the woman's voice, the diction, the stench of political power made Smith sick.

"Yes."

"Good. The senator will be pleased. You come highly recommended, Mr. Smith."

As he hung up the phone, his heart ached as if he'd been shot through the chest.

The next morning, Grace made a decision. She was going to call Blair and ask the woman to come take a look at her father's office. *Her* office. It was time to make that space her own. Lighten up the walls. Throw some drapes around the windows.

She'd already ordered a replacement desk. It was going to take two months to make but it was just what Grace wanted. Made of pale yew wood, it had clean lines and drawers on rollers so she wouldn't feel like she was going to dislocate her shoulder trying to get at her files. The chair was likewise on wheels and kitted out in cream leather.

And there were some other things she was going to do. She'd always wanted a dog.

A golden retriever, she thought. Something big and happy.

Her father had disapproved of owning a sporting dog if they weren't used to hunt. Her mother had despised anything that made noise or shed fur and, for his part, Ranulf hadn't wanted anything that competed for her attention.

That's what she wanted. A dog.

As she fantasized about floppy ears and kindly brown eyes, Grace realized she was finally taking control of her life. Courtesy of the change, she was reexamining everything she'd once simply accepted as *the way things were*. She'd lost her father's domineering hand when he'd died and now she was questioning everything she'd ever known about him. She was slowly learning to stand up to her mother. And thanks to what John had dug up about Ranulf and the von Sharones, she'd gotten a divorce settlement that seemed reasonable.

The losses that came with the recent events in her life were hard to bear, but they were balanced by her sense that it had all been inevitable and overdue. And she'd definitely take the hard truth over appearances any day. Like youth, illusions faded and withered, but the trade-offs, of wisdom and independence and freedom, were well worth the degradation of a pretty exterior.

Buck up, Starfish. Let's see that smile.

"Not anymore. Not unless it's real," she said out loud.

She picked up the dress she was going to wear at the Gala and her jewelry case, and left her room. John was waiting in the foyer, and she walked by him with a stiff nod. She kept expecting his partner to arrive at any moment and felt as though the netherworld of him being on the verge of leaving would never end.

They got in the Explorer and she made an effort to chat with Eddie about his writing. He'd started a manuscript as his final project, a children's book about safety, and she told him she knew an agent who might read it when he was done.

Grace spent all morning down in the atrium, supervising the arrangements for the Gala. The audiovisual people had erected a small stage near the entrance to the museum and brought in a screen on which to show the brief homage to her father's life. The caterers were milling around, setting up tables for the food and bars, and the florist had arrived with thousands of fragrant blooms.

It was early afternoon by the time she was satisfied with how things were progressing. After a quick lunch with some members of the press, she and John went back up to her office.

The elevator doors had just opened when his cell phone rang. She didn't pay much attention to what he said until she heard, "You have him in custody?"

She stopped walking as John's eyes bored into hers.

"When did you apprehend him?" There was a period of silence. "Can you make it stick?"

As soon as he hung up the phone, she said, "Did they find . . ."

He nodded and she was surprised when he didn't look relieved.

"So tell me," she prompted, feeling a sweet rush of release.

"Isadora came around early this morning. She identified the man who attacked her as an associate of her husband's. Marks and his boys arrested the guy."

"Who is it?"

"Someone named Margis. You ever heard that name before?"

She nodded, dumbstruck by the news. "Of course I have. He's an investment manager and a real bon vivant. He was always chasing after women, especially the richest ones. I know he worked with Mimi's husband on a deal and I think he took care of some of Cuppie's money. I'm not sure if Suzanna had any contact with him but it wouldn't have surprised me if she had. As for Isadora, he was very close to Raphael Cunis. They were partners."

"What about you? Did you ever deal with him?"

Grace thought for a moment.

"Now that you mention it, he did approach me right after my father's death. He told me with the change in my net worth, I needed more personal attention and he wanted to take care of things for me. I told him no. I'd heard that his firm was struggling because of the downturn in the markets and there was something I didn't trust about him."

John seemed to be thinking deeply.

"What's the matter?" she asked.

He shrugged. "Marks says that Isadora admitted to having had an affair with the guy. Evidently, she was trying to break it off, which was why she came back to town. That's a very personal connection, unlike the business ones Margis had with the other women. Although I suppose it's possible he'd been having affairs with them, too."

"His name was on the list," Grace blurted. "Those lists from the buildings—I saw his name on them that day you were looking at them."

"Yeah. Marks's boys checked and the man had been in van der Lyden's and Lauer's buildings on the days of those murders."

"Well, I'm relieved," Grace said. As she measured John's

expression, she felt almost defensive about her optimism. "What does Marks think?"

John shrugged. "He thinks the guy did it. Apparently they found a collection of weapons in Margis's house. He likes knives."

"So it's over," she murmured. "And I can get back to my life."

She stared at him and his eyes met hers intensely. For a moment, she held her breath in her chest as all of her painful, secret hopes came back.

Tell me you've changed your mind, she thought. Tell me that you love me and you're going to stay. Tell me that I was right and you were wrong and you can't imagine a life without me. Tell me that I'll be waking up next to you tomorrow.

Not wondering where you are.

But when he remained silent, she turned away and walked down the hall. There were no tears. They would come later, she was quite sure.

Kat looked up from her desk. "There's a man here to see you."

Grace glanced over her shoulder and saw the blond giant, Tiny, get to his feet. Her heart sank as he came forward, a duffel bag hanging off one heavy shoulder, a bright smile directed toward John. The man's expression became downright suspicious when he looked at her.

Smith clapped his partner on the back but Grace didn't hear what was said between them because of a loud ringing in her ears.

She walked into her office and sat at the desk. Moments later, the men came in, John with a serious expression on his face and Tiny looking like he'd been asked to take charge of a ticking bomb. The man's luggage hit the floor with a dull thud.

When the door was shut, she addressed them in her most commanding voice. "Although I appreciate you coming all this way, Mr. . . . ." She waited for the man to fill in the name.

"Just call me Vic," he said.

"Vic. But I don't believe I require the services of a bodyguard any longer." She started to shuffle papers around, trying to look busy.

"Yes, you do," John countered.

"No"—she flashed him an angry look—"I don't."

"Grace—"

She ignored him. "So, Vic, you can pick up that duffel and haul out. No doubt you're relieved by the dismissal. You don't look happy to be here."

The guy flushed.

Smith came quickly across the room. "Tiny's staying and that's final."

"Why? They have the man behind bars so the danger is gone. I'm not a minor and I'm not a mental case so I don't need a guardian. I also didn't ask for your opinion."

Without looking away from her, he said, "Vic, give us a minute."

His partner disappeared without a word.

But left the damn duffel.

"I don't think we have anything else to say to each other." Grace was having trouble meeting his eyes so she picked up a piece of paper from the desk. It was a memo she'd written about the new expense account policy.

"Look at me." When she refused, Smith slammed his fist into the desk. She jumped and caught a pen before it rolled on the floor. Reluctantly, she shifted her eyes to his. "Dammit, it's not like Marks has a confession from the guy. He may not be the one. You've got to take care of yourself."

"I am. I'm dissolving my relationship with Black Watch. The exposure I've had to you boys so far has been as traumatic as anything else in my life lately." She let out a tense laugh. "You know, I always figured there'd be some dramatic moment when you'd come out of nowhere and save me. Somehow, I don't think the job you did on that porch door quite counts. But then real life doesn't have much in common with the movies, does it?"

Because in Hollywood, they would have ended up together, she thought.

She reached for her purse and pulled out the check she'd written before, the one he'd turned down. "Are you ready to accept this now?"

"I don't want your money."

"But you will take it, won't you? So there'll be no ties left between us, so the cut will be a clean one."

John took the check, looking grim.

"Now, take your buddy and get out of here," she told him.

"Tiny is staying." John's jaw was set but she refused to be intimidated by the force of his will. Or swayed by it.

"Tiny or Vic or whoever he is can go to hell and so can you. I don't need another tough guy in my life or in my bed. From now on, I'm sticking to my own kind."

"I don't give a good goddamn what you say. Tiny is going to be here tonight."

"Oh no, he isn't. I fired you and your whole team!" She was being totally irrational but had no way to stop herself. She'd lost sight of everything but the hollow core in her chest. "Black Watch is off my payroll."

"So he's going to do it pro bono."

"I'll have him arrested for trespassing."

"I'd like to see you try," John countered coldly. "The NYPD won't touch one of my boys, Countess."

Grace leapt to her feet, balling her hands into fists. Her body was trembling. "Get out! Just get the hell out of my life!"

He was silent for a long time.

And then she was surprised when he acquiesced, simply turning and striding across the room. When he got to the double doors, he paused. His head went down, as if he were bracing himself.

"Good-bye, Grace."

And with those two simple words, he left.

She took a deep, shuddering breath.

Blindly, she began shuffling papers on the desk, pulling out sheets from files at random, making a mess. Faster and faster, she riffled through them, searching for nothing at all.

The tears fell from her eyes onto her father's desk, leaving water spots on her memos and contracts, policies and reports.

She was still crying silently twenty minutes later when Kat buzzed.

"Yes?" Grace cleared her throat. "What is it?"

"That man is still here," Kat said quietly.

Tiny. Vic. John's partner.

Another hard man with a gun.

"Well, he can sit and rot for all I care."

24

AFTER TALKING with Tiny about the Gala, and hearing the man decide to let Grace go ahead with attending the event, Smith hopped in a cab and went to her home. On the way there, he was thinking that Tiny was probably right. The risk to her was small, especially with Marks's men there, and Tiny promised to cover her like she was the president of the United States, the Pope, and Nelson Mandela all rolled into one.

As soon as Smith opened her front door, a compelling urge not to leave her kicked off a wave of self-doubt that had him cursing. Rushing through her home, he gathered his things while doing his damnedest to ignore the subtle smell of her perfume lingering in the air. Before he left, he took a last look at the photo of her and her father.

Then he put his key on a side table, activated the alarm, and walked out.

When he got to the street, he hailed a cab and asked to be taken to the hotel down on Wall Street that was so close to the Hall Building. The minute he got to his room, he picked up the phone and dialed Senator Pryne's private line. He needed to confirm locations and do a little cyber legwork and he was hoping both would distract him.

It rang only once before he hung up.

Sitting down on the bed, Smith put his head in his hands.

Everything felt wrong. The hotel room. The whole idea of flying off to a different part of the world. His goddamn duffel and his metal briefcases.

When he lifted his head, he caught himself staring back in the mirror over the dresser. Looking at his face, he saw a man who was missing his woman. A man who, quite possibly, would always feel lost without her. A man who was making a mistake.

She was right. He did love her.

So what the hell was he doing leaving?

But he had to let her go, he told himself. To keep her safe.

In a flash, he heard Grace calling him a coward.

Or was he just keeping himself safe?

The next thing Grace knew, Kat's voice came over the speaker. "I'm going down. Are you ready yet?"

Grace glanced at her watch. Hours had passed and she was close to being late for her own party.

"I just need to get dressed. I'll meet you in the atrium."

She changed quickly into the gown she'd brought with her, not really caring how she looked. In the bathroom, she slipped a ring of diamonds around her neck, clipped a pair of earrings on, and touched up her makeup.

After spraying on some Cristalle, she stepped out of her office and was surprised to see Tiny still in the waiting area. She'd forgotten the man was even there and the reminder of John brought fresh tears to her eyes.

Tiny got to his feet like he was coming to attention and nodded, stiffly. He'd changed into a tuxedo.

"You need to leave," she told him.

He just shrugged. "Nowhere to go except here."

"So get creative. This town is full of tourist attractions."

"Sorry, Countess. I've got my orders."

She squared herself and sent him a withering glance. "Not from me you don't and I run this place. You are not welcome here."

"I've got a lot of experience not being welcomed places."

"I imagine that's true. But you still need to leave."

Before he opened his mouth again, she went over to Kat's desk and dialed security's number. She knew she was being extreme but, with a suspect in custody, she could see no reason to torture herself by keeping the other man around.

"I have an intruder up in my office," she said in a half-dead voice. "Please come immediately."

When she hung up, Tiny was giving her an indulgent look. "Do you really think that's necessary?"

"If you leave now, it won't be."

Moments later, her head of security and three other men flew down the hall. What happened next was a blur. The Foundation's officers swarmed around Tiny only to be sent down to the floor or over against the wall, hard. John's partner was a whirling dervish of fists and legs and it was obvious he was going to win even though he was outnumbered.

As she was watching the melee, and wondering how many of her men were going to need medical attention, Grace remembered Eddie's present. Reaching into her evening bag, she pulled out the Mace just as two men grabbed on to Tiny's shoulders. She felt conflicted about using it but then decided he'd already done enough damage to her security detail. Tiny was showing no signs of tiring and she worried that someone was going to get hurt.

"I'm sorry to do this," she yelled over the din. All of the men briefly stopped moving and she took advantage of the opportunity, letting a stream off, right into Tiny's face.

The man cursed and started blinking furiously as the fight resumed. Though he kept on lashing out, the security officers had the upper hand now and were finally able to subdue him.

"We'll take him down to dispatch," her head of security said between heaving breaths. He was straddling Tiny's back while an officer put cuffs on the man. "And then we'll have him arrested."

"That's not necessary. Just get him out of the building." Grace paused. "Will he be okay, though?"

"I'll be goddamn fine," Tiny said from underneath the pile of men. "As long as you call off your dogs and let me protect you!"

The man on Tiny's back looked down in confusion.

"Just make sure he's all right," Grace said, feeling incredibly numb. "I really got him a good one."

"Countess," Tiny protested, lifting his head off the carpet. His eyes were watering and he'd started to retch. "Don't do this. You don't know if they've got the right man or whether they can keep that suspect in custody."

As she looked into his red and swollen eyes, she took a deep breath and addressed the sergant. "Carmine, I'd like to have one of our officers around me at all times tonight."

His thick eyebrows rose. "Sure. But you don't need to be afraid of this guy. He's not getting away from us. Not with what you did to him. And Marks's men are here. We've got enough blue uniforms to make a quilt down there."

She groaned. "Unless they're in plainclothes, tell them to leave. I don't want everyone scared that the terror alert has gone up or something. I do want someone with me at all times, though."

The man nodded and assigned one of the others.

As Grace went down to the party, she was perversely relieved that she was feeling so numb. Under more normal circumstances, she would have been nervous as hell about the outcome of the evening. The kind of people who went to expensive galas like the Foundation's had as much of a herd mentality as any other group of humans and they regarded a decline in prestige like a bad stock tip—as something to be avoided at all costs. The night was going to be a test of the Foundation's strength. Of people's faith in her.

Grace emerged into the atrium and saw that everything was arranged in time for the guests who had already started to arrive. Tables had been erected in an ever widening circle around the marble entrance to the museum and, in the center of each, magnificent bouquets of white and red roses mixed with stalks of deep blue foxglove lent a dramatic air. Uniformed waiters were already passing trays and getting drinks and a string octet had begun to play.

Before she could greet the first arrivals, Kat came up to her and they ran through some last details.

A half hour later, the lobby of the Hall Building was positively packed. The great, glittering masses, it turned out, had rallied around the Foundation. And Grace. She was astonished by the number of people who genuinely seemed to wish her well and were offering their support as she took over her father's role. They also had a lot of good things to say about the Walker painting, the food, the change in venue.

Even the old fogies on the board seemed eager to be in her good graces, now that the evening was proving to be a success. As they came up to her one by one and proclaimed their support, she nodded and smiled. She noted that not one of them protested Lamont's departure.

She was thinking she should have been feeling some kind of triumph, but nothing broke through her fog. In the face of the success she'd wanted and worked so hard for, she had to fall back on her breeding with a vengeance just to get through the night and be who all the people wanted her to be: Grace Woodward Hall. The beautiful daughter of Cornelius and Carolina Woodward Hall. The trendsetter and the social star, now the head of the Foundation.

As she looked over the crowd, seeing the beautiful clothes and the jewels, the wide smiles blooming out of well-known faces, she realized she was standing in a roomful of people who all looked like her—and yet she was totally out of place.

Even though the reaction was logical, given everything that had happened recently, the dislocation seemed somehow more permanent than the growing pains that inevitably came with big changes in life. She was starting to view her world differently and what once was familiar was beginning to seem foreign.

Where the new direction would take her, however, she had no idea.

At the appointed time, Grace went up onstage and introduced the video montage of her father's life. As she watched, she remembered the places and the times and the circumstances of each photograph. Though she was familiar with all of them, she saw each one differently now, as if the colors had been recalibrated. When the last photograph appeared, she regarded the image of her father, sitting at his desk with a pipe between his teeth, through eyes that were strained from conflicting emotions.

She knew that any resolution about the lies he'd lived would have to come without explanation or apology from him. She had to wonder if the remembrance of the love he'd shown her would be enough to help her find some kind of peace with it all. But she wasn't sure.

As the picture of her father dimmed, she had to swallow a few times before she was able to speak.

When the lights came back on, Grace looked down and saw her mother standing in the front of the crush of people, back ramrod straight, neck elegant as a swan's, black dress hanging perfectly from her dainty shoulders. The expression on her face was one of regal forbearance, although the light in her eyes was something close to warm.

When the Walker portrait was unveiled, the crowd fell into a hushed silence. Jack and Blair came up front and a battle ensued between her friend and a media mogul whose fondness for American art was well known. As the two took good-hearted jabs at each other, the price climbed over $3 million, with Jack finally taking the painting with a bid close to $5 million.

The crowd burst out in applause. As flashbulbs went off like firecrackers, Jack came up and embraced Grace, his austere face showing pleasure at his success.

Sometime later the guests began to disperse and Grace's mother was among the first to leave.

"I think it went well," Grace said, as she kissed Carolina good-bye. "Although of course, Father's parties are a high standard to meet."

Her mother reached out and squeezed Grace's hand with surprising urgency.

"It was just perfect, darling. You did a perfect job." Their eyes met. "Your father would have been very proud of you tonight."

"Why, thank you, Mother." But she felt more relief than pleasure at the praise.

"I am also very proud of you. And I told Bainbridge the same thing." Carolina leaned forward and kissed Grace's cheek. "You are going to make a fine president."

With a parting wave, her mother turned and disappeared into the crowd.

Grace shook her head. It was hard to comprehend that, after having given up on ever hearing a supportive word from the woman, her mother had finally come through with one. At a moment when Grace actually needed it. She knew better than to think this was the start of a trend, but she appreciated the gesture.

And then the Gala was all over.

Grace lingered afterward, talking to the caterers for a while and watching the cleanup crew start to reclaim the atrium from the detritus of the party. She thanked the security guy who'd tailed her discreetly all night long and was about to dismiss him when she decided that being escorted home was probably a good idea.

She asked the man to call them a car while she went up to her office to get her bag of clothes and daytime purse. As she rode up in the elevator, she felt solitude and silence push into her.

The distraction offered by the Gala had been a relief, but, like all Band-Aids over fresh wounds, its effects were transitory. Listening to the electronic beeps as floors were passed, she couldn't help but wonder where John was and what he was doing. She pictured him on a plane, somewhere over the ocean, heading for God only knew where.

A part of her refused to believe it was truly over. Common sense told her she'd better get with the program and embrace reality.

Her office was dark as she entered but she found the desk easily, sidling around the conference table and various chairs. She turned on the light next to her phone.

She was getting her purse from a drawer when a man's voice cut through the quiet.

"What a great success it all was."

Grace looked up to see Fredrique standing between the open doors. He shut them as he stepped into the room.

Smith came back from the hotel's gym in a grim mood. He'd deliberately beaten the hell out of himself, but even after miles of running and having lifted enough weights to make his shoulders scream in pain, he still hadn't gotten what he'd been looking for. He'd been shooting for the kind of dead, exhausted state he remembered from his combat days. Instead, he was still keyed up, only sore now.

He knew he had to call Pryne's office. They were expecting to hear from him.

He took a shower first.

Smith was drying off when he heard his cell phone ringing. His instincts came alive, his first thought of Grace.

When he answered it, an unfamiliar voice said, "Mr. Smith?"

"Yeah?"

"It's Joey. The countess's doorman."

Smith gripped the phone. "What is it?"

"You, ah—you told me to call you if anyone wanted to get into her apartment. Well, this guy showed up here a little while ago."

"Tell me."

"He's a caterer. I've seen him here before. Fredrique-something. He said the countess needed a change of clothes after the Gala and that he'd been told to pick them up and take them to the Foundation for her. I mean, I've seen him with her before. Last year, as a matter of fact. But you did say to call you."

"Did you let him in?" Smith shot back.

"No. He got a little steamed. I hope he doesn't screw me for this."

Thank God.

"You did the right thing, Joey. Is she home yet?" Smith rushed to the phone next to the bed.

"No, she's not back."

"Tell me what he was wearing."

"It was a chef's outfit. Whites. He said he'd been at the Gala cooking, but they were clean, which I thought was weird."

Smith was dialing Tiny's cell while they talked. "Tell her to call me the moment you see her. Thanks, Joey."

When a woman answered Tiny's cell, he had a feeling the shit had hit the fan. A minute later, Tiny finally got on the line, sounding hoarse and breathing harshly.

"What the hell's happening?" Smith yelled.

"Ah, shit, Boss."

"Talk!" Smith held the phone to his ear as he started to throw on clothes and strapped his gun holster across his shoulders. "Where's Grace?"

"I don't know. I spent the evening in the ER and this is the first time they've let me use the phone. Look, she's not alone. I think she's got one of the local yokels with her and I know Marks and his boys are around. She's fine."

"The hell she is! They've got the wrong man." Smith slammed the phone down and redialed the number on his cell phone while he left his room. He was pounding down the hall to the stairs when Tiny answered again. "How the hell did you end up in the hospital?"

"She Maced me."

Smith looked at the phone as if it had malfunctioned. "She what?"

"And I had a reaction to the shit."

"Christ. Take care of yourself."

"I'm sorry about this, Boss."

By this time, Smith was halfway down the building. He hung up and dialed the lieutenant's cell phone.

As soon as Marks answered, Smith said, "How many boys do you have at the Foundation?"

"None. We took them off the detail at her request. She said she was going to use her own men tonight and considering we have—"

"Get some cops over there *now*. Whoever you have in custody isn't the guy killing those women."

Smith broke out of the hotel through a side door and began running flat out. He was only three blocks from the Hall Building, but it felt like miles.

"What the hell are you talking about?"

"It's the goddamn caterer. Fredrique."

"The caterer?"

"He's already tried to get into Grace's apartment tonight. Her doorman called me. I don't have time to give details. You've got to trust me on this."

"Do you know what he looks like?"

Smith gave a description of Fredrique. "And he's in chef's whites."

Marks was already barking orders as he was hanging up.

When Smith flew into the lobby of the Hall Building, a security guy he recognized looked up from the front desk with a smile. "Hey there—"

"Where is she?"

"The countess? I think she left already. To go home."

Grace retreated until she felt the chair hit the back of her legs. "What are you doing here?"

Fredrique smiled.

"I couldn't miss the season's biggest event. The canapés were nice, though I wouldn't have done something so common, of course. Your guests could have been much more impressed. But then you *didn't use me.*"

He came toward her, his squat body moving in a jerky way from anger.

"You've ruined me. All of you," he said, his voice intensifying, "have *ruined* me. You froze me out. I've lost *everything.* You think you can just take someone's life and crush it because you're rich and you're powerful. People are toys to you. *Toys.*"

Grace was measuring the distance to the door when she caught sight of the knife in his hand. The blade reflected light with a flash and made her physically ill.

Fredrique's rantings got shrill. "When I was new and fresh, you needed me for your parties to make them good. You demanded me. You wanted me. And then someone else came to town and none of you knew my name. It was like I didn't exist!"

Grace glanced across the desk, searching for something to defend herself with as he got closer. She wished like hell she'd left her father's sturdy crystal bowl of peppermints out. It would have made a fine weapon.

Smith was almost at the revolving doors that led to the street when another security guy called out. "Hey! You looking for the countess? She just went upstairs to get her purse. I ordered a car for the two of us."

Smith cursed as he wheeled around and rushed for the elevators. "The police are on the way—get them to her office as soon as they arrive."

The ride to the top floor was an eternity. He was thinking that he'd give up anything he had to have her safe. Unharmed. Alive.

And that included Black Watch, his lifestyle, the whole thing.

She'd been right. He was protecting himself because loving her was the single most threatening thing he could think of. But the alternative was worse. He'd much rather be with her than without, even if the price he paid was the bogus sense of security he'd had when he was by himself.

All he wanted was her. All he needed was her.

She'd told him she wouldn't wait. Well, he wasn't going to ask her to. He was going to stay by her side.

Oh, God. Please let her be safe.

When he leapt out of the elevator, and saw the light in her office glowing under the doors, he felt a painful surge of hope as he ran silently down the hall. She'd probably gone up to change clothes. She was probably stepping out of her high heels and sighing as her bare feet hit the carpet at this very moment. She was probably fine.

Please let her be fine.

He was about to push open the double doors when he heard a man's voice. The threat behind the words was obvious, even through the wood, and Smith went from anxious to deadly.

Silently, he pushed one side open a crack. He saw the man, the knife and the stark fear on Grace's face.

That was all Smith needed to know.

With a massive lunge, he burst through the door. There was bloodlust and nothing else running through his veins as he tackled Fredrique, taking him down hard onto the floor. Smith was heavier and had the element of surprise working for him, but with all his rage, he didn't need the advantage.

The man began to fight but it was amateur stuff. Smith grabbed the knife and quickly took control. In a matter of moments, he had Fredrique dazed and flat on his back.

But Smith didn't stop there. Before he was fully aware of what he was doing, he had one hand around the man's throat and the other tight on the grip of the knife. For what the murderer had almost done to Grace, he was prepared to eviscerate him on the spot.

Smith raised his arm high over his head and angled the blade so it would hit Fredrique's chest square in the center. He felt an animal growl come out of him as he started to move.

"John! No!"

Smith froze as he heard Grace's voice. He shook his head to clear it and looked at her. Her face was an unnatural gray color and her hands were reaching out to him.

"Put the knife down," she told him gently.

He became aware of his pounding heart, the sound of the breath coming out of his mouth, the feel of the weapon in his hand. He looked back down, into Fredrique's eyes. The lids were peeled back with terror, the pupils dilated by fear.

Smith looked up again at Grace.

"Are you hurt?" he asked her hoarsely.

"No, I'm okay."

He returned his attention to the killer. The guy was beginning to choke and Smith pictured Grace's life gradually leaving her body. He tightened his grip and raised the knife higher, prepared to show Fredrique everything his victims had felt.

"John, put that down! *Please*, don't kill him."

The urgency of her voice snapped him back to reality. He knew damn well he was a hairbreadth away from murder so he threw the knife across the room, flipped Fredrique over, and roughly wrenched the man's hands behind his back.

Smith looked over at Grace. "Are you sure you're okay?"

She gave him a shaky smile. "Yes."

When Fredrique started to protest, Smith bared his teeth and got down real close to the man's ear.

"You better shut the fuck up before I cut your tongue out."

Fredrique didn't say much after that.

"Grace, call your security guys. Marks's men should be arriving soon, but let's get some handcuffs up here."

As she nodded and went over to the phone, all he wanted to do was hold her, but there was no way he was letting the man under him get loose.

Within minutes, two uniformed security officers came into the room. Smith got off Fredrique after they'd handcuffed him and immediately went to Grace. He curled himself around her, surrounding her with his body, and when her arms came around him, he felt a relief that made him lightheaded. Breathing in her scent, feeling her living warmth against him, he thought it was nothing short of a miracle.

With the arrival of Lieutenant Marks and his men, Grace's office turned into a bull pen of cops. Fredrique was carted off, looking dazed and stammering about there having been some kind of mistake.

"Could you give us a sec, fellas," Smith said over Grace's head to the police and security officers milling around. The men in blue were waiting to take her statement, but he needed to be alone with her.

When they were by themselves, he was surprised to feel her stiffen against him.

"So you saved me, after all," she murmured, pulling away. "Burst through the door . . . and saved me. Just like a bodyguard should."

She went over to the windows, moving slowly as if she didn't trust her legs. The hand she raised to her neck was trembling and she looked at her fingers curiously, as if she was only just now realizing how badly she was shaking.

Smith frowned, thinking about the recovery she had in front of her. She wasn't physically injured, but she was going to be rattling around in her own skin for a while. He'd seen it before. Had been through it himself.

"Grace, you're going to need help getting over this. I can recommend someone you can talk to."

"I'll be fine. Although it's kind of you to worry." She stood rigidly while looking out at the twinkling city. "Would you mind calling the police back in? I'm feeling rather tired and would like to go home."

The words were formal, her voice a false calm that told him she was two inches from the cliff.

"Grace—"

"And by all means, you should go now. You've more than served your purpose. You've saved me."

There was a little hiccup after that last word.

"I'm not going anywhere."

Her hand went to the base of her throat. "There's no reason for you to stay."

"What I'm trying to say is—"

"Or are you going to have me arrested for what I did to Tiny?"

Smith frowned. "We'll talk about that later."

"There is no later for us."

"Yes, there is." He went over to her and turned her around. "I don't know how it's going to work but I can't leave you. Walking away from you this afternoon felt wrong, like I was leaving a part of me behind. I don't want to be without you. I don't know if I can . . . live without you."

Her eyes were wary. "What about Black Watch? What about your past?"

"Like you said, we'll work it out together."

"Oh, really?" She stepped out of his reach. "You were very worried about it before. What's changed?"

He shook his head. "Nothing. Everything."

"Now there's an answer." She smiled sadly. "Actually, that's just what I would have expected you to say."

He frowned. "Grace, I—"

Her voice was tired as she cut him off. "I'm sorry, John. But I don't think there's anything you could say that would convince me that all of the problems you saw between us have disappeared."

"How about this." He waited until she looked up. "I love you."

Her eyebrows rose and her mouth opened slightly.

"I love you. And I don't want to live without you." He paused. "I won't pretend I've handled any of this well. But

I promise to improve over time. And I am trainable. That's how I made it through the army."

He offered her a lopsided smile, hoping like hell she would believe him. Believe in them. Now that he finally saw everything they had together, he prayed that he wasn't too late.

Grace just kept staring at him. As the silence stretched between them, a cold dread formed in the pit of his stomach. She'd told him it would take a hell of a lot to open her heart to him again and he wondered if his love was enough.

He was getting ready to beg when she lurched forward.

With an awkward lunge, she grabbed on to him, almost taking him down on the floor with the force of her body. She held on to him so hard, he thought he wouldn't be able to breathe and didn't care if he suffocated or not.

When her hold loosened, he bent down and kissed her softly.

"I love you," he whispered, relishing the glow radiating from her face. He ran a finger down her cheek. "And I want you to know that I'm ready to change. It's not going to be easy but—"

"Stop talking and kiss me again," she murmured with a smile.

"You don't have to ask me twice, lady," he said, as he put his lips down on hers.

Epilogue

THE NEXT morning, Grace smiled as she lay in bed and watched Smith get out of the shower. His big body was hers to have and to hold, she thought. Every last rock-hard inch of it.

And she'd held on pretty hard last night, she remembered with satisfaction.

As he pivoted to dry off his legs, she caught a glimpse of where she'd scratched his back with her nails.

"Look what I did to you," she said with a grimace.

He glanced over his shoulder toward the mirror. When he turned to her, his smile was full of masculine approval.

"I'm wearing your marks with pride and hoping for more tonight."

He wrapped a towel around his tight waist and, when she held her arms out, he joined her. His hair was still damp and he smelled like a clean man.

Her man.

I've chosen well, she thought while staring into his dark blue eyes.

When he chuckled deep in his chest, she raised an eyebrow.

"I'm just thinking of Tiny," he said. "I can't believe you Maced him."

Grace flushed. "I feel really badly about that."

"Don't worry about it. He's tough enough to handle it. I'm laughing because right about now, he's choking back some plastic eggs on a plane headed for the Middle East. He hates eating on planes."

She frowned. "Was that going to be your next job?"

When John nodded, she felt her nerves stir.

"Do you wish you were going?"

He shook his head.

"I don't. Undoubtedly, I will sometimes but this morning, I want to be here." He dropped in for a kiss.

"I love you, John," she whispered.

He pulled back, a serious look on his face. "I have something I want to do."

"What?"

"I want to take you to dinner."

She smiled. "Dinner?"

He cleared his throat. "I want to show up on your doorstep with flowers and some little trinket from Tiffany's. I want to take you out, hold your hand, pull back the chair for you. Treat you like a lady. Be your man."

Grace laughed softly.

"You've always treated me like a lady. And I don't need flowers or dinner or jewelry. I only need you."

He rolled her over on top of him. "Well, you've got me."

She was about to kiss him, when he took her face in his hands.

"Grace, do me a favor." He paused. "I want you to call me Ross."

Her breath caught in her throat as she looked down into his eyes.

"It was the name I was born with. Seems fitting I should use it, now that I'm starting out all over. My last name's gone forever but at least I can resurrect the first half."

"Ross," she repeated. "I love you, Ross."

He brought her lips to his. "Oh, God, say that again."

Read on for a sneak peek of Jessica Bird's

AN IRRESISTIBLE BACHELOR

Coming from Signet

THE WOMAN came to him from the shadows and he knew her by the red of her hair. She moved slowly, deliberately, toward him and he released his breath with satisfaction. He'd missed her and wanted to ask her where she'd been.

But the closer she got, the less he felt like talking.

As she stopped in front of him, he reached out and ran a finger down her cheek. She was achingly beautiful, especially her eyes. They were a fiery brown, a shade darker than the auburn waves that fell past her shoulders. He wanted her. No, he *needed* her.

Her smile deepened, as if she knew what he was thinking, and she tilted her head back. Staring at her upturned mouth, at her parted lips, a wave of urgency shot through his body. Giving in to the hunger, he put his hands on her shoulders and pulled her close, wanting to take what she was offering quickly before she disappeared again.

Bending down, he felt anticipation and something else, something that made his heart pound with more than lust.

Jack Walker's eyes flipped open. Still caught up in the raging hunger of his body, he wasn't sure whether he was truly awake. Or where the hell he was. He knew the bed wasn't his own, but not much else.

He looked around at the dark shapes in the room. After a few deep breaths, the patterns made sense to him. He was at the Plaza Hotel in New York, in the suite he always used when he was in town.

And the woman he still wanted so badly it hurt had disappeared into thin air. Again.

He stared up at the ornate ceiling in frustration. He hadn't slept well the last two nights and he needed some sustained shut-eye soon. He didn't have much patience to begin with and lack of sleep wasn't getting him any closer to Mother Teresa territory.

The dream was driving him crazy. Every time it was the same. Just as he was about to kiss her, right before he was able to taste her, he'd wake up slick with sweat and in a hellacious mood.

Restless, he had to fight his way out of the sheets that had gotten tangled around his body. When he was finally free he walked over to a bank of windows and looked outside.

He'd met the woman only once and he hadn't thought she'd made that big an impression on him. She'd been backing out of a doorway and she'd turned around, her deep red hair swinging over her shoulders. Their eyes had locked. He'd been intrigued, as any man would have been, but it wasn't like she'd struck him dumb with her charms.

At first, he'd laughed off the dream, seeing it as verification that at the age of thirty-eight his sex drive was as strong as it always had been. But the dream kept coming back to him, planting her face more deeply in his memory each night. It was getting harder to blame his infamous libido—this was about Callie Burke.

"Jack?"

He turned to the bed and looked at the dark shape of Blair Stanford. His fiancée.

"Sorry I woke you."

She reached a hand out to him. "Come back to bed."

Jack slid between the sheets and felt Blair slip her arms around him.

"You're tense," she said softly, stroking his chest.

He wove his fingers through hers. "Go back to sleep, sweetheart."

"Is there something wrong?" she murmured. "You've been tossing and turning every night for the past few days."

"There's nothing to worry about."

He stroked her forearm, trying to soothe her but she propped her head up on her hand.

"Jack, we know each other too well for secrets."

"True. But who says I'm hiding anything?" He smiled at her short, blond hair, which was sticking out at right angles. He reached up and smoothed the sides down, thinking she wouldn't have stood for that kind of disorder if she'd known about it. Even in the middle of the night.

Blair stared down into his face for a long time. "Are you rethinking our engagement?"

"Not at all. What makes you say that?"

She hesitated, and that's when he knew she was upset. "I was very surprised when you asked me to marry you two weeks ago and we haven't really talked about it since."

"We've both been busy. That doesn't mean I'm having second thoughts."

What he really wanted to say was that she should know he didn't do "second thoughts." Having made the decision that it was time to get married, and having found a woman he wanted to be his wife, he had everything arranged.

She shook her head. "Jack, this engagement—"

"Is exactly what I want. You are exactly what I want. As a matter of fact, you're perfect."

He heard her sigh in the dark. "I just want you to be sure."

"You know how I feel about you."

"You don't love me, Jack."

The quiet words hit him hard. He opened his mouth, not sure what he was going to say, but she put a slender fingertip on his lips.

"It's okay," she whispered. "I've always known."

He grabbed her hand and kissed it, wishing he could tell her otherwise.

There were so many things about her that he liked and respected. She was a business success in her own right, running a thriving interior decorating company. She had fantastic style and grace. And she was, at her core, a very decent person.

He valued her. He enjoyed her being in his life. The fact

that he didn't love her was the only thing missing, but he didn't consider it a problem. That particular kind of passion just wasn't something he had in him. For any woman.

Jack squeezed her hand. "So maybe the question is more, why are you marrying me?"

"Because I love you and I think we make a good team."

"We are a *great* team."

"So tell me what's wrong."

He shook his head resolutely, not about to tell her he was dreaming about some other woman. "Blair, please trust me. There's nothing going on that you need to be worried about."

"Okay, okay." She ran a soothing hand over his shoulder which was something she did a lot. She had a way of handling him that he liked. Calming but not patronizing. "But I hope you'll tell me at some point. I prefer to know bad news sooner rather than later."

She settled in against him and, as she fell back to sleep, he stared at the ceiling.

It was just a dream, he told himself. The images, the sensations, had more to do with his libido than some redhead he'd met for how long? Ten minutes?

Besides, he'd always preferred blondes and he had a loving, wonderful one right here in his arms. He was a man with a plan and nothing was going to change the course of his life.

J. R. WARD

LOVER MINE

THE NEW NOVEL IN THE
#1 *NEW YORK TIMES* BESTSELLING
BLACK DAGGER BROTHERHOOD SERIES

*At last, the story of John Matthew has
finally been told...*

John Matthew has come a long way since he was found
living among humans, his vampire nature unknown.
Taken in by The Brotherhood, no one could guess what
his true history was—or his true identity.

Xhex has long steeled herself against her attraction to
John Matthew. Until fate intervenes and she discovers that
love, like destiny, is inevitable.

**Available wherever books are sold or at
penguin.com**

FROM

#1 *NEW YORK TIMES* BESTSELLING AUTHOR

J. R. WARD

THE BLACK DAGGER BROTHERHOOD SERIES

Dark Lover
Lover Eternal
Lover Awakened
Lover Revealed
Lover Unbound
Lover Enshrined
Lover Avenged
Lover Mine

Available wherever books are sold or at
penguin.com

#1 *NEW YORK TIMES* BESTSELLING AUTHOR
J. R. WARD

COVET
A Novel of the Fallen Angels

THE START OF A BRAND-NEW SERIES

Redemption isn't a word Jim Heron knows much about—his specialty is revenge, and to him, sin is all relative. But everything changes when he becomes a fallen angel and is charged with saving the souls of seven people from the seven deadly sins. And failure is not an option.

Vin DiPietro long ago sold his soul to his business, and he's made his peace with with that—until fate intervenes in the form of a tough-talking, Harley-riding, self-professed savior. Then he meets a woman who will make him question his destiny, his sanity, and his heart—and he has to work with a fallen angel to win her over and redeem his own soul.

Available wherever books are sold or at
penguin.com